SOMEDAY SOON

BY JULIAN FONT

Forever dedicated to the ones who feel stranded.
Have faith, for *help is on the way*.

CHAPTER I

Fuck heartbreak.

Actually, you know what? Fuck the person who *invented* heartbreak. I wish I could meet that person. I have a running list of questions for them, starting with *why*? Why did they create heartbreak? Did they suffer from heartbreak? Does the heart actually break? Do tiny bits of the heart tear over time, or is it one first and last tear that leaves the heart forever broken? Then there's the most important question of all: *If a heart has been broken, can it be fixed?*

"We need to get you laid," Mac says as we prepare to board the cruise ship.

The woman in front of us covers her kid's ears, then glares back at Mac.

I raise my hand apologetically. "Easy, Mac," I whisper. "There are kids here."

"Oh, fuck." He innocently covers his mouth. "Sorry, kid!"

The sun shines against the Miami city skyline as we shuffle toward the cruise ship towering over the docks–a steel giant patiently awaiting its voyage into the Caribbean. It's too bright out, and everything about this impending "vacation" grates on my every nerve. On the other hand, Mac is all smiles, oblivious to the fact that everything about this vacation makes me want to bolt back to the safety of solid land. *And we haven't even boarded yet.*

"I don't need to get laid," I state with an eye roll. "Let's just try to have a good time, the two of us."

My words hold very little conviction, but I can't help it. There's no way this trip is going to dig me out of the shithole that's been my love life for the past four months. I know Mac has the purest of intentions, and I'm grateful he's taking the time to help me get over the breakup, but–

"Of all possible trips we could take, why a cruise?" I ask as the cruise hostess returns my ticket.

"Welcome aboard, Roman," she greets with a smile.

I force a smile back at her, then nod. "Ma'am."

Mac nudges my side as his eyes trail the backside of two girls crossing our path along the deck. "You got two reasons right there," he says with a raised brow. "Not only are cruises perfect for meeting girls, but the girls have slim pickings. I mean, they're stuck on a boat with two handsome guys like us and nowhere else to go."

The hostess scoffs at Mac's remark, her open palm awaiting his ticket. He snaps out of his trance and hands her the ticket.

"You're a dog," I exhale, holding back a laugh.

Within seconds of stepping onto the ship's promenade, we're each handed some of the most colorful cocktails I've ever seen. The chilled glass sends a current up my arm, forcing me to accept that we're actually doing this. This is happening. Four whole days on a Caribbean cruise. Mac read somewhere online that cruises were ranked one of the best places to meet women, and not long after my breakup, he called me with the idea. Given his long track record of pitching dumb ideas that never come to fruition, I was convinced he would shut up about it if I just nodded and said it was a good idea. To my demise, he actually brought this idea to life.

As we walk along the promenade, I admire the city skyline in the distance, the sun beaming across the shimmering bay. The weather couldn't be more perfect, though I would rather enjoy the perfect weather from the safety of land. Look, I don't do well on the water. All my family and friends know that, but Mac seems to prioritize his love for women above my fear of the ocean.

BZZZ! BZZZ!

As the elevator ascends to the seventh floor, I pull out my phone to see my ma's face flooding the screen. The elevator doors open.

"FaceTime?" Mac asks as we step into the hallway.

I nod. "It's Ma again."

"Man, you're 22. Chicks don't like mama's boys." Mac smirks

at a girl before she enters her room. "How you doin', baby?"

The girl cringes before slamming the door in his face.

"Seems chicks don't like you either," I tease, raising my phone. My face fills the bottom corner of the video call. In an instant, Ma beams at me as if I wasn't with her just yesterday.

"There he is!" she shouts, squinting her eyes behind her glasses.

"Hey, Ma."

"Pa's here, too!" She lifts the phone to reveal my pa standing over her shoulder.

His thick mustache curls up into a grin. "Roman," he greets with his signature stern undertone. "Your mother insisted on us calling to wish you a safe trip."

Ma nudges him. "Don't say, 'Safe trip.' You're implying the trip is dangerous!"

They bicker until I raise my cocktail to change the subject. "Check it out!"

As if on cue, they cheer. "Party time!" Ma shouts. "We wanted to say we love you, have a *fun* trip, and we also want to make sure you didn't forget your medicine."

I adjust my front camera to show the duffle bag hanging from my shoulder. "Got it all here," I say, giving the bag a shake.

Mac forces his face into the screen next to mine. "Don't worry, Mrs. Consano. I saw him pack his pills this morning. They're in his bag next to the extra small condoms!"

I open my mouth for a rebuttal, but I'm interrupted by Pa.

"My son is gettin' laid! Hoorah!" Pa shouts, raising a celebratory fist. "Nice mustache, Mac."

Mac licks his fingers and runs them over the coarse black hair coating his upper lip. "You too, Sergeant C.!"

Pa has always shared a special bond with the friends I served in the military with, considering he's a veteran himself. There's something about risking your life alongside your friends that instantly makes you family. True bonds are formed during difficult times, and Mac and I faced quite a few while deployed overseas.

My pa was deployed a whole lot throughout my childhood, and while his absence over a year at a time was hard on Ma and me, seeing him walk through our front door in one piece makes me never take his presence for granted. To this day, I keep in touch with friends who can't say the same about their own fathers and that breaks my heart. Unfortunately, Mac is one of those friends.

"This is it," Mac says as he places our room key against a door lock.

"Alright, y'all," I exhale. "I have a cruise to cruise."

Ma and Pa begin rattling off their parental send-offs.

"Enjoy yourself, Rome!" Ma shouts. "Remember, your guardian angel is always with you!"

I nod.

Pa leans toward the screen. "What do I always say, Roman? If you don't feel it in your mind, heart, and gut…"

"Then don't do it," I finish.

"Thatta kid." He smirks. "Be good, do good."

I wave goodbye, hang up, and my jaw drops when I lift my eyes to see our room—well, it's more of a penthouse?

"Mac." My breath hitches. "You didn't."

"Oh, but I did!" Mac throws the blinds open at the end of the room, and the afternoon light floods in as he spreads his arms. "I know you hate the ocean, so I thought booking one of the biggest suites on the ship would make it a bit more enjoyable for you."

I throw my bag on the living room couch, feeling the blood rush to my cheeks. Mac picks up on my excitement, and we clink our cocktails together and chug what's left of them. "You son of a bitch!" I wrap my arm around his shoulder, the two of us staring out at the open ocean. "You didn't have to do this!"

Mac shrugs. "I know the breakup was hard on you, brother. You deserve better, and I wanted to give you better. Tough times create tough men, and tough men deserve fun times every once in a while."

The tension drains from my shoulders as I pan around the spacious suite and our private balcony. It's hard to maintain my hatred for this trip after being slapped with Mac's comfort and consideration. Maybe, just maybe, I can find a way to enjoy this after all.

I grab a champagne bottle from the mini-fridge and fill two new glasses. I'll admit that at first, I was against this whole cruise thing, but maybe it won't be so bad. I clink my champagne glass against Mac's. "Here's to fun times."

𐰼𐰼𐰼

As the cruise ship sets off, Mac and I spend an hour freshening up. Our suite is made up of two bedrooms bordering a living room. The living room has a couch on one side and a flat-screen T.V. on the other, which we use to blast our favorite Country songs while we get ready. An L-shaped bar top counter is tucked in the corner of the living room by the front door, which is where we spend some time pregaming for the night.

"Thoughts on this fit?" I ask, eyeing my reflection in my bedroom mirror. I adjust the lapel of my black suit jacket, then run my hands down the front so that it falls over my black slacks. I point one of my loafers in Mac's direction.

Mac brushes over his tight black curls with one hand and swirls his fifth or sixth cocktail in the other. While leaning sloppily against the bedroom door frame, he says, "You can't wear that. You look like you're going to a wedding."

His dig does more damage than he might think. This was the suit I was planning to wear while proposing to my ex-girlfriend. With things ending the way they did, I never got that chance. For a second, I thought it'd feel good to meet someone new while wearing it tonight, that it would lead to some kind of redemption. I also don't know what the hell guys wear on cruises. Us country boys just aren't built like them beach boys.

I face my reflection again. "Is the suit really that bad? It's brand-new."

"Right, right." Mac stumbles into the room and falls onto my bed, spilling some of his drink on the white sheets. "But, 'wedding' dress code isn't the same as 'cruise' dress code."

I shake my head and sigh because I won't be able to escape the lecture Mac is about to give me.

"Here's the thing about fashion, Rome," he slurs, struggling to stand beside me. We study my outfit through our reflection. "You need to tailor what you wear to your environment, or you're gonna stick out like a sore thumb. For example, check me out." He raises a hand toward his hair. "A fresh fade along the sides and back to show the ladies I care about my looks, but a loose Hawaiian shirt and linen pants to show I can let loose. My mustache? Well, I just look good with a stache."

"So, what would you change about my appearance?"

Mac suddenly yanks off my jacket, untucks my shirt, and unbuttons half the buttons. My silver military dog tag shimmers through my open shirt, reflecting the light shining from directly above us. He tousles my hair, though the short length doesn't allow much tousling. "Hmmm." He steps in front of me, separating my view of the mirror. I purse my lips to keep from laughing at his serious expression and unwavering focus on my appearance.

While we were serving in the military, Mac always spent his downtime studying. Cinema, medicine, science, fashion–he read article after article and watched video after video. While he certainly has a unique and unsuccessful way with women, I won't deny that he knows a hell of a lot about random shit.

"I should bill you for this," Mac declares, stepping aside.

My eyes land on the man in the mirror, and I can hardly recognize him. I've never looked this casual in my life, but I like it. My short brown hair is just the right amount of messy on top, some strands hanging over the sides of my head. My baby-blue dress shirt is loose-fitting, untucked, with the sleeves rolled halfway up my tan forearms. My black slacks hug my waist, dropping straight down to the tops of my bare ankles above my black loafers.

It's been months since I've cared about my appearance, which means it's been months since I've looked this good and felt this good. I subtly flex my clean-shaven jaw as I slip a hand into my pocket. This isn't the same Roman who's been mourning his past relationship. This isn't the same Roman who's been avoiding any sort of romantic connection since his last. This isn't even the same Roman who boarded this ship. He's new, he's improved, he's…

"Ready," I say. "Let's get out there."

We make our way down the hall in high spirits and with fresh cocktails. I lost count after my fourth. Or was it my fifth? Regardless, I'm feeling damn good and in a position to make some new friends. The hallway carpet we strut over is a deep blue with golden coral branches weaving elegantly in and around each other. Dark wood lines the walls and borders the white ceiling, where mini-chandeliers hang every few feet. Mac points out the various paintings of old ships on the walls. As we pass each painting, he shares what each ship is named and what year it was built.

"I wish I knew as much as you," I say, stepping into the elevator. "I feel like knowing all this random stuff comes in handy."

Mac laughs, combing his mustache as he looks in the elevator mirror. "Just be thankful you're good-looking. It means you don't have to be smart like me."

I lean back against the elevator mirror, watching the floor

numbers on the screen decrease.

6, 5, 4...

The elevator suddenly halts on the third floor and my heart drops when she steps into the elevator. My world slows so I can be completely present as she glides into the elevator with such grace that I'm convinced this girl is an angel. Her caramel-colored hair falls past her bare shoulders, some strands straight while others curl like they have minds of their own. Her hazel gaze locks on mine for what feels like an eternity. The elevator is dimly lit but still light enough for me to worship the swirling flecks in her eyes. The moment around me fades to insignificance, and to my downfall, the elevator continues descending to the main deck.

The angel's eyes flick to her friend, who stepped in after her at some point.

Keep looking at me, I want to tell her.

By the angel's looks alone, I would throw myself off the side of this ship to save her from drowning, and I don't even know how to swim. I woke up today the same way I wake up every day, which is convinced I may never love again. I was done using my heart—finished—convinced that I wasn't able to take a chance on somebody again. And yet, there's something about the way this girl carries herself that makes me believe both God and love are real again.

The angel's white sundress is loose over her tan frame, her legs sunkissed with a subtle shine. I bet they're soft. I bet chills dance along the surface if a man treats her the way she deserves to be treated, which is like the angel she is.

"Do you have a name, or can I call you mine?" Mac asks the angel's friend.

The friend tucks a few tight black curls behind her ear just so she can glare back at Mac. "You could have said anything, and you chose that cheesy pickup line?" The fire in her deep-brown eyes forces him back a step.

The angel holds back her smile.

Smile, I want to say. *For the love of God, let me see you smile.*

"What pickup line would have worked on you?" Mac asks, smirking.

"Nobody uses pickup lines anymore." The friend turns her back to us, staring at the elevator doors. "I promise to find you more attractive the farther you are from me."

Mac laughs. "Our kids are going to find this story hilarious one day," he teases.

The elevator opens to the promenade, and the angel takes one last look at me before she steps out, before I can thank her for letting me breathe her air.

"I'm Mac!" Mac shouts to the angel's friend as they walk away.

"Doesn't matter!" the friend shouts back.

Mac nudges me, then exhales. "I think I just met my wife."

Me, too.

CHAPTER II

After far too many drinks and a few dances with strangers, I realize I might have judged cruises prematurely. Even for a guy who wants nothing to do with the ocean, it's hard to resist the beauty it holds. The way the vast, black sky above merges seamlessly with the black waters below, dotted with twinkling stars that scatter like spilled diamonds. The way the calm water catches the moonlight in a silvery flash, creating a pathway to the edge of the earth.

I'm having much more fun than I thought I would. The people here are more relaxed, more open to connecting with one another. It's as if time stops in the middle of the ocean as the horizon stands still, the moon and stars shining their brightest. The fruit is sweeter, the drinks are stronger, and the music is better.

The middle section of the main deck has been turned into a nightclub surrounding a circular pool. Two bridges extend from the pool's edges to a floating stage in the middle, where a D.J. plays tropical music that breathes life into the night air.

I thank Mac with every smile that spreads across my face, and we reminisce about the good times we've shared, both in and out of the military. And believe it or not, with every corny pickup line Mac uses on a girl, we actually manage to make a few friends. The people we meet steal my attention for a moment, but none leave an impression like the angel from the elevator. I'd be lying if I said I wasn't looking over my shoulder for her whenever I see a flash of white.

The club suddenly goes quiet as the music fades. A man wearing a bedazzled denim vest and a swimsuit takes the stage, shouting into a microphone. "WHAT'S UP, PARTY PEOPLE?!" The crowd roars, from the elevated V.I.P. sections above to the people swimming in the pool below. The man continues. "I go by '*High-Tide*,' and I'm gonna be the captain of this party tonight! How we feelin'?!" The crowd goes fucking wild. "Hell yeah! I know you're all enjoying yourselves, and it's time to enjoy yourselves even more with some entertainment! But here's the catch… the entertainment is you!"

The crowd's cheers become hums of excitement and whispers while Mac and I drunkenly raise our glasses with our new friends.

High-Tide lifts his hand. "So, here's what I need from y'all! I need six couples to come up on stage and compete to win a free whale-watching experience at our first stop tomorrow! That's right. You and your partner will be spending an afternoon off the coast of the Bahamas with some of the ocean's most fascinating creatures!"

People raise their arms to get noticed, while others shy away. I don't blame them. The thought of being close to a whale sounds terrifying. Colorful lights dance around the main deck as couples are escorted to the stage by nightclub hosts. A handful of couples take the stage, and High-Tide does a headcount.

"We need one more couple!" he shouts, raising his arm. "Come on! We're talkin' about seeing some mother-fuckin' whales up close! That's bad-ass shit! Get some crazy pics for your Instagram while you're at it."

People in and around the crowd turn their heads. They jokingly volunteer one another until High-Tide says, "How about this? Just give me two people. It could be anybody. Just get two more good-lookin' people on my damn stage!"

A hand locks on my arm and then lifts it straight up in the air. Before I can process what's happening, Mac is already screaming across the pool. "OVER HERE! PICK ROME! PICK THIS GUY! PICK ROME! OVER HERE!"

I fail to break free no matter how hard I try. "Mac! What're you—"

"Yeah, pick Rome!" a stranger shouts, laughing at my embarrassment.

People around us feed on Mac's intensity, chanting my name.

I've known Mac for years, and I don't think I've ever seen him this determined to embarrass me. He jumps up and down, getting people to chant my name in unison. At this point, I give up. I can't stop laughing. Partially because only Mac would be able to rouse up a crowd of strangers like this and partially because I know that with my shit luck, I'm about to be chosen.

"WE GOT ONE!" High-Tide's voice floods the deck as a white spotlight beams at me from the stage.

Mac releases my hand to applaud himself for embarrassing me within 24 hours of us getting on this ship. Heads all around turn in my direction, cheerful eyes fixated on me as they form a path for me to approach the pool's center. I throw my hands up, making my way across the bridge and onto the stage with the other five couples. The crowd roars as I wave in all directions, soaking up the moment.

"What's your name, my man?!" High-Tide extends the microphone toward my lips.

"Roman," I reply, flashing a smirk.

A loud, flirty whistle from somebody across the deck draws laughter from the crowd. I usually don't do well in front of crowds, but whatever. I'm drunk and on a ship in the middle of the ocean. It's not like I'll ever see these people again.

"Let's find Roman a partner, everybody!" High-Tide urges into the microphone.

The crowd's shouts form a singular sound until the word "Bachelorette" is chanted behind us. The couples, High-Tide, and I turn back to see a commotion just behind the lit pool. Arms are raised, each hand pointing in one direction.

"We've got a bachelorette over here!" a girl screams.

"Pick her!" another yells.

"Get this girl on stage!" a third shouts.

High-Tide leans across me to the lighting technician and whispers, "Get me a spotlight on white dress over there in Section 3." The technician nods, using both hands to point the spotlight across the pool. "WE HAVE OUR FINAL VOLUNTEER!"

The crowd parts down the middle and my heart nearly leaps from my chest when the light illuminates the angel's white sundress. The bottom trim of her dress flutters like a ship's sails kissed by a gentle breeze with each step she takes. Her beauty shimmers like the sea itself–boundless, mysterious, stirring my soul to its depths.

Hello again, angel, I want to say when she reaches the foot of the stage. *Tell me you remember me.*

My hand is already offering itself to her before I realize I want to help her onto the stage. It's the first time we touch, and while I want to bask in this moment, it's ruined by the diamond mocking me from her ring finger. It can't be. It shouldn't be. Just when I thought I caught a glimpse of the light, I get dragged back into the abyss. The angel folds her lips between her teeth, her hazel eyes meeting mine–soft and unreadable, like she's keeping a secret she isn't ready to share. A current lingers between us as we stand side by side.

"What's your name, sweetheart?" High-Tide asks her.

The angel smiles. "Bella." Her name leaves her lips coated in divinity, carrying the weight of Heaven itself.

Bella.

"Alright, now we can get this party started!" High-Tide shouts over the crowd. A crew member hands a coconut to each couple standing on stage as High-Tide explains, "Each couple is being handed a coconut. The coconut is going to be placed between the stomachs of the couples as they stand face to face. Without using their hands, the couples will need to get the coconut from their stomachs all the way up to their lips. If they use their hands, they're out! And if they drop the coconut, they'll have to start all over again! Now, let's hear it for our couples!"

I'm pretty sure the crowd is cheering, but it's the least of my concerns when I realize Bella is now looking up at me. I suppress the thought of the ring on her finger as we hide our hands behind our backs. I feel the pressure of the coconut against my abdomen, which sends chills down my arms. Bella looks down at the coconut between us, holding back a laugh.

"READY... SET... GO!" High-Tide shouts.

Music cascades across the ship's deck as the competition starts.

"Do you remember me?" I ask Bella, my voice competing with the crowd's cheers. "We were in the elevator together."

She giggles. "I think we're supposed to start the game."

I lift my eyes to see the other couples breaking a sweat trying to move their coconuts up their bodies. I keep my stomach pressed against the coconut, lowering myself to her eye level. "Your name is Bella?"

"That's the name my parents gave me," Bella replies, her gaze fixated on the coconut. She stands on her tiptoes, and the coconut rolls a bit higher up our stomachs. Pushing her chest into the coconut, her hazel eyes meet mine again. "And I do remember you. Your friend was flirting with my friend, Tish."

"He does that," I exhale. With the slight roll of my shoulders, the coconut rises between us. "I hope your friend didn't take offense."

"She thought it was funny," Bella admits. "Which is surprising. She hasn't found men funny for a while now."

The crowd laughs at a nearby couple who drops their coconut, which cracks in two. We turn at the commotion, and our coconut suddenly loosens against our chests. In an instant, I grab her arms and force our bodies closer to keep it from falling. "Shit," I mutter, my lips inches from hers. "Sorry."

Bella laughs. "It's okay. We can do this."

We can do this.

The words cement themselves to my will, giving me no choice but to give Bella my all.

After a few subtle shimmies and sliding movements, we gradually work the coconut to our necks. The crowd hums excitedly and Bella's contagious laugh makes me laugh. We feed on the energy swirling around the deck. Winning becomes inevitable when I realize winning this competition will give me an excuse to see Bella again tomorrow. At this point, I couldn't care less that the excuse has to do with being on a small boat near whales or that Bella is engaged. All I know is I boarded this ship fearing the ocean and love itself, but both of my fears seem to get weaker the closer I get to Bella. *So, I can't help but want to get closer.*

We lift our heads, using our chins and cheeks to push the coconut up to our lips. Bella's eyes widen and a high-pitched squeak leaves her throat. We throw our hands up in the air, consumed by the wave of applause coming from all around.

"We have our winners!" High-Tide shouts. "Make some fucking noise for Roman and Bella!"

The coconut falls into my palm, but I don't look down. Instead, I look at Bella who looks at me looking at her and I have no desire to look away because I don't remember the last time I've enjoyed the simple act of looking at such a beautiful girl and now I feel the urge to kiss her but I don't know where this urge is coming from and my thoughts are racing or is it my heart or both or–

Bella throws her arms around me. "We did it!" she screams, jumping up and down. I open my mouth to speak, but nothing comes out. She pulls away and laughs at my blatantly obvious infatuation with her. "Earth to Roman! Are you there?"

I lower my head and laugh, surrendering to whatever is happening right now. "I'm here," I chuckle. "I'm here."

She smirks. "Whatever you say."

High-Tide escorts us off the stage, through the crowd, and to the side of the deck. "Alright, lovebirds," he says, handing Bella a white envelope. His scripted, upbeat demeanor back on stage dissolves as he pulls out a cigarette and lights it. "Here's how this is gonna work," he adds between puffs. "We dock in the Bahamas at sunrise tomorrow morning. I have two vouchers for a whale-watching boat thing that departs at noon. The boat is called 'The Voyage.' Before you ask any questions, just know I don't have any answers–I was just told by my boss to give this to the winner. All the information should be on the tickets. So, have fun, enjoy yourselves, aanndd I'm gonna go get drunk." High-Tide exhales a cloud of smoke between Bella and me, then turns back into the crowd.

Bella purses her lips, looking down at the envelope. When her eyes meet mine, we burst out in laughter. "What just happened?!" she exclaims.

"I couldn't even tell you. All I know is that we're damn good at moving coconuts without our hands."

Bella twirls and caresses the guardrail with both hands, then gently leans over. The breeze plays with the waves in her hair, her gaze lost in the beauty of the glistening waters that stretch infinitely before us. As I immerse myself in Bella's presence, the club music in the distance is replaced by the gentle hum of the ship and the soft lapping of waves down against the hull.

"Did your mom ever teach you it's not polite to stare?" Bella asks without looking my way.

Shit. Was I staring?

I look down.

"Sorry," I say. "I'm just a little surprised."

Bella leans against the railing, resting her chin on her hands. She finally looks my way. "Surprised?"

I grip the railing a few feet from her hands. "I'm not big on the ocean. It took a lot of convincing to get me on this ship, and I guess I'm surprised–"

"To actually be having a good time?"

I nod.

"Same," she says, her voice delicate. "What brings you out?"

I hold my tongue, saving her from my sob story. Sure, I could be honest and tell her I'm pretty sure Mac forced me out here because he knows I've been depressed since the breakup. I could tell her I've considered re-enlisting because there's nothing worth living for outside of the military, or that I've lost all faith in love and life itself. Instead, I settle for a lie. "My friend and I won tickets in a raffle, and I couldn't pass up the free booze."

"You won tickets for a cruise and whale-watching, huh?" Bella's brows rise. "You might be the luckiest guy I know." Her laughter sparkles in the air, light and infectious. "How do you even manage to get that lucky? It's like you're the main character and every chapter is written just for you."

"Every chapter written just for me?" I shake my head, the two of us now facing the ocean. "If that's the case, my story better have a happy ending."

"If yours doesn't, I'll write you one myself," she replies smoothly.

I tilt my head. "You a writer or somethin'?"

"I'm a reader. But, yeah. I'm sort of writing my first novel, so I guess you could say I'm a writer."

A smile spreads across my face. I haven't known Bella for very long, and she's already impressed me in more ways than one. Her contagious laughter, her unbridled enthusiasm for life, her ambition. I can't help but want to know more, to dive deeper into her world.

"What about you?" I ask. "What brings you here?"

"Adventure."

"So, you're not on some bachelorette party trip?" I ask, wanting to eat my words. As much as I want to dive deeper into this girl's life and find a way to mold hers to mine, I need to know if I actually have a shot with her. "I heard the crowd chanting, '*Bachelorette*,'" I add.

"Something like that," Bella exhales. While her words make me want to jump off the side of this ship, I notice a trace of reluctance in her voice. She continues, "Tish and I thought it would be a good idea to get away from our hometown for a bit after I was proposed to. And I've never been on an adventure, so I guess you could say I'm out here looking for one. We're doing it for the plot."

"*Doing it for the plot*," I repeat with a grin. "I like that."

She smirks. "Every good story has a good plot. So, if our life is a story and we're the main characters, it's up to us to live out a plot worth reading about. Right?"

I tap my finger against my chin. "But, if we're characters, we don't get to decide what happens in the plot. Isn't that the author's job?"

"Good point." Bella takes a few slow steps from the railing, holding my gaze. "Hopefully, the author will be kind to us in the next chapter."

With every backward step she takes back toward the crowd, the void in me grows larger, reminding me of its everlasting presence.

Don't go, I want to say.

"What's next?!" I call out, the question scraping against my tongue. "I mean, what happens in the next chapter?!"

"Well, you and I won a prize I'm sure most people in the world wouldn't want to throw away, so I guess we'll have to make use of it." Bella looks down at the envelope in her hand, then back at me. "Let's meet on the dock at sunrise; that way, we can explore the island before whale-watching."

As Bella continues toward the crowd, each elegant step pulls at my mind and heart. I embrace the bittersweet moment, understanding the inevitability of my time with Bella coming to an end for now. She's getting married. There's no way in hell anything can happen between us. But, as the moonlight drapes over her, highlighting her grace as she drifts away, her lingering presence gives me hope that I'll see her again at sunrise.

My mind reminds me that she's in love with another man...

My heart tells me I still might have a chance...

My gut warns me to stay away...

But the plot urges me to meet Bella in the morning, anyway.

"*Do it for the plot*," she said.

So, "*Do it for the plot*," I will.

CHAPTER III

BEEP! BEEP! BEEP!

I slam my palm over my phone, silencing the alarm. I wipe the drool from my face, my jaw dropping at the sight of the island outside my bedroom window. It's all I can see from my bed, and I'm too excited to spend another moment under these sheets.

Even after the inhumane amount of cocktails Mac and I drank last night, no amount of alcohol can blur the moments I shared with Bella. I still see her–the way she gracefully stepped into the elevator, the way her presence alone brought me peace. I'm ready for more, so I throw the bedsheet aside and jump to my feet.

The island shore greets me just below shades of fiery orange, soft pink, and delicate lavender, all colors making up the morning sky. Palm trees gently sway below, their shadows playing on the white sand. As I get ready for the day, I occasionally look out the window to see that as the sun climbs higher, its rays illuminate the tropical greenery and nearby town. It's only been a day at sea, and still, I'm excited to be back on land.

I adjust my denim shorts and loose-fitted, white T-shirt. Before heading to shore, I sneak out of my bedroom and through the living room to check on Mac. After Bella left last night, looking for Mac was the only thing keeping me from going to bed. It was only right for me to call it a night after spending an hour trying to find him at the club. With no luck, I came straight back to the room and passed out.

I quietly push his bedroom door open, and a laugh escapes me when I see Bella's friend, Tish, cuddled up next to Mac in bed. Leave it to Mac to somehow win over a girl who once wanted nothing to do with him. I shake my head, knowing I'll soon be hearing him say, "I told you so," for the rest of the cruise.

After quietly shutting Mac's bedroom door, I grab my wallet and head out the–*shit, I almost forgot.* I rummage through my luggage until I find my pills. It only takes a day off my medication for the pain to set in. The doctor back on our military base was adamant about me taking these pills for as long as I wanted to "remain sane." I took his advice. It's hard not to take advice that keeps you from going crazy after a near-death experience in combat. I know I wasn't the first soldier to suffer a life-threatening head injury while on a mission, and I wouldn't be the first veteran to lose his mind because of it.

The pills clatter against the bottle as I pour one out. I swallow the pill, and feelings of normalcy and sanity slide down my throat with the help of some water. I fill my backpack with random things I might need on the island. High-Tide mentioned whale-watching would be at noon, and I assume it won't last more than a couple hours. So, I pack some sunscreen, a bottle of water, and a couple of protein bars.

A few cruise hostesses greet me as I reach the edge of the promenade. My palm glides over the smooth handrail of the bridge connecting the ship to the dock. The sky is still a canvas of painted shades of pink, orange, and lavender, forcing me to come to terms with everything being more breathtaking out in the middle of the ocean–even the clouds. We've only sailed for a night, and it seems we're far enough away for these types of clouds to appear foreign. They're different from the ones I grew up seeing back in Georgia. The clouds out here are soft and billowy, floating effortlessly across the sky.

My head is on a swivel when I reach the dock, looking for any sight of Bella. I haven't once stopped to consider that the main reason she's out here is because she's celebrating being married soon, locking in a relationship for the rest of her life. But, I cling to her first answer when I asked what brought her out: "*Adventure.*" With all my power, I force the thought of adventure to replace the thought of Bella being on the brink of matrimony. Is that selfish of me? Maybe a little bit, but being selfish is fine by me if it means I found someone to love again. Plus, I would be a fool to let our prize tickets go to waste. It's not every day you win a contest in front of hundreds of strangers in the middle of the Caribbean. It's also not every day the thought of someone can pump new life into a broken heart the way Bella did mine.

When I spot Bella across the boardwalk, my legs begin walking for me. My chest grows light as I approach the spot she's sitting, smiling–that smile–I just want to keep looking at that smile because it makes me smile and I haven't smiled in so long that–wait. Easy, Rome. She's married. I mean, she's about to be married. Is this stupid? Am I stupid to think that there's something that could actually happen between us? Do I even want for something to happen between us? Adventure. That's right… that's what we're here for. *Adventure*. That's it. Maybe that's all this can and will be. An adventure for the day. Maybe that's all I need to get my mind off the breakup, once and for all. Maybe one day with Bella is the way out of my misery.

"Morning," I greet, standing over Bella.

She beams up at me, instantly dissolving all second thoughts and traces of guilt. "I was starting to think those cocktails got the best of you." She closes the journal she was writing in and jumps to her feet. "You ready for our adventure?"

"I'm here for the plot," I say, the words not sounding as smooth as I would like for them to.

"Ah, he remembered what we're here for," Bella teases with a wink.

I nod, watching the top of her head as she skips around me toward the town. "Where are we going?" I tighten my backpack straps, watching her glide from the dock onto a cobblestone road. "Do you know where you're going?!"

"No idea!" Bella shouts back. With a subtle tilt of her chin, she gestures for me to follow. "But, that's sort of the point of an adventure, Roman."

I struggle to catch up to her, feeling the weight of my hangover creeping in. "Call me *Rome*," I exhale between heavy breaths.

"Rome," she repeats softly. "Your nickname?"

"The people closest to me call me that," I admit, shielding my eyes from the sun that ascends above the ocean horizon.

Bella twirls, side-eying me. "So, we're already close?"

My eyes widen. "I, uh–I didn't really think about it like that."

"I'm messing with you…" she giggles. "… Rome."

We make our way toward the colorful town, and I accept my fate without even knowing what it is. The town unfolds in hues of sun-bleached whites and pastels, a stark contrast to the uniform life I've grown used to in the military. I'm used to dark shades of beige and green, shouting drill sergeants and the possibility of death around every corner. I don't usually let loose, though I'm finding it hard not to when Bella seems to find the beauty in not knowing what happens next, while I find the beauty in Bella.

"It's so beautiful," Bella tells a woman selling crafts at a market stall.

The elderly woman lifts a necklace with a tiny wooden cross made from a slender, flexible wood. Dangling gracefully from the base of the cross are several strands of thin threads, each adorned with tiny feathers. The feathers catch the light as Bella receives the cross in her hand. She holds it up to get a better look.

"What do you think, Rome?" she asks, dangling the cross between us.

I shrug, forcing an interest. "It's nice." I drag my eyes over the other necklaces and designs lining the market stall, hoping she'll pick out another.

"Just nice?" Bella asks skeptically.

"I used to have one."

"Used to, huh?" She tilts her chin, eyeing the silver military dog tag hanging over my shirt. "Sounds like a story to me."

I smirk, tucking the dog tag back into my shirt. "Maybe for another day."

"Cross," the woman chimes in from beside the stall. The corners of her eyes crinkle above her grin. She marvels at Bella's beauty, rightfully so. "For an angel," she adds in a thick accent, closing Bella's palm over the necklace.

"It's very beautiful!" Bella chirps, dropping her shoulder to dig through her backpack.

The woman places a gentle hand on Bella's arm. "You keep. For you, it is free. Los angeles nunca cuentan dinero."

Bella lifts her gaze to meet the woman's, and she thanks her with the utmost sincerity. As we turn back through the bustling marketplace, I tease, "Do pretty girls always get things for free?"

With an eye roll, she says, "I haven't known you a full day, and you're already flirting with me?"

I shrug as she tucks the tiny wooden cross into her backpack. "I mean, this is technically your bachelorette party. You might as well enjoy a bit of attention before you get hitched."

Bella gives me a playful shove. "I'd rather not think about getting hitched right now."

"You'd rather not?" I pinch my brows together, caught by surprise. "You'd rather not talk about getting married?"

Bella ignores my question, hopping from one cobblestone to another on her tiptoes. Everything about this girl is light, from her white linen romper to her hazel eyes. Even the way she carries herself is light.

I'm startled as she suddenly stops and squares her stance to mine. "Listen, 'Rome,'" she states with air quotes for some reason. "Soon, I'll be married to a man who loves me very much. So, I have the rest of my life to think about him. Right now is all about adventure." She pulls out the envelope and taps it against my chin. "Now, we can explore the rest of this beautiful town, see some whales, and have our adventure, or you can join our friends back on the ship. What do you say? Adventure or back to the ship?"

An audible gulp makes its way down my throat.

Bella tilts her chin and raises a spunky brow. "What will it be?"

"Adventure," I state.

A silent beat passes before a smile plays across her face. "Good answer."

As Bella continues through the town market, I can't help but smile. It's cute that she made it seem like I have a choice. In reality, there's no way I'd let her roam around this island all by herself. Sure, I'm also attracted to her in more ways than one, but all that is beside the point.

Right now is all about *adventure*.

The sun is at its highest when we reach the northern edge of the town. After a morning of weaving through a maze of pastel-colored buildings, exploring museums, and eating fruit I didn't know existed, we find ourselves standing on a beach lined with boats.

"The tickets in the envelope said the boat should be docked here at noon," Bella says.

She squats and rummages through her backpack as I pan around the secluded beach before us. Boats of all sizes are lined side by side, their hulls nestled in the sand while wooden stakes anchor their bows in place. The boats range from simple row boats to complex fishing vessels. Regardless of the size, each boat has one thing in common: *They're old.*

"Found it!" Bella's voice is overflowing with enthusiasm as she lifts the envelope to her eyes. "Okay, so it says the boat is docked on the beach north of town, so we got that right. Set to sail at noon, so we are…" She checks her phone. "Pretty much right on time. We just need to find the boat named 'The Voyage.'"

"The Voyage," I repeat. "Pretty cool name for a boat."

Bella leads the way up the beach. "What's fascinating is that boat names always carry meaning. It's kind of like when authors name book characters after loved ones."

"You would really get along with my friend, Mac," I chuckle. "You two seem to know a lot about things I know nothing about."

"You learn a lot the more you read," she replies, then giggles. "Also, I'm sure Mac and Tish are having an interesting morning waking up together. You think they're looking for us?"

I shrug. "Something tells me they'll be just fine without us."

I'm stopped by Bella's arm as she points to our right. "Look at this one!"

The tip of her finger is aimed at a weathered boat, its paint peeling off in large flakes. The boat is smaller compared to the others, and the hull shows signs of the many repairs needed to keep this piece of junk afloat for what might be decades.

My shoulders tense. "I'm not getting anywhere near that thing."

"What do you mean?" Bella asks. "This is so cool! Hello?!" she shouts over the front of the boat. "Anyone up there?"

I reach for her arm. "Bella, I don't think we should–"

CRASH!

The sound of a glass bottle shattering against the boat's deck sends us into a panic. A head pops out over the side. Long blonde dreadlocks hang over the man's filthy face, a layer of dark mud and sand making his golden eyes pop. His beard is unkempt, and his smile suggests he's never used a toothbrush in this life or the last.

"What da wybe?" he greets–well, I think it's a greeting.

Bella places her palms on the side of the boat, lifting herself on her tiptoes. "We're looking for a boat called 'The Voyage.'" The man lifts his chin, confused. Bella uses her hands to help him understand. "We..." She points at me. "Are looking..." She points at the boats. "For a boat called, 'THE VOYAGE.'"

The man's bushy brows straighten over his flattened lips. "I speak English, woman," he blurts aloud. "And even if I didn't, you say same ting twice."

Bella flicks her eyes to me for backup. I lower my head to keep from laughing. "Sorry about her. We're from the cruise ship right over there and we won a free whale-watching trip from a contest."

Bella raises the envelope for the man to see.

"Ah, contest." The man nods, raising himself so that his elbows are resting on the boat's edge. Bella hands him the envelope, and he skeptically observes the tickets and then our faces. "Dis is whack! You don't want to do dis. Da Voyage is boring. I take you somewhere betta for cheap."

"Somewhere better?!" Bella asks the same time I ask, "What's cheap?"

The man's dreads bounce as he tilts his head. "How much you got?"

Bella turns to me. "Do you have any money on you?"

The pleading look in her eyes instantly has me feeling my pockets for cash. I pull out a couple of twenty-dollar bills.

"This is all I got," I say, holding up the cash. The man reaches for it until I pull it back. "But the ticket says we need to board The Voyage."

"Ahhhh, forget dat, man." The man sighs and mutters something in a language far from English. His wild eyes suddenly flick between us. "Voyage is for da tourists, da people who are too scared to see da real deal. You want to experience da ocean, 'Oathkeeper' with Azrael is da way."

"Hi, Captain Azrael!" Bella chirps with a salute. "I'm Bella. This is Roman."

"Bella and Roman." Azrael leaps over the boat's edge, landing in the sand before us. Keeping his knees bent, he lifts his palms and paints an imaginary picture. "Picture da clearest waters, like glass all da way down to da ocean floor. Colors you never seen wit ya own eyes, calling you by name. Dey whisper, 'Roman, Bella.'" He leans forward, placing a musty hand on each of our shoulders. His breath reeks of rum as he adds, "Come wit me if you want to see da sea for what it is–*a goddess*."

The words glide effortlessly from his tongue, his voice rich with remnants of untold adventures. Gold strands make up his clipped dreadlocks, complementing the weaving curls in his tattered beard. His eyes want to leap from their sockets, glowing against his leathery skin. His malnourished complexion and narrow body contrast the intense energy radiating from his sweaty pores. He stands grinning ear to ear, eagerly waiting for us to accept his invitation.

While this morning was serene, the colorful clouds were joined by darker clouds in the distance. I pinch my eyebrows together, feeling a sensation wrapping itself around the pit of my stomach. It's an undeniable gut feeling, a deep-seated unease whispering a warning through every nerve of my body. My pa's words make themselves known in the forefront of my mind, words I've lived by since I can remember: "*If you don't feel it in your mind, heart, and gut, then don't do it.*"

"Let's do it!" Bella shouts.

I wince at her blind enthusiasm. "Let's?"

Azrael beams at us. "Mudda sick!" he cheers, pulling himself up onto the boat with ease. He looks back down, offering Bella his hand.

Bella reaches for it until I yank it to my chest. I flash her a disappointed glare. "A word?" I pull her up the shore before she can respond. "Are you insane?!" I whisper-shout with my back to the boat. "We're not getting on that death trap with that whack job."

"Don't be dramatic." She rolls her eyes. "What happened to 'Doing it for the plot?!' What about adventure?!"

I bite my lip, my eyes flicking between Bella and the boat. *Be smart, Rome. You obviously don't feel this one in your gut.* There's no denying the long list of variables working against me now: I can't swim, something is off about this Azrael guy, and the clouds in the distance seem to keep getting darker.

My eyes meet Bella's, and her pleading gaze somewhat settles my uneasy stomach. I don't know where her unwavering desire for adventure came from, but regardless, it's pulling me in. There's something about her that dominates my fears and dissolves my worries. I haven't known her a full day, and I can't deny that my pitiful life has already become more exciting. There's more beauty, more adventure.

I turn to catch a glimpse of our cruise ship docked on the opposite side of the small town. "The trip can only be a few hours," I declare loud enough for Azrael to hear. "We need to be back on our ship before the sun goes down."

"Yes!" Bella cheers. "Imagine the story we'll tell Tish and Mac, imagine the adventure! Roman and Bella sail out to open waters with Captain Azrael. It's already a novel in the making."

"Jus' chill, brudda!" Azrael shouts playfully. He straddles the upper edge of the boat's deck, one of his filthy legs hanging over the side. "You give me da cash for gas, and I give you adventure," he adds, pulling Bella onto the deck. I reluctantly slap the cash into Azrael's hand, then he pulls me up. "And you will get to meet Marelia."

"Who's Marelia?" I ask, finding my footing.

The boat's deck is a patchwork of weathered planks, each telling a story of countless adventures and the relentless assault of sun and salt. The once-vibrant paint is now chipped, exposing the grayed wood beneath. There's a tang of old fish and engine oil, the air thick with the smell of the sea.

"You meet Marelia soon," Azrael says into a beat-up cooler as he pulls out two beers. He uses his teeth to crack open the bottle caps, then hands us each a bottle. "For you beautiful people." He pulls out a copper flask and takes a long swig, adding, "For Azrael."

The bottle is cool against my palm. I take a swig and feel myself loosen up when I see Bella do the same. I exhale, pressing the chilled beer against my sweaty forehead. "You're insane," I mutter, holding back a laugh. "I can't believe you talked me into getting on this thing."

Bella gets comfortable on the bench next to me. "My dad once said, '*The adventure begins the moment the characters lose control.*'"

VROOOM!

The motor suddenly growls, and the boat lurches backward. I grab a nearby railing and catch Bella with my free hand. "And so the adventure begins," I whisper, suppressing the ache in my gut.

CHAPTER IV

"Are you sure we should even be out here?!" I ask Azrael from the front of the boat. "Those kind of look like storm clouds!"

"I'm sure Captain Azrael would know whether or not it's safe to set sail!" Bella replies innocently.

Regardless, Azrael ignores my question, slurring a sea shanty to himself between sips of his flask. Thick clouds loom in the sky as the boat departs from the harbor, casting long, ominous shadows over the water. The motor roars, stirring a frothy wake as we leave the safety of the shore behind. I can feel my unease stirring in my gut, and I imagine my parents and Mac telling me this is a bad idea. Azrael is a complete stranger, not to mention he's drunk off his ass and I'm pretty sure I've caught him talking to himself a few times.

The next hour becomes a mental battleground. For every moment I find myself suspicious of Azrael, there's a moment where my connection with Bella grows. My stomach turns every time Azrael sips from his flask, while my heart flutters when Bella tells me about some book she brought on the cruise. I break into a cold sweat when Azrael continues talking to himself, while warmth flows under my skin when Bella laughs at one of my jokes. As the island and cruise ship fade in the background, I'm left with a heart that wants to satisfy Bella's deep yearning for adventure and a mind that wants to find out if Azrael can be trusted.

"You want to hear a crazy thought?" Bella asks between sips

of her beer.

I fixate on the way her wavy locks become one with the wind. "Let's hear it."

"Book characters don't know their purpose; only the author knows. Whether the character appears for the entire book, a chapter, or even just for a single page, the character just does what the author needs them to do, and *poof*! Either they get killed off or they live until the story ends. And while the author knows every detail about the character and their fate, the character only knows what happens as their story is told."

"You're interesting, you know that?" I say. Bella presses the beer bottle to her lips to hide her grin, and that's when her engagement ring reintroduces itself to me. I ignore its sting. "I've never met somebody so obsessed with books."

Her expression softens. "I was raised in a bookstore." She loses herself to whatever thought crosses her mind. I watch her gaze roll over the waves lapping against the side of the boat, as if the waves tell a story Bella can't resist submitting herself to. "Is my obsession annoying?" she asks, returning to the moment.

"Far from it," I assure her. "It's cute."

Bella rolls her eyes, then looks to the clouds ahead. "You're trouble, Rome."

"I'm not trouble. I'm just a side character in your book," I tease. "In a couple chapters, you'll be on your way to getting married and finding your happy ending, or what's it called in fairy tales? Your '*happily ever after*?'"

Bella purses her lips, remaining fixated on the horizon. Her demeanor shrinks as she raises her feet atop the bench and wraps her arms around her legs. With her cheek resting on her knees, she repeats, "*Happily ever after*," in a whisper that feels ever so distant.

I sip my beer, contemplating what I just said to make her retract from the conversation. As my eyes follow the moving water along the side of the boat, I begin to envision what Bella's fiancé is like. Is he fit? Is he smart? Cunning? Rich? Does he love books the way she does? Maybe he's all of the above. Or maybe he's the opposite. Maybe he's out of shape, dumb as a rock, has no personality, and lives off her paychecks. It's probably a mixture, considering she seems to have mixed feelings about getting married to this guy.

"When did you start sailing?" Bella asks Azrael.

"I was born on a boat," he replies from behind the steering

wheel. "I sail before I walk."

"Exciting," Bella replies. "Do you have any wild ocean stories?"

Azrael laughs. "Those stories are for land. I don't want to scare you two."

Thank you, Azrael.

"Tell us one!" Bella shouts. "You have to!"

"Okay, okay." Azrael sips his flask. "Years ago, I sail for good fishing alone. Motor stop working, so I drift. One day, two day, three. After a week, da ocean start to speak to me. Da waves call my name. 'Azrael,' dey say. 'I want you to serve me.'"

Bella leans forward. "The ocean talked to you?"

"Clear as day," Azrael exhales in a shaky breath. "Da ocean introduce herself as Marelia. She say, 'Do what I tell you from now on, and I will save you.'"

"And what'd she tell you to do?" Bella asks.

"Marelia wanted me to make an oath. She told me dat one day, greedy fishing company will take over da ocean. She told me to promise to protect da ocean by telling da fishing company to go away." Azrael lowers his head. "Da current picked up after and took me back to da shore. Since dat day, I tried to keep my oath to serve Marelia." He lifts his chin, eyes fixed on the sky. "I tried."

"Oathkeeper," Bella exhales. "That's why you named your boat 'Oathkeeper!'"

"I was going to die, but Marelia save me," Azrael says softly. "I'm not crazy. I keep metal box on da boat. Inside, I have item to keep me from going crazy."

"What kind of item?" I ask.

"An hourglass," he says. "It is a sailor's trick. At least once a day, you turn da hourglass, and as da sand falls, use da time to remember memories like stories. Dat way, you stay connected to da past, connected to da land. Otherwise, memories get lost. Then, you lose reality da way you lose da land. You go insane."

Bella pulls her journal from her backpack and begins taking notes. "This is perfect for a book."

A low growl makes itself known in the distance, stealing Azrael's attention. "Marelia, have mercy," I hear him mutter to himself. "Be good to us."

"Be good to us?" I ask.

Azrael's eyes drift over our shoulders. The distant growl

continues, forcing us to turn our heads. "Have mercy," he continues, his eyes fixated on the dark clouds ahead.

"Azrael!" I call out. He raises his brows as he looks our way. "What's going on?"

He raises a shaky thumbs-up. "We are fine!"

"Then why are you telling the ocean to have mercy?!" With my head on a swivel, it becomes more obvious that the farther we've sailed from land, the more aggressive and murky the ocean appears to be.

Azrael turns his back to us, and the boat slows to a stop. The sound of the roaring motor is replaced by waves beating against the sides of the boat. "Many people don't understand," he says between quick sips of his flask. "Marelia–da ocean–you can tell if she is happy by da waves."

Bella leans forward, noticing the boat rocking over waves which hold an underlying aggression. "Is she upset? The waves are getting… bigger."

"Good question," Azrael replies. He points at the dark clouds gathering ominously in the distance, then leans over the side of the boat. With his eyes closed and weathered hand trailing in the water, he asks, "What is it, my old friend? What is stirring you?"

Chills cover my arms as the waves begin to lift and lower the boat. Its response to Azrael is subtle but undeniable. I glance at Bella, who now also has her hand over the side of the boat. After a few silent beats, Azrael quickly stands and darts to the back. He curses under his breath, rummaging through random buckets and bins.

"What's happening?!" I ask, startled by his fear-stricken expression.

Judging from Azrael's erratic movements, it couldn't be more obvious that something is off. Azrael knows something we don't. Having served in combat, I've been faced with alarming situations time and time again, and this seems to be no different from every time before, only *we're far from being in control.*

"What did Marelia say?!" Bella asks.

"She is not happy! Not good for us!" Azrael shouts with his back still to us. "Not good, not good."

I jump to my feet and make it to him in a few quick steps. "What's happening?"

"Not good. Marelia still upset wit me. Not good."

"Azrael," I say sternly, but it's no use. "Azrael!" He keeps searching through random junk. "AZRAEL!" I growl, now gripping his forearm. His breath hitches, his frantic eyes meeting mine. "What do you mean by, '*Marelia* still *upset*?!'"

Azrael's breaths are shallow. "We should not have left da shore," he exhales. "Da storm is too big."

I release his arm, panic manifesting within me when the words leave his lips. My gut was right. I shouldn't have trusted this drunk lunatic. I didn't feel this was right in my mind, heart, and gut, and now we're in the middle of the ocean with nowhere to go but back to shore, which hasn't been visible for at least an hour now.

"The clouds!" I hear Bella shout in the background. "They're moving this way!"

My heartbeat pounds against the inner walls of my skull. As Azrael goes back to digging through junk, I fight the urge to throw his drunk ass off this boat and drive us back to shore. The sound of surrounding waves grows louder, demanding our attention with little effort.

"We need to go back!" I shout across the deck. "Turn on the motor, and we'll race the storm back to shore!"

Azrael slams a metal box on the deck, then kneels over it. "You cannot outride Marelia!" he says, sifting through random junk. "Marelia is still angry wit me. We must surrender. If we surrender, she will have mercy."

I clench my jaw. If I'm going to get information from him, I'll have to speak his language. "Azrael, why is Marelia still angry with you? What did you do to her?!"

Azrael pauses, flicking his eyes between Bella and me. As we crouch beside him, he finally confesses, "Months ago, I made a deal wit an American fishing company. It was da company she warned me about. Big company, big money. I show dem da rhythm of da local waters and where to find da most fish—dey make good money. Dey pay me good money, lots of good money, then guilt took over when da company sent many, many boats later. In only months, a few of da local fish go extinct. I say, 'No more.' But, da companies don't listen. I give da money away to da local town. Still, Marelia is mad at me. She will not forgive me for my sins."

Bella clenches her backpack to her chest. She subtly lifts her chin and eyes me apologetically. *We fucked up*, she wants to say, but she refrains because our only hope is a drunken homeless man disguised as a captain.

A laugh escapes me. "I knew you were insane," I mutter over Azrael. "You're insane and this was a terrible idea and now we're gonna get caught in the middle of a storm because you don't know what the hell you're doing!" I'm suddenly on my feet, pacing from one side of the deck to the other. I begin hyperventilating, failing to find the path that leads to survival. "We're not gonna die," I exhale with each breath. "We're not gonna die, we're not gonna die."

"It's not up to us," Azrael whispers. "Marelia decides."

Bella sits back on the bench, her eyes exuding terror as they flick left and right. She lifts a shaky hand over her mouth. Her first tear falls, and I swoop the second with my thumb. She fixates on me, my hands now caressing her flushed cheeks. The booming clap of thunder sends chills down my spine, but I keep calm for Bella. If there's one thing I took away from the military, it's keeping my composure in the face of death.

"You wanted adventure," I exhale, inches from her lips. "Well, we found ours."

I shift to face Azrael, who is taking inventory of his metal box. He briefly picks up each item—an hourglass, a knife, a coil of rope—sets them back in the box, and then slams the box shut.

"Azrael." His name leaves my lips calmly this time around. "I know you think Marelia decides our fate. And I respect that, but while there is a chance we can make it back to shore before the storm hits, I need to try. Let me try."

Azrael nods. "You can try, my friend. Marelia must know dat I surrender, but you can try."

I stand to my feet and struggle to balance over the shifting surface as the boat rises. The wind howls, tugging at my clothes until I'm forced to the boat's edge. I grip a nearby rail, guiding myself to the steering wheel in the back. The wet, chilling metal stings against my palm. I tighten my grip, seeing hills of water become mountains on the horizon. Hints of baby-blue peek through the black clouds now lingering above us, and I begin to understand the magnitude of Marelia's frustration with Azrael. I let go of the rail, and the boat suddenly tilts from the right side, sending the three of us sliding across the slippery deck.

"Roman!" Bella screams.

Pain shoots through my side when I slam into the opposite side of the boat. A growl escapes me. I grit my teeth. "We're not gonna die," I repeat. "We're not gonna die." I leap for another rail before the boat's violent rocking nearly sends me back across the deck again. With one hand on the rail, I reach for the crank on the motor. My fingers graze it once, then twice. If I'm going to be able to start the motor, I'll have to let go of the rail again. And if I let go of the rail again, my fate will be determined by God, Marelia, or Bella's stupid "author."

New mission: *Resist letting my fate be determined by anybody but me.*

"Tie yourself! You don't want to be thrown off da boat!" Azrael screams over the wind. I look over my shoulder to see Azrael and Bella clinging to ropes fastened to the front of the boat. "Tie your wrist! You will survive if we ride it out!"

"Roman, tie yourself!" Bella shouts, following Azrael's orders.

I fill my chest with air and face the motor once more. *We're not gonna die.*

I fix my eyes on the crank. *We're not gonna die.*

I let go of the rail. *We're not gonna die.*

I leap across the back of the boat. My chest slams against the top of the motor I cling onto for dear life. Bella's words wrap my conscience, and I refuse to be the character whose story is cut short–the character who doesn't find his own happily ever after. The boat dips, and we begin sliding down a mountain of a wave. I pull the motor's crank again and again, waiting to hear the roar. "START, MOTHERFUCKER!" I scream. "START!" I'll break this damn motor before I let the ocean take my life. "Please."

VROOOM!

"YES!" I scream.

The sound of the roaring motor becomes music to my ears, our saving grace, our last hope. With a smile on my face and newfound adrenaline coursing through my veins, I pull myself up by the steering wheel. The raindrops and wind work together, the drops stabbing my face while the wind makes it hard to stand straight. The boat reaches the bottom of the wave, and I try to safely glide across the next. All traces of a blue sky have been drowned out by darkness, the only light stemming from jagged rivers of lightning running across the sky.

I grip the wheel with both hands and try to turn, but the strength of the ocean causes the wheel to turn me instead. I tighten my grip, the muscles in my forearms contracting as I force the wheel left and we carve down the slope of a wave. Sharp, cold droplets form a spray across the right side of my face.

I wipe my eyes, catching sight of Bella at the front of the boat. Her soaking wet hair is plastered across her face, tendrils whipping wildly. Her white romper clings to her frame, her eyes wide with fear and regret. Sheets of rain separate us, but I still see her mouth the words, "I'm sorry." She reaches out to me while the rope keeps her fastened to the boat by her wrist.

SNAP!

The steering wheel aggressively spins to no end, now completely detached from the motor. Our saving grace, our last hope–gone. I look up to see Bella still reaching in my direction. The front of the boat gradually rises, revealing nothing but the black sky.

We're gonna die.

"Roman!" Bella screams at the top of her lungs.

My lip quivers. *I'm on my way, angel.*

Without wasting another second, I pull myself around the spinning wheel. My feet slip in every direction but Bella's, though I refuse to let the ocean win. Azrael shouts random words toward the sky, laughing and crying all at once.

Bella reaches for me. *I'm on my way, angel.*

I fall onto all fours and slide across the deck, hitting the right side. Lightning strikes, illuminating the madness for a mere moment. Bella's hand is all I see. My breath steadies as I'm finally able to stand to my feet again. For a brief moment, it's easier to stand than it was before. And that's when I realize it's only because we're at the top of the wave. The boat dips forward, and miles separate us from the bottom of the towering wave. My eyes meet Bella's for what might be the last time, and I lean toward her because it's all I can do.

I lean, and I lean…

until I'm falling for her…

and

then

over

her.

For a brief, surreal moment, I'm flying. My world becomes nothing but wind and rain as I fly over the front of the boat with weightless grace. And as time slows and I find myself having lost control once and for all, I embrace the harsh reality that we have no control over reality itself.

I slam into the water headfirst, and the pain is so unbearable I'm convinced I'm dead. All I see is black, and I feel ice-cold water slithering through every hole in my head as I flail my arms, looking for something–anything–to hold on to.

I'm pulled in every direction.

I think I'm crying.

I know I'm dying.

And all I can do is surrender to the ocean.

1 DAY STRANDED

"KHOOAAGGHH..."

The salt water leaves my throat with so much force that it tightens my core. The abrasive sensation of sand covers the left side of my face as I lift it from the ground. Each grain is sharp against my skin, and every muscle in my body screams in protest as I try to move.

Where am I?

I blink rapidly to clear my vision, only to be met with the blinding sun overhead. My mouth is dry, my tongue tracing mini cuts from sand and saltwater remnants. I throw up again. "KHOOAAGGHH!" Less comes out the second time I throw up, but it's just as painful as the first. My core tightens again, and it takes a few seconds for me to inhale air long enough to steady my breathing.

It's when my heartbeat slows that I realize I'm still half-underwater.

SPLASH!

I'm struck by a moving wall of chilling whitewash, the wave covering me from head to toe. I lift my arm toward the beach, but it merely falls flat. With the little strength I have, I swing my arm to the opposite side of my body so I'm lying face up. My entire body is fatigued, and I'm so exhausted I can hardly move my limbs.

I open my mouth to shout for help. Nothing comes out.

I open my mouth again, this time managing a whisper.

"Help."

My body braces itself at the sound of another incoming wave.

"Help."

The word leaves my lips in the form of another whisper. The second wall of whitewash consumes my body, salt water forcing its way back into my head. *Get the fuck up, Rome.* I jerk my body to lie face down, then drag myself up the shore. My head is too heavy to lift, so I keep my eyes on the sand and watch it move under me as I pull myself farther.

I hear a third wave coming.

My body tightens.

I brace myself.

Here

it

comes…

Nothing.

I exhale a sigh of relief, realizing I pulled myself far enough up the shore to avoid the incoming waves. Still lying face down, the left side of my face meets the sand.

And I black out.

🌴🌴🌴

I'm lying parallel to a blurry horizon when I wake up again. For a second, I'm convinced that I dreamed of washing up on this shore. But, the more I blink the blurriness from my eyes, the clearer it becomes that I have no idea where I am.

"No," I exhale in a shallow whisper. "No, no, no."

I lift my head, feeling slightly stronger than I was whenever I last woke. As my vision gradually clears, I can see the storm clouds now in the distance. The sun is just now setting between the clouds and the ocean. As I struggle to sit up on my knees, my hands sink into wet sand, fingers curling around cool grains that make up land I've never been so grateful to reunite with. My chest rises and falls as I think through what could be memories or dreams, each feeling equally as real to me in this moment.

I was on a cruise with Mac.

I left the ship to explore the island.

I was on a boat with… *Bella.*

"BELLA?!" I force myself to stand, my legs wobbling beneath me. "BELLA!"

I scan my surroundings, dread creeping over me as my new reality sets in. I push through the pain in my ribs and chest, staggering up the desolate beach. I'm on a fucking island, a painfully small island. From where I stand, I can see both ends of the small strip of land surrounded by the vast, unending ocean. The beach is made up of white sand, circling a small peak of dense greenery in the middle. Scraggly bushes, plus three palm trees rustling faintly in the gentle breeze. It's a pathetic excuse for an island, as if it was trying to hold on to some form of life while losing the battle against the encroaching sea.

I turn slowly, forcing myself to take it in. Panic gnaws at my chest, air filling my lungs in the form of crackling gasps. The realization hits me so hard that I fall back down on my knees. Tears blur my vision, and I fight coming to terms with the fact that my current situation may be worse than death itself.

I'm

stranded.

"HEELLPP!" I scream over the ocean, my voice cracking. Between shaky sobs and dry heaves, I scream again. "HELP!" I'm so exhausted that I hardly recognize my own voice, one of pure desperation. The rhythmic crashing of waves mocks me as a response. How could this happen? How could I let this happen?

I cover my face with my sandy palms before lowering my head to the sand, and I cry like never before. It's a loud cry, one buried inside of me for the 22 years I've lived on this earth. Faces flash through my mind: Mom, Dad, Mac, Bella, Azrael, even faces of people I haven't spoken to in months. Past teachers, drill sergeants, my ex. If there was a face I've seen at any point in my life, it becomes part of the rapid-fire mental slideshow playing in my mind. And the sad truth is, I would do anything to see just one of their faces because it would mean I'm no longer where I am now.

When I'm out of tears to cry, I wipe at my eyes and look at the last sliver of the sun setting before me. The clouds above become pillows of dark pink and some purple, calming me enough to focus on standing without wobbling. With every wobbly step, I wiggle my fingers and toes as if I'm regaining my sense of touch for the first time. My strength is slowly returning while my breath has regained its rhythm. While any sign of hope seems to be a world away, I can only think to breathe and walk.

Inhale.

Left, right, left.

Exhale.

Right, left, right.

My steps are slow and deliberate, the twilight air cool against my skin while my face is hot with the effort to hold back another rolling set of tears. Even the sound of waves crashing gently on the shore does nothing to soothe the turmoil brewing within. In my short life, I've faced death a few times, though nothing compares to looking in all directions and seeing an eternity of nothing. My eyes pan around the beach that curves around the patch of green. The sand seems to be untouched by human feet or hands other than my own. Delicate shells and pieces of coral dot the shoreline down to the waves that have calmed since the sunset.

And that's when I see it.

A faint shimmer catches my attention seconds before the water recedes from the shore. Adrenaline courses through me. *Azrael's metal box.* I sprint toward the box, racing the next wave to it. I dive onto it, clinging to its sharp edges as the wave washes over me. I'm soaking wet again, but I don't care. I have a box. I have a metal fucking box.

I set it down near the palms, lusting over what's inside and how I can use it to survive. After looking down at it long enough, hope that was once distant is now within reach. If this washed up, what else washed up? My head is suddenly on a swivel, my eyes flicking in every direction for anything that isn't already part of the island. I make a beeline for a large wooden plank floating nearby in shallow water.

I grab the large plank, then drag it to shore.

I find another plank, then drag it to shore.

I find an old bucket, then drag it to shore.

I pace left, then right, squinting my eyes to find anything I can before dusk turns to night, before it's too dark to see anything at all. All I can find are more wooden planks that once made up Azrael's boat. My heart drops when I notice the last plank is a fragment of a larger piece, its jagged edge suggesting it was snapped in half during the storm. And it suddenly dawns on me that if the ocean could do this to our boat, what could it have done to Bella?

I shake my head, suppressing the thought of Bella being tied to a boat that has been shattered to pieces. By the time I finish my last sweep of the island, the sky is its darkest shade of blue before turning black. I lay out each item I could find, then stand over the spread. With a hand on my hip, I take inventory. "Seven-and-a-half wooden planks and an old bucket, plus Azrael's metal box filled with an hourglass, a coil of rope, and a knife."

I sit back on the sand and turn to face the open ocean. The adrenaline that once fueled me has seeped from my body, bringing my attention to the sides of my head, which gradually begin to throb.

"FUCK." *My medication is back on the cruise ship.*

The longest I've gone without taking my meds was only a few days. I have no idea what could happen if I go longer than that amount of time off my meds. But now isn't the time to worry about that. Even in a place where there's nothing I can do but worry, now just isn't the time.

I sit crisscross. With my elbows on my knees, I rest my chin on my palms and close my eyes. I wince at the pain that continues consuming my head. Maybe I can't cure the pain, but I can try to keep myself from fixating on it.

I straighten my posture, resting my hands on my knees. With my eyes closed, I resort to Box Breathing, a technique we used in the military to keep calm under pressure.

I inhale slowly and deeply through my nose. *1, 2, 3, 4.*

I hold my breath. *1, 2, 3, 4.*

I exhale slowly and fully through my mouth. *1, 2, 3, 4.*

After repeating the cycle, my heartbeat and the pounding in my head slow down. I lay back on the cool sand, listening to the breeze play with the palms. The sky is all I see, the stars shining with piercing clarity. Their patterns form across the sky, contributing to the vastness of space. I don't cry anymore, not because this is the most peace I've felt today, but because I have no tears left to cry.

My entire life, I've been in control.

My entire life, I've had a routine, a plan, a mission.

What am I supposed to do now?

Is this really how it ends?

Is this really how I die?

I close my eyes, fill my chest with air, then exhale. "Send help."

The words escape me before I realize I'm praying. I was once religious, faithful to a God I once thought cared about me. But that all changed when He robbed me of my only love. And as I lie here in what might as well be both a prison and death sentence, my unbelief is only strengthened. What kind of God punishes the innocent like this? What kind of God takes the life of an angel and leaves an innocent man to die a slow, painful death in the middle of the ocean?

I study the sky, letting my gaze drift until my blinks become slower and heavier. The stars form a tapestry of dreams, fragments of my memory that shimmer, some brighter than others against the black. The twinkle puts me in a calming state until I'm consumed by my own physical, mental, and spiritual exhaustion–my savior being sleep itself.

2 DAYS STRANDED

I wake, opening my eyes to the blinding sun overhead. I prop myself up on my elbows, blinking until my eyes adjust to my surroundings. "Damn," I mutter, realizing I'm waking up exactly where I was the night before. *Still stranded.*

I push myself to my feet, wincing as grains of sand cling stubbornly to my raw skin. My sunburnt forehead, cheeks, and arms ache with every move, the sting biting deep into my skin. My back is sweating through my white T-shirt, the humid air mingling with my sun-scorched body. I press the tip of my finger into my burnt forearm, and my skin flashes white before it turns back to a deep red.

My mouth is the driest I think it's ever been, my muscles still fatigued from yesterday which feels like a chaotic blur. I still have no idea how I ended up here. Being thrown off a ship in the middle of the Caribbean without knowing how to swim and then waking up on an island unharmed? I'm not the smartest when it comes to probability, but the odds of me surviving had to be below zero. It's one of those situations that make more sense if you just refer to it as some kind of miracle. And I've never been one for believing in miracles.

I swear more and more sand clings to my skin, clothes, and hair by the second. The salty air fills my lungs as I scan the shore feeling slightly more agile than before. I'm also a whole lot hungrier. I won't be able to survive on the hopeless thoughts seducing my mind yesterday. I can't survive on hopeless. I can't dwell on people who aren't here or life back home. I need a new plan–a mission.

New mission: *Find food and clean water.*

I feel the burn as I wipe the sweat from my forehead while approaching the greenery that makes up the middle of the island. The shade of the palms offers me relief from the sun, a newfound luxury. The air is thick and humid out here, much more humid than back in the South. I move cautiously over the crisscrossing vines and roots below me, looking for any sign of edible fruits or plants.

I sift through the bushes. *Nothing.*

I yank on vines and roots. *Nothing.*

I look up. *COCONUTS.*

A laugh escapes me and I'm convinced my mouth would water if I wasn't so dehydrated. I shield my eyes from the sunlight seeping through the palm leaves to count the coconuts. Eight coconuts are nestled up against the three palm trees. Without wasting another second, I take off my damp shoe and throw it at one of the coconuts. I miss, and the shoe falls with a disappointing thud. I slowly pick up the shoe, then crane my neck back. Determination courses through my veins, my eyes now narrowed at the coconuts.

I steady my breath, fix my focus, aim, and throw.

DIRECT HIT.

I drop to my knees the moment the coconut hits the ground. I cradle it like a newborn baby, its rough shell my only lifeline. Now that something edible is in reach, my stomach twists with hunger. I run my hands through vines and roots until I find a decent-sized rock, then set to work. I sandwich the coconut between my thighs and hammer at the top of it with the rock. A growl rumbles low in my throat, each strike sending vibrations up my arms. The shell finally cracks, and after a few more hits, it splits open.

The sweet aroma of coconut water fills my nose. I lift my chin, raise the coconut to my lips, and chug without thinking. The water is cool, softening my dry throat as the chilling sensation reaches my core. I'm strengthened by every last drop that makes it between my lips. Once I finish the water, I use the rock to crack the coconut in half, then begin scraping out the white flesh inside. Each bite is a revelation, the sweetness overpowering the harsh realities I've faced over the past 24 hours. The world around me fades into the background as I focus solely on the next bite.

When there's nothing left of the coconut, I lift my gaze to the palms once more, then close my eyes. A smile spreads across the bottom half of my face. The taste of coconut is overcome by a new aftertaste that makes itself known–*hope*. I taste hope on my tongue, and though it's still not much, it's enough to convince me that maybe I can do this. Maybe, just maybe, I can survive.

Over the next few hours–or at least, what feels like a few hours–I start a new mission: *Build shelter*. I break the larger wooden planks into smaller pieces and fasten them together with the rope from Azrael's box. I prop one plank straight up, then fasten a longer plank so that it slants from the top of the standing plank down to the sand. I fasten the sturdiest sticks I can find over each side of the slanting plank, the shelter's opening facing the ocean as the shelter narrows toward the back. My eyes land on the palm leaves, taunting me from above. The leaves would make a far better roof for my shelter, but I'm not strong enough to climb. Not yet, anyway.

I crawl into the only open end of my shelter, where I've placed the metal box beside a bucket filled with three coconuts. Other than the coconut I ate and the three I've set aside in the bucket, I left four hanging in the palm trees. I take off my shirt and drape it over the front of the shelter. Not because I need to, but because it gives off the illusion of a front door. I'm not sure if it can be this simple, but homes usually have front doors. And though it's the last thing I want to consider, I have to consider this my home for now.

The light seeping through the crevices of the shelter wall reflects off the metal box I run through again. Each time I sift through the random supplies, I cling to a small hope that something new will present itself–something that can get me off this island or help me contact someone who can. Instead, I'm left with the knife, the coil of rope, and the hourglass.

I lift the hourglass, remembering Azrael's story about how he used it to remain sane while lost at sea. "*At least once a day, turn the hourglass, and as the sand falls, use the time to remember memories like stories,*" I remember him saying. "*That way, you stay connected to the past. Otherwise, memories get lost. Then, you lose reality. You go insane.*"

I gently shake the hourglass, the grains of sand collected at the bottom now eager to be on top. My mind is all I have out here; the last thing I want is to lose it. I hope Azrael is right when he says it's a good idea to stay connected to the past. He doesn't know my past, and though he proved himself unreliable once, I have no choice but to give him the benefit of the doubt.

I take a deep breath, flip the hourglass, and as sand begins to slip through the center tube, I dive back into my past...

"SO, TAKE ME DOWN A ROAD THAT'S A LITTLE BIT WIINNDDYY!" I scream the lyrics over the car speakers. "TO A PLACE THEY STILL PUT SUGAR IN THEIR ICCEE TTEEAA!"

Clem's laughter fills my truck, competing with my God-awful voice as I keep on singing. "One thing's for sure, Rome!" She grabs my hand and rests it in her lap. "You were not born to be a Country singer!"

My brows furrow, and I suck in an audible gasp. "Why, Clementine, you've gone stone-cold. Ma loves my voice!"

Clem shoots me a half-glance, struggling to hide her smile. "And what's your pa think?!"

I close my eyes and nod. "Pa thinks that I should keep my mouth shut and stick to bein' handsome."

"Not bad advice, if you ask me," she teases, tightening her grip on me. "Turn left here, baby."

The sun has set behind us, the clear blue sky making room for the stars as we turn into our old high school's parking lot. I lower the music, the school's brick facade looking smaller than it did the last time we pulled into this same lot. It's been a few years since we graduated, and I don't miss it in the slightest because the best part about high school has been by my side ever since. *And I love her more by the day.*

"You're taking me back to school? I didn't study."

Clem ignores my joke, but I feel her silently appreciating me with her eyes alone. With my hand still held tight in her lap, she says, "You know where to park."

I pull into the middle of the parking lot, counting out the 12 spots before backing into the spot I claimed for my entire senior year. My muscle memory takes over as I back into it with ease, then kill the engine. I lean back in my seat, finally finding the time to take in Clem's beauty. Her strawberry blonde hair cascades down to her shoulders, her feathered bangs framing her dark brows just above her kind eyes. Out of all the sundresses she owns, the one she's wearing tonight is my all-time favorite.

She smiles at me smiling at her.

She appreciates me appreciating her.

She loves me loving her.

Clem is so damn beautiful it hurts sometimes, especially now, knowing I'll be deployed overseas sooner than I would like to be. My throat tightens, and I glance back at the school to keep from giving in to the pit forming in my stomach. We've had our fair share of ups and downs in this parking lot, the ups higher than Heaven and the downs lower than hell.

Her voice is soft as she asks, "You okay?"

"Yeah." I force a smile. "You just got me thinkin' about how different things are about to be."

"We'll cross that bridge," Clem whispers. She traces the tip of her nail up my forearm, her touch sending ripples of warmth down my legs. "Right now, I need you to do something for me."

I pick up on the sincerity in her tone. "Anything," I say.

Without letting go of my hand, Clem places her elbow on the center console and rests her chin on her palm. "I ask, you answer," she whispers, smiling.

I salute her, and she sits straight, the two of us now facing the front of the school.

"Where did we meet for the first time?" she asks.

"Biology," I answer, pointing at the brick building to the left.

"Where was our first kiss?"

"Right under there," I answer, pointing to the old oak tree in the yard.

"Where did you ask me to be your girlfriend?"

"Right up there," I answer, pointing to the bleachers lining the football field to the right.

"Where were you when you told me you loved me?"

"We were parked right here," I answer, pointing between us.

Clem's red lips curl up on one side as her blue eyes flick to mine. "We met here. We fell in love here." She sits up, her excitement infectious as she says, "Close your eyes."

I obey.

"Last question," Clem says. "You ready?"

"That was a weird last question to ask," I tease.

I hear her giggle. "Be serious!"

"Yes, I'm ready," I answer *seriously*.

"Where were you when you found out you're going to be a father?"

I open my eyes faster than a man can blink, but I don't see Clem. I see her fragile palm between us, and in the middle of it, a cheap plastic stick with two little pink lines staring up at me. I blink. Then, I blink again. Then, I blink again and again. It's still there. It's real. It's right there, right in front of me.

"Rome," Clem whispers, tears pooling in her eyes. "You're gonna be a daddy."

I feel like I've been punched in the chest, all the air knocked out of me. "You're... you're serious?"

My heart is all I can hear, somehow banging on the inside of my head. A million thoughts flood my mind, none sticking for more than a second. The love of my life is sitting in my passenger seat with our baby growing inside her. *We're having a baby*. I stare at Clem. It's all I can do. Her tearful smile, the pregnancy test in her hand. Suddenly, it all hits me at once.

My hand finds hers, squeezing tight. A laugh bubbles out of me, a blend of disbelief and joy. "We're having a baby." I laugh, shaking my head. "We're having a baby."

"You're happy?" Clem asks, relieved.

"Happy?" I shake my head. "Clem, I–" My throat catches. "I'm gonna be a dad. I'M GONNA BE A DAD."

She exhales a sigh of relief she's had buried for what might've been days.

"I love you," I say, showering her with kisses. "I love you, I love you, I love you."

I pull back, seeing the love in her eyes.

The weight lifts from my chest, replaced by something brighter...

something bigger...

until...

The final grain of sand reaches the bottom half of the hourglass. I feel for the silver dog tag hanging around my neck. Sweat coats the sides of my face, my head throbbing as I return to the present moment, staring at the shelter's ceiling. It's the first time I've relived a memory from what marked the beginning of the toughest part of my past, and in this moment, I'm reminded why. Joining the military cost me the love of my life in more ways than one. While I don't feel any better now than I did before replaying that memory, I can only hope it will keep me sane like Azrael said it would.

As I step down to the water, looking back at what could now be my home feels oddly comforting, a fragile semblance of normal life in this unpredictable place. I shield my eyes from the sun, scanning the ocean horizon for a boat and the sky for a plane. The ocean is smooth as glass up until it rolls into tiny clear waves that tickle the tops of my bare feet. I walk along the line that divides the water from the shore, looking out for any sign of help or a way out.

It's been a day since Bella and I left the cruise ship. I wonder how Mac reacted to me being gone. Did he wait for me to come back? Did he leave the ship to look for me? Is he still looking for me? Is Tish with him? Is Bella with him? Will they or anybody else find me before I die out here? I have so many questions, I'm starting to question which I'll lose first: *my mind or my life.*

Chills suddenly cover my arms when something reveals itself just above a small wave. The world slows and time stops so that it can glide toward the shore with such grace, I'm convinced it's a gift sent by an angel. The olive green fabric has been darkened by the seawater, the straps gently swaying with the motion of the waves as if they have minds of their own. *Bella's backpack.* The moment around me fades to insignificance as I step deeper into the water, reaching for the bag. To my downfall, I would have to swim to it and I don't know how.

I inch closer, the water now at my shoulders. I reach as far as I can, then shovel handfuls of water toward me in hopes the backpack will move in my direction. Instead, it continues bobbing just out of reach, taunting me. The small waves tease me by moving the backpack closer, farther, then closer, then farther again. I clench my jaw, stepping deeper to the point where my chin dips beneath the surface. The tips of my toes graze the sand below until… *shit.*

I'm overwhelmed with panic when my feet lose the ground. I start kicking in every which direction, my eyes now below the surface. I squint, catching the blurry sight of a loose backpack strap. Nearly blind, I flail my arm toward the bag and snatch it. The air leaves my lungs in a quick burst, my core tightening as I sink deeper. I kick out, desperately searching for the ground with my feet. *Don't you dare die, Rome.* My heart pounds in my ears. The thought of my life ending over a backpack becomes believable until I finally feel the loose sand below.

I lower myself over the ground and begin trudging back toward the shore until I finally break through the ocean surface. I gasp for precious air between coughs. The shore is only a few feet away, and the thought that I almost died just a few feet from land is humbling. One trembling step at a time, I inch back up to land and drop the backpack between my feet. The waves become a distant whisper behind me, the sun warming my wet skin.

Just as I gather my strength, a sound cuts through the crashing waves–*a cough.* It's faint, and I'm convinced I hallucinated it until I hear it again. My feet are cemented to the sand, my head on a swivel. I strain to listen, scanning around the shore. The shallow shoreline is empty, the white sand curving around both sides of my shelter and the palms.

Am I already going crazy?

I hear another cough. My eyes widen. My heart skips a beat.

I'M NOT ALONE.

My legs are still shaky, but I force them to move anyway. I bolt straight up the shore and past my shelter. Branches scrape at my bare torso and denim shorts as I weave through the lush bushes separating me from the other side of the island. I trip over the last bush, and I find myself looking down at her.

It can't be.

It shouldn't be.

But, it is…

"BELLA!" My voice is a blend of relief and disbelief. I sprint down to the water where she lies lifeless on her side. I kneel over her. "Bella, how did you…? Where did you…? Are you okay?! Bella."

I gently turn her face up. Her eyes are closed, her skin pale in the afternoon light. Dark strands of hair are fanned out around her fragile head. "Hey," I whisper. "Can you hear me?" I lower my ear to her parted lips and hear her shallow breath. "I've got you. I've got you."

Bella's eyes flutter open. Her gaze is on the sky above before it meets mine. I press a hand to her delicate chest, just above the trim of her white romper. I look up, scanning the beach for the boat, a piece of wood, or anything she could have used to survive up until this moment, but find nothing.

"You're okay," I whisper, wiping long, wet strands of hair from her forehead. "I'm here."

Her eyes are closed again, but she's alive. She's here, she's alive. I place my palm over my lips, and while forcing back a flood of tears, I silently thank whatever brought her here.

Together, we can now find a way to survive.

Together, *we can do this.*

3 DAYS STRANDED

The sun is rising by the time Bella's hand moves from her chest to her side. It's the first movement she's made other than breathing. I spent the entire night watching her sleep inside the shelter I built yesterday. Even with no sleep, my energy reaches an all-time high at the sight of her moving her hand. I crawl toward her, now halfway inside the shelter. As if feeling my presence, she slightly tilts her head up from the shirt I have her using as a pillow. She opens her eyes.

Hello again, angel.

I smile, raising a coconut between us. She tries to lift her hand, but I stop her. "Let me."

Bella nods, opening her mouth so I can pour her some water. Her head falls back onto my shirt, and within seconds, I'm convinced she's back asleep. The cycle continues for some time. Bella moves her hand, I give her some water, she goes back to sleep, repeat. Each time she moves her hand, it's with a bit more strength than the last.

After each pour, I return to a stick I've been sharpening into a spear. Now that Bella is here, the six-and-a-half coconuts will only last us half the time they could have lasted me alone. That's fine by me because it means that I have company.

I noticed a few small fish darting between shallow waves last I was down by the water, so I figured I would learn how to add them to our survival diet. The stick is nearly as long as my arm, sturdy and strong enough to deliver a lethal blow if my aim is anywhere near as good as it was back in the military. While sitting beside Bella, I drag the knife's sharp edge along the edge of the stick, sharpening its point. The scraping sound is oddly therapeutic, and focusing on the slices of wood peeling from the edges almost takes my mind off of this island entirely. It becomes a game, managing to keep my mind from any thought that could lead to panic. It also helps keep my mind off my peeling face and arms from the sunburn.

The sound of rolling waves continues in the background, and I've accepted that they'll never cease to break. The sound of each break is an entity of its own at this point, one that I naturally tune out and begin to appreciate when I'm reminded of its presence. When I first washed up, the waves mocked me. They reminded me that I'm alone, on a fast track toward my impending death. But as I've gotten to know them, a mutual respect is becoming known. The waves respect that I'm still trying to survive despite my circumstances. And I respect that I have no control over the waves themselves. After all, they brought me here. They saved me, and now Bella, too.

"Where are we?" Bella's voice is raspy, though her angelic undertone is still more prominent than ever.

I look up from my stick and see her lying on her side, looking at me. Her gaze is attentive. Through her eyes alone, I can see her curious mind struggling to form conclusions. I want to lie, to give her some form of hope by saying that we're not far from the last island we were on, and that help is on the way. But I decide against it. She would find out soon enough.

"I don't know," I reply, setting down the stick. I fondle the knife in my hand, choosing my next words carefully. "Regardless, we're alive."

Bella's eyes drop to the sand between us. "Are we going to die out here?"

"No," I snap, reaching over her for the wooden bucket. I pull out one of the pre-cut slices of coconut meat I carved. "Here, you need to eat something."

She holds up a shaky palm. "Thank you." Upon taking a small bite of the meat, she sighs with relief. A subtle smile plays on her lips, which makes me do the same.

"Good, huh?"

"Who would have thought something so simple…" She lifts the piece of coconut meat. "Mmm."

I exhale a laugh, then go back to sharpening my stick. "We got lucky with those three palm trees. We're down to only six coconuts after this one, so I'll have to learn how to fish."

"Rome," Bella murmurs faintly between bites. "How are we gonna get home?"

I stop sharpening, pondering a response that will keep her spirits high. "Do you remember when you said, '*The adventure begins the moment the characters lose control?*'"

She nods.

"Whelp." I raise a hand to the open ocean before us. "We found our adventure." The words leave my lips coolly. They aren't necessarily fueled by optimism, but they're not entirely pessimistic either. I suppose it's the realest thing I can say in a moment like this.

Bella cracks a smile. "We can do this," she says the way she did the night we met on that stage.

"Your backpack washed up," I say, changing the subject. "I wrapped it in my shirt so you could use it as a pillow."

"Thank you."

"No need to thank me. I found you right after it washed up, so I didn't have time to really go through it. Is there anything in there that can help us?"

Bella props herself up on her elbow and looks down at the T-shirt-wrapped backpack beneath her. There's a slight tremble in her hands as she unzips it and pulls out a pen, the cross necklace she got back in the Bahamas, and a journal. I stop sharpening my spear and sigh. *So, nothing that can help us.*

I go back to sharpening. "We'll need to ration the coconuts until I catch a fish."

"What happens when we run out of water?"

I point my stick toward an array of dark clouds in the distance. "Never thought I would say this, but we'll have to hope another storm comes our way."

Bella nods. "I want to help."

"You need to rest," I state.

She sighs. "Give me something to do, anything."

The knife glides off the edge of my stick, this time without me having to put in any effort. I lift the point to my nose, observing the tip. It's sharp against my palm, ready to pierce anything in its path.

"There are bushes under the palm trees," I say, standing to my feet. "It might be best for you to gather as much wood as possible. If we can somehow get a fire going, it will make the nights easier. That's when it gets colder."

Bella's eyes fall from mine to the silver dog tag hanging around my neck. She gives me a weak but playful salute. "Gather wood. Roger that, Sergeant Rome."

"At ease, soldier," I chuckle. "Just 'Rome' will do."

I turn down the beach and pull the hourglass from my pocket before I reach the water. I exhale, preparing to reconnect with memories I've yet to make peace with. I take a deep breath, flip the hourglass, and as sand begins to slip through the center tube, I dive back into my past…

I grip my M4 Carbine, the assault rifle's hard metal cold against my bare palms. Even with the extensive training up to this mission, my nerves are getting the best of me. Makes sense. It's my first raid since being deployed three months ago. It's a wild thought, having just been in my hometown with the love of my life. And now, just three months later, death is in my scope.

My eyes flick over the rifle. The selector switch is set to "safe." The magazine is in the magwell. My sights are aligned. And the harsh reality kicks in: *I'm ready to kill.*

I place my palm over my chest for a moment, feeling the wooden cross dangling from my neck under my armor. In a whisper, I pray, "*Lord, keep Your hand on me, my girl, and my baby back at home.*" I put my faith in God because that's all you can do when the devil is knocking on your front door at a moment like this.

My heart pounds in my chest as I follow our point man from the hummer to the back of the abandoned warehouse. Even in our heavy military gear, our footsteps are muted over the cold, moonlit dirt road. The point man lifts his right hand, a signal for us to halt at the sound of two voices coming from around the corner. With our backs pressed against the warehouse wall, I turn back to Mac and another squad member.

Mac keeps a low profile, his dark eyes darting between me and the point man as the moon's eerie glow shines overhead. We drop lower as the warehouse's garage door slides open, headlights now flooding the dirt road in front of us. The point man keeps his hand up, still signaling us to wait. After tightening my grip around my rifle...

I inhale slowly and deeply through my nose. *1, 2, 3, 4.*

I hold my breath. *1, 2, 3, 4.*

I exhale slowly and fully through my mouth. *1, 2, 3, 4.*

Just last night, we received intel that an enemy cell is planning to bomb our local military base. The details we gathered were sparse, but the stakes are high. Regardless, our mission is clear: *Infiltrate the enemy hideout, gather the evidence, and neutralize the threat.* Our squadron, consisting of two seasoned veterans, plus Mac and myself, was deemed best for the job. And we're about to find out if that was the right choice.

A silhouette steps out of the warehouse, standing in the headlights of a truck still parked inside. The silhouette becomes a man holding his own rifle, its bullets prepared to land in one, if not all, of our bodies or heads. That's if he's lucky. Our point man lowers his right hand to the trigger of his rifle. We do the same.

According to our intel, this warehouse is supposed to be abandoned. To the demise of either the enemy or ourselves, it's filled with who-knows-how-many enemy soldiers. As the headlights of the vehicle inside move forward, the man steps backward and in our direction. He directs the vehicle with his free hand until he notices our squad. He looks right at us.

My heart rate picks up as we await the point man's mark. He quietly aims his rifle, then calmly gestures for the enemy ahead to lower his gun. I raise my own rifle, my finger hovering over the trigger in the event that we don't get the outcome we want–their surrender.

Drop the gun, I want to say. *Just surrender, and we'll all live.*

With his rifle still aimed at the enemy, the point man whispers into his walkie-talkie, "I got eyes on the threat. We've been compromised. Warehouse confirmed as enemy-occupied. Requesting air support. Over."

The enemy raises a cautious palm, preparing to surrender. Relief begins to wash over me until the enemy suddenly screams in his native language into the warehouse and raises his rifle at our point man.

BANG!

In a blink, our point man puts a bullet in the enemy's skull. He drops dead.

It's on.

"MOVE!" our point man shouts. In a single-file line, our squadron jolts forward. "CONSANO! ON PERIMETER!"

I obey his orders, stepping out to his right as we turn the corner. The headlights of what quickly becomes a semi-truck appear, its engine deafening.

It's closer than I expected.

The truck whips out of the warehouse, its headlights becoming all I see before…

I stand at the edge of the shallow water. "That's enough for now," I whisper, slipping the hourglass back into my pocket.

I tighten my grip on my new spear, my heart pounding in anticipation of catching my first fish. A spear is a whole lot different from the wide range of guns I've used. The sharpened stick fits awkwardly in my palm as I hover over the shallows with light footsteps. The sun is at its highest, and while no clouds hover above, thick clouds form pillows on the horizon. Cool, clear waves lap my legs, revealing the silvery bodies of fish flashing beneath the surface. I steady my hands, positioning my spear just above the water. My stomach growls with hunger, reminding me that I'm six coconuts away from starving to death. I need to strike and I need to strike soon.

The fish lurk innocently beneath the clear surface, oblivious to my looming wrath.

I tighten my grip around the spear.

I aim.

I strike.

I miss.

"Dammit."

The fish scatter in all directions, leaving me standing empty-handed. I inhale a calming breath, then exhale. This isn't going to be easy. I step out of the water, waiting for the fish to return to the same spot. After a few minutes, they show, and I'm creeping back into the shallows.

I crouch slightly, shrinking my shadow as small as possible to keep from scaring them away again. Instead of being quick to strike this time, I decide to watch in hopes that I'll pick up on a pattern that makes up their movements. If I can strike not in the spot they're in but rather in the spot they'll be, maybe I won't have to return to Bella empty-handed.

My muscles tense when I see a fish swim into view. It darts left, right, then stays still for three seconds. I fill my chest with air, gripping the spear more firmly than the first time. The fish does the same pattern: *left, right, still for three seconds*. I subtly lean forward, keeping low.

Left.

Right.

Still.

I stab to its left.

I miss.

"FUCK!"

Time stretches on as the attempts pile onto one another. I stab, I miss, I stab, I miss. I eventually lose track of my failures, my confidence now a pathetic mound of wet sand. Stab, miss. I'm noticing that fish don't swim in patterns, so it was pretty stupid to think that would ever be possible. Stab, miss. Something is telling me there's no way in hell I'll ever catch a fish. Stab, miss. And not only will I die of starvation out here, but now I'll also be the reason for Bella's death. Stab, miss.

I stand straight, a cold sweat coming over me as I stare through the empty shallows. There isn't a fish in sight now, forcing me to come to terms with the chilling thought of now being responsible for our survival or death. I turn back over my shoulder, seeing Bella gracefully gather sticks near our shelter. Impending deaths aside, she still moves with calm, quiet elegance. It's as if our dire circumstances don't faze her in the slightest.

I exhale a long, defeated breath as I head back up to shore. "I hope you're okay with coconut for dinner," I mutter. I manage to successfully stab my spear into the ground without missing, then sit beside it, facing the water. "This is gonna be harder than I thought."

A silent beat passes before Bella responds, "There's always tomorrow."

I force a smile at her blind encouragement.

It's a scary thought, realizing we could eventually run out of tomorrows.

I'm quickly learning how volatile emotions become when you're grappling with survival. Every little move you make has the biggest impact on your mind. With every little win, you find yourself on top of the world. And with every little loss, you find yourself dragged to its depths. Survival is when you become the rope in a game of tug-of-war between Life and Death. You're being pulled in two different directions, each force fighting for your mind, heart, and gut. And all you can do is feel the tension, the pressure.

Bella drops some sticks by the shelter, then sits beside me. As gentle waves continue rolling in, we look over the gradient of purples and blues, which are starting to darken under the sun's dying light. "I might be saying this a bit early, but I think there are worse places to be stranded," she says. She's made a lot of progress since this morning. By another miracle, she's just as vibrant as the first night we met.

I fold my lips between my teeth, humming a sound in agreement. The truth of the matter is I don't know how to process Bella's positive outlook on this situation. I've been a ball of mixed feelings since I washed up on this island. Part of me–a big part at that–is happy I'm not alone. But another part of me wants to blame her for putting us here in the first place. It was her thirst for adventure and blind optimism that led us onto Azrael's boat. All this talk about "doing it for the plot" got us here, and now it could kill us both.

In my peripherals, I see Bella's finger begin drawing something in the sand between us. "Do you know what a story arc is?" she asks innocently.

"Bella," I murmur. "I don't think now is the time."

"A story arc is the journey that the characters in a book go on. It starts at the beginning of the story, obviously, but there's all these things that happen–"

"Bella," I try to interrupt.

"... Between the beginning and the end. Even when I journal about my life, I write as if it's a book and I'm the main character. Since I started doing that, I noticed that our lives have their own story arcs, their own journeys where–"

"BELLA."

Bella winces at the abruptness of my voice, pulling her finger from the sand. In a swift motion, she nearly folds into a fetal position, raising both of her arms to shield her face. Between her raised palms, her wide-eyed, frightened expression reveals a past filled with trauma.

I used to see this in the military all the time. People hide their past traumas until they're triggered by the smallest gesture, a single word, or a subtle thought. Some people picked up their traumas before the military, while others picked up their traumas during the military. *Where did Bella pick up* her *trauma?*

Before I can say a word, Bella stands, forcing a not-so-convincing smile as she wipes the sand off her legs. "I'll get all the sticks together, and we can try to make a fire."

"I…" I raise a hand toward her, and it falls as she heads back to the shelter. "I'm sorry," I whisper.

My eyes drop to the line she drew in the sand. It's a crisp arc that starts low, gradually rises to a peak, then slopes gently at the end. Just a few days ago, I was infatuated with this girl, following her into the depths of the ocean, submitting my fate to her own. But I'm finding it hard to love when our survival is my responsibility. There's no time for love now, no time to let my heart soften when I need it to pump hope and determination through my veins.

I don't care to love.

I just want to survive.

🌴🌴🌴

The sun has dipped below the horizon, casting a deep orange glow over the island. Bella and I dug a fire pit in the sand, filling it with dry leaves, twigs, and sticks. It takes me a while to find a couple of stones I can start the fire with. When I finally come across two, I kneel over the pit and begin striking them together.

"Where'd you learn how to do that?" Bella asks, watching me strike.

"My friend, Mac, taught me back on deployment," I reply softly.

Nothing comes of the first attempts, just the bland sound of stone hitting stone. As my hands start to strain, I realize I need to push on. I refuse to let myself fail again after not being able to catch a fish.

"You went on a deployment?" Bella wraps my shirt tighter around her shoulders.

"Yes, ma'am."

I strike the stones again, this time with more force than before. A tiny spark leaps from the stone, and I can hear Mac's voice coaching me through this the way he did years ago. *We tell stories by the fire or spend the night fighting off the wolves. The choice is yours, Rome,*" he once whispered between chattering teeth as he shivered at my side. "*The choice is yours.*"

I strike the stones together again, then again, and again.

Each time with more force until…

"You did it!" Bella exclaims as a bright spark lands on the leaves.

"Quick!" I shout, cupping my hands over the flame. "More leaves! More twigs!"

Bella scurries to the shelter and back, fueling the fire with small twigs and crunchy leaves. The flame grows, licking at the larger sticks. I lean over the flame and give it a gentle blow. In a few seconds, it becomes a steady blaze warming our palms.

The moon is just now rising in the distance, piercing between countless stars keeping us company tonight. A silver ribbon has formed under the moon, stretching from the horizon to the calming waves at the shore's edge. My gaze follows the ribbon up to the white sand until I catch Bella admiring the fire from across the pit. Her eyes reflect the flickering flames, illuminating the joy and gratitude over something as simple as warmth and light.

I've faced death before, and I *still* find myself panicking out here at times, so I can't imagine what Bella is feeling. The least I can do is try to cheer her up or get her to find a sense of peace. Even if it's just for a moment.

My eyes drop to Bella's backpack lying beside her. "Your journal," I say softly. "Are you still able to read the pages?"

Bella offers a subtle nod. Her once-chirpy demeanor is now masked by a more timid expression. She raises her knees toward her chest, wrapping her arms around her legs. She's wearing my T-shirt over her romper, and the fact that it's way too big on her makes her look even smaller than she already is. "Why do you ask?"

I pick up a coconut and crack it in half. *After this, we'll be left with five.*

"Well, you said you want to be a writer." I give her the coconut. "I'll be your first reader."

Bella sips from the coconut, her eyes curious. She wipes her lips with the back of her hand, then says, "I've never let anybody read my writing before."

As she hands me the coconut, I look left toward the bushes and palms, then right toward the moonlit sea. "I don't see a better way for us to pass the time," I reason between sips. "Come on, writer. Read me a story."

Bella purses her lips, the warmth of the flames painting her pondering expression with a soft, golden glow. Her eyes narrow, then I catch her smirk as she slowly reaches into her backpack. She carefully pulls out a worn, brown, leather-bound journal. Her eyes meet mine once more, a flicker of excitement swirling in their depths. She balances the journal on her lap, then turns to the first page.

And she reads…

Laguna Beach, California
Saturday - May 11th, 2019

"Do you see it?" Ms. Rivera asks from the foot of the ladder.

I run my finger along the spines of each book on the top shelf until I find the book she's looking for. "Jane Austen." I exhale a sigh of relief, gently pulling the book from the shelf. I lower myself from the ladder. "Great choice, Ms. Rivera. *Pride and Prejudice* is a classic."

Ms. Rivera flashes a genuine smile, her silver necklaces complementing her neatly coiffed silver hair. She beams down at the book when I place it in her palms, then looks up at me with the kindest eyes. "I sure am looking forward to this one," she says softly. "Thank you, Bella dear."

I smile. "My pleasure, Ms. Rivera. Would you like me to ring you up at the front?"

She blushes under her thick, colorful glasses. "I saw your father is in today."

"He is," I giggle, pointing to the front of the store. "He's right up front at the register."

Ms. Rivera smiles, brows raised. Her lavender dress sways, and her freshly-polished shoes tap against the light-wood floors as we make our way to the front of the bookstore. Dad is slouched over the countertop, whispering the words he's reading under his breath. Ms. Rivera approaches the counter excitedly, holding her book with both hands. I lean against the nearest bookshelf and watch their interaction play out.

Ms. Rivera's eyes crinkle above her wide grin. "Good afternoon, Donald."

Dad keeps mouthing the words from his book, oblivious to the rest of the world. Ms. Rivera turns to me for help, and I quickly walk behind the counter. I pretend to rummage through the shelves behind Dad, then give him a shove. His whispering stops, and after a beat, I hear his stool skid back as he stands. "W-well, hello, Ms. Rivera! I—sorry, I didn't see you."

"Don't you worry, Donald," Ms. Rivera chirps, raising a shaky palm. "That must be a good book."

Dad nervously runs his hand over what's left of his thinning hair and pushes his glasses up the bridge of his nose. His cheeks quickly turn to a rose-red. "It's r-really good."

The two smile innocently at each other for what starts to feel like a little too long, so I help them out. With a hand cupping Dad's shoulder, I chime in. "Ms. Rivera is buying *Pride and Prejudice*, Dad." I give his shoulder a light squeeze.

"Oh! Oh, right! Yes! A classic!" he says, snapping out of his trance. "This one is on us."

"No, no!" Ms. Rivera's many silver bracelets jingle as she waves off Dad's offer. "That's very kind, but I'm a paying customer like everyone else should be." She reaches into her purple purse and gently pulls out a 20-dollar bill.

Dad smiles, reluctantly taking the 20 dollars. "That's very kind of you, Ms. Rivera."

She playfully waves him off. "20 dollars is nothing compared to the adventure that comes with your books. You know that better than anybody." Her giddy eyes flick between us. "Before I go, I think I need to hear one of your infamous quotes."

Dad blushes. "Oh, I don't know."

"Please," Ms. Rivera whispers, anxiously waiting.

After a silent beat, Dad clears his throat. "Life is a precious, fleeting story. Make the most of yours," he says smoothly.

Ms. Rivera lifts a shaky hand over her forehead and pretend-swoons over one of the many wise, bookish quotes Dad shares with our customers. I hold back a laugh, and after she tucks the book into her purse, I'm nearly shoved across the store as Dad shuffles around the counter to open the door for her. The bell above the door jingles with a familiar, melodious ring, the only constant in my life since I can remember. Dad walks back inside the store and watches Ms. Rivera return to her car.

"She doesn't read that fast, you know," I say.

"Huh?" Dad replies, still fixated on Ms. Rivera.

"Have you not noticed she comes into the shop almost every single day to buy a new book? Dad, she's not buying the books to actually read them. She's just buying them so she can flirt with you!"

Dad turns back toward the counter. His walk has turned into more of a waddle over the years. A poor diet and sedentary life in a bookstore will do that to you, but it somehow suits him perfectly. This might sound crazy, but I think it also adds to the bookstore's charm. Who wouldn't want to buy books from a story-obsessed, jolly old man?

"Ms. Rivera doesn't flirt with me," Dad murmurs, adjusting books that don't need adjusting.

I shrug, making room for him to return to his stool. "Whatever you say."

"If she even was flirting with me like you say she is…" He picks up his book, returning to the page he left off. Before he continues reading, his eyes flick above his glasses to meet mine. "What would you think about—you know—all that?"

"*All that?*" I place a comforting hand on him. "I think it's time for all that, Dad."

Dad folds his lips between his teeth, his plump cheeks lifting into a warm, heartfelt smile.

Being the daughter of a bookstore owner, the afternoon becomes what it's always been. Ordering new books, stocking bookshelves. Greeting customers, cleaning the stocked bookshelves. Balancing the cash register, setting up new window displays. Even on a busy day like today, the tasks are never daunting. By now, it's in my nature. It's routine, it's life.

Dad opened Seaside Books 16 years ago, and while I was only five years old at the time, I remember those days more vividly than I remember even more recent times. The aroma of paperback books is ingrained in my memory. The sensation of flipping pages has a home in my fingertips. And the sound of the bell above the front door brings promise of a reader about to embark on a new adventure.

The bell above the door jingles. "Hello, introverts!" Tish shouts across the store.

Customers turn their heads. Dad continues reading at the counter, unfazed. I apologize to the customer I'm speaking with before meeting Tish at the front. Her tight black curls have been pulled into a top bun, her cream-colored bikini peeking through her knitted beach dress.

I check my phone, then whisper, "I think I need another 10 minutes."

Tish's eyelids droop into a lazy gaze. "You texted me that 10 minutes ago."

"Right, but we just had a rush and—"

"Nope," she snaps. "We're going to Brooks Street. So, grab a good beach book to keep you busy down there while I watch the surfer boys do the surfing thing."

I sigh, but I know Tish is just looking out for my best interest. Growing up an only child, I prayed and prayed for a sister. God gave me Tish in elementary school, and we've been looking out for each other ever since. Tish never had the best relationship with her parents, which is why she spends so much time at the bookstore. Being my oldest friend, she also understands that if I don't make time for life outside of the book world, I won't have a life at all. She balances me out, keeps me rooted in the real world while my imagination wanders anywhere and everywhere my characters take me.

"Let me get my bag," I say.

Tish claps. "Also, grab me a book that will make me look smart. Doesn't matter which one. Surfer boys are dumb, so they probably won't care what book it is."

I skip behind the counter, grab my bag and a book for Tish, then kiss Dad on the cheek. "We're going down to Brooks! I ran through the to-do list an hour ago. Do you have everything you need?"

With his chin lowered toward his book, his eyes flick up to mine. "Have fun."

"Love you!" I shout, running back around the countertop.

"Hi, Donald!" Tish shouts as I grab her hand and pull her to the door. "Bye, Donald!"

"Be good, Tish!" Dad chuckles.

"No promises!"

The beach is crowded like any other Saturday in the summer. Tish and I always head down to Brooks Street because the beach has a private feel, the way it's tucked between two cliffs. Brooks is usually filled with Laguna Beach locals, considering you have to cut through a neighborhood to get to the sand. It has the best waves for the local surfers and the best local surfers for Tish to drool over.

"That one! That's the one!" Tish whispers as she hits my arm and points at a wave with the other.

I lower my sunglasses to catch sight of a surfer on top of the wave. "That's the third boy you called 'the one.'" I look back down at my book.

"I don't think this stupid book is working," Tish groans.

I turn to face her. "That's probably because you're holding it upside down."

Tish raises the book, just now realizing the words are upside down. "Whatever. Being smart is dumb." She flips onto her stomach, yanks up her bikini bottoms, and undoes her top. "I'd rather be hot," she says with a smirk.

A couple surfers make their way past us.

"Aye, what's up, Tish?!" one of them greets.

"Lookin' good!" adds the other.

Tish waves and the two of us burst out laughing. She turns to face the ocean. Atop the shimmering surface, a cruise ship crosses the horizon. "Have you ever been on a cruise?"

I lift my eyes from my book. "I've never left Laguna Beach."

"You're always reading about adventures. You've never wanted to go on your own?"

I stick out my bottom lip, pondering her question. "I never really thought about it like that." I've always considered myself a homebody, and while I never saw anything wrong with escaping reality through books, Tish may have a point. Most books are based on real-life adventures, and if I'm going to one day write my own book, it would probably make sense for it to be based on my own adventure. "I've never considered going on a cruise, but if anyone is going to talk me into it…" I lower my chin, eyeing Tish from over my glasses. "It would be you."

"Noted," she replies casually.

The sun is at its highest, the air filled with the rhythmic sound of waves crashing on the shore. Just as I'm about to get back to reading, my eyes hover over a rolling wave. *And that's when I spot him.* His tan skin stands out against the vibrant blue, his surfboard one with him as he glides effortlessly over a wave that doesn't seem to end. His figure is striking, his deep-red wetsuit clinging to his muscular frame. He smiles, he laughs, he becomes one with the ocean.

He attracts both the sunlight and everything in me capable of being attracted. Every move he makes is precise yet natural. It's as if his ability to surf is a blend of a thousand hours of practice and a God-given gift all at once. Even from a distance, I can see the smile on his face. Every droplet of freedom and joy clings to this man for dear life, begging for just a few more moments of him before they return back to the ocean.

A sensation suddenly sweeps my lower lip, and it takes me a second to realize that it was Tish's thumb. "Wasn't going to let that drool linger on your lower lip," she teases.

I cover my face with my book to shield the beach from my embarrassment, then I subtly lower the book so I can see the surfer peel out the tail end of the wave. As he reaches the top of the wave, he gracefully leaps off his board and into the water headfirst. "Red wetsuit," I say into the book. "Who is he?"

"Red wetsuit?" Tish squints. "That's Luca Genova."

I lean forward, waiting for Tish to continue, but she doesn't.

His name alone is already more than I can handle.

"I think I need to meet Luca Genova," I say in shallow breaths.

Tish lowers her glasses, now sitting up beside me. "Then you're going to need to join his band or learn how to surf because he doesn't care about anything other than his guitar and surfboard. I'd stick to your little book boyfriends."

I bite my lip. "Why have I never heard of him?"

"His band is only in town for the summer. They're driving up the coast, performing at bars and house parties in all the beach towns." A mischievous grin plays on Tish's lips. "Ask me how I know that."

I exhale a laugh. "How do you know that?"

With a smirk, she whispers, "I've been texting the lead singer, Abel *Genova*."

"Brothers?!"

"Twins." Tish nods, eyes closed. "I know. Two hot twin brothers who are in a band. They were made for you and me."

"Why were you keeping this from me?!"

She shrugs. "You're always in your little fantasy-book world. A boy like Luca would be an adventure of his own."

"An adventure of his own," I repeat under my breath. "That's exactly what I need right now."

I'm not surprised that Tish knows Luca and Abel. Tish has always been the social type, always in the know. She's the first to know the name of any hot guy she comes across. And being the beauty she is, the hot guy's number always finds a way into her phone.

Laguna Beach is a small enough town for everyone to know each other by first name. The kids who grow up here either move far away or set roots and stick around forever. There's usually no in-between. It's one of the few reasons I don't already know Luca and the reason I'll need to get Luca to fall in love with me before the end of the summer. He can be my adventure, we can fall in love, and when it's all said and done, I'll have a story worth writing about.

"I have an idea," Tish says with a devious grin. She wraps her arm around my shoulder and presses her lips against my ear. "If you go out there and pretend to drown, he'll have to save you."

"You're insane."

"I mean it! Bella, every boy wants a girl he can save. It makes them feel important, and if you can make Luca Genova feel important, well, of course he's going to want you."

Every boy wants a girl he can save.

I inhale a few deep breaths, letting Tish's wisdom seep through my better judgment. Her arm releases me as I stand to my feet. I adjust my white bikini and take a few cautious steps toward the water. Sand volleyball players and beachgoers tend to their activities while I fixate on the man in the red wetsuit. He's sitting upright on his board between the other surfers, the red popping against their black wetsuits.

Tish's little guilt trip about me not wanting to go on my own adventures fuels my determination.

"Do it for the plot," I tell myself.

Fake-drowning. That can't be hard, right? Just get deep enough and swim, but like don't swim well enough for someone to think you're not in any trouble. That's it. That's all it should be. Swim, but don't swim. Live, but also almost die. Don't actually die. Just get close enough to dying where you need Luca to come save your life. Easy.

I take a deep breath, feeling the salty breeze ruffle my hair. The water is cool as it washes over my toes. Without turning my head, I glance in Luca's direction. His white teeth shine against his dark, striking features as he jokes with the other surfers. Determined to get him to notice my existence, my breath catches as the chilling water hugs my waist.

Luca paddles into position to catch the next wave. The clock is ticking. If I don't time this right, I could be saved by the wrong man. After a few more steps, the water is at my chest. I turn back to Tish for a thumbs up or some signal that confirms what I'm doing isn't actually insane. Instead, I see her lying face down with her bikini bottoms hiked up her ass again, talking to some guy. "It's all you now, Bella. You got this," I whisper under my breath. "For the plot."

The water tickles my chin, and just as I'm about to shout my first cry for help, I catch sight of a towering wave curling over my head. In an instant, my lungs are stripped of all oxygen and my face scrapes against the ocean floor. I hold my breath, fully submerged underwater, not knowing which way is up or down. I splash and thrash among the whooshing of water pushing and pulling from all directions.

My world becomes chaos, my fate now decided by the ocean itself. I reach toward the sky and when I grab a handful of air, I kick myself up to the surface. I can hardly catch a glimpse of the shoreline between dark strands of my own hair. I gasp, and I'm swallowed by a wave bigger than the last. My lungs are burning, fear gripping my heart. Suddenly, nothing about this is romantic. Nothing about this is part of a fairy tale. This is a tragedy in the making.

I've always been an amazing swimmer, but this is another story. I open my eyes underwater, my vision overwhelmed by the darkest shade of green. I can hear the waves crashing mercilessly above, and it scares me to even think that trying to breathe may lead to being tossed again. It's a battle I'm losing, my strength quickly fleeting.

Just when I accept that I can't hold my breath any longer, a strong hand grabs my arm. Eyes closed, I submit myself to the hand as I break through the surface, swallowing air because my life depends on it. I cough. I sputter. I'm pretty sure I cry, all while clinging to the solid presence beside me.

"I've gotcha," he says, his voice low, firm.

He keeps his arm around me, maneuvering us over another wave opposite the shore. I hold on. It's all I can do, not because I want to but because I need to. With powerful strokes, he moves us farther out to sea. We move over the next hill of a wave before it breaks, and that's when I see the surfboard. He throws one arm around the board and hoists me onto it with the other. I continue coughing, stuffing my chest with air.

"Hold on tight," he says. The veins on his hand demand my attention as he forces my hand to grab the board's edge. His voice is calm. Between the dark strands of hair hanging over my face, I catch a glimpse of his red forearm. *RED.* We're deep enough for the waves to roll harmlessly beneath us, the ocean current causing us to sway. "You're safe now," he adds.

My breath steadies, my chest lying flat over the board. I open my mouth to speak, but the words refuse to slip between my chattering teeth.

"You okay?"

"Y-yeah," I manage in a whisper. "Th-thanks, L-Luca." My eyes widen in horror when I realize what I've just done.

Luca laughs. "How'd you know my name is Luca?"

I slowly lift my chin to see his unwavering, blue eyes. His hair is soaking wet, each long strand gold until they turn brown against the top of his head. He patiently awaits my answer. I want to run, hide, and kiss him all at once. At the very least, I need to come up with an answer that doesn't make me sound like a hopeless romantic who almost killed herself fake-drowning just to get this guy's attention.

"You, um—you look like you'd be named Luca?"

Luca laughs again. *I like Luca's laugh.*

"You took a nasty fall." He tucks my hair behind my ears, then thumbs my cheek. When he pulls his thumb away, my eyes drop to the blood coating the tip. My jaw drops and I lift my fingers to my face. "No." He catches my hand before I can touch the scratch. "You'll irritate it." Our eyes fall to our hands, his nearly twice the size of mine. "Sorry."

A piece of me dies the moment he lets go. We peacefully tread water for a few silent beats, our bodies side by side, our arms wrapping the polished wood. The people standing along the shore go about their day, oblivious to my having almost died and fallen in love within seconds of each other.

The cliffs on either side of the beach stand tall against the bright blue sky, the water below a deep green. The moment is surreal, serene. I feel the warmth of Luca's body to my left, his presence comforting. I turn my head to look at him and notice his eyes are closed. His cheekbones are pronounced under his fluttering lashes, his long hair tousled along his forehead and down his neck. It feels like we're miles from the shore, and it's a feeling I could get used to.

"You're not from here," I say, breaking the silence.

Luca opens his eyes and faces me, a smirk playing on his lips. "And how would you know that?"

"It's a small town, and I know everyone in it."

He squints at me, trying to read my mind. "What's your na—"

"Bella," I reply before he even finishes asking.

His eyes crinkle above his smile which I stare at with no remorse. I can't help it. This man is a work of art, the son of a sea goddess, the main character straight out of a romance novel. Just when I realize I'm probably drooling again, he says, "If you feel up for it, I'll take you back now."

I look over my shoulder at the distant shore. "But, I don't wanna go back."

Luca's gaze softens. "We should go back."

Once the waves have calmed, we swim back to shore where Tish is the first to greet us. "Hi!" She extends her hand to Luca. "I'm Tish."

Luca shakes her hand. "Luca."

"Thanks for saving my best friend," she chirps, her eyes bouncing between Luca and me. "She's cute, right?"

Luca lets out what might be a laugh. Regardless of what it is, he avoids the question. I fold my lips between my teeth and shake my head at Tish. *He's not interested,* I try to say with my eyes.

"I would get a Band-Aid on that scratch," Luca says, looking down at me. The sun casts a golden hue across his flexed jaw as he examines my face one last time. "I'm glad you're okay. It was nice meeting you, Bella."

I force a smile, feeling completely and utterly rejected. Maybe I didn't fake-drown well enough. Maybe he has a girlfriend. Or maybe, and worst of all, he's just not interested in me. I hold his gaze for a few steps before he turns away, paddling back out.

"I can't believe it worked," Tish whispers excitedly.

"Right," I reply shakily. "Glad I could pull it off."

She grabs my shoulders with both hands, squaring my stance to hers. "So, tell me what he said out there! Did he think you're cute? Did you make him think he actually saved you?"

I glance over Tish's shoulder at Luca as he sits on his board alongside the other surfers again. He's not smiling like before, and I can't help but notice him looking right back at me. "I don't think he's interested," I mutter. "So much for my adventure."

"Oh, bullshit," she snaps. "I told you Luca only cares about his guitar and his surfboard. Maybe you couldn't pull his attention away from surfing." She looks out at Luca, then back at me with a smirk. "We'll just have to try pulling his attention away from his guitar at his next show."

Tish walks back up the beach.

I follow her a few steps, then turn back to catch Luca still staring at me.

Maybe I really did pull it off.

4 DAYS STRANDED

It's my fourth day on this island.

We have five coconuts left.

Soon, we'll be out of food and water.

My stomach churns as I watch Bella sleep from outside the shelter. Since she washed up, I've let her sleep inside, considering it's not big enough for us both. Lying on my side, I adjust the pair of shorts I use as a pillow. It's becoming a tradition for me to give Bella my shirt so she can use it as her own pillow. Even back at home, it doesn't take much for me to be able to sleep, so I don't mind letting her have a more comfortable setup.

My hunger is beginning to manifest itself into something I can actually hear. My stomach growls, demanding me to feed it. My shoulders and arms are so burnt that the mere rub of my palm sends dead skin falling to the floor. I'm aching on the inside, breaking on the outside. And still, what hurts the most is the thought of Bella falling for another man the way I fell for her the night we met.

Since Bella read her journal last night, I keep hearing her say Luca's name. *Luca, Luca, Luca.* I was gutted while listening to her read, but Bella's journal is our only entertainment on this island. It was the first time I was able to get my mind off this new reality. It's also a love story that will keep me from dwelling on my own twisted failure of a love story.

For what it's worth, I'll admit that Bella is one of the best writers and readers I've ever met. Sure, I don't come across many, but hearing the way her own words pour from her lips–I can't help but want to find out what happens next between her and Luca. And to find out why she's so reluctant to talk about marrying him.

Judging from the time we've spent together, I can tell Bella loves her sleep. It doesn't come as a surprise to me. She's good at it. Her smooth legs extend over the soft sand, peeking out from under the shelter. Despite where we are and the madness of it all, there's beauty in the simple moments I spend watching her sleep. The purity, the innocence. Her breathing is so silent, I'm sure silence itself gets envious the moment Bella closes her eyes.

A sliver of light appears on the horizon, casting a gentle, golden glow across the island. I study the trim of Bella's white romper at the top of her legs. Even after being torn from a boat, abused by the ocean current, and washed up on a deserted island, the white fabric that wraps her looks brand-new. I smile at the sight of her unharmed, safe. If she wasn't here, my will to live would be a dimming light. Instead, it's a burning fire that yearns to keep her warm. But even then, no fire burns forever.

I turn onto my back, facing the fluffy clouds that drift lazily over the island. Pink, orange, and lavender–all colors I see myself eventually learning to love. It's interesting how when you're stripped of most things in this world but a few, you learn to love the few, become grateful for the few, and you realize that the few are all you may need to keep you going. Sunrises and sunsets are part of the few things I'll admit I took for granted back in Georgia.

My stomach churns again, the growl rattling my core. I lift the hourglass between me and the clouds, studying the grains filling the bottom bulb. As painful as reliving my past may be, it's the only thing that will distract me from my hunger until Bella wakes.

I take a deep breath, flip the hourglass, and as sand begins to slip through the center tube, I dive back into my past…

BAM!
The semi-truck strikes me. In a mere blink, I'm lying face up on the dirt.

"ROME!" Mac's voice is muffled by the ringing in my head.

I hardly make out the sounds around me. Muffled shouts, muffled pops–gunfire. "STAY DOWN, ROME! STAY. DOWN."

I can't move, I want to tell Mac. Panic clings to my swelling brain. *I can't speak. Holy shit. I can't speak. Mac, I can't form fucking words.*

My mouth opens, and I try to say something–anything.

It's as if my brain has been detached from my voice.

Distorted sounds echo from all angles above me. Just a moment ago, I was making my way around our point man as we approached the enemy base. And the next, I'm struck by the unyielding force of a literal semi-truck. My bones scream in protest as I lie flat on my back. All I can do is breathe, silently praying to God that the dim sound of gunfire doesn't lead to my body catching a bullet.

MAC! I want to shout. *Mac, help.*

In my peripherals, I see the silhouettes of my squad move forward. Small bursts of fire flash as they continue shooting over me. The world slowly grows distant. With every passing second, staying conscious becomes a greater struggle.

"MAC, ON CONSANO!" The point man shouts through the ringing.

Awareness is slipping through my mind like sand through a hand. A chill seeps through my bones, and each heartbeat reminds me that I'm still alive for now.

Through the haze, I feel a hand grip my backpack strap. "Hang in there, Rome," Mac whispers over me. My world tilts as he drags me across the dirt. "God, no. Rome, you're gonna be alright. Stay with me."

Mac, I can't speak I can't move I'm trapped I'm trapped in my own head.

Mac slides me to the warehouse wall and sits me up against it. The gunfire in the distance is relentless until it's replaced by Mac's heavy breathing. His panicked face swarms my view as he kneels before me. "Stay with me," he whispers urgently. "Can you see this? Follow my finger."

I blink, trying to focus on his finger, which slowly blurs the closer it gets. I follow the blur left to right, then left again.

"Good! That's good," he exhales, leaning closer. He shines a small light in my eyes. "Pupils responsive."

I open my mouth to speak, but it's just a jumbled outpour

of sounds.

Mac, I can't speak. I can't move.

A sharp pain overwhelms the front of my head and shoots through my body. I wince.

Mac's gaze softens when he notices tears of frustration welling in my eyes. Keeping low, he tightens his grip around my hand. "I know, Rome. Just stay awake. Don't fall asleep on me." He reaches into another pocket and pulls out a syringe. "For the pain…"

I feel a sharp pain in my arm, and in an instant, the waves of pain are replaced by a cool sensation. *Morphine.* The once-rapidly growing pain is dulled as I'm detached from my body. The scene unravels before me as I hover above Mac and myself. The gunfire is now taking place in the warehouse, leaving Mac and I in blissful silence just outside.

Mac's voice becomes slightly more audible. "IMMEDIATE BACKUP NEEDED. WE HAVE A MAN DOWN, STRUCK BY AN ENEMY AUTOMOBILE. SERIOUS HEAD TRAUMA, POTENTIAL BODILY INJURIES."

He kneels in front of me, shielding my body. A silhouette appears in the distance and before they can shoot at us, Mac fires a bullet into their chest. More silhouettes rise from the shadows, and Mac shoots down one at a time. He puts his life in jeopardy to save mine, and I can't even thank him for it. I make it my mission to survive just so I can.

The concept of time escapes me. After what feels like a few seconds and also an eternity of Mac fending off enemy threats, headlights appear. Dirt swirls all around as a helicopter hovers just over the warehouse. A medical Humvee skids in front of us, and Mac urgently stands to brief the medical squad.

I blink, and I'm sprawled on a gurney.

I blink again, and I'm lying in the back of the Humvee.

Still slightly numb from the morphine injection, I see the medical team's heads popping in and out of my ceiling view. They remove my helmet and unstrap my uniform. I.V.'s are jammed into my wrists. Cool sensations mix with the warm, and my blinks grow heavier.

My view of the ceiling is interrupted by flashes of strawberry blonde and floral patterns. I can see Clem and our baby. I pray, *Lord, keep Your hand on me, my girl, and my*

baby back at home.
My head tilts to the left, my eyes landing on Mac.
He's leaning forward, tears trickling down his dirt-covered face.
I try to thank him, but my mind still won't connect to my voice.
Mac nods. "Don't worry about it, my brother," he whispers, his voice cracking. "You would've done the same for me."
"Rome," one of the medical team members says.
I can't speak.
"ROME," she says louder this time.
I CAN'T SPEAK.
I try to look at her, but the others keep me pinned down.
"ROME! ROME! ROME!"
I fade in and out of consciousness until…

I suddenly open my eyes.
"ROME!" Bella shouts over me.
"I CAN'T SPEAK!" I shout. "I CAN'T MOVE!" I'm blinded by the sun shining overhead as she pulls away. I slap my palm over my face, sucking in heaps of air. "I'm trapped in my—I'm trapped in my body," I panic, eyes closed under my open palm. Dread washes over me, knots forming in my stomach. I try to focus, piecing together fragments of the memories.
"Rome, listen to me." Bella's voice is soft, gentle. Her hand caresses my bare shoulder, pulling me from the edge of panic. "Calm down. Breathe."
I take another deep breath. My heart is racing, all while the present moment returns, bit by bit. *I'm not in the back of the Humvee anymore.* I'm not with Mac. I pull my hand from my face and blink against the harsh sunlight. When my vision clears, I notice the teardrops seeping into my palm. In my other palm, I hold the hourglass.
"I'm sorry if I scared you," Bella says. "You were crying in your sleep."
She pulls back as I sit up and wipe my runny nose.
"I'm fine," I blurt aloud.
Her eyes land on the hourglass. "You're doing what he said to do."

"I have to," I reply, fixating on the ocean. "Azrael said remembering the past will keep us sane."

Bella rests her hand on my thigh. "I don't know what you just remembered, but whatever it was, it's in the past. It can't hurt you now."

A part of me wants her to drop what she just witnessed. The vivid nature of these memories is forcing me to realize that they're so powerful it's like living them all over again. Just a minute ago, I was deployed on a mission. I was lying under gunfire. I was paralyzed from the neck down, bound to die. And now, I'm back on the island.

Bella hands me a half-cracked coconut. *After this one, we'll only have four left.* The rough shell is cool against my palms. It dawns on me that we might not be rationing smart enough. Once we run out of coconuts, finding water is going to be a whole new challenge. I subtly lift the coconut, feeling the water sloshing inside, then lower it. "Take a sip," she says. "We'll slow down until we get rain."

I scan the sky for any sight of rain but find none. "I don't think we'll see rain for a while."

"Take a sip," Bella urges again, raising the coconut to my lips.

I glance down at the coconut, then at her. She forces a smile. I force one back, then fake a sip. Deep down, I want to chug it. I want to chug this coconut and every one after. I want to eat. I want to shave my face and take a shower and live a normal fucking life again.

"You're a good writer," I say, avoiding the thought of my struggles. I pick up my shorts I used as a pillow, and slide them back on. "You have me wanting to know what happens next in your story."

Bella blushes. "I'll read to you again tonight."

I raise my chin, letting Bella's words manifest into a promise, a glimmer of hope amidst our dire situation. It's amazing how something as simple as a bedtime story can have such a profound effect on my mindset. In a mere moment, my excitement brings out the beauty from all around–the shimmering water ahead, the vibrant greens of the bushes and palms. My low becomes a high. Bella's presence alone is grace incarnate, giving me a reason to keep moving. Despite the painful memories, despite our struggle to survive.

"Where's my spear?" I ask, standing to my feet.

Bella beams up at me. "You're catching one today."

"I'm catching one today."

The spear no longer feels foreign in my hand as I approach the water. The cool waves lap over my ankles, then shins, then knees. The silver bodies of tiny fish dart in different directions, far enough to rule me out as a threat while also in my spear's reach.

"You've got this," Bella encourages softly from behind. She steps beside me, her movements so light that she doesn't cause a single ripple over the water. "You can do this."

"*We* can do this," I correct her. "We can do this."

I adjust my grip on the spear. Seconds pass, my anticipation causing my heartbeat to double over. My eyes strain while fixating on the fish. Some move quickly while others stay still. I fill my chest with a final breath, then thrust the spear through the surface. I miss.

Come on, Rome. Do good, be good.

Soon, we'll be down to our last coconut. Our last source of food. Our last source of water–of life. At this rate, survival is entirely dependent on my precision. Two lives will be lost if I can't carry a dead fish back to shore. We stand still, waiting for the fish to return.

"Rome," Bella whispers, stepping toward me without moving the water beneath her. Her gentle hand caresses the arm I use to hold the spear. Her touch sends chills down my spine. "Water exaggerates your movement." Her hand tightens around my bicep, and she jerks my arm forward a few inches. "If you don't move like water, the fish will know to avoid you."

As a wave rolls behind us, she carefully pulls my arm back. As the wave rolls back out to sea, she carefully pushes my arm forward. "Move like water."

I lower my chin, relaxing every muscle in my body. I carefully shift my weight backward, mimicking the small wave as it rolls toward the shore. Keeping low, I carefully shift my weight forward with the wave as it pulls out toward the sea.

Move like water.

I continue swaying with the movement of the ocean. Silver flashes beneath the surface, beckoning for my attention. It's the quickest the fish have returned after my miss and the closest they've been.

I sway, they gather.

Move like water.

I sway, more gather.

With a swift motion, I shift my weight with the rolling wave. I inhale, then exhale until my lungs no longer hold a trace of oxygen. When the wave pulls back out to sea, I shift my weight forward.

"YOU DID IT!" Bella shouts.

I pull the spear from the water to see a wiggling fish impaled on the end. It takes a second for me to realize... "WE DID IT!" I scream in laughter. Bella and I jump up and down, overwhelmed with excitement. "WE DID IT!" With one hand holding the spear, I hoist Bella up with the other and spin her.

I set her down, and she looks up at me with pure joy. Her face glows, her smile wide. Without wasting another second, I pull her into a tight hug. Her body is warm against mine, her heartbeat lightly thumping against my lower chest. It's as if our heartbeats synchronize–fast then slow, hard then soft. It's validation, it's triumph, it's peace. Above all, it's Bella. She's the reason I'm here and she's quickly becoming the reason "here" isn't as bad as it should be.

"Tonight, we feast," I exhale, lifting the spear.

We make our way up to our shelter with a newfound pep in our step. I shove the dull end of the spear into the soft sand, then begin gathering sticks, dry leaves, and twigs for tonight's fire. The sun eventually begins its descent, casting long shadows over the beach and bathing our reality in its golden light. Bella giggles as she lifts a big stick triumphantly over her head before setting it down. I grin ear to ear, her joy over something so simple becoming infectious.

"I can't believe you almost actually drowned while fake-drowning in front of your fiancé," I chuckle while striking stones together over the stick pile.

Bella plops down beside me. "Okay, maybe it wasn't the best idea," she admits playfully. "Real or fake, Luca saved me, which is all that matters. Right?"

"I guess." I strike the stones, causing two embers to fall over the dry leaves. They slowly burn. "Tish sounds–"

"She's a lot," Bella interrupts.

I exhale a breath. "I was gonna say she reminds me of Mac."

She shrugs. "Both of them are smart–"

"And insane at the same time," I interrupt this time.

We laugh, then Bella tilts her chin and says, "Is what she said about boys true?" She observes me nursing the new flame, gently blowing until it becomes a small fire. "That every boy wants a girl he can save."

I purse my lips, watching the fire dance as I ponder her question. "I don't think so." I reach for the spear and drag the dead fish off the edge. "Clem never really needed saving."

"Who's Clem?"

Bella's question forces my heart to drop into my stomach. I sit crisscross, holding the fish by its tail as I drag the back end of my knife across its scales. With each drag, a thin slice of scales hangs over the fish's head. "Clementine, she's my ex," I share reluctantly.

She looks away as I begin gutting the fish. "Is Clementine the reason you cry in your sleep?"

"She's the reason for a lot of things," I reply dryly. "I would have done a lot different if I knew things would end between us the way they did."

Bella lifts her gaze to the sky. "So, if Clementine didn't need saving, did you find yourself looking for a girl to save while you were with her?"

I squint at the gutted fish in my palm, though I no longer see it. I see myself years ago, falling in love with Clem, a girl who lived for loving me back. She never needed saving. She just needed me. And after looking back, she made that known throughout our relationship. And I just took her for granted until it was too late.

"I joined the military," I murmur.

Bella leans forward. "Huh?"

"I joined the military," I state, sliding two chunks of fish onto the spear's tip. "Shortly after we started dating, I enlisted to join the army."

We exchange looks as we come to the same realization. Bella raises her palm over her mouth to hide her shock. "You didn't need to save Clementine…"

"So, I left Clementine to save my country." The chunks of fish catch fire. "Shit!" I stand, blowing small gusts of air over the flaming fish.

"Tish was right," Bella sighs, looking at the fire pit.

I offer her a piece of burnt fish. "I'd rather not get into all this right now."

She thanks me, then takes a bite. "I'm sorry. I didn't mean to overstep."

"You didn't. We're stranded out here with nothing but our

pasts, so we might as well share 'em with each other." I sit back down beside her, taking a bite of the burnt fish. A sigh of pleasure escapes me upon tasting something other than coconut, regardless of how poorly it was cooked. "Mmm."

As much as I want to take the second bite, I savor the first along the top of my tongue. I can feel Bella watching me absorb the moment. With my eyes closed, I take the next bite. Upon opening them, I see Bella now sitting across the fire. She's holding her journal, flipping through pages. When her eyes flick up to mine, we both smile. She balances the journal on her lap, and she reads…

Laguna Beach, California
Saturday - May 18th, 2019

"You ready to lose, kiddo?" Dad teases, shuffling a deck of cards. I pour a bag of chips into an empty bowl. "You wish."

The faint murmur of crashing waves seeps through the open window of the apartment, blending with the smell of the salty air. It's Saturday night, or "*Game Night*," as Dad and I like to call it. Since Mom passed, it's been our weekly tradition. I will admit that there are few things I look forward to in my simple life, and Game Night is one of them.

I make my way from the kitchen to the corner of our apartment, where Dad is slouched over an old, round table. I set the chip bowl over the weathered slab of wood adorned with scratches and coffee rings that tell stories of card games and late-night snacks shared between the two of us. The antique lamp casts a warm glow across the gentle lines on my dad's face as he smiles at the chips.

"Did we lock up the store?" he asks before he pops a chip in his mouth.

"I'm not too sure," I reply, making sure we have everything we need.

Snacks, soda, poker chips, and a deck of cards.

"I'll go down and take a look." The chair creaks under him as he stands.

I place my hand on his shoulder. "I'll go check."

Dad smiles and sits back down, already out of breath from merely standing up. In the back of my mind, I've made it a point to talk to him about his rapidly growing weight. It's getting to the point where he can't make it up and down a bookstore aisle if someone is already in it. I know my gathering of late-night snacks and soda only fuels the fire. It's just hard to tell your own father that he can't enjoy something while he's still grieving.

I cross the living room, which is sandwiched between our two bedrooms, then head down the narrow staircase and into the bookstore. The wood planks ache beneath my bare feet, a sound I've hated since I was a little kid. The apartment and bookstore are decades old, and while I remind my dad that this place needs a serious facelift, he says Seaside Books needs to maintain its "antique feel." Don't get me wrong. It's cute during the day, just scary at night.

As I reach the bottom step, I squint at the front door through the narrow bookshelves. The store is nearly pitch-black, but I can still see the old lock glinting in the moonlight from the countertop. I step between the aisles until a silhouette appears just outside the window. My breath catches, sheer panic forcing my back against one of the shelves.

I subtly lower myself, trying to make out who the silhouette belongs to. Their face is darkened by the shadows. As they peek through the window to scan the shelves, I notice they're wearing an oversized black hoodie and baggy black pants. I take a deep breath, trying to calm my racing heart. The figure leans toward the window, cupping their hands to look inside. When they pan left, I sneak closer to the lock. I wait. When they pan right, I sneak just a bit closer.

If I can lock the door before they try to open it, they won't be able to get in. The figure slowly reaches for the handle, and as they gently push the door open, I lunge forward.

WAM!

I slam the door shut, startling the intruder. I grab the lock, fasten it over the handle, and yank the curtain over the window.

"Jesus, Bella!" a familiar voice shouts in a whisper.

I scrunch my face. "Tish?!"

Tish shushes me from the other side of the door. I slowly lift the curtain to see her removing the hood from her head. The moonlight reveals her curly hair, which has been pulled into a tight low bun. I eye her from head to toe, my panic slowly replaced by relief.

"Are you crazy?!" I whisper through the narrow crack separating the door from the window. "I thought you were trying to break in!"

"I *was* trying to break in," she snaps, observing her hand. "I think you broke one of my nails."

I roll my eyes while digging through a nearby drawer for the key. When I undo the lock, she slips inside. "What are you doing here?!" I snarl, locking the door behind her.

"You weren't picking up your phone, so I had to come tell you in person," she whispers.

"Tell me what?"

Her frown curls up into a cheeky grin. "Guess whose band has a show tonight?"

"Luca's band is playing tonight?" It's been a week since Luca and I met down at Brooks. It's been busy at the store, so it was easy for me to pretend like I hadn't been thinking about him. But I'd be lying if I said the memory of him wasn't a scene I replay every night before bed.

"It's nothing big," Tish warns. "Abel said they're playing at a house party a few blocks up the hill. It'll be small enough for you to see Luca up close. And more importantly, for Luca to see you."

Warmth flows through me as a mix of excitement and anxiety—*exciety.* As much as I want to see Luca again, I don't know what another rejection will do to me. "We've been through this," I say softly. "He wasn't interested."

Tish's eyes narrow. "We're going to the party." She rubs my stained, oversized T-shirt between her fingertips. "After you throw this away and put on something tight."

I pull my shirt from her grasp. "It's comfortable, okay? And I can't tonight. It's Game Night."

"Bella?" Dad's voice calls from upstairs. Tish and I turn to face the dimly lit staircase at the back of the store. "Everything alright down there?"

"Coming!" I shout in the most casual tone I can manage. "Picking up some books I knocked over!"

"You know I love your dad, but you'll have plenty more Saturday nights to play games with Donald," Tish reasons in a whisper. "Luca and Abel's band is only in town for the summer. Let's just go watch them play, then you can come back and play Go Fish."

I put my hands on my hips. "We're playing poker."

"Whatever," she scoffs, making her way to Dad's stool behind the cash register. "I'm not going alone, so I'll be sitting right here feeding off the attention I get in my Instagram D.M.'s. Come down when your dad falls asleep, and we'll go."

I purse my lips, weighing the risk. I'm old enough to make my own decisions, and I've been a good enough daughter to sneak out one night. Maybe I deserve a night out. Maybe I deserve to experience the type of night where I don't know what will happen next—to experience a bit more of my own adventure.

I tilt my chin toward the books lining the shelves behind Tish. The light from her phone screen illuminates the spines of the novels, each with its own unique storyline and each storyline with its own characters, conflicts, and climaxes. Regardless of the stories told in each book, they all have one thing in common: *a good plot.* And the better the plot, the better the book.

So, I decide against my better judgment because that's what makes for a better story, right?

I decide to do it for the plot.

Within only an hour of playing poker, I notice Dad starting to doze off across the table. "Getting sleepy, are we?" I ask, holding back a giggle.

"Mmhm," he manages.

"Come on. I'll help you to bed."

The apartment is quiet except for the subtle hum of the refrigerator and creaking floorboards under our feet. The dim lamp light casts a faint hue across the living room, bringing out the patterns lining our antique furniture. Dad leans against me, forcing me to guide him to his room using both arms. It kills me inside to think about the times he used to carry me to my own room in this same apartment, and how our roles have reversed over the years.

Dad's room is small, lit only by a bedside lamp that highlights the photographs framed on the walls. I sit him on the edge of the bed and take off his shoes one at a time. His sleepy eyes pan around the room until they stop at the photo of Mom on his nightstand. Even as his mind drifts toward tonight's dreams, I see the secret mourning he carries.

"Thank you, kiddo," he exhales as I remove the second shoe. I help him lie back, then pull the blanket to his chin. With his eyes now closed, a content smile plays across his face. "You're the perfect daughter, you know."

I smile, sitting on the edge of the bed.

"I know she'd be so proud of you," he adds in a whisper. "So, so proud."

An emptiness reveals itself in my heart, a reminder that it's by faith alone that I believe Mom is watching us from Heaven. While I miss her more than words could ever describe, I understand why God would want her back. Mom was a saint.

My eyes flick to the photo of Mom, her smile forever frozen in time on Dad's nightstand and along the walls of this apartment. I would do anything to share just another hour with her. I want to hear her soothing voice read me to sleep like she used to. I want to walk down the stairs and see her organizing the books as the sun rises. The mere thought causes the hole in my heart to grow just a bit more. *I need to fill it, and I need to fill it now.*

When I notice Dad's chest rise and fall to the rhythm of sleep, I turn off the light and get ready in my room. My room still clings to my childhood, the walls painted a soft blue with scattered white birds flying in different directions. My twin bed in the corner of the room is covered in a fluffy, white comforter, the only update I've made to this room since I was a kid.

My phone lights up between the scattered jewelry on my dresser, and I check it to see a text from Tish.

TISH: Is he asleep yet? The band is about to go on

I open my closet, revealing a wall of mostly white clothes. White has always been my preferred choice. I don't have any cool black, oversized hoodies like Tish. I've just never been comfortable in any color other than white. Remembering Tish instructed me to wear something tight, I dig until I pull out a white crop top. It has sleeves and only shows a sliver of my stomach, so it won't be Tish-approved, but it's the only shirt that makes my boobs look big enough to be considered boobs. I slip a pair of distressed, baggy white jeans over cream-colored flip-flops.

"Almost done," I whisper when I see my phone light up again.

I look in the mirror, studying my reflection. My hair has been pulled back into a high ponytail. My dark brows contrast the white fabric I'm wearing, and I couldn't be more proud that I actually put makeup on and look… hot. It's a pretty rare feeling, given I've always been the small-beachtown girl who works at the local bookstore with her dad. I usually don't get much attention, but tonight will mark the beginning of a different story. Tonight will be the start of a story actually worth reading about.

The street is littered with poorly parked cars and red solo cups lining the sidewalk. The few streets we walked up the hill were quiet, but the house at the end of this street is the opposite. Teenagers and young adults are scattered along the street, laughing and shouting at one another under the streetlights. A crowd gathers on the front lawn of the house, random colors spewing from the windows and doors on both floors. As we weave between the crowd to get closer to the house, the music grows louder.

"Do you know any of these people?" I say to Tish's back.

She unzips her hoodie, and people turn to catch a glimpse of her black lace bralette. "None!" She twirls around to face me, throwing her hands in the air. "Isn't it great?!"

I follow her up the path, splitting the crowd of dark, shifting figures against the flashing lights coming from the house. A wave of intimidation consumes me when I realize most of these people are older than me—more confident. We squeeze through the front door, and the once-muffled music nearly becomes too much to bear. The walls and ground below me vibrate, the music so loud that people don't even bother trying to talk inside.

We near the living room where flashing lights hover over bobbing heads. *It's for the plot,* I remind myself. *You're doing this for the plot.* Most of these people tower over me, some of them covered with tattoos from head to toe while others have pierced parts of their bodies I didn't know were pierceable. The crowd's cheers form a thunderous roar when the song ends. Drinks are raised, smoke gathering above people's heads. My chest tightens when I look around for Tish, but she's nowhere to be found.

"Oh no," I gasp. "No, no, no."

The living room suddenly goes black. The crowd packs in, forcing me in the direction of God-knows-what. With all my strength, I tread through the sea of partygoers. The sound of a low bassline hums through my body, strengthening the drunk bodies that close in on me. I push toward what I now pray will be a back, side, or front door. White lights flash as the bassline grows louder. The sound overwhelms my ears, then my head, all the way down my core. The place reeks of cheap beer, weed, and degeneracy. *Forget the plot. I'm perfectly fine with reading books for the rest of my life in the safety of my bookstore.*

I'm suddenly halted by a table as its edge digs into my side. I wince at the sharp pain, then climb on top of it as the flashing white lights turn blue. With each flash, faces are revealed in the crowd. All strangers, no sight of Tish. The room stays the color blue, and three crisp white spotlights shine from the back of the room to the front, illuminating the three men on stage.

Smoke looms overhead, and as it clears, I catch sight of Luca. His golden hair hangs over the sides of his jagged jawline, his fingers dancing over the guitar with effortless grace as the song starts. The sound of his electric guitar is raw and grips my heart, each note pulling me deeper into his allure like a boat dragged out to sea by the ocean's merciless tide. Without him having to say a word, he becomes all I see, all I hear, all I feel. And all I want is more. More Luca.

For a moment, I forget that I'm at a party surrounded by strangers. I forget that I'm standing on a table in the dark. Life itself is replaced by this man I hardly know anything about, and I welcome the thought of losing control with open arms. Without even trying, he becomes my adventure.

The band chimes in, their instruments melting together in perfect harmony. The bass pulses through the walls, the beat of the drums replacing the beat of my heart. Abel presses his full lips to the microphone, the music forming a tidal wave that drowns out my conscience. I don't fight it. Instead, I submit myself to it, becoming one with the crowd.

Even with each bandmate carrying their own weight, I follow the rhythm of Luca's guitar. He stands beside Abel, his soft smile contrasting the profound hold he has on me. I now understand what Tish meant when she said Luca doesn't care about anything other than his guitar and surfboard. I wouldn't care either if I possessed the skill he possesses with both. It makes me wonder what comes first for him… the *love for what he does best* or the *skill*. If it's love, then I'll make this man love me. If it's skill, then I'll let this man play me until he becomes the best at it.

I close my eyes, swaying to the music. When the song picks up, I open my eyes and meet Luca's gaze. His soft smile becomes radiant, a beacon of light. In a room full of strangers, we're alone. He notices me, and the intensity in his eyes forms an invisible thread that connects us from across the party. As Luca's final note hangs in the air, our connection remains undeniable. He keeps his eyes on me as Abel thanks everyone for listening.

"We are *The Babylon Brigade*!" Abel shouts, pointing a finger to the ceiling. "You guys have been fucking great! Thanks for listening."

Everyone cheers, and the stage goes dark. As the lights turn back on, hip-hop music begins playing from the speakers and people go back to their party festivities—conversations, drinking games, drugs, more drinking, more drugs. I'm nearly gutted when Luca finally breaks eye contact with me to put down his guitar.

A hand grips my arm, nails digging into my flesh. "Bella, what the hell?!" Tish pulls me off the table and nags me for leaving her. As she runs her mouth, all I can hear is the sound of Luca's guitar still echoing in my mind. And all I can see is Luca stepping off the small stage and up the stairs with his bandmates. "Are you even listening to what I'm saying?" Tish's words eventually make it to me.

I face her, unfazed.

"I ssaaiidd…" She palms the sides of my head and leans forward.

"Abel wants us to go upstairs."

I squint at Tish. "Upstairs?"

"Are you picking up what I'm putting down? We pretty much got invited backstage to hang out with them."

"Take me," I command. "I need to talk to Luca."

Tish laughs, grabs my hand, and pulls me through the crowd. Two massive men stand at the foot of the stairs, one stopping us with his hand. "I'm going up to see Abel," Tish states.

"Name?" one of the men replies with a brow raised.

"Tish." She smirks at me, then adds, "And tell Luca that Bella is here, too."

He gestures for the other man to go upstairs. After a few seconds, he waves us up. With each step, I try to improve myself in a way that might attract Luca. By the third step, I've fixed my ponytail. By the fifth, I've pulled down my shirt to show just enough of my collarbone. By the seventh, my lips are glossed. And by the ninth, I'm convinced that the author of my life is ready to give me a chance at love.

The man opens the door, and I'm overwhelmed by a thick wave of smoke. I hold my breath, but Tish doesn't mind it. She's the first to strut into the room with her head held so high that you would think she's the one performing tonight. It's a spacious room, the walls covered by vintage art pieces and posters. People are sprawled out on a few couches while some play a game of pool in the corner.

A wide sliding glass door lines the back wall, which opens up to a balcony overlooking the hillside and ocean beyond. The moonlight spills in, casting a silver sheen over the people leaning against the railing as they smoke cigarettes. I follow Tish, feeling like her shadow as she looks for Abel. We find a spot with our backs against the wall and while I feel like we're sticking out like sore thumbs, I realize nobody has once looked our way.

"There's Luca!" Tish whispers.

I pan around the room until my eyes land on Luca stepping up to the pool table. He leans over the table, his black T-shirt hugging his biceps as he readies the cue to take his turn. I'm moving in his direction, feeding on the undeniable pull he's had on me since I saw him last week at the beach. The closer I get, the more aware I am of the flutter in my chest and the tremble in my hands.

Luca lines his shot, the intensity of his focus unwavering. By now, I know that anything he does, he does while tuning out the world around him. He hits the cue ball with a satisfying crack and sinks the

8-ball in the corner pocket.

His stern expression loosens into a smirk. "That's game," he says softly. "A bet is a bet." The guy he's playing against sighs and tosses a hundred-dollar bill on the table. Luca stands tall, and the cue stick tightens between his pecs as he crosses his arms. "Keep your money, Dane. Beating you is worth more to me than taking your cash."

Dane rolls his eyes. "Drinks on me later then," he blurts out. "Good game, dickhead."

The two shake hands, joking lightheartedly. I swear I blink, and when I open my eyes, they're both looking right at me. *How long have I been standing at the edge of the table?*

Dane raises a brow over his thick mustache. "You alright?"

I open my mouth to speak, regretting the words that will come out of my mouth before I even think of what to say.

"You're Bella," Luca says with a head tilt. The corners of his lips curl up into a grin. "The bad swimmer."

"The bad swimmer." Dane's eyes flick between us until they widen. "That's right." He smirks, and I blush at the thought of Luca telling Dane about how we met. He sets his cue stick flat on the table, then grabs his money. "I'll let you two crack on."

Luca ignores Dane as he leaves. His gaze remains fixed on mine as he rests his chin on the tip of his stick. "Balcony?"

I nod.

He sets the stick down.

He takes my hand.

He leads me to the balcony.

The ocean breeze sweeps Luca's hair as he's the first to step through the sliding doors. The hillside slopes down to the beach below. The sound of crashing waves is soothing, the air between us humming with an unspoken tension. The few people smoking cigarettes congratulate Luca on a great show before heading back inside.

Luca flashes a smile their way. "Thanks for listening." When the sliding doors close, the silence becomes deafening. Don't get me wrong. It's sweet, just deafening. He leans back against the railing and crosses his arms. "Are you following me?"

"What?!" I snap, stepping up beside him.

"I'm teasing," he says.

Luca gently strokes my arm, and I think I might melt through the floor. He's taller, much taller than me when we're standing on even ground. Whether he's just getting out of the ocean or finishing a show, his hair somehow falls perfectly each time he runs his hands back through it. It falls down to his shoulders, which are so broad I couldn't wrap a full hand around them to save my own life. He also looks hard—I mean strong—but also hard? But his voice is so soft. How can someone be so hard and soft at the same time?

"Hello?" His voice derails my train of thought.

Shut up, Luca. I'm busy falling in love with you.

"Huh?" I ask, admiring how wide his chest is.

Luca's laughter dominates the balcony. "I asked if you knew I would be here tonight."

I blush. "No, I—"

"Just keep popping up," he interrupts smoothly. "Hey, I'm not mad about it."

I let out an exhale. "Tish is talking to the singer in your band and he said you guys were having a show tonight."

"So, what'd you think?"

I shrug, downplaying my infatuation. "You're pretty good," I lie. *You're incredible.*

"Pretty good?" Luca tucks a few golden strands of hair behind his ear. He does it in a way that's so nonchalant. I don't think he realizes how something so simple can still take my breath away. "It must take a lot to impress you."

I feel him studying me as I lean against the railing. We stand shoulder to shoulder, now looking over the edge. He places his large hand on the smooth surface near mine. The heat radiates, a tickling sensation rising from my fingertips, up my arms, down my core, and settling between my legs.

"I can be a harsh critic," I tease, somehow keeping my eyes on the ocean.

A silent beat passes before Luca's pinky grazes mine. "Fine," I hear him say. "I like a challenge." His hand envelops mine. He pulls me away from the railing, opening me up to him. My lips part as he grazes my cheek with his thumb. "The scratch from the beach has pretty much healed up now."

I cringe, replaying the memory of my embarrassing ploy to fake-drown. "That was embarrassing."

Luca smiles. "Is it wrong for me to say that I'm glad it happened?"

"You're glad I almost drowned?" I flash a smirk. "Sounds a bit wrong to me."

"If it didn't happen, I might not be standing here with you right now. And standing here with you right now feels right. So, yes. I'm glad you almost drowned."

Luca's interest in me seems sudden compared to the way he cut our time short the last we spoke. While I'm not complaining about it, I want to find out what's different this time around.

His eyes drop to my lips, and my breath gets caught in my throat. The warmth of his hands nearly becomes too much to bear, the closeness of his body sending chills down my spine. He relaxes his lips while slowly lowering himself to mine. The smell of booze is on his breath, but I'm so overwhelmed by the possibility of us kissing that I suppress every one of my senses but touch just so I can feel more of him.

It's happening. It's actually happening.

Until it doesn't.

"Abel, stop!" Tish's laugh causes Luca to pull away as she stumbles onto the balcony. Standing behind her is Abel, a slender man with a shaved head. "You're terrible!"

Abel drags his eyes up Tish's body, and I can't help but notice that he has Luca's face. *Twins.* He's handsome, though he's not the same type of handsome as Luca. Abel is a dangerous type of handsome, the type of handsome that could lead a girl astray.

Tish slaps the tattoo-covered arm Abel wraps around her waist. I bite my lip to keep from scolding her for robbing me of my main character moment with Luca. Luca seems to feel the same way. Abel lowers himself to lick the side of Tish's face. She laughs even louder while lifting her chin for him to do it again. I clear my throat to make it known that they're not alone and the balcony is already taken.

Tish gasps. "Oh my, Bella!" She points a finger at Luca. "And Luca?! It's about damn time."

Abel looks up from Tish's neck. From the looks of him, he's on more drugs than I can count on one hand. Even in the night, his pupils are so obviously dilated that they become an abyss, home to any vice a man can possess. "Well, aren't *you* a little angel?" His words leave his lips in the form of a hiss. A malicious grin spreads below the tattoos under his eyes. "She looks fun, Luca."

Luca's eyes narrow. I watch his shoulders roll back as he puffs out his chest. "This is Bella."

"Little Bella," Abel says to my chest, sizing me up.

I feel Luca's arm wrap around my shoulder. He pulls me close, sending a message to the group: *Bella is mine.*

Abel sneers at Luca. He lifts a tequila bottle, takes a swig, then offers it to Luca. "Loosen up, little brother. We had a good night."

Luca reluctantly accepts the bottle, takes a sip, then hands it back.

Abel smirks. "That's a good boy." He glances at me, then back at Luca. "Tish, let's go back inside." He lifts Tish over his shoulder and turns back into the room.

Tish drunkenly giggles, mouthing, "Oh my God," in my direction as she's carried back through the sliding doors.

When they're gone, Luca lets go of me. "You and Tish should leave," he warns, turning his back to me.

What the hell?

"Leave?" I ask, gutted the way I was back at the beach last week. "I don't get you."

Luca rests his elbows on the railing. He looks down, his golden hair hanging over the sides of his face.

"I can't figure out if you're interested in me or not," I confess. "We flirt, and just when I feel something may happen between us, you send me away." I lean against the railing, tilting my head to try and see his face, to get some kind of response. "Look, I'm obviously attracted to you, but it seems like you don't feel the same way and—"

Oh.

His lips are on mine.

My.

Luca's lips are on mine.

God.

Luca is kissing me.

My eyes are still open for the first few seconds of what has become our first kiss. The world stops spinning, or at least that's what I want more than anything. Because this is the moment I didn't know I needed to experience until I finally experienced it. The distant crashing of waves becomes all I hear, while Luca is all I feel in every fiber of my being. His kiss is gentle yet firm. His hands are soft against my cheeks, yet they plead for me to submit myself to their embrace. I reach up, threading my fingers through his lush hair. When he pulls away, I search him for answers to questions I never knew I needed answered.

Who are you?

Where have you been all my life?

What are you doing to me?

"I didn't mean to send you mixed signals," Luca whispers. "I just don't normally do whatever this is."

"Neither do I," I admit. "I usually just read about it."

He kisses me again, this time more deliberately. When he pulls away, the sweet moment becomes subtly tainted by the lingering taste of tequila. He raises his phone between us. "I need your number so I can take you on a proper date." He nervously looks over my shoulder, then at me. "But, right now your friend is drunk and you should take her home before things get out of hand." Still trying to think straight after that kiss, I put my number in his phone and hand it back. He reads the number back to me, then smiles. "I'll text you."

"Good," I say, still trying to regain my composure.

Luca palms the small of my back and guides me inside. The room is filled with half the amount of people once in it. Tish and Abel are making out on the couch until I tap Tish's shoulder. It doesn't faze her. I tap again, and she can hardly look straight when she pulls back from Abel, who is just as wasted.

"The fuck are you doing?" Abel slurs, folding over Tish's lap.

"We need to go," I whisper to Tish.

Her eyes flutter back while she tries to nod. Abel remains face down on the couch as Luca and I carry Tish down the stairs and outside. All that remains of the party are passed-out people lying between piles of red solo cups. We gently sit Tish down on the curb and I call an Uber.

"Is she going to be okay?" Luca asks.

I turn to face him. "She's fine."

"Will *you* be okay?" He smirks, running a thumb over the scar on my cheek. "I promise not to wait a week before seeing you next."

"Don't make a promise you can't keep," I tease.

"I keep my promises," Luca replies before kissing me once more.

I hold up a pinky. "Pinky promise."

He wraps my pinky with his, then lifts our locked hands to his lips and kisses the top of his fist. Pinkies still locked, I then kiss the top of mine. He smiles down at me, saying, "It's a promise I look forward to keeping."

It's in this moment that I see my story being written for the first time, and it may finally be one worth reading about.

One filled with adventure…

One filled with love…

And Luca Genova.

5 DAYS STRANDED

I drive the tip of my spear through the fish with ease. Its silver body shimmers, reflecting the morning sun as I lift it from the water. I take a moment to admire my first catch of the day. It's larger than the one Bella and I shared for dinner last night, but my hunger gets the best of me. *I want my own.*

I fasten the fish to the rope I tied around my waist, then sway with the ocean current the way Bella taught me. As I wait for the fish to return, I notice the ocean is choppier than normal, the waves lapping over my shins with more aggression. It's been five days since I washed up on this shore. It's safe to say that my low moments have kept from getting any lower, while the highs just keep getting higher. Even in the chaos of the wilderness, Bella and I have found order. I'm now responsible for catching the fish while Bella makes sure the wood is prepared for the fire and our shelter remains intact.

I look back to see Bella sleeping peacefully under the shelter. Since I've been on this island, I've found myself grappling with thoughts of life back home. After I lost Clem, I suppressed some of my most painful memories. I couldn't find the strength to face them, to think about what went wrong. And with each day I've spent on this island, I've felt those memories pulling at me like never before. It's like my past is forcing its way into the present while my vision of the future is fading. I guess that's just one of the consequences of being stuck in solitude. It's hard to distract the mind in a place like this. No phone, no drugs, no alcohol, no friends or family or people at all for that matter. Just a mind full of insecurities, struggles, and regrets you forgot were there.

When you're stranded, the mind does what it does best. It wanders through everything it knows, which is made up of the past. Every experience, every moment, every word spoken, and all the times the heart's been broken. It's all stored in the mind, and I'm starting to realize that isolation quickly forces you to take inventory of every thought your mind has recorded.

So, the same way Bella fake-drowned for Luca, I fake-smile for Bella. I do my best to remain in high spirits, but I have limited control over our lives out here. I can only catch so many fish. We can only drink so many coconuts. At the end of the day, we're limited out here. We've been getting by, but my gut says we may not get by for much longer.

"Good morning," I greet Bella from beside the fire I made.

She rubs her sleepy eyes, stepping out from the shelter. "Morning, Rome." Her head pans left to right over the open ocean. "Another day in paradise."

I laugh under my breath. We're so far from civilization that it's hard not to find the situation somewhat humorous at times. No sight of a plane or boat in five days; we're completely off the grid. "*Another day in paradise*," I repeat.

Bella sits beside me, staring into the fire. I lift my spear, revealing two charred slabs of fish hanging from the end. Her tired gaze meets the fish, and her eyes widen, her smile spreading from cheek to cheek. "You caught two?!"

I shrug, smirking. "I learned from the best." There's a light tremble in my hand as I offer her the spear. She takes a slab and looks at me for permission to eat. "Go on," I chuckle. "I think we've earned breakfast."

She lifts the fish to her lips, pausing to savor the smell and sight of it before taking her first bite. She closes her eyes and moans while chewing with gratitude. The moment she hands me the spear, I do the same. Being able to eat is no longer expected. It's earned–no–it's a gift. There's no guarantee that fish will always be within reach, nor is there a guarantee that I'll always have the strength to catch them.

Even as we're able to eat more, I'm getting weaker. Simple tasks like standing up or holding the spear over the fire are strenuous for me. My hands are trembling more often, and my head is, at times, overwhelmed by the dull ache that keeps reminding me that I've gone five days without my medication. I'm surprised by the lack of side effects that have come with not taking my pills, but then again, the struggle to survive may just be distracting me from them.

I point at the four coconuts lying between Bella and me. "Got them down from the tree this morning," I sigh. "We're down to four now."

"You climbed one of the trees?!"

"Hell no, I'm not crazy." I laugh. "I threw my shoe at 'em until they came falling down."

Bella nods, handing one to me. "You got a lot done while I was sleeping."

"Easy for me because you sleep a lot," I tease, breaking the coconut open with a rock. "Let's drink. Being hydrated is more important than being fed."

I lick my cracked lips, the rough shell scratching against my palms. It's roughly the same size as the others but feels twice as heavy now. I turn it, observing the once-lively green husk that's turned brown. How long will it take for our bodies to do the same? How long will it take for us to rot away before finally drifting into whatever awaits us on the other side of death? How long before the trembles, aches, and hunger become too much?

"How do I look?" I ask after sipping. "Be honest."

Bella forces a faint smile, studying me. "Well, for starters, you look like you wouldn't be able to win the game we played back on the ship," she teases.

"Sounds like a challenge," I snap playfully, handing her the coconut. "What else?"

Her smile fades as she studies me harder this time. "Your beard is growing in, and your sunburn is turning into a bit of a tan." She sips the coconut, her eyes dropping to my bare chest. "You're looking leaner than you were when we first met, but other than that? Nothing too different."

Disbelief works through me like a gentle fog. I glance down at my arms, raising my palms. My sunburn has been replaced by a darker shade. I didn't even think I could get this dark. Even while under the shade of the palms and shelter, the sun's rays reflect off the ocean, so I couldn't escape the sun if I tried.

I gently graze a finger over my ribs, wondering how long it will take before they start to show. I run my hand over my jaw, feeling the beard that's replaced the clean shave I've always maintained. Sure, we're surviving. We've found a way to catch food and live off coconuts up until now, but it won't be enough to keep us alive for another few weeks.

Bella's voice pulls me back to the moment. "Your eyes have changed the most since we first met."

"What do you mean?"

She sets the coconut down, leans forward onto her hands and knees, then stares deep into my eyes. "Your eyes are like the ocean. Sometimes, you look at me, and I see waves of fear and frustration–a storm. And other times, I see serenity–the ocean at sunrise and sunset. Before you look at me, I have no idea which it's going to be... the storm or serenity."

I lower my chin, jaw clenched. My breaths grow deeper as I battle my own exhaustion. Bella is right. I'm losing the foundation of who I am. My moods are volatile; they ebb and flow based on the state of hope I feel within. I could feel entirely at peace in this moment, eating fish while having a conversation. But I have no idea how I'll feel in a matter of minutes when there's nothing to do but find the next source of food and water.

"*The storm or serenity,*" I quote Bella aloud. "By now I know you're good with words, and still, I'm impressed by that line."

"Why, thank you." Bella sits back and lifts her knees to her chest. A gentle smile plays on her lips as she says, "Your turn."

I squint at her, taking her in the best I can. Her caramel-colored hair is wavy at her sides, somewhat tangled as it drops just past her shoulders, but it's not messy. Despite everything she went through to get here, her white romper is still whole, hardly showing any sign of distress while my clothes are weathered. After five days, the fabric she wears is still the purest white. Even her legs shine the way they did when I first saw her.

Warmth flows through me when I find her eyes staring into mine. Her iris is the perfect blend of hazel and all things pure. Even after being stranded, even after accepting the circumstances of our situation–there's a sparkle of hope and adventure. Just below her cheek, I notice the tiny scar Luca mentioned in her journal. *How did I miss that before?*

I lean forward and gently graze the tiny scar on her cheek. "From the day you met Luca at the beach?"

Bella closes her eyes, welcoming my touch. "You never noticed it?"

"Not until you read about it," I admit, remaining on my knees before her. "I'm not lying when I say I don't think you've changed at all. You're just as beautiful as you were the day I met you. The moment I saw you in that elevator, you moved with such grace, like the world bends itself in your favor while all you do is simply exist. You have this pureness about you. You had it on the ship and you somehow still have it now. I can't begin to explain how you give me peace when I need to be at peace. And when I feel like dropping dead, you motivate me to stand up and keep pushin'." She tilts her chin, her eyes locked on mine. "I would be dead if you weren't here with me. I would've given up. You're saving my life in real time."

Bella's chest rises and falls faster with each breath. I can hardly recall what I said because I didn't even think about it before saying it. I spoke how I feel based on what I see, and I don't even care what I hear back because I can cling to a better future thanks to her presence alone.

She suddenly looks down at her ring, reminding me that my words can't hold a candle to her commitment to Luca. As her eyes flick toward the ocean, I shake my head, admitting defeat. Her ignoring my subtle profession of admiration is a battle I might've lost, but I refuse to lose the war.

"Have you used the hourglass today yet?" Bella asks.

I reluctantly pull it out of my pocket. Her hand meets my shoulder, and she lowers me onto my back. *It has to be done.* I close my eyes.

I take a deep breath, flip the hourglass, and as sand begins to slip through the center tube, I dive back into my past…

I blink, my eyes struggling to adjust to the light that hangs above me. The humidity clings to my skin like a blanket, my bare arms resting at my sides. The more I blink, the more obvious it becomes that I'm in a medical tent. The tarp stretches above me, sloping to either side of the beds positioned side by side. The faint smell of disinfectants sweeps my nose.

I try to sit up, but I'm stopped by the sharp pain in my

head before it shoots down to my ribs. A groan escapes me as I sink back into my cot. I have no idea what time it is, but I have some idea of where I am when I see the massive American flag draped across the tent's back wall. I'm back on base.

Even though my head feels like a trillion pounds, I let out a sigh of relief because I can move my body again. After being hit by that truck, I was afraid I wouldn't be able to speak or move ever again. I now know I can do at least one of the two.

I hear muffled voices coming from the other side of the tent wall, accompanied by boots crunching over gravel just outside. The muffled voices become clear as two men step through a fold in the tent's wall.

I can't turn my head too far, but I recognize the first voice I hear as it says, "Good morning, Sleeping Beauty." Mac steps in front of me, standing straight at the foot of the bed. "You look like shit."

I smile even though it hurts.

A medic stands next to him, his eyes hovering over whatever machines are beeping behind me. "Told you he'd be awake after a night's rest," he says, opening his palm.

Mac scoffs and places an unlit cigarette in the medic's palm.

"The bet was two," the medic states dryly.

Mac places a second cigarette in the medic's palm without taking his eyes off me. "How you feelin', Rome?"

I feel a cold sweat come over me. If I can't speak, I don't know what I'll do. The last thing I remember is being in the back of the Humvee, not even being able to thank Mac for saving my life. I was trapped in my own body, with no way to communicate to the outside world.

I inhale a deep breath, then exhale. "I feel like I was hit by a truck," I reply.

Mac and the medic's jaws drop at the sound of my voice, then they laugh in celebration of what may or may not be a miracle.

The medic taps the top of my foot. "Glad you're in high spirits, Consano. You should be dead right now." He steps around the bed and holds down a button. The top half of the bed slowly rises so that I'm sitting straight up. "When you got here, you were hardly breathing from the broken ribs. Good news is no punctured or collapsed lungs, but you're lucky because it was a close call. Our biggest concern was your head after the collision. There was a good amount of swelling, but we won't need to perform surgery because you seem to be responding well to the meds we got you on. You're going to be in here for a few days so we can monitor the swelling and adjust as needed. We've also got you on medication to help with the hallucinations."

My brows bunch up. "Hallucinations?"

The medic nods. "It's common after suffering a head injury like yours. You might hear or see some things that aren't real–just part of the healing process." He points at the side of his head. "We have you on a low dose of Risperidone. It's an antipsychotic to keep you from..."

"From going crazy?" I ask.

He pauses. "I know it sounds unsettling. If you stick with the meds, you shouldn't get much, if at all." I flatten my lips, lowering my head. *I'm at risk of losing my mind?* "Head up, Consano. If you believe in God, now is a good time to thank Him. I've seen a lot of men lose their lives over a lot less."

My fingers graze the edges of the wooden cross hanging around my neck. The medic squares his shoulders to Mac. He and Mac salute each other before he leaves the tent. Mac silently picks up a chair and positions it to face the foot of the bed. With a grunt, he takes off his boots and kicks his feet up onto the bed's edge. The corner of his mustache curls up as he smirks at me. His dark features crease in a way that says he's been going through hell since our mission.

"We succeed?" I ask. He dodges my question by looking away. "Mac, was the mission a success?"

"We're going back in tonight," Mac says. "We have a mission brief in an hour." I grab the railing beside me to sit up even straighter, but the pinch in my head forces me back down. "Rome! Chill out."

"You can't go back in without me," I reason. "I'm going with you."

"You're not doing shit." Mac laughs. "Are you insane? Rome, this is your chance to go home on medical discharge. You can be with Clem, supporting her through the pregnancy."

My mind teases me with the thought of going home. I

imagine walking through the navy blue front door of my family's home. I imagine Ma and Pa embracing me before I see Clem on the white bench in the backyard. I see her strawberry blonde hair falling over the baby bump under her floral sundress. It's the sweetest thought, and while there's no place I would rather be, I couldn't be there while Mac is out here. I can't leave Mac, not after he saved my life. We've fantasized about walking back through that front door together, being embraced by our family and friends as heroes. I don't want to fantasize about our return any other way.

"I'm not going back without you," I state. "We've talked about this for months. We go back together."

Mac's gaze falls to his lap. "I was afraid you would say that." He lifts his phone between us. "She'll be expecting your call."

My eyes flick between his and the phone. "You told Clem what happened?!"

"I didn't know if you were gonna make it," he admits, handing me the phone. "I'm sure she won't be happy to hear that you're choosing to stay, but she'll be happy to know you're alright." He stands and makes his way to the exit. "I'll leave you two to talk."

"Mac," I call out. "Thank you."

"You would've done the same," Mac replies softly.

"One more thing," I say before he steps out. He turns. "Shave that mustache before you start to think it looks good on you."

"Too late," he says with a wink.

After he leaves, I look down at the phone. Clem's contact is already open on the screen. As excited as I am to tell her I'm okay, I'm nervous to break the news that I want to finish my deployment. Whether or not she knows the collision was bad enough for me to be offered a medical discharge, I gave Mac my word that we would see this through. And I keep my word.

After a few rings, Clem's face appears on the screen. My heart takes flight, soaring through the pain at the sight of her. Her hair falls in soft waves beside her face, catching the light to form a shimmering rose gold. I smile, then my heart shatters at the sight of the tears gliding down her red cheeks.

She blinks, a whirlwind of emotions spurring in her gaze when she sees that it's me. Those baby-blue eyes widen, then send even more tears falling–tears of excitement, joy, shock. "Rome, is that you?" she asks, piecing it all together. Her lips curl up, the brightness of her smile giving me life through the phone. "Oh, Rome. Look at you."

"Hey, baby," I greet smoothly.

Her face suddenly becomes devoid of all doubt. She beams at me while smiling, laughing, and crying all at once. When she realizes I'm alive, her sadness becomes a state of bliss, like the sun breaking through a storm of worry. She leans closer to the phone, the look on her face full of love and concern.

My voice quivers as I push through the pain. "You and the baby doin' alright?"

Clem lifts the camera to reveal the curve in her belly below her dress. "Doin' just fine. Missing daddy, of course."

Her background sways and it dawns on me that she's sitting on the swinging bench in my family's backyard. Countless memories between us two have been made on that bench, and it brings me to tears, thinking that soon, more memories will be made between the *three* of us in the same spot. Ma's daffodils flood the ground just behind the white bench, the color popping in contrast to the dark green, beige, and dirt I'm used to seeing out here.

"What happened, Rome? Mac called earlier and said it wasn't good."

"We were on a mission and it went south." I spare her the details. She's worried enough. "Nothing more than a mosquito bite."

"Was it enough to...?" Clem cuts her question short, but I know what she's asking.

With her father also having been in the military, she knows that if I were medically discharged, I would still be able to keep my benefits, even while coming home early. I could be there with her for the remainder of her pregnancy, to love on and support all while getting the financial aid I deserve for coming so close to death.

"I wish I could jump right through this screen and hold you right now," I say, avoiding her question.

"Soon, you won't have to," she chirps. "It could be sooner if–"

"Clem."

Clem's mood shifts. "You're not gonna at least try?"

I bite my lip to keep from crying. I already see the realization killing her.

"Mac and I aren't finished out here yet."

"You're not going to try?" Her bottom lip trembles, tears welling. I look up to help me keep from feeling down. My silence isn't the response she wants to hear. "Roman, I have our baby in me, and even when you don't have the chance to come home early to be with us…" She presses her palm to her forehead, her breaths coming in quick bursts.

I've lost all control at this point, crying my eyes out while she does the same. "You know I can't come home early, Clem."

"Why not?" Her voice cracks in anger. "Why not?!"

"BECAUSE I CAN'T!" I shout. My head pounds mercilessly. "If I come home without Mac and something happens to him, I'll never be able to forgive myself. And I can't wake up one day feeling to blame for him losing his life while I just left him behind."

Clem freezes, and for a moment, I question if the service cut out. But then, she blinks. "You left us behind," she exhales. Her words are a bullet in the head, piercing my skull before splintering into a hundred sharp fragments. As if that wasn't enough, she says, "And one day, you might wake up feeling to blame for leaving us behind."

My jaw drops. "Clem…" A drop of water suddenly lands on the phone screen, causing it to flicker. "Clem?"

I look up to see the tent ceiling.

How is it raining?

"Rome?" Clem asks through the screen as it flashes white. "Can you hear me?"

I feel a raindrop land on my forehead, then another.

I cover the screen, but the rain somehow makes it through.

"Rome, I'm sorry," I hear her say. "I didn't mean it. I–"

The call cuts out, and the raindrops become a soft pour until…

I open my teary eyes to a tickling sensation against my face, neck, and bare chest. I lift my head from the damp shirt that's been folded neatly under me. My fingers curl under the soft, wet fabric. Wet. WET. THE SHIRT IS WET.

I look up at the sky and feel raindrops dancing over my face, neck, and body. Dark clouds blanket the sky overhead, sending a rhythmic patter of rain over the palm leaves and our shelter. Bella stirs beside me, her long lashes fluttering as she wakes to the same sensation.

"It's raining," I say. "IT'S RAINING!" I scream. I shake Bella, then jump to my feet. "BELLA, IT'S RAINING!"

A genuine smile spreads across her face. She closes her eyes, lifts her chin, and parts her lips to the sky. "It's raining," she whispers under her breath. The corners of her lips curl up as she kneels. "Thank you," she exhales toward the sky, her fingers now laced under her chin.

I scramble to my feet and bolt to the shelter. I dump everything out of the metal box, grab the bucket, and then set them in the middle of the beach. Around the bucket, I place half-open coconuts face up to collect as much water as we can. After a few trips up to the palm trees, I'm able to fasten a few broad, dead leaves around the bucket to catch more precious raindrops. It's a heavy pour now, each drop of rain a gift that gives promise of a new day.

"Our clothes!" I shout. I strip down to my briefs and spread my shirt and shorts over our shelter. "Our clothes will catch more water, and we can wring them over the bucket."

I gently pull the corners far and wide to cover the low, slanted roof. Bella follows my lead, lying her white romper next to my shirt. I stop short upon catching sight of her in her bra and underwear. Bella stands there with that unassuming grace I discovered when we first met. Raindrops cascade down her shoulders, illuminating the soft light from the stormy sky.

My world stops, my mind a jumbled mess of all things Bella. The light she embodies, her yearn for adventure, her love for stories, her kind nature. The way she cares for her dad, how she values her friendship with Tish, even the way she loves Luca. As much as I hate to imagine it, I love the way she loves, even if the someone she loves isn't me.

Bella notices me staring and looks down shyly. "Anything else?"

I blink myself back to survival mode. "Right. Yeah, no. We're... yes." I'm betrayed by my own words as they spew out of my mouth as nonsense. Her laughter overpowers the sound of rain, and I want nothing more than for her to never stop laughing. I clear my throat. "We should, um–the bucket and box. Let's make sure they're collecting the rain."

Bella's eyes twinkle behind the wall of rain separating us, her voice light as she playfully agrees. "Good idea!"

We work silently for a bit, pouring the water-filled coconuts into the bucket, then placing them in the sand again. As we kneel over the bucket, I steal glances of Bella every chance I get. I notice her do the same when I pretend to look away. Her soaked hair frames her face, pronouncing her straight brows and cheekbones. I follow a water droplet as it glides from a hair strand along her jaw. It settles at the curve of her tiny chin, then drips into the bucket with the rest of the divine droplets.

The few dark storm clouds that have gifted us at least a few more days of survival continue their journey past the island. The rain lessens, the sun now reintroducing itself.

Hope you got what you need, the sun mocks. *Because you're stuck with me until further notice.*

Bella and I wring our clothes into the now-filled bucket, then move the bucket, metal box, and refilled coconuts inside our shelter.

"That was nice of the author," Bella says as she hands me a coconut filled with rainwater.

We sit beside each other under the shade of the palms. I take a sip, then hand her the coconut. "The author put us on this island in the first place. After doing something like that, I think anything the author does will seem nice."

Bella nods, lifting the coconut to her lips. She sips, then says, "Those clouds weren't anywhere in sight before we fell asleep." She hands me the coconut. "I think it's safe to say the author still needs us for the story."

While Bella's writer talk never struck a chord too deep for me, what she says suddenly resonates on a deeper level. With all this mention of taking risks "for the plot" and being "characters with our own arcs in our own stories," I ponder the double meaning behind her mentioning of the author. Before I lost Clem, I was a God-fearing man. I didn't fear death because I had faith, but that faith died with my relationship.

What kind of author forces his main characters to suffer?
What kind of God leaves his creation stranded on an island?

I take a moment to observe the rainwater. I swish it in small circles to make sure it's real and not something I'm hallucinating because Bella was right when she said those clouds weren't anywhere in sight before we fell asleep.

"It'd be real nice of this author of yours to send help," I joke dryly, setting down the coconut.

Bella laughs under her breath. "If characters wrote their own stories, everything would go right. And stories are boring when everything goes right."

"That's a good point," I exhale. "I hate that that's a good point."

My eyes find Bella's before they drop to the tiny scar under her eye. She gently grazes it with her fingertip. I force a smile, struggling to suppress the thought of Luca when I now see the scar. For the first time since Bella started reading her journal, the idea of Luca carries a bit of a sting. I can't shake the thought of how she looked in the rain, how her hair clung to her face, her laughter blending with the pouring rain. It's as if every raindrop that met my skin today rejuvenated my mind, heart, and body. And now, Luca feels like an intrusion on the beautiful moment I shared with Bella.

Bella picks up on my discomfort. "What's wrong?"

I look out at the horizon, where the sky meets the ocean in a sharp line. The clouds have retreated, shrinking in the distance as our world prepares for dusk. I wonder if something has changed in her the way something changed in me. I wonder if she sees a future the way I'm starting not to. Life on this island could be our new reality for who-knows-how-long, catching fish and praying for rain. Eventually, we will have burnt our last piece of wood. We will have read the last page of Bella's journal. We will have scared away all the fish we couldn't kill. *We will have run out of life to live.*

"Do you think you'll ever see Luca again?" I ask.

I can feel Bella's gaze settle on my cheek, searching for something deeper in my expression. "I do."

Her words hurt, her hope a sharp thorn in my side.

"Do you even want to see Luca again?" My question scrapes against my tongue. "Since we met, I noticed you change the subject whenever I bring him up." I turn to face her. "But, you write about him like he's the love of your life. Is he?"

"Is he the love of my life?" Bella's eyes drop to the ground between us.

"It's a yes-or-no question," I add.

"Not really. Love is too complicated for yes-or-no questions," she replies quickly. "You can't possibly think love is simple."

I lie on my side, keeping myself propped up on my elbow. "It can be simple," I say softly, grabbing a handful of sand. I wrap my fingers over the grains, tighten my grip, then let them fall back to the earth. "I was in love, then I wasn't. Pretty simple to me."

"I would argue that you still love Clementine. It's just a different kind of love."

I squint at Bella, trying to process what kind of love I could still have for Clem. Bella doesn't know Clem. She doesn't understand the damage done in my past. She can't comprehend the sacrifices I made for my country, only to return to a girl who took my future in the palm of her hand, crushed it into broken pieces, then let the broken pieces fall back to the earth for me to put back together.

The little fantasy-book world Bella lives in doesn't translate to the cruelty the real world embodies. I've experienced war, true hell on Earth. I've watched men die while Bella experienced sunsets and neighborhood parties. Before being on this island, she had never known Pain or Struggle; all while I had become good friends with both Pain and Struggle, and now the two are my friends for life.

"I don't think we'll get off this island," I mutter, sitting up. I lift my knees to my chest, wrapping them with my arms. "The world isn't kind to the kindhearted. There is no karma. It's like the storm that stranded us, inconsiderate of how good of people we are. You saw how big those waves were. Nature kills."

"Nature also gives life," Bella adds. She places a hand on my knee. "Nature didn't kill you, Rome. Nature brought you *here*."

"Well, I don't wanna be here anymore," I state, eyes fixated on the horizon. "My entire life, I've been in control. When things went wrong, I found a solution. Back at home, I solved problems for my family. I solved problems for Clem. I solved problems for the damn country, for Christ's sake." I drag my palms down the sides of my face. "Out here, time is passing us by while we can't do a damn thing about it. All we can do is wait."

Bella's expression softens. She feels my frustration and somehow doesn't feed on it. Clem used to feed on it from time to time, telling me that I was wasting my time whenever I felt like I pursued a path to better myself. But Bella is different. Bella is like a kid who hasn't been corrupted by the world. It's as if her books have kept her in the dark. Better yet, *it's as if her books have kept her in the light*. She's remained far away from injustice and cruelty. She's been protected, saved by her books.

"How about this?" Bella gets on her knees. Her hand is cool on my shoulder, chilling my heated nerves. "In a lot of romance books I read, there are these little games the main characters play. It's a way the author develops their characters. It's a way they grow closer, and even stronger."

I shoot her a half-glance. "Bella, not everything is about books."

"Oh, come on. Please!" Her gentle fingers turn my chin toward her. "We can play a game that gets our minds off this island. It'll be fun, I promise."

The playfulness in her eyes slowly draws me in. It breaks through my anxiety, and I can't help but smile at her optimism. I inhale, then exhale a calming breath. I relax my shoulders and turn so that we're sitting crisscross, face to face.

"What's the game?" I ask, shaking my head and smiling at the same time.

Bella sits, deep in thought. "I'm making it up, so don't hate on it. This is a 'Bella-Original.'"

I nod for her to continue.

She smirks. "We're going to go back and forth. I'm going to say something that I plan to do when we get off this island, then you're going to say something you plan to do. And we're going to keep going until one of us smiles. The first to smile loses. We'll call the game, '*Someday Soon*.'"

"Hope you're ready to smile then." I narrow my eyes. "Because I'm playing to win."

Bella covers her smile. "Okay, that doesn't count! I'll go first."

"Go for it."

She adjusts herself to sit more comfortably. "Someday soon, I'll see Tish again."

"Someday soon…" I ponder for a moment. "I'll see Mac again." As the thought of seeing Mac again fills my mind, the weight on my shoulders lessens.

"See, that's good!" Bella nods, forcing back her grin. "Okay. Someday soon, my first book will be published."

"Someday soon, I'll fix up my parents' house." The weight lessens just a bit more.

"Cute," she says. "That would've made me smile if I wasn't trying to beat you in this game. Where do they live?"

I lean back, my hands now in the sand as I straighten my legs. "Blue Ridge. It's a small town back in Georgia."

"Someday soon, I'll visit you in Blue Ridge," Bella says.

I clench my jaw to keep from smiling. I somehow manage to keep a straight face, but I can't resist the butterflies that manifest themselves within. I imagine Bella meeting my parents and seeing their small home. I imagine her telling them all about books like she does with me. I imagine Ma throwing her arms around Bella when Ma learns the only reason I survived out here is because of Bella.

"Blue Ridge isn't anything special, you know."

Bella purses her lips, then says, "If it's special to you, then it's special to me."

How can you not smile at that? Damn, this is tough.

We continue back and forth, learning more about each other as the game goes on. It becomes about the little things, like hobbies we miss, types of food we want to eat again. And as we continue, more serious topics arise, like goals we have and parts of the world we never got to see but will someday soon. With each turn, Bella's light embraces the anxiety and looming depression threatening me since the moment I woke up on this beach.

I look down, then mutter, "Someday soon, I'll learn how to swim."

"Wait." Bella's eyes widen. "You're joking."

"I mean it," I reply. "Someday soon, I'll learn how…"

"Yes, I heard what you said!" she snaps. "But, like, how did you serve in the military and not learn how to swim?!"

I itch the side of my head, thinking through the best way to phrase this. "I sort of made a deal with the drill sergeant. If I aced all the land drills and did all of his busy work, he'd let me skip the water drills."

"So, you've never wanted to learn how to swim?"

I shake my head. "I don't do well in water. I like to be in control, which I have a lot more of on land. That's one of the reasons I didn't want to go on the cruise."

"But you went on Azrael's boat with me."

"Because you were so excited to go," I admit. "I did it 'for the plot.'"

Bella inhales a sharp breath, turning red. She refrains from smiling with all her strength, then releases the breath. "You almost got me there." She claps sand from her hands, and we watch the grains fall. When my eyes meet hers again, she says, "Someday soon, I'm going to teach you how to swim."

I smile.

"Aha!" She points at my face. "You lose, sir."

I keep smiling. I can't help it. "Fine by me."

🌴🌴🌴

The sun has set and surrendered to twilight when I get the fire going. The light from the twinkling stars is mirrored over the calm water surrounding our island. Nothing but the crackling fire and soft laps of waves can be heard until Bella sits beside me with her journal in hand.

"Where did we leave off again?" I ask, finishing my last bite of fish.

Her fingers lovingly trace the edges of her leather journal. "Tish just got way too drunk at the party Luca's band performed at, aanndd Luca promised not to let a week go by before he saw me next."

"Hmm." I lie my head on Bella's backpack. The full moon hangs low in a sky speckled with an abundance of stars. "Did he keep that promise?"

"No spoilers," Bella teases, finding the page we left off. "You ready?"

"Ready."

She reads…

Laguna Beach, California
Monday - May 20th, 2019

"I'm not your daughter anymore," I say right to Dad's face. "You're no longer my father."

Dad shrugs from his stool behind the cash register. "I meant what I said."

"You *do* realize that what you just said is bookish blasphemy," I state, leaning against the nearest bookshelf. I cross my arms and squint at him. "How could you think that classic books are better than the books coming out now?"

"It's in the name!" Dad chuckles, pushing his glasses up the bridge of his nose. "The books are considered 'classics' for a reason."

It's been a slow afternoon at the bookstore, lending more time for organizing, cleaning, and having a heated debate over who has better taste in books.

"You're stuck in the past, old man," I tease. "New books are more exciting. They're more relatable!"

Dad rolls his eyes, then points at the Classics section. "The themes written about in the classic novels are universal, Bella. They stand the test of time. The books written nowadays are about whatever is popular in the moment. You kids and your TipTop trends."

"The social media app is called 'TikTok,' Dad," I correct him. "And I'll have you know that I've found some really good books on TikTok."

He raises the book he's been reading and taps the cover. "Just promise me that when you publish your first book, it becomes a classic." His words make me blush. "Promise me."

"I promise."

"Good." The stool creaks under him as he leans back against the bookshelf. He opens his book and pulls the bookmark from the page. "Anything you write will be a classic, kiddo. And I can't wait to be the first to put it on a shelf."

"Thanks, Dad."

The bell above the front door suddenly jingles, and Ms. Rivera walks inside with a warm smile on her face. Her purple glasses magnify her kind eyes as she gets a good look at Dad while he reads. The door shuts softly behind her, and she innocently scans the entryway as if I don't realize she is only here to flirt with Dad again.

"Hi, Bella dear!" Ms. Rivera greets. "Just coming in to pick up a new book!" She twirls, showing off her freshly trimmed bob cut. "Do you mind lending me a hand?"

"Ms. Rivera!" I greet loud enough to get Dad to look up from his book. "You look very beautiful today. Right, Dad?"

Dad's eyes widen at Ms. Rivera, the stool skidding from under him as he stands. "Y-yes! Hello, Ms. Rivera."

She playfully waves him off, then winks at me. "You're too kind, Donald."

I giggle, watching Ms. Rivera acting so calculated while Dad doesn't even know what planet he's on. "I'm gonna be in the back office catching up on emails," I say. "I'm sure my dad can help you out today."

I tilt my chin, hoping Dad picked up on my wing-woman efforts. The two begin their small talk while I head to the small office in the back of the bookstore. I click through one email after another, each from an indie author looking to have their book sold in our store. As a bookstore employee, I skim through each blurb until something sparks my interest. As an aspiring author, each email forces me to question my aspiration just a bit more. We get hundreds of emails per day from writers with books that may never land on a shelf. To think I may soon be one of these authors makes the journey appear nearly impossible.

Bleh.

The bell above the front door jingles again. The sound of slight mumbling can be heard from the front of the store while I keep clicking through emails. A pit starts to grow in my stomach when I realize some of these book blurbs are actually better than anything I could ever come up with. I've wrestled with idea after idea for my own book, but nothing has ever really stuck. So, I journal when I can, hoping that one day inspiration will strike or I'll be able to pull inspiration from an entry.

I reluctantly reply to the emails, asking them to send a copy for us to read before we make any commitments. Upon hitting Send, I look through the glass separating the office from the store.

Oh my…

No it can't be there's no way how did he find me here what is going on?

Through the window, I catch sight of Luca browsing the shelves. His white linen shirt hangs loosely over his shoulders down to his beige linen pants. He's barefoot, which isn't uncommon in Laguna Beach, peacefully scanning the shelves, his finger gently brushing over the spines. The late afternoon light spills through the windows, accentuating his curious eyes and the grace of his subtle movements.

My heart swells as I read him like I would my favorite book, a book I never want to end. Books have always been an escape for me, and I'm realizing that Luca is starting to have the same effect on me. When he's around, reality becomes less intriguing, less important. He carries himself like captivating prose, drawing me in when the chapter begins and leaving me wanting more when the chapter ends. I already want to read Luca forever, and I've hardly even begun reading the book that makes up his life.

Watching how he tucks a few golden strands of hair behind his ear reminds me of the last time I saw him. The party was only a couple nights ago, and here he is. He promised not to wait a week before seeing me next. He couldn't even wait three days.

I crave the warmth of his nearness, the memory of his melodic laughter bringing me to my feet. I approach the door frame separating the office from the store and lean around the frame just enough to study him with one eye. He's skimming through an adaptation of *Romeo and Juliet* by William Shakespeare. In an instant, his eyes flick up and catch mine. A slow, knowing smile spreads across his face. It's as if he can read the chapters of my heart, piecing together parts of our story that are yet to be written.

Luca tilts his chin, a golden strand of hair falling over his face. "Do you usually spy on your customers?"

I shake my head, then point at the book he's holding. "Do you usually pick the most cliché love stories?"

Luca laughs, tucking the golden strand behind his ear. "Hey, don't knock the classics. It's got everything. Love, drama, tragedy. What's not to like?"

"*Don't knock the classics,*" I repeat his words, joining him between the shelves. "Did my dad tell you to say that?" I ask, pointing to the front of the store.

Dad and Ms. Rivera silently watch us, hiding their smiles. Luca and I laugh.

"I thought you would have better taste, Luca," I tease.

He grins, eyes twinkling with playful mischief. "Even the best stories have their clichés."

I giggle. "I think I'll stick to my new-age, more exciting reads, thank you very much."

Luca raises a brow, closing the book. "Then I'd love to see which books are worthy of your time."

It becomes impossible to hold back my smile. As he follows me to the next aisle, my heart and mind are overwhelmed by my overflowing love for books and newfound love for Luca being felt all at once. I lead him to the Contemporary Romance section, each a hidden gem.

We browse, pulling out one copy after another. I make Luca try to guess what the books are about just from reading their titles or by the looks of their covers. The banter between us grows more playful with every passing second, the bookstore fading into the background as we share our love for written words. I've seen Luca obsess over his waves. I've seen Luca obsess over his guitar. But I'm enamored by the version of Luca that obsesses over books, or at least the version that tries to obsess over them.

"You should know I'm not a big reader," Luca says, raising his hands in surrender. "But, I want to be."

I flash him a skeptical look. "And what made you want to be?"

"I met a cute girl who works at a bookstore," he says with a smirk. "And I want to continue this conversation over dinner with her."

The way he lays out his thoughts between us nearly makes me lose my breath. Luca is direct. I like direct. No time wasted, no games. Just a simple invitation that gets my heart racing. I pan along the bookshelves, making it seem like I have to think about getting dinner with him.

"Dinner sounds perfect."

Luca exhales a sigh of relief. "Glad you said so because I already picked it up," he says. "It's in the van. Can you get off work early?"

I open my mouth to speak, but my words get stuck. I haven't finished the checklist of chores and errands for the store. "I…" Luca's grin starts to fade. "Let me ask my dad!"

I cringe, realizing how childish that sounded. Being 21, I shouldn't have to ask my father for permission to go out with a boy. As I approach the front counter, I notice Dad and Ms. Rivera enjoying their chat. I take a few cautious steps toward them, thinking through the best way to ask. Before I can string the right words together, Dad says, "Of course you can go." His rosy cheeks slowly rise into a smile as he side-eyes me. "Be safe, kiddo."

"Oh, to be young and in love again," Ms. Rivera sighs.

I turn back to Luca and smirk. "Where are we going?"

"It's a surprise."

My world is black under the blindfold covering my eyes. I lost track of left and right turns within the first five minutes of our drive, so I have no idea where we are or where we're going. Luca's van gently rumbles beneath me, my fingers tracing the weathered fabric wrapping my seat. As we drive, I feel the soft afternoon breeze seeping through the cracked window.

"I swear I'm not kidnapping you," Luca says playfully from the driver's seat.

"That's something a kidnapper would say," I tease. "You know, I haven't read a book where a bad thing happens to somebody blindfolded."

I feel us turn left as he asks, "Oh, yeah?"

"Yeah. In all the books I read, the blindfold usually comes out when the characters are about to get spicy."

Luca laughs, making me fall for him just a bit more. "And what happens when characters 'get spicy?'"

I adjust the blindfold. "It's bookish slang for when characters get intimate."

"Good to know," he says smoothly. "In that case, I'll make sure to keep the blindfold close."

"Patience, Romeo." I find it hard to suppress my butterflies. At this point, I've seen just about every part of Luca worth seeing. The way his golden hair seamlessly catches the sunlight, framing his chiseled face. The way his blue eyes sparkle with warmth and mischief, making me feel safe and in danger all at once. His lean body, muscular enough to do what he pleases without overpowering. I've seen enough, and now I think I need to feel.

"Almost there," he says, breaking the silence. The car comes to a slow halt, then it climbs up what feels like a curb. The old van tilts left and right over bumpy terrain. I'm itching to take off my blindfold, but I would hate to rob myself of any spoilers for what may happen next in our story.

"Do you usually let guys blindfold and take you places in old vans?"

"Never," I admit. "I'm only doing this for the plot."

"The plot," he whispers. "I like that."

The van makes a sharp left, then beeps as he shifts it in reverse. I lean forward as we inch backward. The keys jingle, followed by silence when the van turns off. The sound of his door shutting makes me brace myself for whatever is about to happen next.

The cool ocean breeze sweeps my white blouse the moment Luca opens my door. He unbuckles my seat belt. "Careful," he whispers, guiding me from the van. I feel for him, praying I touch his face, chest, abs, every part of him I can. After a few shaky steps, he sits me on what feels like the back of the van. He removes my blindfold, and I gasp. "What do you think?" he asks.

Lanterns hang from inside the back of the van to the open doors on either side of us, their dimmed glow becoming pronounced as the sun dips over the ocean horizon ahead. The van is parked in reverse, facing the edge of a cliff overlooking Brooks Street beach. The view from up here nearly takes my breath away, seeing the surfers below as specs in the distance. Their movements are slow over the vast, shimmering ocean. The sound of crashing waves is a serene backdrop to a book-worthy moment unraveling before us.

Luca sits next to me and places a to-go box of Chinese food on my lap. "I probably should have asked if you like Chinese food before getting you Chinese food."

I beam at him, feeling my cheeks turn red. "I'm not picky."

"Thank goodness," he exhales before pointing to the opposite end of the cove. "Look! That's where we met."

Luca's words attach more meaning to Brooks Street than I could've imagined. I follow the white linen covering his arm to the finger he points at the shore. The memory floods my mind, though it never left. I remember his red wetsuit popping over the waves he effortlessly made his own as he surfed them. I remember cautiously stepping into the water. I remember drowning, and I remember him pulling me out of my own panic.

In an instant, Brooks Street becomes so much more than a beach. It becomes *our* beach.

"I have a confession," I say, setting down my chopsticks.

Luca swallows his food, then blows his hair out of his face. "Uh oh."

"Nothing bad. I just sort of was pretending to drown so that you would save me."

Luca freezes, holding a piece of chicken inches from his lips. He drops it back onto his plate, then shoots me a half-glance. "You were pretending?" A line shows between his straight brows, and I can see him replaying the moment in his head.

I prepare for his response. *Is he somehow taking offense to this?*

"You put your own life at risk so I could save it?" he asks, now facing me.

"Okay, when you put it like that, then I just sound crazy." *Back it up, Bella. Get yourself out of this mess you've just made.* "I swear I'm not crazy. I just saw you out there and I thought there was no way you would even know I exist."

Okay, wow.

Before I know it, Luca's lips are on mine. I'm really starting to love this whole random-kissing-thing he does. He's good at it. My eyes flick between his as I admire the delicate fringe of his long lashes.

He pulls away and smirks. "You *are* crazy," he states. "And I love crazy."

I don't even care that Luca just called me crazy.

If Luca loves crazy, I'll be crazy.

"If I'm crazy, what are you?" I ask before taking another bite of chicken.

"I'm impressed."

I tilt my chin. "Oh?"

"Yeah." He sets his to-go box beside him, attaching words to his emotions. "I've never been so interested in somebody I hardly know," he admits. "I've always been so obsessed with surfing and music. I never thought it was possible to be so amused by somebody outside the water or off the stage."

"So, I'm not distracting you?" I ask.

Luca squints at me. "Not at all. It's refreshing. You're just not what I'm used to."

"What are you used to?"

"Not following my own heart." Luca's words leave his lips in a disheartened tone. "My brother and I pretty much share everything now. The van, the band, our lives."

Growing up an only child, I have no idea what it's like to share anything, let alone my face the way Luca and Abel share theirs. I always wanted a brother or a sister, but I never thought about how suffocating it must feel to have a twin with the same aspirations, goals, and life.

I meet Luca's stare. "I feel like it's good that you and your brother are so close."

"A little too close," he says in an exhale. "Growing up, our parents went through a divorce. It got pretty ugly, and our parents made us choose between them."

I nearly choke on my food. "Oh my."

"Yeah." Luca's gaze hovers over the beach. "We were young and didn't know any better, and well, Abel chose to live with our dad and I chose our mom."

"You were separated?"

My heart breaks for the childhood version of Luca not only being separated from his own twin but being forced to choose between his parents. While I spent my childhood on the beach with two loving parents, Luca was being used as leverage in a legal battle between his own parents. No child deserves that, let alone the boy pouring out his heart beside me.

"Abel got the worst of it," Luca continues. "Our dad is an alcoholic, just a bad guy overall. Which is why Abel turned out the way he did." He gestures to his arms and face, a subtle nod to Abel's sporadic tattoos and intimidating facade. "We came back together not too long ago and formed a band with our childhood friend, Dane, the drummer."

I smile, remembering Dane playing Luca in a game of pool at the party. "I remember Dane."

"Sweet guy," Luca adds. "Anyway, since then, we've just focused on music and what's best for the band, which I guess could be considered the only family Abel has left."

"And your parents? You don't keep in touch?"

"We cut off our dad. Mom moved east to take care of our grandma." He turns from the beach to face me. "And we're out here, 'riding the wave.'"

Our smiles break through a conversation that went much deeper than I thought it would. It's baffling to see a guy like Luca turn out to be so beautiful inside and out after going through all of that. I suppose if it were the other way around and Luca lived with his dad instead of his mom, he would've turned out like Abel. I wonder if Abel thinks the same.

Luca raises his hand to his hair, but I beat him to it, tucking the golden strands behind his ear myself. "I just trauma-dumped on you," he whispers apologetically. "Some first date this turned out to be."

I lean forward, and he dips his forehead to mine. "Since we met, I've wanted to know more about you." Our eyes lock. "And you made me realize you'll always leave me wanting more."

The food falls from my lap, splattering over the dirt as we embrace each other. His tongue sweeps my lip, his hands gripping the small of my back. Our kisses grow more intense by the second and though he's so much stronger than me, he lets me push him onto his back. His lush hair forms a tapestry over the scattered pillows and blankets taking up the back of the van.

Acting off of sheer attraction to the strength and grace Luca embodies after surviving such a troubled past, I straddle him and let my breaths deepen against his lips. He slides his hand through my hair and grips the back of my neck before pulling me in. His tongue sweeps mine again, a low moan speaking volumes of his feelings toward me.

A whine leaves my lips as he flips me so that he's now on top. Golden rays of sunlight flood the back of the van in perfect contrast to Luca's tan, prominent features. His golden locks reach for me as he slowly lowers himself, the sensation from his soft lips overwhelming my neck.

How can one man be so polite yet reckless?

So perfect yet broken?

So whole yet hurt?

"Bella," Luca breathes into my chest.

He looks up at me and I'm overwhelmed by the view of his piercing blue eyes and the ocean beyond. He doesn't break eye contact as he undoes the string on my blouse so slowly it's painful. I want him to tear through it, to put me before all of the passions he obsesses over. I want him to learn me, play me, turn me into art the way he does with every one of his obsessions.

Luca carves through waves like he can't live without them.

Luca strums his guitar strings like he can't live without them.

And Luca will make love to me like he can't live without me.

He separates my blouse, his lips forming a trail of kisses over my chest and down my abdomen. I watch him study every detail of my upper body, the obsession forming in his gaze as he ponders how to make the most of me in however much time we have left. He slides backward, using his tongue to claim the string of my linen pants. He looks up again, clenching his teeth and undoing the string with no hands.

Only a sliver of light is left of the setting sun behind him, lending more attention to the hanging lanterns lining the back of the van. My chest rises and falls more aggressively as he unbuttons his shirt. It separates, and my attention is pulled to the muscles over his bare stomach. With a sadistic grin, he pulls my pants off and lays them over one of the pillows.

Luca's breath grows unsteady with desire as he stands outside the van. He drags his eyes up and down my nearly naked body. "I want you." *Good.* "No…" *No?* "I need you." *Oh.*

He steps up into the van and shuts the doors behind him. I rise to my knees, unable to wait for him to come down. The intensity of our kisses escalates as we both kneel face to face. I pull his shirt from his body like it's on fire, then throw it against the wall. He gently nips my bottom lip. The second I feel his finger graze the inner lining of my thong, my legs nearly shutter. I bite his lip, pulling his chest into mine. His finger's graze becomes a sweep, then a stroke, which forces my jaw to drop. He slides my panties to the side. He's not even inside me yet, and I'm ready to—

"OH." My entire body trembles against his, my hands tightening around his arms. I tilt my head back, eyes closed as the sensation manifests in my chest, its ripple overwhelming my lower body.

Luca smiles against my neck. I feel his stubble against my skin as he whispers, "You finished, didn't you?"

I blink at him, not knowing what to say, do, or feel besides embarrassed. Can I really be so infatuated by Luca that I can't even keep myself composed enough to have sex with him?

I clear my throat. "I don't know how that even happened."

"Well, regardless, I'm glad you enjoyed it," Luca says, holding back a laugh.

His grip on me lessens until I grab his forearms. He looks at me, confused. Without saying a word, I kiss him with more passion, more aggression, more grit. I pull him into me, forcing him to match my energy, which he does without hesitation. Warmth flows between us as he grows hard between my legs, and that's when I pull him back on top of me.

"Fuck, Bella." He draws back a few inches, his eyes flicking between mine. "I need to feel you." He nips my bottom lip again while pulling my panties down my legs.

Luca straightens himself while still on his knees. He unbuttons his pants. Lanterns hanging along the inner walls of the van cast sharp shadows across the ripples and contours of his muscular frame. I open myself up to him as my eyes fall from his long, tousled hair to the striations on his pecs, his abs between the V-lines pointing to the length of him.

My breath catches. "Luca."

"Yeah."

"This is my first time."

Luca pauses, his fingers resting on his lowered pants. The air in the back of the van thickens with a mixture of anticipation and burning lantern oil. His expression is deep, reflective. "That's okay," he whispers smoothly. He slowly crawls over me, a twinkle in his eye as he whispers, "We'll start slow. Then, all at once."

And so we start slow, and I cling to the hope that Luca will fall even harder for me, the way I'm already falling for him. *All at once.*

He gently leans into me, and I wince at first. The first inch is already overwhelming. How am I supposed to take the rest? Our kisses deepen, the warmth and passion making it easier for me to receive all of him after a few light thrusts. He applies more pressure with the full weight of his body. His hips finally reach mine, and when we both realize we've become one, we exhale satisfaction against each other's lips.

"See?" Luca whispers. "We start slow." He thrusts into me, the pleasure whirling in my core before it moves through my body. "Now, all at once."

It may be my first time, and already his thrusts instantly become a drug. Intoxicating, euphoric, in some ways medicinal. He slides inside of me, then out, then in again with a mastered sense of rhythm. *It's the way he mastered his own guitar.* His tongue sweeps mine, exploring me by forming paths with a mastered sense of spontaneity. *It's the way he mastered the waves.* And as we climax together this time, our bodies tightening around one another, I smile at the thought of Luca mastering me.

"Too bad we weren't able to eat," I tease, watching Luca put his clothes back on.

"Have you seen my phone?" he asks in a panicked tone. He starts flipping pillows and blankets. "What time is it?"

I adjust myself so I'm sitting up. "Is everything alright?"

Luca's breath shallows. "I need to make sure—just… where's my phone?" His panic fills the van, infecting me like a virus. "I need to get the van back before he knows." He throws on his linen shirt, and I'm pretty sure his pants aren't even zipped up as he opens the back doors.

"Luca!" I whisper, shielding my naked body.

It's nighttime now and too dark for anyone to see me, but some consideration would have been nice before he almost made me flash the entire beach. His footsteps echo outside the van. I slip on my pants and tie my blouse as he opens the door on the driver's side. I step outside the van and shut the back doors. A blue hue illuminates his stressed facial expression as he reads his littered phone screen.

"You need to get the van back before *who* knows?" I ask, cautiously approaching him. He doesn't respond. "Luca."

"Huh?" Luca turns to face me. As he opens his stance, I catch sight of the half-empty liquor bottles that have been stuffed into the shelf lining the car door. He notices me staring, then steps in front of it. "I had an amazing time tonight," he blurts out, forcing a smile. "And I hate to do this, but we have to go right now."

I suppress my suspicion and get in the car. It's not the first time Luca cut our night short, but I'm left wondering if his wanting to leave has anything to do with me. Did I do something wrong? Was I not enough? I know it was my first time, but was it that bad?

Luca is silent the entire way home, driving like a madman. No music, no conversation. No hand-holding or flirty comments like characters do in the novels. Nope, just screeching tires and speeding through yellow and some red lights.

"Bella, I'm so sorry," Luca says as he skids to a stop in front of the bookstore.

"It's fine!" I downplay my confusion, having no idea what the hell is happening. "I hope everything is alright."

"Me, too," he replies softly.

I open the car door, step out, and shut it.

He rolls down his window and forces another smile. "Come here and kiss me goodnight."

I catch a glimpse of light amid the looming darkness that set in not even 10 minutes ago. I step up to his door, and he runs a hand back through my hair, then pulls me in for a kiss. This one feels different from the others. It's rushed, quick, an obligation.

Luca's phone lights up on his lap. Someone is obviously trying to get a hold of him. A friend? A bandmate? Another girl?

"Next time, I'll let you eat before making love to you," he teases.

I laugh. "I think Romeo would have made love to Juliet before they finished their Chinese food, too."

He smirks. "Goodnight, Juliet."

We kiss again, this one a little better than the last. *Okay, we're back on track.*

Luca pulls out, and the van skids up the street and around the corner, leaving me wondering whether or not this is supposed to happen. We do things for the plot. And as I've opened myself up to

Luca and already feel myself falling for him, I'm forced to come to terms with the plot having thickened.

Someone has a hold on Luca.

And I'm not sure if I'm ready to find out who just yet.

6 DAYS STRANDED

The fish are learning to keep their distance from me. Either they're getting smarter, or I'm getting worse at this. I sway with the tiny waves that lap around my shins, but it's just not doing it for me. I feel more sluggish, even weaker than before. I grow more tired by the day, regardless of how much I sleep and eat. My arms and legs are beginning to lose their definition. I'm starting to think that pretty soon the people back at home won't be able to recognize me. That is, if they ever see me again.

I itch my beard, observing the water for any flashes of silver. The sense of peace I was beginning to find out here is threatened by returning fears of starvation. I squint against the sun as it continues its ascent among dense clouds above the horizon. A silver flicker catches my eye, and I spot a school of fish a few feet away. I sway with the waves, mimicking their movement as I inch closer. Upon leaning forward, I swiftly stab at the fish. They scatter, leaving me alone with my thoughts.

I look up, and a defeated sigh leaves my chest. It's been months since I last prayed. Given my current situation, you would think I'd be a full-blown Christian again just to get on God's good side. "Hey," I say, eyes locked on the sky above me. *No response.* I clear my throat, twiddling the dog tag hanging around my neck. "It's, uh… been a while, so forgive me for being a little rusty. I know I haven't prayed much since Clem and I split up." I cringe, shaking my head. "No. Nope. Too soon."

I give up and look to the beach for Bella's support, but she's nowhere in sight. About an hour ago, she insisted I leave her alone this morning, so I'm pretty sure she's on the other side of the island doing God-knows-what in a place where there's already nothing to do. Despite my growling stomach, I decide to take a break and lie in the shade under the palms.

I stab my spear into the soft sand and sprawl myself so I'm lying face up. The palms sway gently in the breeze, rustling whispers I'm yet to cipher. I narrow my eyes at the leaves, trying to see what Bella sees in Luca. Based on her writing, he seems like a handsome guy, sure. I get that. But, for her to fall as quickly as she has for a guy she knows so little about? I just don't get it. Or, maybe I'm just jealous she doesn't feel that way toward me.

I wonder if Clem fell for me as quickly as Bella fell for Luca, or if she would fake-drown for me. Judging from Bella's journal, the love Bella feels for Luca makes me question how much Clem loved me. It kills me to think that I may never be loved the way Bella loves Luca. And considering the way Luca just up and left Bella after they made love for the first time, I'm starting to think I'll soon understand why Bella is so reluctant to marry this guy. How do you go from giving somebody your everything to wanting nothing to do with them? The way Clem and I ended left my heart in shambles, and I think Bella might be right when she argued that I may still love Clem; it's just a different kind of love.

I don't know Luca well enough yet. Hell, I may never know Luca at all. But I know something is seriously wrong with him for cutting a moment short with a girl like Bella. If I find out he hurt her, that may be the final source of motivation I need to get me off this island, just so I can kick his ass for it.

I pull the hourglass from my pocket, resting it on my stomach. I brace myself for another day of submitting to this routine I'm not even sure is really keeping me sane. With every day stranded comes a new memory to relive, painful or not.

I take a deep breath, flip the hourglass, and as sand begins to slip through the center tube, I dive back into my past…

"You ready, Rome?" Mac asks, tossing his bag into the truck bed. "Let's go, man. I'm hungry as hell!"

"That's the third time you ask!" I shout back. "Just wait one goddamn minute!"

I drag my eyes over the flower display lining the wall of the small store. Set against the backdrop of the brick storefront, the colorful display is a testament to the charm of a small Southern town like Blue Ridge. It's been six months since we left for deployment overseas. After nearly dying out there amid the chaos, being back home just doesn't feel real.

"Lookin' for somethin' in specific?" a voice squeaks from behind. I turn to see a girl looking up at me with eager eyes. She twirls her golden blonde locks with one finger and points at my uniform with the other. "Thanks for your service," she adds kindly.

"This country's been good to me, so I thought I'd return the favor," I reply with a nod. "Do you have any sunflowers?"

"We do, but only if they're for your mama." She raises a brow before turning to another shelf. "Because I'll be giving them to you with my phone number."

I lower my head to keep from blushing. "I'm honored, ma'am. But I have a girl back at home."

"Well, that's a shame for me." The girl hands me a lush bouquet of sunflowers. "I won't give you my number then. As much as I hope things go your way, you'll know where to find me if they don't."

I nod, then feel my pockets for my wallet.

"Don't," she says. "The bouquet is on us, soldier. I hope she loves 'em."

"Me, too." With a hand over my heart, I thank her and run back to Mac's truck. He honks again before noticing me. "Dammit, Mac!" I yell, opening the door and climbing in. I slam it shut, then face him. "We spent six months dodging war, but if you rush me one more time, you're gonna find it!"

Mac busts up laughing as he turns the truck onto the highway. "Couldn't resist."

The sun hangs low, flooding the countryside separating us from our neighborhood in the distance. Mac's old, beat-up truck rattles over the worn asphalt, the low hum competing with the Country music blasting on the radio. His hand drapes casually over the steering wheel, the other resting on the open window frame. I lean back in the passenger seat, twiddling the wooden cross hanging from my neck.

Nostalgia and excitement wash over me as our neighborhood nears. It's been months since I've seen these roads, fields, the small shops and bars that make up Main Street. We're both overwhelmed by the familiar charm that comes with friendly faces, white picket fences, and everything else that makes up the simple life. We pass the old diner and our old high school, but I know that nothing will compete with seeing Clem again.

Clementine. Just thinking her name could give me the energy I need to conquer the world, dissolve any fear, and see again after having gone blind. My grip tightens around the bouquet as I close my eyes and picture her feathered hair cascading in small waves, framing her face in ways that make her look ethereal. Her eyes, always expressive. I picture the floral dresses she always wears, her hand resting on the curve of her belly. The day I was deployed, she was nearly two months pregnant and already showing. She held the promise of our future together, a future for a baby of our very own who would embody the same love and beauty she holds.

"Almost there," Mac says, picking up on my impatience.

I rest my head against my seat, forcing back a smile. "You think she's really showing now?"

"Has to be," Mac snaps with his eyes on the road. "You're a big boy, which means Clem's got a big baby in her. At this point, what's it been? Seven months?"

I exhale as we turn onto our street. "She'll be going on eight."

"She's gonna look like she's ready to pop," Mac chuckles.

Things got a little rocky after my injury, but it wasn't anything we can't overcome. It hurt Clem when I chose to finish my deployment instead of coming home early, but it had to be done. She knew I promised myself that I would serve for the time I set out to serve. Nothing more, nothing less. Plus, I couldn't leave Mac behind. Our calls were less frequent during my three-month recovery, but now I'm back home and ready to pick up where we left off while embracing a new beginning at the same time.

My parents' place comes into view, just as old as it is cute. The slightly weathered, white paint speaks years of love and care, the porch decorated with hints of red, white, and blue. The truck's rattle comes to a stop, and we grab our bags from the truck bed.

"Your parents know we're back today, right?" Mac asks from over my shoulder.

I walk cautiously up the steps onto the porch, then tease, "They wouldn't be my parents if they didn't know."

The front door is hanging slightly open. I quietly pull the screen back and push the door.

"SURPRRIISSEE!!"

The cramped house shakes as people cheer at the top of their lungs. My eyes widen at the sight of family and friends throwing up their hands to greet Mac and me. Within seconds, Ma throws her arms around my waist while Pa stands right behind her, his chin held high. His smirk translates to the utmost respect and pride for filling some pretty big shoes.

When Ma finally finishes showering me with kisses and reminding me that this better be the last time I leave, she leaps over and does the same to Mac. Pa fills the gap Ma creates, holding out a firm hand for me to shake. I nod, and when my hand meets his, he pulls me in for an unexpected hug. *Well, that's a first.*

He gently caresses my cheeks and whispers, "How's the head?"

I flatten my lips, looking down at my duffle bag. "I'll be poppin' pills till further notice," I explain. "Doctor prescribed a pill a day to keep me sane."

Pa nods slowly, almost apologetically. "You're alive. That's all that matters," he assures me. "I couldn't be more proud of you, Rome."

It was a scary time after getting hit by that truck. The doctors monitored me closely, checking for any more swelling or complications. By the grace of God, they didn't find anything out of the ordinary and neither did I. No swelling, no hallucinations. Only an answer to my prayer. *Lord kept His hand on me, my girl, and my baby back at home.*

Every doctor made it known that if Mac didn't do what he did to protect me that night, he would be the only one returning home to Blue Ridge and it'd be to break the news to my parents–news that they would no longer be parents. Instead, God had other plans. I know deep down that I was kept alive to be the best father I can be.

My eyes flick between Pa's. "Where is she?"

"Out back," he states, taking my bag off my shoulder. When I try to step around him, he grabs my arm. "Rome." His eyes drop to the flowers in my hand.

Ma steps beside him, sympathy pouring through her gaze. "Maybe make your rounds before talking to Clem," she urges. "Settle in a bit."

"Make my rounds?" I pinch my brows together, exhaling a nervous laugh. "I'm gonna see my girl and our baby. That's what I'm gonna do."

Pa lets go of my arm. I walk between them, and after a few quick "hello's" and "good to see you's," I'm heading for the backyard. As I pass through the kitchen, I catch a glimpse of strawberry blonde out the window.

I approach the sliding door with a smile on my face. She's even more stunning than I remember, sitting in the corner of the yard on the swinging bench, watching the kids play. As I slide the door open and step outside, the sound of music is replaced by the kids running around the backyard. Clem's light sundress sways gently in the afternoon breeze.

I can't help but notice her posture is relaxed yet distant. I step closer. Her focus is still on the kids, her eyes following them but with an air of distraction. I step closer. Her reserved demeanor sends a cautionary ache through my heart. I stop, now standing over her.

"Clem," I say softly.

Clem's eyes flick to mine, then down to the flowers. Her lips part for her to speak, but nothing comes out. The world around us fades to the background. The laughter, the rustling leaves, the nostalgia. Everything is put on pause.

"I'm back," I add as if she can't see it for herself.

Since the day I left, I've imagined this moment. One time after another, and every single time, she meets me halfway with her hand resting on the curve of her belly, tears of relief trickling down her rosy cheeks as we celebrate my homecoming. It was the thought that kept me alive out there, even when the odds weren't in my favor.

Instead, I've walked all the way across the backyard and she can hardly speak to me. But, when she stands, she doesn't have to speak at all. My eyes fall to her stomach, the absence of the curve forcing me to come to terms with my new reality. She shakes her head, tears rolling down her cheeks. I look around her for any sign of our newborn baby.

Clem keeps shaking her head, and as if in slow motion, the flowers I once held meet the floor. This isn't how I imagined coming home. There's no love in her eyes. There's no pride, gratitude, or promise of a new chapter I could look forward to. None. Just sorrow, pain, and blame.

I see Clem standing before me while the vision of our future vanishes into thin air.

I'm not going to be a father.

I look up to see three palm trees reaching for the sky, and they whisper my name, their voice blending with the breeze until...

I open my eyes, the sun shining through the palms overhead. I look down at the hourglass, each and every grain having made its way through the center tube, now resting in the bottom bulb. I don't know how long it's been, but I don't care. I decide to check on Bella to help get my mind off Clem.

"Bella?" I call out to the other side of the island. I step through the bushes, seeing her sitting peacefully near the water. She's looking down, focusing on something in her lap. I cautiously approach her from behind.

Bella flashes me a quick glance, then covers her lap. "Don't look!"

Her urgency forces me to keep my distance. "What're you doing?" I ask.

"Nothing," she says, shielding my view. She stands to her feet, keeping her hands behind her back. "It's a surprise."

"Just wanted to check in." I raise my palms, looking around the empty beach. "Pretty boring place, so I figured you could use some company."

"Company would be nice," she says softly. "But, first you need to close your eyes so I can hide your surprise."

I close my eyes.

"No, no," she says. She gently holds my hand, and presses it over my eyes. "Use your hands so I know you're not peeking."

I hold back a laugh, obeying her command. "Roger that."

"Good, soldier," she teases.

A few silent beats pass. I get lost in the soothing sound of waves lapping against the shore, echoing the island's solitude. The thought of Bella taking time out of our day to make me a gift makes me cherish her all the more. I haven't done anything to deserve being treated so kindly by a girl I didn't know existed just over a week ago. And here she is, putting others before herself in circumstances that would bring out the selfish in even the most selfless individual.

"You can open them now." Bella's voice is closer and more soothing than ever.

"Hi," I greet while blinking the sunlight from my vision.

"Hi." She beams up at me, her eyes filled with excitement. "So, I was thinking." Her hand envelops mine, tugging me toward the water. "Do you remember yesterday when we were playing Someday Soon, and I said I would teach you how to swim?"

My stomach turns. "Y-yeah."

"Well…" She leads us to the edge of the shore. "Someday is today."

Someday is today?

I release an anxious breath. "I don't know."

My jaw nearly drops to the floor as Bella strips down to her bra and underwear. She flashes me an innocent grin, and I habitually avert my eyes, fighting the urge to admire her natural beauty. Even as I avert my gaze, I steal glimpses as she steps out before me. The shimmering water reflects a golden hue over her smooth skin, her presence divine, as if her being is supernatural, not of this world. Her laughter is a melody, a chime carried by the afternoon breeze. She's so light on her feet that she doesn't even leave footprints in the sand as she runs down to the ocean.

Bella's laughter echoes, sending a nervous energy coursing through my veins. *Get out there, you son of a bitch.* I can no longer resist. I run after her, giving in to the magnetic force pulling me in her direction. I pull down my shorts, hopping on one foot as I kick them across the sand. My heart beats excitement and fear through my body. My shins are consumed by the chilling water, then my hips, and eventually my chest.

Bella dips her head under the water, and emerges facing me. Her hair becomes its darkest shade of brown as she slicks it back, complementing the brown, green, and hints of blue in her eyes. She looks at me with that infectious smile of hers, offering me her hand. I hold it, and we take a few steps deeper into the ocean until we're just about neck-deep.

"First thing's first," Bella says as she gracefully floats inches away. "You'll need to relax. Or you're going to sink like a rock."

I exhale a nervous laugh. "You make it look so easy."

"I'm just floating." She effortlessly swims around me, now separating me from the shore. When she finds her footing, she says, "Floating is easy. Here, lean back. I'll show you."

While Bella's movements come naturally, I couldn't be more robotic. I've lost all remnants of coordination, surrendering myself to the same body of water that nearly took my life before leaving me stranded on this island. I suck in a heap of air and lean back, fluttering my arms at my sides. Warmth flows beneath my skin when her hands press firmly against my back. Floating becomes even easier.

"Trust the water," Bella whispers, holding me up.

I fight off the thought of the mountainous waves that destroyed Azrael's boat, the merciless force that tore it apart, leaving shattered wood washed up on the shore, the abyss that's home to creatures unknown and undefined. Water might be the greatest mystery to me. Without it, we die, and at the same time, it claims the lives of whoever underestimates its authority over our planet.

"*Trust the water*," I repeat Bella in a whisper. My fluttering hands maintain a slower rhythm, my body finally letting loose.

"I've got you," Bella assures me. "I won't let anything happen to my favorite student."

"I'm your only student," I tease, my eyes flicking from the sky to her.

"Only and favorite." She nods, studying my body as it hovers over the surface. "You can do this."

"*We* can do this," I correct her.

She smiles. "We can do this."

We continue like this for a few moments. The sound of the waves rolling over the distant shore becomes so soothing, my mind begins to wander. I imagine how Bella learned to swim back in Laguna Beach. I picture her parents, her mom alive and well, admiring her angelic nature as she becomes one with the water as a kid.

It dawns on me that I've done myself a disservice by going through life without being able to swim. With the ocean being as vast as it is, I'm robbing myself of an abundance of adventure. It's no wonder Bella carries such light and grace at all times. She's one with water, one with nature. I spent years a part of a system, serving to maintain order in the military. I've been a number, collateral damage in a grand scheme. All while Bella lived a care-free life becoming one with Earth and Heaven right above it.

"How're you doing over there?" Bella asks.

"Pretty good, I guess." My eyes widen when I realize Bella's voice came from a distance. I look around but can't find her anywhere. "Bella?!" I catch sight of her standing in the shallows. "Bella!"

She cups her hands beside her mouth and shouts, "You're doing it! You're swimming!"

I'm swimming.

I'M FUCKING SWIMMING!

My arms maintain a newfound rhythm, my hands cupped as they push water under me. My strokes become more natural as I steady my motion. *Keep goin', Rome. Keep goin'.* I keep my knees bent while kicking out from under me. I could touch the bottom if I needed to, but I do the best I can to stay afloat for as long as I'm able to.

"I'm swimming!" My voice cracks between laughs. "Are you seeing this?!" I can't stop smiling. I can't stop laughing. This may be the best I've felt in a long time, and I have Bella to thank for it. "Get back in here!"

Bella giggles. "How about you meet me halfway?! And no touching the ground! You have to swim."

I lean forward, doggy-paddling my way to Bella. Like the natural she is, I watch her leap into the water and swim effortlessly toward me with a commanding grace. When we reach the halfway point, I stand to catch my breath. The ocean stretches endlessly behind us, the horizon a blend of billowing cushions of clouds. Bella and I face each other, taking each other in with our eyes.

"Thank you," I say softly.

Bella tilts her head, lowering herself so her chin rests on the ocean surface. "What are you thanking me for?"

I lower myself to her level. The sunlight reflects off the water, illuminating the side of her face. "I'm just thankful for you."

Bella blushes, and my gaze drifts to her lips. I can't wait any longer to feel them on mine. My heart pounds as I decide to risk it all. I part my lips, leaning in ever so slightly. I wouldn't have lasted on this island without her. I wouldn't have an ounce of hope, and here she is, a living, breathing reason for me to make it out of here alive. I have to convey my feelings in a way words just can't express. My subtle lean becomes known, and I notice her lips part, too.

A sudden, thunderous rumble forces our heads to turn. In the distance, a gathering of storm clouds makes their way in our direction. *Did nature really just kill the mood?*

"More rain," Bella whispers excitedly.

I sigh. "If we're lucky."

The two of us face each other once more. A playful grin slowly spreads across her face and before I try to kiss her again, she playfully splashes me. "I'll race you back!"

Bella turns and begins swimming back to shore.

I bite my lip, then swim after her.

🌴🌴🌴

I've heard people describe the ocean in positive ways: Calm, beautiful, serene, breathtaking, refreshing, crystal-clear. I've also heard people describe the ocean in negative ways: Choppy, restless, intimidating, dark, dangerous, murky. What's interesting is that each and every one of these descriptions is true.

I tighten the rope around our shelter's roof, fastening the wood planks and branches together. Since we returned from our swim, the sun has retreated behind the dense, black clouds hovering toward the island. The horizon–once serene–has become a violent scene of thrashing water, causing choppy waves to crash against the shore. I grow more anxious with each crashing wave. Our hands move with urgency, racing against time with the hope that we prepare for nature's wrath. Bella twists the wooden bucket into the sand just in front of our shelter. We lay our clothes over the roof, except for my shirt, which I hang across the opening.

"If we can't both fit, I'll sit through the storm under the palms," I say.

"We'll fit," Bella assures me.

I look at the sky when she bends over to crawl inside. The thought of weathering a storm with Bella in a shelter hardly big enough for us both sounds more dangerous than the storm itself. I've been attracted to Bella since the moment I laid eyes on her in that elevator. And while my survival mode takes over from time to time, that attraction has nonetheless grown over the waking moments I spend with her.

I can hear Bella moving things behind my hanging shirt. "We have a few coconuts and a few bites of fish left," she says.

"What about your journal?" I ask, refraining from fixating on Bella's white thong as her back arches in front of me.

"Journal, too!"

The palm trees begin to bend and sway in the chilling wind. Their creaks hint at the power behind the gusts, each slightly more violent than the last. I tighten one last knot as the rain starts pattering over the leaves and our shelter. Lightning tears through the darkened sky, which I use as a cue to join Bella inside. I gently push my shirt to the side and crawl in, embracing the thickened scent of damp wood and sea salt. Thin beams of white light are filtered through the gaps in the wood branches and planks I used to build the walls.

Bella is lying on her side, her back to the wall. She pats on the sand making up the thin strip of open space beside her. I release a nervous exhale, knowing how difficult it's about to be, being this close without me acting on my attraction toward her. We huddle together, the warmth from our bodies contrasting the cool breeze that seeps through the cracks and crevices.

"Are you comfortable?" I ask.

"Hmm." She sits up, pondering through different positions. Her hand is cold against my forearm as she pulls it under her. "Lie down."

Bella lifts her hair over my arm and rests the back of her head on it. Now lying side by side, I wrap my arm around her naked shoulder. It's been months since I last lay next to a girl. Then again, Bella has made me realize that it's been months since I've done a lot of things with a girl. We stare at the ceiling, and I can only hope for the sound of the falling rain to distract us from my rapidly beating heart.

"Better?" she asks.

"You have no idea," I say softly.

I become hyper-aware of my feelings, lying this close to Bella. Her breath grazes my neck, the rhythmic thrum of her heartbeat against my side. I've never been this close to her, never been this present. Her damp hair brushes against my cheek, and I want to cement every subtle movement and flinch she makes into my mind for the rest of my life. Being this close to her makes me realize I never want to be far again. Her presence roots itself to me, wrapping and intertwining with my being.

I'm so fixated on the euphoria that comes from feeling her, I don't know how much time passed between the moment we laid down and the moment she asks, "Did she break your heart?"

I squint my eyes at the ceiling. "That was random."

"I think it's fair to ask random questions after a week of being randomly stranded on an island together."

I let out a soft chuckle. "That's fair." I think through the best way to package the trauma that consumed my life just months ago. I fail to come up with any response other than a direct one. "Yeah. I guess Clem did break my heart."

Bella grazes my chest hair with her thumb. "How did she hurt you?"

My breath catches. "Do we have to do this right now?"

Thunder growls from above, the low-pitched roar shaking our bones.

"We don't have to right now," she says. "But I don't see us finding a better time soon." Bella is right. And as much as I've grown to like her, I don't like that she's right. She turns and rests her chin on my chest, her curious eyes studying me. "Maybe there's a reason we were put on this island, and it's not just to survive. Maybe we're supposed to do more than survive."

"What's there for us to do other than survive?" I ask.

"Heal."

Bella's response strikes true the second it leaves her lips. The thought of healing embraces my soul like the final piece of a puzzle, a piece once lost. But this isn't just any ordinary piece. It's heavy, riddled with pain and unspoken truths. My natural instinct is to leave out the piece, to keep telling myself that I'll eventually put it in its rightful place. Eventually, not now. I find that putting this piece in its rightful place is more difficult than any of the struggles we've faced on this island so far. More difficult than catching my first fish, building fires, assembling our shelter, and learning to swim. Healing is different.

"I was going to spend the rest of my life with her." I lace my fingers behind my head, eyes locked on the ceiling. Reliving my memories in silence is one thing, but voicing them here and now is entirely different. Regardless of how tough it is, I continue with the same blind faith that got us here. "Clem and I met when she first transferred to my high school. She was the sweetest, kindest girl I ever met, nothing like the girls I grew up with in Blue Ridge. There was something about her that was so gentle, so precious. Before she came around, I kept my head down. Wasn't smart, so I got by the best I could in class and played football till I was old enough to enlist in the army.

"First day of senior year, I see Clem for the first time. She walked right into my Biology class wearing this yellow sundress, yellow like a sunflower, with this strawberry blonde hair like those Southern Belles you see in the movies or read about in books. It was her first day at our school and the only open seat was to my right, so that's where she sat. Right next to me." I blink in and out of the memory, and it's as if I'm seeing Clem for the first time again. I clear my throat. "Wasn't long after she sat that she asked me about the dog tag I was wearing at the time. I told her it's my pa's and she did the sweetest thing. She told me to thank him for his service. We got to talkin', little whispers during the lesson where she told me her pa was still in the military, deployed overseas. She liked that I wanted to be a soldier like her pa and mine. And I liked that she liked that.

"We got along real good after that, and I found myself not eating lunch alone with Mac anymore because Clem would join us. All the other guys would look her way, but she always had her eyes set on me and I had mine on her. Mac and my parents took a liking to her, and before I knew it, she was spending more time at my house than she was at her own. Before graduation, I made her my girlfriend, and boy, did I fall quick."

I hold my breath a moment, rubbing my dog tag between my fingertips as the thunder roars just outside. "After graduation, Clem went to a local college while I enlisted. We did long distance for a bit, making the most of the time we spent together when I would come back into town. Things were getting more serious between us, and I found myself preparing for a six-month deployment overseas when she called me, devastated. Her pa had passed away, one of three lives lost in a helicopter crash while he was on a mission. She begged me to stay home right then and there, but I couldn't. Everything I worked for up until that point was leading to my deployment. Being a military hero like my pa was all I had wished for, being the small-town kid I was.

"That next trip I made home, we had our first argument ever. We were in my truck in the parking lot of our old high school, just screamin' at each other. I told her I would never forgive myself if I stayed and she said she would never forgive me if I left. That night, I learned to compromise. I told her that one deployment was all I would do. The deal was for me to go overseas for six months, serve the best I could then come home to be with her. Like night and day, she went from cryin' to smilin'. We never made love the way we did that night. Not even the times after could compare to that one time. A month later, I found out why that time was different."

"That's the night you got her pregnant," Bella chimes in, her chin warm against my bare chest. I can feel her attentive eyes still studying me, but all I see is Clem as I remain fixated on the ceiling.

I inhale a deep breath, then exhale. "I came home a month after. It was my last visit before I was set to deploy. She picked out the most beautiful sundress. It was my favorite out of all the others she wore. She asked me to drive her to the high school parking lot, and that's when she broke the news to me."

"Were you excited?" Bella asks.

"Shocked, then ecstatic," I reply. "I let her know that I loved her, over and over again. And I'll never forget the smile on her face fading before my very own eyes when she asked if I was still going on deployment... and I said *yes*."

Tears well in my eyes, blurring my vision. I close them, feeling the tears form streams down the sides of my face. Bella's thumb sweeps my cheeks, catching the tears before they reach the sand.

"I couldn't stay," I confess. "This was a promise I made to myself, and I keep my promises. She didn't fight me on it, though. Instead, she cried in my arms all night. The last damn night I had with her before leaving for six months was spent making her cry." I exhale a shaky laugh. "I was making myself out to be a villain and I didn't even realize it yet. Not a day went by out there when I didn't think of Clem and the baby. Not a day went by when I didn't pray for them both. Even when the calls became less frequent toward the end. The thought of her and the baby got me through. Even after I almost died on a mission myself, I saw her and the baby. We both knew that after the collision I was in, I could've come home early, but I chose to finish the deployment. It was the third time I chose the military over her. The first was when her pa passed, the second was when she told me she was pregnant, and the third was after my injury. It shattered her, and we weren't the same after. Then, I came home."

Bella props herself up, tears now welling in her eyes, too. "Was she there?"

"She was there," I reply, my voice cracking. "But, the baby wasn't. She had a miscarriage, lost the baby within days of my injury. And she kept it from me because she was so devastated, she didn't know how to cope."

"Did you break up because she kept it from you?" Bella asks.

I shake my head. "She didn't know how to cope at first, but she eventually found a way while I was recovering."

"How?"

"By falling in love with someone else." My words are venomous, poisoning the air between us. "The guy was in her class back at her college. When she lost the baby, I wasn't there to save her from the pain. So, she turned to another man who could."

I wait for a response from Bella. Anything. To my knowledge, there's no combination of words in the English language she could string together to make me feel better. Instead of using her words, she does something far more powerful.

She lifts her head, and with apologetic eyes, she runs a hand back through my hair. Then, she leans over me and pulls me into a warm embrace. Her actions speak more than anything she could say, and I give in to my urge to cry. Bella's embrace is a lifeline, as if God's forgiveness manifests itself in her touch. What I did to deserve sharing this moment with Bella, I may never know. But I know that it's all I'll ever need, and I'll never ask for more. She's already a blessing, a gift I could never deserve by my actions alone. When no tears are left for me to cry, nothing is heard but the rain.

My thumb grazes Bella's hip. "Bella?"

"Yes?"

"I think I've shared enough for the day. Will you read to me?"

Bella sits up and tilts her chin, a gentle smile playing on her lips. She reaches over me, grabs her journal, then lies face up by my side. Thin strips of light cast through the cracks, illuminating the words on the page she opens to, and she reads…

Laguna Beach, California
Saturday - May 25th, 2019

It's one thing to read about characters falling in love.

It's another to fall in love yourself.

Falling in love is a lot easier than I thought it would be, and I'm starting to understand why people use the term "falling." It's because falling doesn't require effort. It doesn't require energy. To fall, all one has to do is surrender. Then it's up to whoever you're falling for to catch you or let you hit the ground.

In the past week it's been since Luca and I made love for the first time, I've surrendered myself to him, fallen for him. I've been so invested in him that I haven't even made time to write. Instead, I read romance books and imagine Luca and myself as the main characters. I listen to his band's music. I scroll through pictures of him on social media.

We've spent most of each day together, and I make the most of every second because he has to spend the nights rehearsing with Abel and Dane. I've watched them perform at a few local dive bars, and every time, I admire Luca's love for music the way I did the first night I watched him play. Even while sandwiched between the sweaty bodies making up the crowd, I get chills when I notice that the way he obsesses over his guitar on stage is the same way he obsesses over me when we make love in his van.

Luca insists that I only hang around Abel and Dane at the shows, never outside of them. At first, I thought it was weird, but I don't mind it because I only want to spend time with Luca anyway. So, I don't ask many questions.

Sometimes, Luca and Dane will come by the bookstore. Dane is a really nice guy, very sweet and soft-spoken which is funny because he bangs on the drums like a psychopath. Like Luca, Dane has never been a big reader but wants to be. So, when he stops by the store with Luca, I always make sure to give him a short book to read during their downtime.

I haven't spoken to Abel since the night we met. I've never told Luca this, but I don't care to speak to Abel. Ever since he told Luca that I "look like fun" right in front of me, I've had no desire to be near him. Luca couldn't be more different from Abel, and that's one of the nicest things I can say about Luca. I think Luca would agree, based on how he described them being raised as polar opposites.

On the other hand, Tish spends every waking moment with Abel. I don't know much about their relationship because since they met, I haven't seen Tish outside of their shows. Even at the shows, it's only for a brief moment. Luca says she's always around their apartment, but that's all he really says about her.

"*She just sits there and watches us play*," Luca told me one day at the bookstore. "*Sometimes, I forget she's even there.*" He said it so casually I didn't really think much of it. Tish tends to withdraw from the world when she falls in love. I'm not complaining, although it would be nice to get a text from her wishing me a happy birthday today. I understand, though. I've withdrawn a bit since meeting Luca, too. Now I don't go to the beach unless it's with Luca, and I don't spend nearly as much time with Dad, which is why I made Luca promise to come to Game Night tonight.

"All I want for my birthday is for you to get to know my dad," I told Luca.

"I'm there," he said, holding out his pinky. "I promise."

I laced my pinky around his, then we kissed the tops of our fists.

It's the first time I'd ever invited anyone over, so I spent the entire Saturday running up and down the stairs to clean the apartment while working my shift. Dad has been glued to his new book behind the counter, not expressing much interest in meeting Luca.

"When are you gonna get ready?" I ask, peeking out from behind a bookshelf. I force a smile to hide my nerves. It's not often the love of your life befriends your dad, and it's not often your dad befriends the love of your life. "You know how important this is to me."

"When we close, kiddo," Dad says without lifting his eyes from his book.

I sigh, then run upstairs to clean the living room for the third time in an hour. As I finish wiping down the round table in the corner of the apartment, I notice the one spot I missed. Dust lines the top of the chair that hasn't been used since Mom passed. A lump manifests in my throat before I get myself to wipe the dust. I swiftly run my cloth over the surface, treading an ocean of memories.

The chair by the window was her favorite spot. It's where she would sit to read and sip her tea. After my final sweep of the chair, I take a step back. I was much younger last I saw her, but I still see the morning light flooding through the window as she would peacefully read. I would run to her, still wearing my pajamas. I can still see her calming smile just before she'd lift me onto her lap. I can still hear her soothing voice as she read to me until it was time to get ready for school.

The floorboards creak under Dad's weight as he reaches the top of the stairs. His sweaty face softens when he sees me standing over Mom's chair, his rosy cheeks rising into a smile. "I'm sure she would have loved to meet him," he whispers.

Without saying a word, I turn and hug him.

"Dad, he's here!" I shout when I hear Luca's van pull up to the curb. I look in the mirror, gently lift my curls, and let them fall over my white top. "Please tell me you're ready!"

BZZZ! BZZZ!

I lift my phone to see Luca calling. I exhale a calming breath, suppressing my nerves. "Hello, Romeo."

"Happy Birthday, Juliet."

"Thank you." I notice myself blushing in my reflection. "Are you coming up? Every year, my dad bakes this marble cake for my birthday, and I already know you're going to love it!"

"Listen, Bella. There's sort of been an emergency."

"An emergency?" I look out the window and see Luca still inside his van. "Is everything okay?"

"Everything is fine," Luca says calmly. "A band backed out of performing at Marine Room tonight, so we got the call to fill in. They want us to go on in 30 minutes."

I release a heavy breath, relieved everything is okay, but I'm dreading the fact that this means I'll have to choose between spending my birthday with my dad and spending it with Luca. "That's amazing." I press my forehead to my bedroom window. "You guys are going to be great."

The line goes quiet. After a moment, Luca replies, "Bella, I need you there."

"Really?" A smile tugs at the corners of my lips.

"Of course," he states. "The only thing I look forward to at these shows is seeing you in the crowd."

I exhale a giggle. "I'll be down in a sec."

We hang up, and I check my reflection one more time. Upon opening the bedroom door, my heart plummets when I see my dad carefully placing the marble cake in the center of the living room table. He hums softly to himself, adjusting each candle. The excitement from seeing Luca wrestles with the guilt from what I'm about to do. Dad's eyes light up when he sees me standing at the doorway. As he stands straight, I notice his red bow tie perfectly tied just under the collar of his plaid shirt. The shirt hugs his round frame, tucked into a chunky pair of brown slacks. *He's ready to celebrate* me.

"Happy Birthday, kiddo," Dad says, gesturing toward the cake. "Just the way you like it."

I swallow hard, then force a smile. "It's perfect."

He takes a step forward, his gaze warm. "I already put the games out on the coffee table. We can start with a board game and then play cards. I hope Luca knows how to play poker!"

BZZZ! BZZZ!

I pull out my phone to see Luca calling again. My eyes flick up. "Dad, I need to tell you something."

His brows part. "What's wrong?"

"It's Luca's band." I brace myself. "They were asked to perform tonight. It's a big show and he wants me there to support."

Dad's rosy cheeks fall. "Well, that sounds like quite the opportunity." He looks down at the cake and board games.

"I know this is tradition." I take a step toward him, conflict tearing me to bits. "But I need to support him."

He slowly nods, pulling his pants up over his stomach. "You should go. We can always celebrate when you get back."

I run forward and throw my arms around him. "I love you. And thank you for the cake." I pull back and kiss his forehead. "Perfect, as always."

Dad blushes. "Be safe."

I make my way downstairs, lock the front door of the bookstore, and turn to see Luca standing outside the van with a single white rose. His black T-shirt is oversized, cropped just above his straight black slacks that drop to his glossy boots. I can't contain my butterflies as I skip over the curb and into his arms. He gives me three sweet, delicate kisses before lifting the rose between us.

"Happy Birthday," he says, handing me the rose. He opens my door for me. "I picked the white one because it's all you ever wear."

"Why, thank you," I giggle. "You know me so well."

As Luca makes his way around the front of the van, a taste lingers on my tongue. *Is that vodka?* The remnants of our kiss are tainted by the sharp flavor of booze again. Just before he gets in, I notice the liquor bottles lining the bottom shelf of the driver's side door again.

They were half-empty a week ago, and now all are empty but one.

"I know I promised I would get to know your dad," Luca says, a subtle slur in his tone. "Maybe after the show?"

I force a smile, still processing the empty liquor bottles and change of plans on a night that was supposed to be important for my dad, Luca, *and* me. "He might not be awake, but we'll see!"

Luca shifts the gear stick. We jerk forward as he sends the car in reverse a few feet. He stops, laughs, then shifts the gear stick again. "Sorry about that. Pre-show nerves."

Nerves? I didn't know Luca gets nervous.

The sun has just set as Luca swerves onto Pacific Coast Highway. Tall palm tree silhouettes contrast a sky adorned with clouds of fiery orange and pink. The rugged cliffs and slopes of Laguna Beach are scattered with the twinkling lights of homes and beachside cottages. The highway curves as we make our way downtown, and while the moment is surreal, I can't help but give in to my suspicions.

"Did you already start drinking?" I ask, trying not to come on too strong. "I noticed the taste when you kissed me."

Luca runs a hand back through his hair, keeping his cool. He remains fixated on the road as he replies, "I was pregaming with the band a bit. We were celebrating, because you know. Playing at a bar like Marine Room is a pretty big deal."

"Totally!" I place my hand on his. "And I'm not trying to be a nag. I just didn't want you to feel like you had to drive if you already had too much to drink."

Luca winces, flashing me a half-glance. "You think I'm too drunk to drive?" he snaps. "Do you not trust me?"

My hand loosens over his when I realize he won't touch me back. Something isn't right, the same way it wasn't right the last night we spent together at Brooks Street. I played dumb when Luca suddenly wanted to leave that night. I still don't know who was calling him or why he was in such a rush.

"Of course I trust you," I say, now watching the road ahead. "I just noticed the bottles on your side door and didn't know if this was an everyday habit or every once in a while."

Luca nods. "You want the truth?" he sighs. "This is Abel's van. The bottles are his, not mine." He envelops his hand over my thigh, and I'm reminded of how big his hands are. They nearly cover my entire thigh. I'm too busy drooling over the veins along the top to realize he might've just said something important after telling me the bottles belong to Abel.

I look up at him. "Did you say something?"

He laughs, having caught me fixated on his massive, smooth, somehow extremely attractive hand. *When did I get so into hands?*

"I said I'm nothing like Abel. You're safe with me, so don't worry." His words leave his lips with stern yet comforting conviction. "You like my hands?"

I literally feel my cheeks turn red. "Is it obvious?"

He runs his palm up my thigh, applying more pressure. Warmth manifests itself within, and I'm beginning to wish I wore a skirt instead of pants. With his eyes still on the road, he whispers, "It was pretty obvious." He presses over me, and it becomes just a bit harder to breathe. "The rose was just the first birthday gift. Are you ready for the second?"

I lift my chin, the back of my head molding against the headrest as he moves his middle finger in a circular motion between my legs. He moves it faster, pressing over my white pants and I can feel the seat between my legs already getting hot and I'm already arching my back so that he can press deeper and—*WHITE PANTS.*

My eyes widen, and I pull his hand away before I let him finish me. "My pants!" The two of us laugh. "They're white! It'll be too obvious!"

A devilish smirk plays on Luca's lips. "Then we'll save it for later."

Luca's band is a hit, per usual. The crowd makes that known as their shouts and cheers shake the walls between each song. Before I met Luca, I never came out to the bars. Laguna Beach isn't known for its bar scene, but that might change after this summer, thanks to their band. The first thing Luca told the owner when we entered was that it's my birthday, and since then, I haven't reached the bottom of a drink. Before I finish a glass, I'm handed a new one filled to the brim. With every sip, the music becomes more intoxicating, more alluring.

I had never been to Marine Room until tonight, and I'm starting to question why it's taken me so long to get myself to go out to places like this. Marine Room is an old-school beach bar with a charm that makes you feel at home. The dim lighting casts a warm glow over the glossed wood lining every wall except for the brick wall at the back of the bar. Across the bricks, massive illuminated letters spell out "MARINE ROOM," just above the stage the band has dominated over the past two hours.

I sway, holding up my drink as I sing the lyrics to songs I've played on repeat at the bookstore. After a song ends, the crowd erupts as Abel chugs what's left of his beer. The sweat glistens over his sharp cheekbones and sporadic face tattoos. His charisma radiates over the crowd, and though it appears as though he was born to be a star, I cling to the thought of his childhood trauma forcing him to use music to escape it. If Luca hadn't opened up to me, I doubt I would've picked up on Abel's instability all by myself.

With one hand gripping the microphone stand, Abel reaches the other into the crowd and pulls Tish onto the stage. The crowd cheers as they make out like they aren't being watched by a hundred people. Abel then grabs the mic and yells, "Make some noise for my girl! Isn't she hot as fuck?!"

The crowd cheers and whistles for Tish as she does a twirl. I can't help but notice the thick blonde streaks of hair she dyed since we saw each other last. It's one of the many things that have changed about her appearance, and even though we haven't talked, I can already tell by how she carries herself that she isn't in her right mind. My eyes wander to Luca taking another shot with a few fans to the right of the stage, and when I pan back to center-stage, I catch Abel staring right at me. I freeze. Tish is so drunk that her eyes are rolling back as she clings on to Abel, but Abel keeps his snake eyes on me. It's as if he knows I love Luca, and he can use his identical resemblance to Luca for his own sick and twisted favor. He delivers Tish back to the crowd, his wired gaze still fixated on mine.

"We're gonna play one more for you guys. This one's unreleased." The crowd roars until his low voice pours out from the surround-sound speakers. While staring into the depths of my soul, he says, "This song is called 'Angel.'"

The band starts to play, and a pit forms in my stomach when I remember what Abel said to me the last time I saw him: *"Well, aren't you a little angel?"*

I grow more uncomfortable as he begins singing. While the alcohol in me makes it harder to cipher the meaning behind his words, I can still make out the lyrics: *"I'm a demon in the dark, with a black and broken heart, I can't have you 'til you fall, 'cause Heaven isn't answering my call. I'll turn your wings to ash and flame, 'til you're cursed to bear my name, only then will we be true, an angel damned, fallen for you."*

The crowd becomes hollow bodies, swaying and bumping into me, invading my personal space. My breaths become unsteady, my head growing light. Abel keeps his eyes locked on me and I do my best to keep mine on Luca who doesn't seem to pick up on whatever is happening right now. He has no idea that his brother is trying to claim my heart or soul or both right here, right now. The walls of the bar are closing in, Abel's voice wrapping me like a vice. Each word feeds a dark connection forming between us, one I become determined to detach myself from.

I glance at Luca again, but he's lost in the music, now fixated on his guitar. I want to call out. I want to shout his name. Not by means of cheering but by means of begging for help. I close my eyes, but it just makes it worse. I'm handed another drink from a stranger, then another shot. I should leave. I NEED TO LEAVE. As I weave through the crowd, I still feel Abel's eyes on me.

The cool night air sweeps my sweaty face as I enter the alley. The music and cheers are muffled now and I give myself a couple seconds to steady my breath. I lean my back against the brick wall, then slide down it so that I'm sitting with my arms wrapping my legs.

What the hell was that?

I'm drunk, but being drunk can't be all that was in that moment. The thought of Abel's eyes haunts me every time I blink, the song still ringing in my mind, chilling my bones. Eventually, I hear a muffled applause from inside, and a few moments pass before the bar's side door opens.

"Bella?" The familiar voice calms me. I look up to see Luca kneeling beside me. "Are you okay? I saw you leave."

I embrace him, the feeling of his body bringing me stability and peace. "I think I had too much to drink."

Luca gently pulls back to get a better look at me, his palm resting on my cheek. "You'll be alright," he says with two smiles—I mean one smile. One? Actually, I don't—I see two smiles now.

"I think I need to go home."

"Bella, you're fine," Luca slurs, his breath reeking of bad decisions soon to be made. "We'll get you some water on the way to the after-party."

AFTER-PARTY? I won't even make it back to the van.

"You promised," I slur. "You pinky promised."

"Here, I'll help you up." Luca's hands tighten around me, and he pulls me to my feet. I find it hard to keep my eyes open, but I manage to see him look left, right, then down at me. After a few silent beats, his lips are suddenly on mine like before, but his kisses are more aggressive. There's no rhythm, there's no romance. There's not even a way for me to stop him. "Fuck, you look beautiful," he whispers against my ear.

"Luca, stop." My arms get weaker the more he leans into me. I'm pinned between him and the wall as he nibbles from my neck down to my shoulder. He tightens his grip on my forearms, the pain quickly setting in as tears roll down my cheeks. "Home." It's the only word I can form as I begin blacking out.

"Shh, I'm gonna give you your second birthday gift before the party," Luca whispers, his fingers tracing my panty line. He yanks at the buttons on my pants, one falling to the floor. "Will you just fucking relax?"

WAM!

The door swings open so fast that it hits the brick wall.

"There you guys are!" a new voice shouts. As sad as it sounds, I'm relieved to hear the voice, regardless of who it belongs to. Luca releases his hold on me, and I slouch forward, throwing my hands up to guard myself. I'm hardly able to hold myself up. "Luca, Abel is asking for you inside."

"Dammit," Luca mutters, stepping toward the door. I fall back against the wall, hearing him add, "Keep an eye on Bella until I come back out. Good shit tonight."

"You, too," the voice replies. "We crushed it."

The door closes. In the silence and stillness of the dark alley, I hear the sound of boots clicking over the cement. The sound gets louder until they stop nearly a foot away. I turn my back to whoever the boots belong to, a soft hand wrapping my bruised forearm.

"Please, no," I slur as he pulls my arm toward him.

"Shh," he whispers, his voice even closer now.

All I ever wanted was to live a life like the characters I read about. All I ever wanted was to find my adventure, to find love. What have I ever done to deserve this? What have I ever done to deserve being taken advantage of in this very moment by the man I've fallen for and this complete stranger?

"It's Dane," Dane whispers. He wraps his own shoulder with my arm, holding me up.

"Dane?" I ask without the strength to see him for myself.

He begins walking us down the alleyway. "I'm taking you home."

I can't walk.

I can't open my eyes.

But, I manage to smile.

I wake up as the van comes to a stop in front of the bookstore. I have no idea what time it is or what happened to Luca, Tish, and Abel. Regardless, I'm just happy to be home and slightly more sober than I was when we left the bar. I undo my seat belt as the passenger door slowly opens.

Now that I can see straight, I recognize Dane. His curly brown hair hangs over his forehead, his thick mustache giving him a retro look. The streetlight reflects off his silver nose ring below his sympathetic gaze.

"I hope you're alright," he says. "Luca doesn't always get like that."

I force a smile from inside the van. "What made him get like that?"

"It's Abel," Dane says carefully. "He's never been the best influence on Luca. And Luca... well... he gets a little out of control when he drinks too much."

"Is it often?" I ask, remembering the bottles and kisses tainted by the taste of alcohol.

Dane presses his lips together, his silence speaking volumes.

I lower my gaze, disheartened. My lip quivers as tears start to well.

"For what it's worth, he's in love with you," Dane adds. "He just gets a little carried away sometimes."

I look up at him, holding back the tears with everything in me. Since I laid eyes on Luca, I've known he's the only love interest in the story that makes up my life. The sad truth is that even the love interests in the novels come with conflict. They're made up of traits, both good and bad. They're put in situations they can't control, and it's up to them to grow or fall behind. Tonight, Luca fell just a little bit behind, but maybe there's still time for him to grow.

"Thank you, Dane."

"Anytime."

When he leaves, I let myself into the bookstore and mope up the stairs. The door leading up to the apartment is slightly open, the lamplight seeping through the crack. When I open the door, my heart aches at the sight of Dad lying peacefully asleep on the living room couch. The board games are still neatly spread across the coffee table in front of him, my birthday cake still untouched. His broad fingers are laced over his stomach as it rises and falls.

I drop my phone. I slip off my shoes, and without waking Dad, I lie on the couch and rest my head on his shoulder. All I wanted for my birthday was for Luca to get to know my dad, and here my dad was the entire time, ready to get to know Luca. I finally find peace in closing my eyes now that I'm with my father, where I should have been all along. And with my eyes now shut, I cry myself to sleep.

STILL
6 DAYS STRANDED

Bella winces as I sit up and tear my shirt from the shelter's opening. The wind and rain sting against my cheeks as I trudge angrily toward the water, but the sting holds no match to the burning pain in my chest. I'm fuming, my mind racing with thoughts of Luca forcing himself onto Bella. My heart contracts and expands with every beat of frustration that's sent pumping through my veins.

It all makes sense why–deep down–she doesn't want to marry this guy.

She can't.

I won't let her.

The missing pieces begin to come together, creating a picture in my mind I can't ignore. I remember Bella's trauma revealing itself the other day when I raised my voice at her, the way she folded, raising both of her arms to shield her face from me. *She's traumatized by Luca.* Even while I haven't heard the full story that's led Bella up to this point, I'm starting to understand why she's expressed reluctance.

I pace from one end of the empty beach to the other, clenching my fists so tight I might draw blood. Luca is not a real man. He's a coward hiding behind a facade. He's an abuser, a manipulator. The choppy waters swirl around my ankles as my footsteps become stomps. I can feel my blood boiling, my head tightening as I envision Luca forcing Bella against the wall of that alleyway. It kills me to think we're still nowhere near finished reading her journal. There's still more to their story and I already know it ends with her still engaged to him.

"Tell me the story doesn't continue this way!" I shout back to the shelter as Bella steps out. She lifts a hand to shield herself from the fierce rain now falling sideways. "Tell me you aren't actually marrying him!"

"Roman..." Bella is nowhere near me yet, but her voice seeps into my mind like a whisper I can feel. "You don't understand."

I trudge in her direction, eyes fixed on her as she slouches before me. "How could you not end it then and there?" I grab her hand and raise it between us, her engagement ring dull under the gloomy sky. "You can still leave him. Leave him."

She looks out over the ocean. Lightning strikes in the distance, followed by a thunderous boom that shakes the earth below. "It's too late."

"What the fuck do you mean, '*It's too late*?'" I snap. "He hurt you!"

Bella pulls her hand away, and it becomes a fist at her side. "He loves me."

"He loves you?! You can't be serious," I laugh, my hands now on my hips. "Don't be an idiot."

Her brows straighten, her once-soft demeanor now hardening. "I'm not an idiot."

I point at her ring. "You obviously stayed with him after he tried to take advantage of you," I explain, my tone competing with the looming storm.

She shakes her head, flashing a bitter smile. "It's not that simple, Roman!"

"Oh, bullshit."

"Excuse me?!"

"BULLSHIT!" I shout over her. "Just like all your little fairy tale book world nonsense you talk about. Wake up, Bella! The real world isn't like the fantasy you live in. There's no Romeo and Juliet. There are no cutesy little love stories with happily ever afters."

"Stop," Bella commands.

It only fuels me to keep going. I step toward her, pointing a finger right at her chest. "*You* stop. It's your fault we're stuck on this island, you know."

"Don't." Her tone softens, a plea for me to be quiet before I say something I'll regret.

But I can't be quiet. I can't shut up when all I see is Luca tainting her purity. "You're everything a man should want and more. I knew that before you even spoke your first words to me. I knew you were different. Everyone seems to know it but you. You're an angel walking among men, yet you bring yourself down to our level. You'll become consumed by it if you don't throw that ring into the ocean right now!"

Bella abruptly brings the ring to her chest, protecting it with her other hand. "I can't."

I shake my head at her, quoting her words. "*Do it for the plot.*" I step away and spread my arms. "Look where your plot has you now! You were so convinced you needed to go on an adventure. Is that what this is to you? Is this the adventure you were looking for?" I watch tears fall from her eyes, feeling an odd sense of satisfaction as they land on the soaked sand. "Be honest with yourself. You aren't looking for an adventure. You're looking for an escape from a loser who tricked you into loving him! You're running from reality because you can't handle it."

She sucks in a deep breath. "Oh, and you have it all figured out?!" Her voice cracks in anger as she closes the distance between us. Her nail digs deeper into my chest with every word that follows. "You're the real coward. You act so high and mighty, using your talk of serving in the military to hide the fact that you have nothing to live for after you abandoned a perfect relationship!"

I clench my jaw. My own tears beg to be set free, but I won't give Bella that satisfaction.

She lifts her chin. Her lips form a trembling smirk when she realizes she struck a nerve. "Second thought, your relationship wasn't perfect, and the only reason it wasn't perfect is because of you. You couldn't find conflict, so you created it yourself." Her smirk becomes a grin. "You say you wanted to be a hero. You're no hero—no—*you* are the *conflict*."

Bella's words are a bullet through the heart, the shell casing falling from her lips to the ground. The impact reverberates inside my chest. A heart once broken and poorly repaired, she lands a direct hit that leaves me dropping to my knees. I grab the sand below me, watching my tears become one with the pouring rain. As I lift the sand and open my palms, each grain becomes a memory I buried. Joining the military to make a name for myself, fueling the chaos that is war, leaving Clementine and not being there to help her heal after I broke her heart time and time again. I watch every traumatic memory play out in the palm of my hands before letting them slip through my fingers.

I was shipwrecked long before I stepped onto Azrael's boat.

I was deserted long before I washed up on this island.

And here I kneel, forced to come to terms with it all.

When I look up, Bella is crawling back into the shelter. She pulls the shirt to cover the opening. I sit back on the sand, overwhelmed by the severe ache in my mind, heart, and gut. The pain becomes nearly too much to bear, and I immediately want to take back every word I said to Bella. I'm nowhere near Luca, and he still managed to ruin any chance I have of a connection with her. Even after he shows blatant signs of abuse and disrespect toward her, his ring remains on her finger. I'm jealous and not afraid to admit it to myself. I know Bella deserves better, and after what I just said, there's no way in hell that I'm any better.

My legs tremble under me as I stand to my feet. With my head hanging low, I walk up the beach to the palm trees. When I reach the palms, I can hardly hold myself up anymore. I've been physically exhausted, and now that I'm emotionally exhausted, all I can do is collapse beneath the trees. The ground is hard and unforgiving, which is what I deserve after what I said to Bella. But now I'm just too tired to care. The storm continues raging around me, the palm leaves above shielding me from the pounding rain.

The restlessness within me stirs with the weight of my mistakes and troubled past. With Bella so upset with me, I have no one to turn to but the One I've neglected since I lost Clem. I slowly push myself off the ground, now kneeling under the tree, and for the first time in a long time, I pray because it's all I can do.

"God, I'm sorry. I'm so, so sorry," I exhale toward the sky. "I've acted like I'm the victim, but I realize now *I'm the problem*. But I don't want to be. Maybe I deserve to be on this island, after all. Every struggle, I deserve it all." I lower my head and close my eyes. "I'm the conflict. I've made so many mistakes with Clem, and now I'm doing the same with Bella. If what she said the other day is true… if You brought us here to heal, just please help us heal. We can't do this, just the two of us. And I promise You that if I ever get off this island, it will be thanks to You."

7 DAYS STRANDED

I wake up feeling the most rested I've felt in a long time. Gentle waves lap against the shore, forming a soothing rhythm after yesterday's storm. I sit up against the palm tree, blinking up at the beams of light that peek through the palms. The sky is a pale blue, dotted with fluffy, white clouds. I have no idea how much time has passed since Bella and I argued, but judging from the sun shining directly above, it's almost noon. I stretch out my arms, feeling the stiffness in my muscles ease a bit. Yesterday's storm battered the island, leaving debris from the bushes and palms littered across the shore. Luckily, the shelter is still standing.

I pull the hourglass from my pocket, swirling the grains of sand in the bottom bulb. After weathering yesterday's storm and reconnecting with a part of me once lost, I find the courage to face Clem head-on all over again. I take a deep breath, flip the hourglass, and as sand begins to slip through the center tube, I dive back into my past...

The sounds of the party are muffled as I follow Clem's hand falling to her stomach. I've been back in Blue Ridge for less than an hour, and I already want to run as far as I can.

I want to leave everything behind, make my way to the edge of the earth, and fall right into oblivion. My vision of the future and my past with Clem shatter into a million pieces as kids continue running around the backyard. The music continues to play, but I can still make out the whispers of family and friends who took the time to welcome Mac and myself home.

"When?" I ask, my eyes locked on Clem's stomach.

Clem's voice is one with the breeze. "A few days after you almost died."

"How?" My eyes meet hers. She tries to speak, but her words get stuck in her throat. Her heart doesn't want to let it out. I ask again anyway because I need to know. "How did you lose the baby?"

Clem keeps her palm firm against her stomach as if out of sheer habit. "They said it was a miscarriage."

Miscarriage. The grass I stand on begins to tilt. I can't stand straight. I'm hung up on a word I never thought I'd be forced to come to terms with myself. For months, I clung to visions of not the two of us but *three*–Clem, me, and our child. A vision is what it was, and in an instant, I realize that a vision is all it will ever be.

Kids funnel back into the house, and it takes me a moment to realize the music has been lowered. Out of all the different ways I pictured my homecoming, this wasn't one of them. Months ago, the thought of coming home to a family Clem and I were starting became my armor. It kept me alive, sped up my recovery, and brought me miracles. But now, the same thought is closing in on all sides. There's no retreat, no backup, no Mac to shoot down the threat while I stand hopeless.

I take Clem's hand from her stomach, now holding it in mine. "It's okay, we're okay! We can get over this. I can help you…"

"Rome," Clem whispers, but I keep going.

"… We'll get you all the treatments you need. We'll find out what went wrong, and we can try again when the time is right. We can–"

"ROMAN." I wince, her puffy eyes piercing through remnants of hope I desperately cling to. "I met somebody."

Clem's words hardly register because I'm numb. Numb,

lost all feeling in my mind, heart, and gut. I can no longer think, no longer feel, no longer trust. Her hand suddenly feels foreign, like that of a stranger. I do us both a favor and let it go.

"You were gone," she blames, rivers of tears gliding down her cheeks. "You could have come home and you decided not to. It hurt so much that I… that I couldn't go on. You know how I felt about you going, and you still went and then stayed, and then when I lost the baby, I needed somebody to be there for me!"

I sit on the swinging bench, the chain creaking with a small sway. I don't know what or how to feel. "You're blaming me for the miscarriage?"

Clem crosses her arms and looks up at the sky. "I wanted to at least have the decency to tell you in person."

"That you fell in love with SOME OTHER GUY AFTER I GOT HIT BY A FUCKING TRUCK?!" My words explode from me in a violent, rageful tone. I didn't see it coming, none of it. The truck, the miscarriage, the infidelity, the blame. "I could have DIED, Clem! And what? You just move on?! Just like that?!"

I stand up, pacing side to side. Betrayal struck me harder than the truck. In fact, it makes me want to get hit by the truck again.

It makes me
want
to
fucking
die.

"Clementine." Mac's voice is thunderous, looming over the yard as he stands just outside the back door. "It's time for you to go."

I turn back to Clem, who drops her head. At some point, I dropped the sunflowers I got her, and I only notice because she steps on them while on her way back into the house. When she leaves, I plop myself back on the bench, placing my elbows on my knees. My cross necklace dangles below my chin, catching a few of my tears.

I trusted You. The necklace snaps as I yank it from my neck. *You were supposed to keep Your hand on us.* I throw the necklace across the yard, then cry into my palms. What good is faith if what you have faith in takes everything from you? What good is belief if all you receive from believing is pain? What kind of God hurts his believers? What kind of God takes a man's family away from him?

I feel Mac's arm wrap me as he sits beside me on the bench. He pulls me into his chest, patting my shoulder. "It's gonna be alright, brother," he whispers, saving my life a second time. "It's gonna be alright."

Teardrops fall to my lap, soaking my denim shorts.

The soaked spots become dirt stains.

And I feel as though all hell is about to break loose until...

I'm staring at my weathered denim shorts while sitting up against the palm tree. Remembering my final moments with Clem is like a wound I've reopened, still raw and bloody. I'm reminded of how fresh the wound is, and though it pains me to have experienced it all over again, the pain is subdued when I see Bella standing down by the water.

I stand to brush the sand off my legs. Her back is to me, the hem of her white romper swaying gently in the breeze. The sun catches the golden strands in her brown hair, and the world blurs around the clarity of her presence. I just watch her for a moment, hung up on the harsh words shared between us.

Sand shifts under my feet with every step I take toward her. I remove my T-shirt from the front of the shelter and put it on. Bella's posture remains elegant and tranquil as she lifts her chin, sensing my presence. When I reach her, she remains still. I don't want to bring up last night. I don't want to disturb her peace or risk upsetting her even more than I already have. Therefore, I don't say a word. Instead, I stand beside her and gently take her hand. Her fingers are cool at the touch before warming against mine. I glance at her, admiring the twinkle in her eye and the tiny scar atop her cheek.

"About last night," I say softly. "I shouldn't have said what I said."

"No." Her gaze softens as she continues staring at the ocean. "It needed to be said, and I needed to hear it." She squeezes my hand. "If we were put on this island to heal, we have to make peace with our pasts."

Bella releases my hand, then turns to face me. In her other

hand, she reveals a wooden cross. Its frame is carved from dark wood, each groove and knick telling a story of its creator's careful work. I remember the lady back in the Bahamas giving it to her. And now here Bella is, giving it to me.

The cross rises above her open palm as she lifts the twine. The twine is coarse, with a few small seashells tied intricately along its length. She dangles the cross necklace between us, the colors of the shells shifting under the sunlight. I become entranced by the cross, remembering the last time I wore a cross around my neck, which was the last time I spoke to Clem.

"It's all I can give you," Bella explains. "I added the shells. It's the surprise I was hiding from you the other day. You deserve a gift after everything you've been through."

My bottom lip trembles. "Bella…"

She stands on her tiptoes and drapes the twine over my head. "It can remind you that God has got His hand on you every moment you spend out here, that just because you and I lost control, doesn't mean we can't be saved."

The cross dangles just above my silver dog tag. Bella's delicate fingers brush over my neck as she makes sure the necklace sits right. The rough twine and shells become one with my skin, and a smile plays on Bella's lips when she sees the tear sliding down my cheek. I glance at the ocean, finding it impossible to look at her.

"You have no idea what this means to me," I exhale. "I had a cross necklace of my own. I prayed for Clem every day I was away, and when I came home and things ended…" I lift the cross in my palm. "I threw away the necklace because I blamed God for everything that went wrong. I've been wearing my own military tag around my neck because I vowed to take control of my own life. But you've made me realize that you're right about there being an author to our story, and you're right about our adventure starting the moment we lost control. We were brought here for a reason." I release the cross, then rip my dog tag from my neck. "Since I took control over my own life, nothing has gone my way. And that's because it's not about my way. It's about *His*–The Author."

I throw the dog tag over the waves, feeling the weight of my world lifted off my shoulders as it lands in the water. After all, it's not my world. It was never my world, plan, or plot. My life is God's story to write, and it's up to me to be the character He needs for the plot He has in store.

"We can do this," Bella says, taking my hand.

I face her, my vision blurring behind tears. "We can do this."

🌴🌴🌴

I return to the fire pit as the sun begins its descent. "The fish are back," I say, holding up a rope with three fish fastened to it.

Bella flashes me a smile while filling the pit with twigs and sticks. "Not bad."

After the past seven days we've spent on this island, today feels like the first. I know that sounds weird, but it's true. It's as if this entire week, we've been adjusting to the land, the water, and each other. We have food, we have water, we have shelter. We've weathered storms, shared laughs, told stories. We've fought and we've forgiven each other. We now look forward to the sunrises and sunsets. We have a routine that we're growing to love. What once seemed like the end is becoming a new beginning.

As the fire comes to life, we sit beside it, facing the horizon. The sky is a blend of fading golds and purples, the fish at the end of our sticks glistening above the firelight. I watch Bella slowly rotate her stick, making sure the fish cooks evenly.

"You haven't finished your story," I say. "I didn't even consider that Luca could have made up for that night."

Bella flashes a faint smile. My eyes fall to my new necklace. A small part of me died when Bella read the last few pages to me. I don't support her relationship with Luca. I can't stand Luca at all, but I respect that she still loves him despite his mistakes. In a weird way, I wish Clem did the same for me. Selfishly, I don't want to hear the rest of Bella and Luca's love story because I want my own story with Bella. But I can't be selfish. I'm healing and Bella needs to heal, too.

"I want to know what happens next."

Bella tilts her chin while chewing a piece of fish. After swallowing, she slowly nods. "Don't move."

"I don't have a choice," I tease while chewing. "I'm stranded on an island, remember?"

She laughs, then stands and makes her way to our shelter. "Are you sure about this?" she asks, returning with her journal in hand.

I nod.

Bella smiles, and then she reads…

Laguna Beach, California
Sunday - May 26th, 2019

I open my eyes to the soft morning light filtering through the sheer curtains. The familiar sound of waves blends with the distant calls of seagulls just outside. I have a headache, and it takes me a moment to realize that it's from all the drinks I had last night. With each blink, the sight of my living room becomes clearer. My fingers tighten around my blanket when I notice I'm on the couch. *Was I too drunk to make it to my own bed?*

I shift slightly, looking for any sight of Dad. Bits and pieces of memories from last night replay in my mind, most making my stomach turn. I remember the look on Dad's face when I told him I was going out instead of celebrating my birthday with him like every year before. I remember Abel singing that terrifying song. I remember Luca pinning me against the wall in that alley. And I remember Dane coming to my rescue. Any other details might as well be lost in the haze of what might be the worst night of my life.

I blink myself back to the present moment. A glass of water, a slice of last night's birthday cake, and a book covered in wrapping paper lie on the old coffee table before me. I smile, leaning forward to take a bite of the cake. A subtle moan escapes me, nostalgia weaving its way through me as I swallow a bite of the marble cake Dad has made for my birthday since before I can remember. He never disappoints.

I set down my fork and lift the book. Written across the brown wrapping paper are the words:

Bella,

You know I love the classics, but never as much as I love you. I picked out this book for you because I think it represents the next chapter of your life, which is one of adventure*. Remember, kiddo… the adventure begins the moment the characters lose control. Give this adventure a read, then go find your own.*

With love,
Dad

I carefully tear through the wrapping paper, making sure Dad's note remains in one piece. My heart races as I'm overwhelmed with curiosity. When I tear the final piece of paper away, *The Wizard of Oz* beckons for me, written in shimmering gold over the green cover. I trace the title with my finger, feeling the raised letters. While I've seen the movie, I've never read the book. I lock onto the cover illustration depicting Dorothy's silhouette on the yellow brick road. The spine cracks as I flip through a few of the aged pages, yearning to read about her adventure while clinging to the inspiration to eventually embark on my own. With a sense of renewal, I tuck Dad's note into my journal, and get ready for a new day.

It's a slow morning at the bookstore, which gives my mind too much time to wander. I know that Luca should probably be the last thing on my mind right now after last night, but I can't get him out of my damn head. I can hardly hear the music in the bookstore. I can hardly focus on *The Wizard of Oz* as I try to start it in the back office during my shift. All I can think about is Luca pinning me against the wall, refusing to let me go.

I gently graze over the bruises he left on my arm.

PING!

My phone sends my heart into a frantic beat. My mind races through every possibility of who it could be, and before I even pull my phone out, I know it's Luca. To my downfall, it is. I read his texts, both messages choking my heart as I read them in his soothing voice.

LUCA: I know I don't deserve a second chance
LUCA: But if you decide otherwise, you know where to find me

My mind and heart begin to wage war against each other. My mind reminds me that Luca crossed the line. If Dane wasn't there, Luca would have had his way with me. I told him to stop. I told him to stop, and he just kept going. My hand tightens around my phone, the bruise on my arm reminding me that loving Luca is dangerous. And yet, my heart holds on to the act of love itself, forcing thoughts into my stubborn mind, thoughts of the romance characters I read about. I see the characters who stumble and fall, the ones who break the hearts of the ones they love but still manage to change for them. Luca can change. I know he can change. He can learn from this, become the main character in my story that I believe him to be. With a shaky breath, I make my decision, knowing that whatever happens next can save us or shatter us to pieces.

As I walk down to Brooks Street, I realize how much love is like the ocean. It's vast, it's unpredictable, it's full of hidden depths yet to be explored. At times, it's gentle like the waves that lap the shore, and at other times, its merciless waves will leave you gasping for air. You can dive into the deep headfirst or take one step at a time through the shallows, but then it's all up to the ocean. The scariest part is that if you want to experience it for what it truly is, at some point, you'll have to swim with the constant risk of sinking. So, I can read about characters who find love the way someone admires the ocean from the shore, or I can put the books down to seek love for myself the way someone charges at the waves head-on.

With every step I take down the gravel path leading to the beach, my decision becomes clear. I dove headfirst for Luca, and although we're sinking, it might not be too late to swim again. My bare feet meet the warm sand as I stop at the base of the cliffs. I look up, squinting at the sun. After returning to the spot we met not long ago, I'm forced to consider that while this place is where our story began, it can be the same place our story ends.

I shield my eyes from the sun, panning the shore for any sight of Luca. The beachgoers tend to their summer fun, families building sand castles while surfers carve the shimmering waves. My heart pounds when I spot him sitting on the rocks just outside of a nearby cove. His back is to me, and I catch a glimpse of his feet dangling over the edge, his eyes fixated on the waves that curl below.

I approach him, climbing carefully over the rocks that lead to his. His long brown hair is one with the breeze, hints of gold reflecting the sunlight. He's wearing a cut-off T-shirt that shows off his tan, muscular arms. His beige denim shorts are frayed at the edges, wrapping his lean legs. The closer I get, the more he looks otherworldly. His wild, unpredictable nature draws me in, even as the small part of me knows I should keep my distance.

When I reach his rock, he gently turns his head. The light catches his eyes and they shimmer like the ocean beyond. I stop a few feet away, afraid that if I get too close, I'll let his beauty blind me to his flaws. And right now, that's the last thing I need.

Luca doesn't say a word at first. He just turns to face me. With a soft smile, he pats the surface next to him. I obey, silently sitting beside him. We face the open ocean, the sea seeming infinite from here.

From up this close, it becomes apparent how easy it must be to get lost out there. I glance at Luca, his profile sharp against the sloping hills lining the coast.

"You scare me," he murmurs, competing with the crashing waves. There's a silent intensity in his gaze as it remains fixed on the horizon. His words catch me off guard. *I scare him?* Wise words coming from the guy who had me pinned against a wall last night.

I squint at him. "An apology will do."

"No, it won't," Luca replies softly, but the regret in his tone is sharp. "What I did was unforgivable, and an apology won't take it back."

Luca's words erode my anger, leaving something softer in its place. I don't know what I was expecting, but it would have been something more along the lines of him making up an excuse for his actions. Instead, he simply acknowledges the damage done and the hurt he's caused.

"Bella, I'm not some Romeo. I'm not like the guys you read about. I'm reckless, I… I don't know how to love at all." His eyes finally meet mine and that's where I find his obsession, the same obsession I had set out to receive. "If you haven't noticed, I'm passionate about the things I do. And I use those things to keep me from women because of what happened last night." He shakes his head, looking down as he continues. "I can't take things slow with you. I want you all the time in more ways than one. I want to hear your voice, see your smile, make love to you at all fucking times. And I'm finding it hard to do anything else."

His confession is raw, stirring something deep inside of me. Since I first laid eyes on Luca, I wanted him to fall in love with me. Now, I'm forced to imagine his love for me leading to the end of us.

Luca's eyes land on my bruise, forcing his lip to quiver. "Did I…?"

"I'm fine." I cover the bruise, watching his world come crashing down.

Strands of brown and gold hang over the sides of his face when he buries it in his palms. Tears fall through his fingers as he whispers, "I'm a fucking monster." He looks out at the ocean, running his hands back through his hair. "I swear I never meant to hurt you. I'm… I'm falling in love with you." He exhales a shaky breath. "It's just that my lifestyle was never one for love. The band, the traveling, the partying. Last night made me realize I was moving in a direction that could ruin you." He turns to face me again, but this time with a fire in his eyes.

"And that changes today. Bella, you made me realize that the life I was living would eventually kill me. So, I'm gonna quit drinking for good. I promise you. I'm gonna drop the party bullshit and just focus on what I love the most—*you*."

Did he just say what I think he said?

A million thoughts come flooding through my mind. I set out to win Luca's love, and now I finally have it. He's choosing me over his vices, offering me a love I've always wanted. I dove headfirst for Luca and although we were sinking, we can swim again. He's promising me a new chapter, one of redemption and adventure and romance and everything I could ever ask for. Tears begin to fall as I reach for his hand. It trembles in mine as I speak the words he once told me. "We start slow, then all at once."

Luca leans forward, dipping his forehead to mine. "We start slow, then all at once," he repeats.

It couldn't be more true. Love starts slow. It begins with a glance, a shared moment on Brooks Street while floating on a surfboard after Luca saved me. Love continued with him kissing me on that balcony and when we made love for the first time above Brooks Street. Then, love rooted itself in the small moments, the short visits to the bookstore, the subtle smiles during his shows. And now, love is suddenly everywhere. It floods my life like waves rushing the shore, inevitable and unavoidable. Thinking of Luca before I fall asleep and the moment I wake. It's now something I live, and even as we weather this storm and we're at a point where all seems lost, we find our way back home.

We will continue to build on this love, wave after wave.

And just like the sea, love will carry us to places unimagined, becoming the adventure I've yearned for.

"I want to make good on my promise from before," Luca says. "If it still means a lot to you, I want to get to know your dad."

I hold up a fist with my pinky pointing toward him. He gently wraps it with his, and we kiss the tops of our fists.

"I would love that," I whisper. "And Dad would, too."

"Luca's here!" I shout from my bedroom when I see the van pull up. A thrill works through me as I see Luca stepping out of the van, the subtle smile on his face one of confidence and vulnerability. He runs a hand through his hair, clutching a single white rose and a book in the other. "Dad! Are you ready?"

"Ready as I'll ever be!" Dad replies from the kitchen.

I smooth out my white sundress, then enter the living room. Outside the living room window, Laguna Beach is bathed in a twilight glow. The ocean reflects shades of lavender and pink as the sun dips beneath the horizon. The palm trees sway lazily, their shapes dark against the vibrant sky. I juggle feelings of excitement and anxiety while Dad hums a song, setting the table for dinner.

My heart skips a beat when I hear Luca's knocks on the front door downstairs. I take one last look in my mirror, then make my way down the stairs and through the bookstore.

As I open the door, he smiles down at me. "For you, Juliet," he greets softly, offering me the white rose.

I rise on my tiptoes to kiss him hello, then open my stance for him to come in. "Come on in, Romeo." I lead him up the stairs toward the dim light cascading down from the living room. As we approach the top stair, I raise my palms. "Dad, this is—"

"Luca!" Dad greets with a chuckle. The floorboards creak under him as he approaches Luca with a broad smile. He extends a welcoming hand. "I've seen you around the bookstore a few times. Please, come in. Make yourself at home!"

Luca flashes Dad a shy smile as they shake hands. "Thank you, sir."

Sir? The words leave Luca's lips as if he's speaking a foreign language. This is the most polished I've seen him, from the black dress shirt and slacks he's wearing to the formal words he speaks. It's not like him, though I can't help but admire his effort to make a good first impression on the only family I have left.

Dad pats his back. "No need for *'Sir.'* Call me Donald."

Luca's shoulders relax. "Thank you, Donald." His eyes pan around the tiny living room until they suddenly widen. "Oh! Before I forget..." He lifts a book between the two of them. "I'm not a big reader, but I found this at the market the other day. I heard you enjoy the classics, and well, the cover says it's a classic."

"Would you look at that?!" Dad blushes, putting on his glasses to read the title aloud. "*Tess of the d'Urbervilles.* You know I read a book a day, and I've never gotten to reading this one! I'm a big fan of Thomas Hardy's writing style, so I'm sure I'll love this one. Thank you, Luca."

Dad suddenly hugs Luca so tight I think I hear a few bones crack. Luca's laugh is muffled by my dad's shoulder. I find it impossible to contain my smile when the two make their way to the table without me, their two worlds becoming one. The mismatched antique plates glimmer under the antique lamp shining from above. I play music off the T.V. speaker, and Luca flashes me a smirk when I play one of his band's songs. I shrug, approaching the table they stand over.

"Your seat is right over there," Dad says.

Chills cover my arms when he points at the seat closest to the window. *Mom's seat.* She was the only person to ever sit in that chair. Since she passed, the chair has remained untouched, the collecting dust a reminder of the void she left behind. Luca sits in the chair, taking in his surroundings without realizing the power of this moment and what it symbolizes for Dad and me.

Dad senses my hesitation and places a comforting hand on my back. "She'd want us to move forward," he whispers.

With a steadying breath, I pull out my chair and sit across from Luca. He smiles, and it dawns on me that this is how we honor my mother. We shouldn't honor her with dust and emptiness but rather allow ourselves to create new memories and share laughs in a space that was once hers. Dad is right. She would want us to move forward.

As we begin to eat, Luca catches my eye, and it's in his gaze that he tells me, "*Thank you.*" I smile between bites. We're exactly where we're supposed to be, rewriting parts of our stories that went wrong, filling empty spaces with new beginnings. And I couldn't be happier to share it all with Luca.

.

8 DAYS STRANDED

"This seems dangerous," Bella warns from behind.

"Well, I don't see myself getting stronger anytime soon." I fasten the rope around my waist while looking up at the towering palm tree. "Eventually, I'll be too weak to cut down the leaves." I loop the rope around the trunk and brace my shoe against the rough bark. "There's no better time to climb than now."

"But, what if you're not strong enough?" she asks.

I rest my forehead against the tree, the sun beating relentlessly through the palm leaves above. With every day that has passed, I've grown weaker. My muscles ache when I do something as simple as standing up. My head hurts when I think too hard about practically anything. Though we're getting by, the gradual decay both inside and out is a reminder that death is like the rising tide, unforgivingly inching closer.

"I can get up there today," I exhale. "I may not be able to say the same tomorrow."

And with that, I climb. My hands tighten around the rope as I inch up the tree. The bottom of my beaten shoes scrape against the trunk. The sound of stretching twine can be heard on the other side of the tree, pleading for me to reconsider doing this. I'm not even halfway up when my muscles begin protesting for me to stop, sweat seeping through my shirt. But I have to keep going, have to keep climbing.

Higher.

"We can do this," I whisper under my breath.

Earlier this morning, I woke up with the idea to rebuild our shelter, to make it useful and one that will start to feel even more like a home. It's the least I can do after Bella made me the necklace. After hearing her read about the comfort of her home back in Laguna Beach, I realized I want her to have something similar here. She deserves it, and I want to give it to her while I can.

Higher.

I continue climbing through the pain. I'm pushing myself beyond what I thought I could handle, but I'm past the halfway point and can't look back now. I grit my teeth, sliding the rope higher. I pull on the rope while simultaneously pushing my feet against the tree. As I climb higher, the wind blows harder. The sound of the palm leaves grows loud as I near them. I'm so close that I could probably grab one of them if I jump.

The rope suddenly makes a sharp popping sound.

Shit.

I pause.

"What happened?!" Bella shouts from below.

I close my eyes, my breath growing unsteady as I remain frozen. The sharp sound came from the opposite side of the tree. Having no idea how bad the potential tear is, I'm left with a choice. I can move up just a few more inches to where the leaves are in reach, or I can give up and make my way back down, hoping the rope doesn't tear.

"Rome?"

"I'm fine!" I blurt out. "We can do this."

I inhale slowly and deeply through my nose. *1, 2, 3, 4.*

I hold my breath. *1, 2, 3, 4.*

I exhale slowly and fully through my mouth. *1, 2, 3, 4.*

I start to feel the rope straining. There's no more time to think, no more time to doubt. So, I leap. The world slows as I put my faith in the branch I reach for. I grab a handful of leaves, my fingers wrapping a few sturdy branches. Bella screams as the torn rope hangs from my waist toward the ground below. Adrenaline courses through my veins, and I can hear my heartbeat pounding in my ears. My feet dangle beneath me. I won't stop. I can't stop. The tree sways under my weight. I fumble for the knife in my pocket, then start cutting. The blade slices through the first branch, and I begin cutting the next as the first falls lazily toward Bella. I slice through another leaf, then another. My muscles burn, and once I've cut every leaf except for the ones I'm hanging from, I desperately cling to the tree. My breathing deepens, but it doesn't steady yet. I still need to get down.

"Rome, I swear! If you survive this, I'm gonna kill you myself!" Bella screams. "You're crazy!"

I manage a laugh, looking down at Bella, who is anxiously watching from the safety of the ground. The hard part is over, and although my body is close to giving out, I begin my new mission.

New mission: *Make it down the tree.*

While I gather what little strength I have left, I look out over the ocean. It's the first time I've seen the world from an angle that isn't the shore, and I must admit it's a beautiful view.

Taking it one inch at a time, I carefully climb back down, my feet finally meeting the sand. Bella throws her arms around me, and I can feel her heart beating frantically against my chest. "I can't believe you."

I smile, falling into her arms. I cherish the warmth and gratitude that flow from her body to mine as my exhaustion kicks in. She suddenly pulls back and slaps my chest, her eyes fierce with protective anger.

"Risking your life for leaves?! Have you lost your mind?!" She slaps my shoulder, then my chest again. "You're insane!"

I can't stop laughing. The tension over the past few minutes, the absurdity of what I just did, and Bella's feisty reaction are a blend of unexpected happiness. "Hey, hey!" I stutter-step around the palm tree and peek around the side. "I'm here, I'm okay."

Bella looks up at me, her arms crossed. A silent beat passes, the sound of lapping waves lending peace to the moment. She purses her lips, then she can no longer hide the reluctant smile that spreads across her face. "Promise me you'll never do that again."

I look up at the palm leaves still attached to the other two trees.

"Rome! Promise me."

"I promise," I say softly.

Bella holds out her pinky. "Pinky promise it," she insists.

I wrap her pinky with mine, and the moment she kisses the top of her fist, chills cover my arms. It's the same way she has Luca make promises to her. And while I can't control the promises he keeps or breaks, I can control mine. "Pinky promise," I assure her.

She nods. "What are the leaves for, anyway?"

"You surprised me with the necklace," I reply, picking up the leaves. "Now, it's my turn to surprise you."

🌴🌴🌴

"Are you almost done?" Bella asks from below the palm trees. Her voice is light, playful.

"If you ask me one more time, I'm gonna start over!" I tease.

I adjust the palm leaves that now hang over our new and improved shelter. I peek over the top to see Bella sitting obediently against one of the trees. My fingers tremble as I smooth over the fastened leaves. I remove every imperfection, tie every loose end. This needs to be perfect. For us.

Lately, I've been trying to think less about surviving. Ironically, it's become second nature. We live to eat and drink. We eat and drink to live. Life has really become that simple. The panic that once poisoned my mind–thoughts of how we would make it out of here alive–is beginning to fade. It's as though we've found a peaceful rhythm, and I like it.

I glance up at Bella again, the breeze stirring her hair as she reads her journal. The sight of her sitting there is a painted picture, a culmination of blues, greens, and pops of white. It's moments like these that make the thought of leaving my world behind seem tempting. Since we washed up, we haven't seen a single plane in the sky nor a single boat on the horizon. There hasn't been a single sign of rescue since we arrived on this shore, and the strangest part is that I'm beginning to make peace with it.

Peace is replacing my desperation.

Bella is replacing my family and my friends.

The island is replacing my hometown.

And this new shelter is looking a whole lot like our new home.

I make my way up to the trees and offer Bella my hand. "You ready?"

"Ready." She closes her journal, then beams up at me.

I pull her up to her feet, cover her eyes with my hands, and guide her from behind. With every step we take toward the water, I feel her cheeks rise higher into a smile. Just before we reach the water, I turn her to face the shelter, then remove my hands. "I know it will never compare to your home back in Laguna Beach, but I hope this will be home enough for now."

I stand back and watch Bella take it all in. With the help of some large rocks I rolled up from the shore and some stray branches, I rebuilt our shelter into one nearly twice the size of the last. The palm leaves I cut down drape over the entrance, lending enough shade to be a cozy front patio. I was able to fasten the ceiling high enough for us to crouch under rather than crawl.

Without saying a word, Bella steps cautiously toward our new home. She lowers herself under the patio and I hear her gasp at the sight of what's inside. Two large plants are fastened by vines along one of the walls, mimicking shelves where I placed the prettiest seashells I could find.

Truth be told, I was never sure how Bella would receive this. I'm sure using survival time to do a home makeover isn't in any sort of shipwreck survival handbook. But I felt it had to be done. It's something to remind us that regardless of the circumstances, we still have a home.

I sit on one of the large rocks by the front, watching her explore inside. "What do you think?" Bella silently pans from right to left. At the sound of her sniffle, I ask, "You alright?"

Her hand rises to her mouth, her shoulders trembling. "You didn't have to do this," she whispers. A warmth blooms in my chest at the underlying gratitude in Bella's voice. She turns to me, the hazel in her eyes magnified by sacred tears that fall down her cheeks. She crawls closer until she's kneeling in front of me. Before I know it, she's wrapping me in her arms, pressing her face to my chest. "I can't believe you did this for me."

"*We* did this." I gently caress her face in my palms, my eyes flicking between hers. "I wouldn't be doing any of this if it weren't for you. And I can tell by the way you read to me that you miss home. I know this isn't nearly as special, but I thought it might help."

Bella pulls back slightly, looking up at me with tear-stained cheeks, and that's when it shifts. Everything, all at once. The island, the ocean, and the sky all fade into the background. All I see is Bella, all I breathe is Bella. Her lips trembling and breath shallow, her presence is nothing short of surreal.

The fragility of life suddenly weighs on me. Upon feeling the fear of wasting another moment, the distance between us dissolves with a kiss I put off for far too long. The kiss isn't careful, it's not considerate. It's a dam that breaks—all desire, fear, frustration, gratitude, and hope pouring out all at once. I feel her fingers run back through my hair, and she presses against me like she's scared I might pull away. I'll never pull away. I'll never pull away, leave her side, or let go. I don't care if she never loves me the way she loves Luca because all that matters is the way she loves me. I feel that love here and now, and it's like she, too, accepts that this kiss is about more than expressing how we feel. This kiss is about our survival.

She's engaged. I know that.

There's still a ring on her finger. I see that.

And still, with the warmth of her lips molding to mine, betrayal is the last thing on our minds. It's about here, it's about now. It's about expressing our love for each other so that we can live and keep pressing on. It's about the lives we're building from nothing. God put us on this island for a reason. Though it's still unclear, it's undeniable that He's using this dire situation to save us from our pasts so that we can pave the way for a better future.

I don't know if we'll ever be rescued or find a way off this island.

But, if we stay here,

if this becomes our new home,

where I wake up beside Bella,

fall asleep beside Bella,

and do it all over every day after,

then I'm okay with these days being my last.

Our lips part, but my forehead rests gently against Bella's, the warmth of our breaths becoming one. Her long lashes cast shadows over her cheeks, and although I can't see her gaze, I can feel her sudden struggle, the weight of regret setting in. A tear wells along the edge of her left eye. *She's thinking about him.*

"Bella." My tone is low, steady. I feel her pulling away. Not physically, but mentally. I don't blame her for a second. Instead, I blame myself. "Open your eyes." She keeps them closed. Another tear wells, following the first down the side of her face. "Bella, please."

Her eyes flutter open, the third tear gliding down her cheek. I let it fall. She needs to feel this, thoughts of *what was* resisting *what is*. I pull back enough for her to see me. Now on my knees, I gesture for her to look at our new home, then out at the beach and ocean beyond.

"I want you to look," I say, my tone rising. "Look around. You see all of this?" I raise a hand toward the swaying palm trees and the white stretch of sand. "This could be it. This is all we have. Right here, right now. And Luca isn't here. Our lives have changed drastically, and we don't owe our pasts anything."

Bella's lips part as if she's preparing to speak, but words refuse to leave her lips. I see war in her eyes, but it's unlike any war I've ever seen. There are no soldiers, bullets, bombs, shouts, screams. It's a war of lives, a war of loves. One side is bound to her past, to promises once made in a world now distant. The other side is bound to her present, to us. It's the love built on empty promises or the love built on survival.

She takes a deep breath, then exhales. Her eyes flick to the journal resting on the sand beside us. The pages curl from the salty breeze, the words inscribed on each page reflecting the memories in her eyes. For a few silent beats, she just stares at it, and I can understand why. It holds pieces of her heart, memories that both killed her and gave her life. And now, those memories stand between us, threatening our present and future together.

"You don't understand. I have to keep reading it," Bella whispers. Her voice trembles. "Part of me is stuck in those pages. If I don't finish it, I can't move on."

A lump forms in my throat. I know it's not as easy as her throwing her ring out into the water after a kiss. It's not as easy as tearing out the pages of her love story to write a new one. As much as I don't want to hear what happens next in her love story with Luca, I want Bella to find peace. And if Bella finding peace will lead to us being together with a guilt-free conscience, then I'll force myself to listen to every word she reads, no matter how much it hurts.

I pick up the journal and rub grains of sand off the cover. "If you need to keep reading, do it." I hand it to her. "You know I'll listen."

Bella takes the journal with one hand while wiping her tears with the other. "Before I read, you need to go back."

"Go back?"

"Your memory for the day." She points at my pocket. "We're in this together, remember?"

I reach into my pocket and pull out the hourglass more reluctantly than ever before. Today was the best day I've had since being shipwrecked. For the first time, the thought of reliving memories feels as if I'm being unfaithful to this new life I've created with Bella.

Bella closes my hand over the hourglass, then holds it up to my heart. "If we were put here to heal, then that's what we need to do. Both of us."

I clench my jaw, staring into her supportive gaze. I take a deep breath, flip the hourglass, and as sand begins to slip through the center tube, I dive back into my past…

It's strange how years of sacrifice, discipline, and facing death itself couldn't prepare me for losing Clementine. My heart feels like it's in fight or flight, but now my life possesses nothing worth fighting for. I've danced with Death and sat with Trauma, and neither compares to my brief encounter with Heartbreak.

It's been three days since I walked back into Clem's life and she walked out of mine. I've replayed our short conversation over and over again, and each time, the ending I imagine is more bearable than what actually happened.

Clem's words poison my mind. "*You were gone*." Not once did I think that enlisting would force her away from me. Not once did I think that the miles separating us would force her into another man's arms. Maybe I wasn't thinking at all. Maybe, I never thought that what I was doing wasn't in the best interest of Clem and our baby, my everything. And as a result, I lost it all.

I sit alone in my truck, parked in front of my old high school. It's the first time I've left the house since I got back from my deployment. After loads of failed attempts made by Mac and my parents to get me out, I finally decided to get my ass off the couch tonight. This was the only place I thought to come, considering it was the only place I would come with Clem if we weren't at her house or mine. That's the only shitty part about living in a small town. You're left with no place to run when you need to get your mind off the pain.

I stare through the windshield at the empty field and weathered bleachers, every shadowed corner reminding me of a time that was so simple. We were young. We thought we had it all figured out. Hell, we *did* until life had other plans. This place held a heartbeat, and now it seems like a graveyard for the good ol' days.

I twiddle my dog tag in my fingertips, dragging it up and down my chain. Without Clem, there's nothing left for me here. And now I've found myself flirting with the thought of re-enlisting because I don't know how to live life any other way. The thought of facing death again doesn't sound so bad when you pour your life into someone and they leave. It suddenly dawns on me that Clem probably thought the same when I left her for my deployment.

Car headlights suddenly sweep the empty lot, piercing through the darkness. I squint at the familiar car as it makes its way toward me. The engine hums until the car parks directly ahead, my heart stumbling when I realize who it belongs to.

I recognize her by her silhouette alone the moment she steps out. "Clem?" I call, stepping out of my truck. "What're you doing here?"

Clem steps closer, her arms crossed. "I couldn't wait any longer to talk to you."

I stand still, having no idea what to say or how to feel. My mind races as she closes the distance between us. I pull my hands from my pockets, readying myself for her embrace. I'm gutted when she stops, my headlights casting a soft glow over her blue eyes. In them, I see fire, vulnerability, and everything in between. At one point, I fell in love with everything over and underneath the surface of this girl, and after we broke each other's hearts, we now find ourselves nestled between new beginnings and second chances all at the same time.

"I didn't think I'd see you again," I whisper, my voice rough from nights of screaming into my pillow.

Clem's lip quivers before she says, "Seeing you again the other day made me realize everything I did, and you didn't deserve any of it." She looks down, a single tear gliding down her cheek. "My God, this is hard."

"It doesn't have to be." I offer her my hand. "I still love you. I'm always gonna love you."

The distance between us dissolves as she leaps into my arms. I hold her like never before because this time is different. This time, I'm here to stay. This time, there's no duty beckoning for my mind. There's no honor fighting for my heart.

It's just Clementine, the way it once was—the way I always knew, and while I did, I wedged distance between us. I left her to save a country that never needed saving, and when I came back, she was the one who needed saving *only because I left*.

"Don't you ever go leavin' again," she whispers against my chest.

I caress her cheeks, kissing her forehead before we lock eyes. "Never again."

"ROME." Mac's stern voice pulls my attention from Clem. I turn back over my shoulder to see him moving toward me. He takes cautious steps, holding up his hands as if to protect himself from me. "Are you okay?"

"We're fine," I reply.

Mac looks past me. "*We're*?"

"Clem and I are fine." I turn to face-... My words hang in the air as my eyes search the empty parking lot. My heart slams in my chest, my hands shaking at my sides as I stutter-step backward. I spin, looking for any trace of Clem. "No, no. She... she was just here."

Mac's hand gently lands on my shoulder, pulling me back to reality. "There's no one here, man."

His words weigh on me. I can't accept them. Clem was here. I just saw her. I heard her whisper against my chest and felt her in my arms. But all I see before me is the silent stretch of asphalt. My stomach turns over itself when I realize the truth.

Mac's worried expression grates at me. "Have you been takin' your medicine?"

I shake my head, numb.

"Come on," he says quietly, guiding me back to his truck. "Let's get you home."

As we make our way to his truck...

it slowly dissolves into grains of sand...

falling toward the earth until...

The sand gathers in the bottom bulb of the hourglass. I look up to see Bella patiently waiting for me to return to the present, to reality. Without saying a word, I place a gentle hand on her thigh and feel her warmth spread through me. I ground myself in her presence, a part of me expecting her to vanish right before my eyes the way Clem did that night. But she doesn't. And instead, I honor the weight of her being, the softness of her skin and the light in her eyes.

"You're here," I whisper, my words one with the ocean breeze.

"I never left," Bella says. Her hands find mine, our fingers intertwining in a way both familiar and new. She tightens her grip, her hold on me so firm and intensely real that I can't help but laugh.

Bella shifts her focus toward the journal in her lap. I lean back against the rock, admiring the profound beauty in this moment. I raise my knees, wrapping them with my arms. When she finds the page she left off, her eyes flick up to mine, and she flashes me a faint smile, one of gratitude. I nod, forcing a smile of my own.

Since I lost Clem, I've come a long way in more ways than one, and I couldn't be more grateful that the long way brought me to Bella. I feel for the cross hanging from my neck, relieved that reliving once-painful memories is starting to heal me. Slowly but surely. Bit by bit, I'm preparing myself to embrace the next chapter, and now it's her turn to prepare for the same.

I can accept that with every page Bella reads, her walls may come down just a little bit further the way mine have for her. Those walls don't need to come crashing down. They just need to be low enough for me to climb over.

"Your turn," I urge.

Bella releases a breath, and then she reads...

Laguna Beach, California
Friday - May 31st, 2019

The sun warms my skin as I lay out at Brooks Street. Waves roll in and out, their constant sound soothing as I get lost in *The Wizard of Oz*. It feels good reading with a clear mind again. Over the past week it's been since Luca came over for dinner, our relationship has become impenetrable.

Luca has made good on his promise to give up drinking for me—for *us*. He's spending less time with Abel and more time at the bookstore and around our apartment. He's smiling more, laughing more. There's a silent strength he now carries that's making our world all the more peaceful. It's crazy how the smallest changes can have the greatest impact on our lives, and now that he's making the changes, we can grow. We can leave the recklessness behind and skip to the chapter where everything is perfect and right and sweet and all the things the main characters could ever ask for.

I watch Luca out in the water, his red wetsuit a magnet for my gaze to latch on to as he surfs across a never-ending wave. I take a deep breath, and the scent of salt water and sunscreen makes its way through my lungs.

"Bella?" A familiar voice pierces the air, pulling my attention from the page.

I turn and there she is. I lower my book, fixated on Tish standing at the other end of my beach towel. I blink, trying to comprehend how different she looks since we last sat on this beach together. It's only been a few weeks, and I can hardly recognize her. Her once-thick and lush black hair is divided down the middle, now bleached blonde along the right side. She's thinner, much thinner since I last stood face to face with her. Her cheekbones are sharp, her collarbone peeking through the stretched crewneck of her gray band T-shirt. She's not as tan as usual, suggesting she hasn't seen much sun. Even her legs look swallowed up by the black denim shorts she wears.

"Tish," I exhale in a whisper, standing to my feet. She awkwardly averts her eyes, wrapping her arms around herself as if to hide how far she's fallen into Abel's reckless lifestyle.

"Hi," Tish says, her voice as soft as the wind. Her eyes drop to her feet. "I thought I might find you here."

I struggle to find the right words to say. It's nearly heartbreaking to see this hollowed-out version of my best friend standing before me. It's like she shrank into herself. She's less of a force, and that's mainly what Tish was known for being before she withdrew from the world.

I blink myself back into the present, realizing there could be a bigger reason for her being here. "You want to sit?"

"Sure." Tish smiles, though it doesn't reach her eyes.

I lay the towel so we can face the ocean while sitting side by side. As we sit, I run through things to say. I want to ask how she is, what she's been doing, why she looks so different. But it's one of those weird situations where you have so much to say you feel as though nothing should be said at all. What should be addressed? What should remain unaddressed? I start to think all of my questions and concerns can be answered with a simple question. "Are you okay?" I ask.

Tish stares straight out at the ocean. Even in her darkened state, the sun reflects remnants of her beauty. *She's still in there somewhere.* There's no movement in her face or body except for the single tear that slides down her cheek. I watch it fall to her shirt. When I look up again, her eyes are closed, her chin raised. "No," she breathes.

I haven't heard much about Tish over the past weeks other than her spending more time with Abel than anybody else. Luca mentioned that she watches their band play and spends more time at their apartment than she does anywhere else.

From the start, I've had a bad feeling about Abel and blame him for having tainted her. Tish doesn't even need to voice that she's hardly been eating while doing more drugs than I can probably count on one hand. I look out at Luca who continues innocently surfing with a smile on his face, and I can't help but be grateful that he's distanced both he and myself from Abel. I could have easily been in Tish's position if Luca hadn't changed his way.

I swallow, now facing Tish. "Is it Abel?"

She nods. "Yeah," she says, her voice hardly more than a whisper.

"Why didn't you call me?" I ask. "Why didn't you tell me something was wrong?"

"I didn't know something was wrong." She lowers her chin. "I don't know, I thought I could fix him. And the more I hoped he would change his ways, the more I found myself changing mine."

I wrap her shoulder with my arm, then pull her close. "Oh, Tish." Her entire body trembles at my touch. "It's not too late to get out."

"I'm scared to leave him," Tish says, her voice cracking. "He's reckless. And he admitted he doesn't know how to love at all."

My heart plummets when I hear the words leave her lips. Luca said the same to me before I forgave him. But, no. Luca is different. Luca isn't Abel. Luca is Luca, and I've fallen for Luca. Abel can't touch us. He can't hurt us. Luca and I will never be what Abel and Tish are. "Come stay with my dad and me," I urge. "Don't go to Abel's anymore. Don't go to their shows."

I feel Tish's arm wrap around my lower back.

"I'm sorry I stopped reaching out," she confesses. "I became someone I'm not."

"Shh, it's okay. I'm just as much to blame for not checking on you," I say softly. "You'll come stay with me and get through this."

"I'd like that," Tish replies between sniffles. She releases me and wipes the tears from her cheeks. After a long exhale, she straightens herself and spots Luca in the water. "Luca's not like Abel. I can tell by the way Abel talks about him."

"What does he say?"

"Abel hates that Luca spends more time with you than he does with him." Tish smirks. "And I love that Luca spends more time with you because Abel hates it."

While I'm flattered at Tish's comment, an unsettling feeling manifests itself within. What do reckless people do to the ones they hate? Would Abel try to hurt Luca? Would he try to hurt me? Would he cut out Luca from the band? Frankly, all I can hope for right now is for Luca to be done with all this recklessness for good.

"Promise me something?" Tish asks, a hopeful smile spreading across her face.

"Anything," I say, placing my hand on hers.

She gestures toward the ocean at a cruise ship in the distance. "Promise me one day we'll leave this place. Just sail away, some place far from here. It could be anywhere. Let's just leave land for a bit and not worry about the people on it. Just us and Mother Nature."

"I'd like that." I smile, squeezing her hand. "I'd like that a lot."

"But, do you promise?"

I turn to face Tish. "I promise."

As the day goes on, the tension between us lifts, every ounce of emotional weight once carried fading with every passing minute. The two of us settle deeper into the sand, sharing laughs and catching up on life. Sure, it's only been a few weeks since we last spoke, but a few weeks apart is an eternity when you grew up spending almost every day together. Tish's presence becomes a gift I wasn't prepared to receive today, and I'm more than happy to receive it.

Tish rolls her eyes, twisting a handful of her bleached hair. "Half of my head is fried."

I struggle to hold back a laugh. "It looks good!"

"Shut up," she says, playfully narrowing her eyes at me. "You're too nice to tell me it looks awful."

"It's very..." I really put thought into this, believe it or not. "'Rockstar chick.'"

"You mean it's very 'mid-mid-life crisis.'"

We both laugh, then find ourselves panning around the beach. The sun is just beginning its descent behind a wall of darkened purple clouds. Seagulls call from overhead, lazily surfing the breeze as it begins to cool down. The weathered cliffs framing Brooks Street catch the light of the setting sun, the ocean sparkling beneath.

Luca is finally making his way out of the water when Tish whispers, "It's crazy how you two began that day, and now here you are making it happen."

I slowly nod, fixated on Luca. "I had my doubts, but yeah. Guess you could say we're making it happen."

Luca's red wetsuit clings to his frame as he approaches, his hair dripping over the surfboard he lies in front of us. He smirks, unzipping his wetsuit and peeling it down to his waist. His muscles are pumped from hours of nonstop surfing, his skin reflecting the dimming sunlight. I catch Tish glancing at his broad shoulders and chiseled torso. I don't blame her. I do the same every time I see him shirtless.

"Juliet," he greets.

"Romeo," I reply. "You've been out there a while," I tease, lifting myself toward him.

He meets me halfway for a gentle kiss. "And you've been right here a while."

"I can't," Tish exhales, rubbing her eyes. "You're too cute."

Luca and I laugh, then he offers me his hand. "You two want to grab dinner somewhere?"

"I don't wanna intrude." Tish begins packing up. "I should probably get going."

Just as she stands, I grab her hand. "Yes. We would love to grab dinner."

The three of us go to a restaurant within walking distance of Brooks Street. As we settle in at a table on a deck overlooking the water, a sense of calm washes over me. The food, the view, and the company of my best friend and Luca. We become one with the moment, Tish and I telling Luca stories about our childhood.

"Remember when I gave that guy my phone number at this bar?" Tish asks between sips of her milkshake. "Biggest mistake."

I laugh. "That's the only time I've ever heard of a bartender giving a customer their number."

"Wait, wait, wait." Luca's eyes flick between us. "Aren't customers usually the ones who hit on the bartenders?"

"First and last time I ever did that." Tish closes her eyes, sighing in surrender. "He texted me every day for a month."

"You never responded?" Luca asks eagerly.

"I did for the first two days," Tish replies. "Then, I saw him at the beach with his wife and kids."

Luca chokes on his soda and begins pounding his chest. He laughs between coughs. "What the hell?! Texting you every day with a wife and kids?!"

"I sure know how to pick 'em," Tish whispers into her straw.

Tish's joke hangs in the air. It's a loaded comment, whether or not she meant for it to be. The three of us look in different directions, almost trying to play it off like she didn't just take a jab at Abel in front of Luca. It's obvious that Abel has done more damage in three weeks than Tish's past flings have done in three years. There's no longer a trace of the laughter from moments ago. Instead, I half-glance at Luca and notice him flexing his jaw.

"I know Abel's not a good guy," he finally says, breaking the silence. "I can't defend him for choosing to live life the way he does after everything he went through growing up." Tish's eyes lock on Luca's. She probably didn't expect him to address Abel's behavior so directly. "I get it," he continues. "You deserve better."

Tish swallows hard, her tear-filled eyes studying Luca. "I'm scared of what he'll do if I try to leave him."

"I wish I could tell you how he would react," Luca sighs. "I've been scared to leave the band for that same reason. I don't know what Abel will do, especially when I'm all he has. But, I will say that after distancing myself from him, I feel so much better."

I hold Luca's hand under the table, and he gives me a light squeeze. It's the first time I've heard Luca's intentions spoken openly, and I feel even more of a shift in him. It doesn't take trained eyes to see that Abel's recklessness has clung to Luca's identity, and because of that, Luca is now slipping through Abel's fingers. I love the way Luca loves music and the way he immerses himself in it without even realizing it, but I know music is also the only connection Abel uses as leverage over Luca.

We both know that loving me could mean giving up a big part of that life. Luca isn't just walking away from Abel and the band. He's walking away from his vices—the drinking, the drugs, running from one town to the next with no responsibilities or true love. And I can give him that love. I can give him true love, an adventure, and a future of our own.

"I'm still figuring it out," Luca says. "But, I already know it's worth it. We don't have to let Abel control our lives."

Tish nods, and it's in the depth of her gaze that I see a glimpse of hope.

It's faint but nonetheless there.

She's not alone in this anymore.

None of us are.

The walk back to my apartment is a long one, though it's one I enjoy more than I thought I would. After parting ways with Tish, we've spent most of it walking in comfortable silence, my hand laced in Luca's as we walk alongside Pacific Coast Highway. There's a silent peace between us, a sentiment to our time spent with Tish. It's hard to think that a week ago, I witnessed a destructive side of Luca, a side that could have led me onto the same path as Tish and Abel if I wasn't willing to walk away.

I glance up at Luca, hearing nothing but the sound of our footsteps and the distant hum of the ocean. He's smiling, and there's an ease about him that adds to the serene atmosphere of tonight.

Until it shifts.

It's subtle at first, a foreign scent threatening the salty breeze. But, then it grows. It prickles at my senses, forcing the hairs on the back of my neck to stand. I frown, my senses now alert as I look around. Luca's hand tightens around mine. He smells it, too.

"What's that smell?" I ask.

"Something's burning," Luca says, panning over the horizon. His expression hardens, the peace from a moment ago threatened by caution.

I follow his gaze as he searches the darkness. We continue

walking, and with each step, the smell of ash becomes more potent. My stomach tightens, but I shake it off. Wildfires are common during California summers. It's usually something the locals brush off because it never really threatens the towns, more so the hills.

I lift my chin to see the streetlights illuminating clouds of floating ash. As we turn onto the street that leads down to my home, the ash becomes so thick that we can hardly make out the faintest glow appearing at the edge of the sky. Before I can even think it, before I can even imagine the slim chance that the fire could be coming from somewhere close to home…

No.

It shouldn't be.

It can't be.

I drop my sandals, then my backpack joins them on the floor. I let go of Luca's hand, and break into a dead sprint down the winding road that leads home. My breath leaves my throat in ragged gasps. I hear Luca's surfboard hit the asphalt somewhere behind me and then his footsteps beside me as he keeps my pace. We turn the corner, and I'm slammed by a wave of terror when I see it.

Flames lick at the blackened sky, dark clouds billowing from the windows of…

THE APARTMENT.

THE BOOKSTORE.

"No, God," I whisper, slowing to a stop in the middle of the street. "Please, God. No, no."

I turn to Luca standing beside me, his profile glowing red from the distant flames, his eyes wide with horror. To say that my hands are trembling is an understatement. My entire body is shaking, and I can hardly look or think straight. People are gathered on the street, watching the flames engulf my home, my life. The heat from the flames is scorching, even from the distance we keep.

"Dad." The word leaves my lips in the form of a final, dying breath.

I look around at the people, most of them dark figures that merely stand and stare at my world as it burns to the ground. An emptiness forms within me at the realization that Dad is nowhere to be found. Luca grabs my arm, a fire smoldering in his iris.

"He's in there, isn't he?" he mouths–says? I don't know I can't hear him anymore. I hear burning. I hear destruction. I hear the shaking in me heart racing beating I can't breathe I can't where's my dad???

All I can manage to do is shake my head. Sirens can now be

heard in the distance, but they're quiet. Too quiet. Too far. If Dad is in there, the firefighters won't make it in time. Luca clenches his jaw and in an instant, I see the decision he makes in his eyes. Before I can stop him, he's moving, running toward the burning building with a desperation that nearly sends me spiraling. Flames dance along the doorway he runs through, and he disappears into the blaze.

Time slows. Upon blinking, I realize I'm on my knees, screaming and crying. Bystanders gather, some helping me to my feet while others openly talk about "*the girl's dad who is trapped inside.*" Somebody is helping me stand, and I only have enough strength to whisper, "Come back." The fire is too merciless, too destructive. The reality kicks in that there's no way my dad could have made it out. If he had, he would be right here next to me, telling me it's all going to be alright.

The sirens grow louder, minutes starting to feel like hours as I stare at the doorway. Suddenly, through the haze, I see movement. A figure emerges, holding another. It's Luca. Luca is alive. Luca is holding someone. Someone. *Dad.*

"DAD!" I scream. I break out of the people's grasp and rush forward.

Luca and Dad drop to their knees on the sidewalk. Luca gasps for air, his face and hair black from the ash. A groan escapes him as he lowers Dad to the ground where he now lies unconscious.

"He was—" Luca wheezes. "Hardly awake—" Luca wheezes. "When I found him at the bottom of the stairs." Luca coughs, his chest heaving.

Sirens and honks are suddenly flooding the street. Firefighters and medics swarm the building. I scream for them to let me go as they pull Luca and myself apart and from my lifeless father. I beg and plead for Dad to open his eyes, but he remains still.

"Get this kid oxygen!" A firefighter shouts as he drags Luca behind one of the trucks.

My eyes sting from the blend of ash and tears, but I can still see a group of medics loading Dad onto a stretcher. As they load him into the back of an ambulance, I'm sat on the back of another truck and forced to wear an oxygen mask. My lungs burn with every breath until the mask forces cool, clean air into my lungs.

"Breathe," a voice says.

I try to breathe. I blink again and again, trying to breathe, trying to stay awake. I begin praying that I'll wake up and this will be some kind of vivid, terrible nightmare. Instead, I remain awake. This is no nightmare. This is no fictional tragedy. This is reality.

I take in the world around me, a world consumed by ash…
and in the distance, I spot a white van…
and sitting in that white van, I see Abel watching us.

9 DAYS STRANDED

For the first time, I wake up with Bella in my arms. She lies still, her body slowly rising and falling to the rhythm of sleep. Her cheek rests softly on my shoulder, her dark hair forming a tapestry over my chest. The morning sunlight filters through the palms and branches making up our roof. Everything about Bella feels light, and I'm beginning to question how. Since I first met her, there has been this undeniable light she embodies. She made walking with grace seem effortless, and now I'm realizing how much of that light has been threatened by darkness. It kills me to think about what could happen next in her journal, whether or not her dad survived and if Luca's brother had a part to play in the fire.

I force my curiosity to the back of my mind, preparing to face whatever this new day may hold. My body feels heavy, a weak grumble consuming my stomach. I need to get used to my body constantly reminding me that I've gone from eating three square meals per day to a single fish per day, two if I'm lucky.

I gently press the side of my face to the top of Bella's head, and the ache in my bones fades for a moment. I lie my head back on the sand and admire our new home. I'm proud of myself for finding the strength to rebuild our shelter into one big enough for both of us. It's brought more peace to a place that once brought pain.

Nine days, I think to myself. We've spent nine days shipwrecked on this island. I'm starting to question whether or not it even makes sense to keep count anymore. Sure, nine days is a long time in comparison to one. Nine days is also a short time in comparison to being stuck on this island for the rest of our lives. With each thought starting to weigh more the way my body does, I can see myself eventually letting go of keeping track altogether. My life may depend on it.

I gently move out from under Bella, making it my mission to keep her from waking. I want to see the smile on her face when she sees me cooking the fish I'll catch for breakfast. As I step out of the shelter, my eyes land on her journal lying next to our fire pit. Though it wasn't her intent when she first wrote it, her story has undeniably kept us going. It's given us an escape when we need it the most. It also keeps her connected to her past, which I'm learning isn't as forgiving as I once thought.

Bella has been through hell and back, and maybe that's what makes her the angel she is. Luca forcing himself on her, her bookstore and home burning down, her dad being taken to the hospital. I don't even know what happens next, and I already admire her for keeping her peace. Lord knows I've hardened myself over a few months of enduring much less than she has over the past year. So far, her story is one of both love and tragedy, and the more she reads, the more I see her letting go of it all. I see it in the way she's starting to look at me. I feel it in the way we touch. The more pages she reads about Luca, the less of a hold he has on her.

As I pick up my spear and head down to the water, I find myself dwelling on my love for Clem. I loved Clem with all I was, and the more time I spend with Bella, the more she's taught me how real that love for Clem was. It was real, true love. And when I lost Clem, I lost sight of love. It wasn't until Bella came around that I found the strength to love all over again. And I can't keep this newfound strength she gives me because it doesn't belong to me. It belongs to Bella, so that's who I intend to use it for.

The morning sun hangs low in the sky, keeping me company while I search the shallows for today's food. I sway with the lapping waves, habitually scanning the clear water below for any trace of silver. The cotton candy clouds above cast round shadows over the open ocean, the air cool and refreshing. I scan the water below, tracking the rise and fall of the water. My muscles coil, my spear slightly raised at the ready.

A sudden flash of silver catches my eye. I move fast, and with two smooth steps, I drive my spear through the fish. I lift the tip of my spear to my chin, watching the fish flail before it goes still. Now lifeless, the body still glistens in the sunlight no less than it did when it was living. Relief works through me when I pull it free and head back to shore. Bella could wake up any moment, and I want a freshly cooked fish ready for her by the time she steps out of the shelter. I kick my feet dry, a smile tugging at my peeling cheeks. *And that's when I see it.*

It's a moving spec in the distance, well above the sharp horizon, a tiny glint of metal. It doesn't register at first, like hearing a foreign word spoken for the first time. But then my heart fucking drops because it's a plane.

A plane.

A PLANE!

"Plane," I say. Then, "PLANE!" I scream.

For a moment, I can hardly breathe. My mind struggles to catch up to my sight. It's been nine days of nothing. No plane, no boat, no sign of life other than trees and fish. And now there it is. Hope in flight, a thin white streak in its wake as it pierces the sky.

I drop my spear to the sand, my head on a swivel. Signal. I need to send a signal. Fire. Start a fire. That's what I need to do fire set a start a fire I NEED TO START A FIRE. I sprint up the beach to the bushes and begin snapping branches. I throw them onto the sand, frantically gathering anything capable of catching fire.

"Bella! Plane!" I shout. "Bella, wake up! There's a plane!"

My hands quiver as I scrape stones together over the pile of sticks and plant debris. Hope and Doubt wage war in my mind, each fueled by the distant hum of the plane. Hope constricts my heart, a new reality setting in, one where we're rescued. One moment, Hope tugs at my heart. *You can do this.* The next moment, Doubt pulls the opposite way. *You won't light the fire in time. And even if you do, the smoke won't be enough to get the pilot's attention.*

"Please," I beg God or the stones or both. "PLEASE!" My teeth grit against each other while I remain on the brink of success or failure. I glance back over my shoulder. "BELLA!"

I strike the stones.

No spark.

I strike the stones.

No spark.

I look up to see the plane now fading in the distance. The stakes have never been this high. I haven't had a more important mission. This could be the ticket to our survival. This could be the answer, the solution. I see Bella and I going home to our parents and our friends. I feel Mac and Tish throwing their arms around us. I taste real food. I hear music.

Bella emerges from the shelter, her relaxed posture in stark contrast to my abruptness as I shout, "THERE'S A PLANE!"

A line shows between her brows. Urgency finally courses through her as she shields the sun with her hand to look over the ocean. "Where?!"

I pause, my eyes wide. I look back over my shoulder. All that remains is the white streak the plane left as it soars away. Far away, never to be seen again.

My gaze drops to the stones in my hands, each coated in my own blood from the failed attempts. My hands still trembling, I drop the stones and lean forward until I'm sprawled over the sand. The adrenaline subsides, and my breaths shallow. The war in my mind has ended, and Doubt stands victorious, having conquered Hope.

Bella kneels beside me and lifts one of my bloody palms to wipe it with her own. "Rome."

"There was a plane," I sigh in defeat. "It was there. It flew past us. I couldn't... I'm sorry."

She runs a gentle hand through my hair, scanning the horizon. "It's okay. We'll get another chance."

Her words don't reach me. I turn my head, my cheek sticking to the warm sand as I stare at the ocean. *Nine days*. It took nine days for us to get this chance. Could it be nine more for us to get another? The uncertainty gnaws at my will to live.

I close my eyes, doing my best to receive Bella's affection as she continues running her hands through my hair. Back in the military, planes and helicopters always moved in strict patterns. It only took me a few days to pick up on most of those patterns, where each aircraft was heading and at exactly what time.

My mind runs through possibilities. The plane I saw was flying too high to be a search and rescue plane. That means it would have to be a commercial plane. If that's the case, we're under a flight path.

I lift my head from the sand. "Flight path," I whisper.

Bella releases me. "Huh?"

"We're under a flight path!" I turn onto my back, then stand on my feet. "Planes don't just fly one way and then never return," I explain, wiping the sand off my face.

I gather an armful of sticks and carry them down the beach.

"Wait, what?!" Bella shouts to my back. "Explain!"

My mind races, wondering how long it will take for the same plane, if not a new one, to fly in the same or opposite direction. A day? Two days? A week? I don't want to think about it being any longer than another nine days. I may not be able to control when we see it again, but I can control how ready we will be. I stack the sticks, then run back to the center of the island to gather anything else capable of catching fire when the time comes.

"We have to be ready for when they fly over again," I state, adding to the growing pile. "I'll keep a big pile of sticks and anything we can burn ready. And when the time is right, we'll set it on fire. If the fire is big enough and the smoke rises high enough, it should work."

Bella lingers a few feet behind me, watching me make a few more trips up and down the beach before she says, "Are you sure this is a good idea?"

I pour more debris onto the pile that's now nearly up to my waist. "Am I sure?" Dead skin sticks to the back of my sweaty hand as I wipe my forehead. "Not exactly, but we don't have any other leads. This is the best chance we have at getting out of here."

I slump down next to the pile, my body aching and hands raw. Bella's eyes remain on the pile as she keeps her distance. I see her thoughts playing out in her gaze, none supporting my new mission. "Do you not think this is a good idea?" I ask, wiping my bloody hands on my shorts.

Her attention drifts to the ocean, her voice faint over the sound of the gentle waves. "It's just… that's a lot you're going to burn for the small chance that they actually see it. What if it isn't big enough? What if they miss it, and all of this goes to waste?"

I frown. "We can't give up on being found."

"But, what if we have to? What if it makes more sense for us to use everything on this island for living on it instead of escaping it?" Bella sits back on the sand, facing me. Her expression softens. "I just don't know how much longer I can see you getting your hopes up and then crushed all over again. And as the days go on, I'm finding it easier to…" She looks down at her ring and slowly takes it off. "I'm finally finding it easier to let go."

Bella stands over me, the sunlight illuminating her liberated gaze. In a swift motion, she takes a few steps and throws her engagement ring into the ocean. Her breaths deepen as we watch it sink along with the past that once held her captive. "When we first kissed, you said, 'This could be it. This is all we have. Right here, right now.' You've made me realize that if this is all we have, then I'm okay with that."

I stand to my feet, staring at the ocean that's now swallowed her commitment to Luca. Her words sink in. She's right. Just yesterday, I felt that this is all we have. Right here, right now. I'm not the same person I was nine days ago and neither is Bella. Our desperation to be rescued was fading before I saw that plane, and that desperation was replaced by a sense of belonging.

Bella looks down at her naked ring finger, then up at me, and I just can't wait a second longer. Our lips meet, and as I kiss her, something settles deep within. Whether we stay or go, I know one thing for certain. *Bella is the love of my life.*

I gently pull back, just far enough to meet her eyes once more. Her lips are parted, our breaths shallow as she waits for me to kiss her again. I don't know what's going through her mind. I don't know how much of it still dwells on Luca and how much of it now dwells on me. But does it matter? Bella is the love of my life and I don't want to wait to prove it to her. This new life may not be temporary. It may be forever, and our forever may not last much longer. So, why wait?

"Bella," I exhale against her lips. Her eyes widen with curiosity. "I know you haven't finished reading," I say. "I know you haven't figured everything out, but you need to know... I love you."

The surprise in her gaze becomes known.

There's no fear, no hesitation. Just understanding.

"I know it's only been nine days. Look, we could get off this island tomorrow or spend the rest of our lives here," I continue, caressing the back of her head. "Regardless of what happens, I want to be with you. I *need* to be with you." Tears trickle down Bella's cheeks, her breath catching in her throat. "Marry me," I whisper. "Not because we're stuck here, not because you're all I have, but because you're all I need. We'll do it right here. I'll marry you right here on this island in the middle of nowhere. Tomorrow."

I can see the emotions swirling in Bella's gaze. The shock,

uncertainty, everything we've been through up until this point. It hasn't even been a day since the idea of "us" became our reality, but your idea of reality changes when tomorrow is no longer promised. My heart begins to pound with more aggression while I wait for her response.

Bella inhales a deep breath, then nods. "Yes." Tears well in her eyes before they trickle over her smile. "Yes, yes, I'll marry you."

I pull her into my arms, kissing her like it's the first and last time.

The pile of sticks and debris beside us is no longer my lifeline. Love is my lifeline.

And whether or not we are found,

Bella and I have found something real, something that will last.

🐦🐦🐦

I crouch over the fire pit, keeping my hands steady as I strike the stones. A spark lights up the moonlit beach for a second, an ember flickering to life as it kisses the pile of sticks and leaves. I cup my hands over the pit, gently blowing until the fire catches.

"You're getting better at this," Bella chirps from behind.

"Which part?" I ask between gentle blows.

"Everything." She nestles up against her backpack, the flames illuminating her admiration. "I think you would do just fine without me."

I lie next to Bella and toss a few twigs into the fire. "I don't even want to imagine life on this island without you."

She smiles softly at the dancing flames while caressing her journal. My eyes hover over her bare feet, up her smooth legs, and along the white trim of her romper until I meet her eyes. Her hair is one with the evening breeze and I have no choice but to appreciate her in a new light. I woke up this morning as a single man, and tonight, I will fall asleep engaged to marry the reason I'm still alive.

"So, little miss writer. Have you ever thought about what your first book would be about?"

Bella slightly tilts her chin, pondering my question. Her eyes drop to the journal in her lap. "You know, I've talked a lot about writing a book, but this is all I've really ever written."

"It's good, Bella." I rest my hand on her inner thigh. "It's really good."

She smiles. "We'll see if you feel that way when we reach the end."

While a small part of me hates that I have to sit through Luca and Bella's love story, I know it still has to be done for her to put it all behind her. She's already chosen me. The story about how Luca and Bella fell in love is now just a chapter in the story about how Roman and Bella fall in love. So, if I have to listen to how the two of them fell in love so we can fall in love, so be it. After we reach that last page, it'll be me. Only me.

Bella rests her head on my shoulder while flipping through pages. She suddenly pauses on the page we left off. "I should warn you, the story gets a little rocky."

I kiss the top of her head. "What do you mean?"

"It's—well…" She releases a shaky breath. "You'll hear for yourself."

I nod, fixated on the dancing flames. Bella clears her throat, and I get lost in her words as she reads…

Laguna Beach, California
Friday - May 31st, 2019

The sirens are loud.

I can't breathe. I can't think. Fire. There was a fire. The bookstore, my home. All of it was on fire. Every book family photo piece of furniture every bedroom every THING we have ever owned burning to ash in front of my very own eyes. I can't breathe. I can't think. How? How could this happen? What did we do to deserve this? Me. Is it me? Is it my fault this happened?

The sirens are so damn loud.

Dad.

I cling to Dad's hand as the sirens scream just outside the ambulance we're crammed inside. His hand is heavy, limp in mine. It's the only thing I feel. The rest of me? Numb. A thick layer of ash coats his swollen fingertips. There's an oxygen mask over his lifeless face as he lies face up. It's helping him, right? It has to be helping him. His chest hardly dips and rises. I breathe shallow breaths just so he can breathe more of the oxygen taking up the ambulance. He'll wake up. Fires don't kill people they don't burn, right? That's a fact? That's a fact. It has to be a fact. He'll wake up. He'll wake up and everything will be okay because this isn't actually happening. This can't be happening.

The sirens are so damn LOUD.

After everything Dad and I have been through, we're supposed to see better days. After everything Luca and I have been through, we're supposed to find our happy ending. This isn't supposed to be a part of our story. We aren't supposed to lose it all. *I'm not supposed to lose you, Dad.*

The smell of smoke is still stuck in my nose. It's everywhere, which means it has to be in Dad's lungs. I set Dad's hand back on the stretcher, then I clasp my own hands together. I close my eyes, rocking back and forth.

"God, please," I pray in a whisper. "You can have the apartment. The photos, jewelry, all of it. You can have every page of every book in the bookstore. Just let me keep my dad." I rock back and forth some more. "You already took Mom. Please don't take Dad."

I wipe my runny nose. I have no idea where Luca is. We were separated the moment the medics and firefighters arrived, leaving me wondering where we're going and who's going to be wherever we end up. Two medics are sitting in the corners near the front of the ambulance. The urgency once written across their faces has been replaced by relaxed expressions. Do they know something I don't?

"Is he going to be okay?" I ask, the sight of them blurred by tears.

The medics glance at each other, then one gives me a subtle nod and a forced smile.

I don't speak medic, but if I did, then that weak nod seemed a whole lot like a "no."

Everything jolts as the ambulance makes a sharp left turn. My body sways forward, the medics remaining still and unfazed. This must be their millionth trip. This is my first. The oxygen tank shifts, the equipment shaking even after we come to a stop. I catch a glimpse of the hospital entrance through the tiny windows in the back of the ambulance.

I'm frozen, watching the medics now standing over Dad. The back doors suddenly burst open, light flooding the back of the ambulance in a mere blink. It's so bright, and everything happens so fast. Too fast.

"Let's move! Let's move!" more medics shout from outside.

Before I know it, I'm following an entire medical team as they roll Dad down the ramp. Even more medics and nurses run outside the hospital entrance like they've been waiting this whole time, helping roll him through the entrance. I follow weakly behind, everything around me blending together as I walk through the sliding doors.

I'm blinded by a wave of fluorescent lights when we enter the emergency room lobby. The white glow and harsh scents overwhelm me, sharp voices and commands being shouted from right to left, then left to right. Metal benches are bolted along the pale blue walls, and a long desk separates worried families from a small group of nurses in the corner.

"Stay here a second, miss." A nurse grabs my arm, dragging her studious eyes up and down my body for injuries. I shake my head. Her grip tightens. "Miss, I need you to stay right here."

"No," I manage. They keep rolling Dad up the hall, his body swaying with every jolting movement. "Dad! Dad!"

Doctors and nurses weave between each other in a way that's both rehearsed and chaotic at the same time. I point a shaky finger at the double doors they wheel Dad's gurney through. This can't be the last I see him. This can't be how his story ends. No, no, no. *I'm not supposed to lose you.*

"Shh, shh," the nurse whispers calmly. She guides me to a nearby bench, my feet cold against the tiles.

"I need to be with him."

"You've done everything you can," she whispers. "Now the doctors need to do everything they can."

I sit back, bringing my knees to my chest.

He can't die. Please, God. Don't let my dad die.

I never got a chance to say goodbye.

The room feels cold, which I suppose is what the room should feel like when it shares a wall with the edge of life and death. The chill lurks through the wall, seeping into my bones. The strong stinge of chemicals and bleach replaces the smell of smoke, but it burns all the same. I press my forehead against my knees. I thought I had all the time in the world, so much time I didn't even consider time itself worth considering.

I stare at the blue and gray tiles, my gaze tracing scuffs and stains that each tell their own story. I see stories of lives saved and lives taken. I see families dissolving the distance between themselves and doctors as they're told what their next chapters entail.

Sounds of shuffling feet mix with whispers, beeping machines, and a baby crying nearby. As the commotion starts to settle, I can think somewhat clearly again. I replay the scene in my mind. The flames, the people standing and watching, Luca running inside and pulling Dad from the burning building, and then I remember Abel watching it all unravel from the van.

The memory lingers, becoming more potent as my racing thoughts release me from their grasp. Just as we were being escorted into the ambulance, I noticed the van parked toward the end of the street. I remember seeing the driver's side door hanging open, and in the light emitted from the flames, I remember seeing Abel just sitting there, watching my world burn. How did he know where I live? And of all the times I could see him outside of my home, why is the one time while it's burning to the ground?

I have no idea how much time has passed when the nurse taps my shoulder. Minutes? Hours? It doesn't even matter. All that matters is that she's standing next to a doctor who may have answers to questions I'm scared to ask. From the look on the doctor's face, I can tell it's bad. I know it's bad. He has that look on his face like the one in the movies where they prepare to be the bearer of bad news. Regardless, he knows something I don't.

The doctor clears his throat. "Are you the daughter?"

I nod.

"I'm Dr. . . ." He sighs, fixating on the looming desperation written all over my face. Then, he sits next to me. "I'm Keith." His eyes drop to my ash-covered feet and hands. He carefully thinks through his next words before speaking them softly. "Your father is stable." His voice cuts out. "But, he's. . . currently. . . in a medically induced coma."

The chill crawls up my spine. *A coma.*

Keith pushes through rehearsed empathy that makes me want to scream. "Your father's lungs were severely damaged from the smoke inhalation. We performed an emergency intubation and put him on a ventilator to help him breathe for the time being." He pauses, fixating on his clipboard. "And his heart," he adds, looking up. "The stress from the fire really took a toll, so we had to perform a cardiac catheterization. It's where we put a thin tube through a blood vessel that leads to the heart to help with circulation."

I sit motionless, still hung up on the first thing he said. "*A coma.*" In this moment, all I'm good for is imagining Dad being kept alive by machines somewhere in this building. If there's one person in this world who doesn't deserve even the smallest bit of pain, it's him. He's done nothing but read books and love me. That's it.

If there is a God somewhere out there, how could He let this happen? Dad already lost Mom and spent years trying to get over that loss. He doesn't deserve to be trapped in his own mind, hooked up to wires and tubes. Not him.

"How long?" I ask in a whisper. My eyes meet Keith's. "How long will he be stuck like this?"

Keith chews on his bottom lip. "I wish I could give you an answer, but every situation is different. It could be days, weeks." His face softens. "Look, what's important is that your father is stable. He's resting. His body needs to recover, and we're going to do everything we can to make sure it does."

I regret asking the question before it leaves my lips. "And what if he doesn't wake up? What then?"

"We cross that bridge when we get to it."

Keith lifts his chin, eyes fixating on a nurse who approaches us. When I look up, she opens her stance toward Luca. I stand and throw my arms around him, tears trickling down my cheeks. He embraces me and I can't help but feel the fragility in his core after pulling Dad from the fire.

"I'm so sorry, Bella," Luca whispers, resting his chin atop my head.

"I did everything I could."

"You saved his life," Keith says to Luca. "And now we'll do everything we can to return him to you healthy and well." He flashes an apologetic smile before continuing back through the double doors alongside the nurse.

Luca lifts my chin. His empathetic eyes flick between mine, then he pulls me into his chest, running his fingers through my hair. Our embrace is warm, steady. It's as if he's holding all of my pieces together, and the moment he lets go, each piece will meet the floor. The stench of ash still clings mercilessly to the fabric of his shirt. Even in the safety of this hospital, I can't rid myself of the tragedy that has made up tonight.

I close my eyes, tightening my grip on him. "I saw the van."

"The van?"

"Your van." I pull back, looking up at him. "Before I ended up in the ambulance, I saw Abel sitting in the driver's seat. It was parked across the street where he was just sitting, watching. It was almost like he was *waiting.*"

Confusion etches itself in Luca's expression. "Abel?" He shakes his head. "Abel what? He was there?"

"I saw him."

"No." He loosens his hold on me. "There's no way. He would have said something. He would have helped." My assumption lingers between us, waiting to be addressed. He turns away, running his hands back through his hair. "Bella, what're you saying?"

I cross my arms, holding my tongue.

"Bella," Luca says more sternly this time. "What are you saying?"

I avert my eyes from his, nervously tapping my foot against the floor.

"You think Abel did this," he states, anger tightening his tone.

"You said it yourself," I reply. "You said Abel isn't a good guy. You said you were scared to leave the band because of what he might do!"

Luca just keeps shaking his head, pacing around the lobby. "He wouldn't burn your fucking house down with your dad inside, Bella. Is that what you're implying?!" The anger pokes through his once-calm demeanor.

My entire body trembles. Regardless of whether or not Abel is behind this, the accusation alone carries more weight than Luca can bear. It's one thing to imagine Abel being the cause of all this. It's another to say it out loud. And there's no taking it back now. "Why else would he be there?!" I ask.

"You're in shock," Luca says as he grabs my arms. "Abel wasn't there. He wouldn't do this to get back at me for choosing you over the band."

"He didn't do it to get back at *you*." I tilt my chin. "He did it to get back at *me* for stealing you from him. Think about it. You're the only family he has left. Without you, he has no family, no band. Without you, he has nothing."

Luca lowers his head and releases a shaky breath. Strands of singed, golden hair hang over the sides of his face. When his eyes meet mine again, they're full of rage. "I'll be back," he snarls before turning toward the exit.

"Luca!" I call out. "You can't just leave me here!" My voice cracks in desperation, but it's already too late. He's already out the sliding doors. "You can't just leave me here alone."

I fold forward, using the bench to keep me from collapsing. Luca's sudden absence strikes me like a tidal wave, leaving me gasping for air. Where is he going? What's he planning to do? Tears sting in my eyes, and I try to force them back. I can't let this break me. Not here, not now. As the doors slide shut, I'm left alone with my thoughts, left alone with the sound of beeping machines, worried families, and whispering nurses, left all alone.

Laguna Beach, California
Saturday - June 1st, 2019

There are 22 panels making up the ceiling of Dad's hospital room. The panel right above my seat has a crack in it. It's a jagged line that stretches halfway across the panel. The panel next to that panel has a smudge. It's a tiny smudge, and I wonder how it even got there each time I look at it. Does it matter? Nope. It's just something I've noticed after an entire night of staring at the ceiling.

The sun is setting outside, forcing me to accept that Dad has been in a coma for almost 24 hours now. *Coma.* The word still sends shivers down my spine. To think that "Dad" and "coma" are being mentioned in the same sentence—well, that's the thing. I don't want to think about it.

My eyes drop to the tray of food the nurse left me almost an hour ago. I haven't left the room since Dad was admitted. Since then, the nurses have started to treat me like a patient. With Dad lying peacefully still while attached to his oxygen machine and a few other machines, the nurses usually come in to replace a few bags, check a few numbers, then ask me how I'm doing. I'm damaged, and I'm as good as damaged gets.

I pull my knees to my chest, resting my chin on them as I watch Dad's stomach rise and fall. As long as he's breathing, he's alive. As long as the beeps remain steady, he's alive. My dad has always been my everything, so as long as *he's* alright, *everything* will be alright.

Abel sitting in his van outside the fire is the clearest memory I have of the night, and I can't force the thought out of my mind no matter how hard I try. I want answers, to know how the fire started. Something tells me Abel might be the answer I'm looking for, and Luca was persistent in finding out for himself. I haven't heard from him since he stormed out of the hospital last night, and I don't know whether or not that's a good thing.

At this point, I don't even know if there's any good left in this world. You begin to wonder where the good went when you see your dad's rosy cheeks go pale, when you see a machine breathing for him, when you...

"How's he doing?" Tish asks, stepping into the room.

"The same," I whisper, rubbing my sleepless eyes. "Have you seen Luca?"

Tish sits in the chair across Dad's hospital bed. With the subtle shake of her head, she says, "You haven't heard from him?"

I lift my phone between us. "My phone died after I called you." I fixate on the rhythm of Dad's breathing. "And there's no rush to hear from him. Everything I need is right here."

Tish glances at Dad for a moment before her eyes flick to the ceiling. "Oh, Donald." Her voice cracks, tears welling. After a few silent beats, she murmurs, "You know your dad's always been like a dad to me."

I flash a faint smile. "Because you've always been like a sister to me."

"Dammit, Bella," Tish's voice breaks, tears now streaming down her cheeks. "How could this happen? You two, of all people. You don't deserve this. Never in a million years."

"It was Abel," I say with steady certainty, hoping that the more I say it, the better I'll feel. "Abel started the fire."

She tilts her head. "You can't be serious. How do you know?"

"Before we were taken to the hospital, I saw Abel sitting in the van outside the fire."

"Abel was outside of your house?" Tish leans forward.

I nod.

She freezes. "Did you tell Luca?"

I nod.

"Did Luca confront him?"

"Luca left as soon as I told him what I saw," I say, forcing down the lump in my throat. "He hasn't been back since."

Tish gets up and sits beside me on the couch. Her presence is warm, grounding. She gently runs her hands through my hair and pulls me toward her shoulder. I rest my head, my tears staining the fabric of her jeans. "Luca will make things right. All we can do is be here for your dad."

I nod, feeling the weight of my accusation lessen. It feels better now that Tish knows what I saw without fighting me on it. But I can't shake the flicker of doubt in the back of my mind. I want to believe that Luca is confronting Abel. I want to believe that someone somewhere knows what put Dad in this situation. And a small part of me wants to go back to the day I met Luca, to convince myself to stay out of the water. Because maybe—just maybe—if I never went in, I would've never met Luca, which means Dad would still be sitting behind the counter at our bookstore.

I hear it before I see it. The sound of an alarm forces me awake, shattering the stillness of the room. I wince at the sound, looking in every which direction as doctors and nurses flood the room. My eyes land on the monitor between the bodies weaving in and around each other before they reach Dad. The green line on the screen erratically spikes and dips.

"No," I gasp.

Tish is slow to wake, then quick to acknowledge the brewing chaos.

"WE NEED A CRASH CART! NOW!" a nurse shouts, standing over Dad.

Another nurse gestures for Tish and me to stand, but I can't move. "Girls, we need you to step out of the room."

"No," I gasp again, my legs rooted to the floor. "I need to stay. Please let me stay."

I can't let them separate us again.

"WHAT ARE THEY STILL DOING IN HERE?" a doctor shouts toward us.

Two pairs of hands grab us by the shoulders.

I scream over the piercing beeps and frantic voices. "I'm not leaving him!"

I straighten my legs, making it harder for the nurses to drag me out. My body folds as I'm held up by arms I can't see because my eyes are glued to the defibrillator they hold over Dad. It's the last thing I see until the door slams in my face.

I struggle to breathe between sobs. Tish pulls me into her embrace and we collapse against the wall, then slide down to the floor. The wall is cold against my back, my head overwhelmed by the sound of my thrashing heart.

This can't be happening. Dad was just breathing. He was right there, right in front of me. He was just sitting behind the counter in the bookstore. He was just sitting across the round table playing cards with me. He was just here.

My world freezes, each second stretching into eternity. I don't know how long we sit there, but I know the ache in my chest isn't going anywhere until I wake from this nightmare. Tish and I tremble in each other's arms, wallowing in disbelief while the hallway clock ticks in the stillness.

After what feels like forever, the sounds from the other side of the wall go silent. The door opens slowly, and a nurse cautiously steps into the hall. "Bella?" I don't even have to look up at her to know. "We did everything we could."

Her words don't reach me because they don't matter.

The words have already been written.

The chapter has already come to an end.

Dad is gone.

10 DAYS STRANDED

I spent all of this morning preparing for what might be the most important day of my life. The first light of dawn has broken over the horizon, a warm glow casting over the shimmering ocean. It's as if God painted the sky in shades of gold, creating the perfect day for the perfect wedding.

I carefully place the most beautiful seashells I could find in two straight lines leading to the water. With Bella making preparations of her own on the other side of the island, I've gone all in on surprising her with a venue for our ceremony, one that will hopefully compete with the weddings in the books she reads. The past 10 days on this island have forced us to feel many emotions—confusion, loneliness, fear, hope, determination, acceptance. We've ridden some low lows and higher highs. And today, we may reach the peak.

My heart hurts for Bella after hearing about how she lost her dad. I once considered myself strong, but I'll confess that losing my parents the way Bella has lost hers? That would kill me, but it didn't kill Bella. It makes me wonder how she can embody such grace and purity despite enduring such a loss. She's fought her own battles, wrestled with God, and still stands with divine strength. It's inspiring, and it's all starting to make sense why she was so eager and willing to seek a new adventure.

By now, I know Bella reads to escape her heart-shattering past.

By now, I know Bella smiles to keep from crying tears she has every right to cry.

I lay out a few rows of rocks on both sides of the center aisle made up of seashells. On one side, I place three rocks side by side. On the other, I place another three rocks. At the end of the aisle closest to the water, I built a mound of sand we'd use as a stage to stand on. I stabbed two palm leaves into the sand on both sides of the mound, each leaf standing tall. I run up the shore toward the palm trees, then look down at my creation. From the aisle bordered by seashells and rocks to the standing palms separated by the hill of sand, it's perfect.

My pride is threatened by an underlying pain when I realize that our family and friends won't be here to witness this.

Ma, Pa, and Mac on my side.

Bella's mom, dad, and Tish on Bella's side.

As I sit at the top of the beach, I see it clear as day. Ma sitting on one side of me, Pa on the other. Pa would be wearing a hideous Hawaiian shirt Ma would've picked out for him. I would burst out in laughter the moment I saw it. Ma would already be a wreck, crying because of how proud she is that I met the love of my life.

Pa would place a comforting hand on my shoulder and ask, "You ready?"

"Yes, sir," I would reply.

"And how do you know you're ready?" he would ask with a smirk.

"I feel it in my mind, heart, and gut."

Pa's thick mustache would curl into a smile, his eyes crinkling as he pats my back. "Thatta kid," he would say. "You did good, been good."

Ma would chime in, patting her cheeks dry. "I knew God always had His hand on you. This is beautiful, Rome. And Bella is even more beautiful." She would lie her cheek against my shoulder, taking it all in.

"Check it out!" Mac would shout, ruining the moment as he steps in front of us in nothing but a bow tie and swimsuit. "I combined 'wedding' dress code with 'island' dress code."

I would stand and embrace him. "My best man."

"But, not the better man," he would reply, pulling back with a firm hand on my shoulder. "That's all you, brother."

I would be holding back tears, grateful to be blessed with a loving family that would never hesitate to stand by me. And as I look up at the sky that's been stroked with soft streaks of pink and white, I understand that everything I have ever done has led me here and now for a reason: to heal with Bella.

After making final arrangements and when the sun is at its highest, I make my way back home to check on Bella. As I step through the palms, I find her sitting just outside our small house, her arms wrapping her knees while she remains fixated on the lapping waves before her. Something in the air has shifted back on this side of the island, thick with an unsettling energy I wasn't expecting after a morning of fantasizing.

"Everything okay?" I ask, crouching beside her.

Bella shoots me a half-glance, then wipes at her cheeks. "Hey!" She forces a smile. "I'm just getting ready!"

Oh, God. I notice the journal lying on the sand in front of her. My heart aches, my mind racing through all the reasons she could be crying. These aren't tears of joy. Tears of doubt? Reluctance, maybe? I begin to feel like an asshole for pressuring Bella into doing something as insane as committing her entire life to a man she hasn't even known for two full weeks. She boarded that cruise engaged to marry Luca, and now I'm expecting her to walk down the aisle for me. Just two days ago, we kissed. Just yesterday, she threw her ring into the ocean. And today, we're supposed to get married?

"It's not you." Bella's voice pierces through my train of thought. She pats the sand beside her, and I sit without thinking twice. "You're perfect," she says, taking my hand and resting it on her lap. "I don't regret falling for you and I don't regret wanting to marry you." Her eyes fall to her journal. "I just need to put my past to rest before I move on."

"That's okay," I say, tightening my hand around hers. "I don't want to pressure you into anything. I know you've been to hell and back, and I would never expect you to just let go of everything you've been through. I know it was–*is*–hard. Regardless, I'm here for you every step of the way."

Disappointment tugs at me, but I force myself to swallow it down. What Bella and I have is too new, and I can't expect her to bury the closure she needs. Her history with Luca and the trauma of her past matter. My eyes drift to the same waves that swallowed her ring yesterday. There was certainty behind her actions, but grief doesn't work that way. I would be a fool to think she could let go of loving someone so quickly.

If there's one thing Bella has taught me, it's that love isn't simple. In fact, it's far from it. I used to think that it was something you could just turn on and off, that you could disconnect from the person you love in the blink of an eye or the turn of your cheek. *If only.*

"We have time, but promise me something," I say softly. "Promise me that you won't look at what's on the other side of the island until you're ready to marry me."

Bella nods, lifting her pinky between us. I wrap her pinky with mine, and we kiss the tops of our fists. "I promise."

"Well, then." I kiss the top of her hand, then get comfortable on the sand. "Ready when you are."

She smiles, runs a hand through my hair, and then reads...

Laguna Beach, California
Saturday - July 6th, 2019

It's been over a month since I last wrote, and it's still hard for me to form words. I feel like my life has been a story that's had its pages ripped out and torn apart, then put back together out of order. The characters don't get what they deserve, not the good or the bad. Loose ends are left untied, singed at the tips so they could never be connected. No matter how hard I try, I can't make sense of any of it.

Usually, when you're reading a book, you get a pretty good idea of what might happen next. It just makes sense. You meet the characters, and you can tell which are destined for greatness and which are destined to set the world ablaze. Regardless of the right and wrong—the good and evil—it's the author's job to restore balance by the story's end. Or at least, that's what you hope for. But we don't always get what we want.

Sometimes, the book doesn't have a happy ending. Sometimes, the characters fall in love with the wrong people. They make mistake after mistake without finding redemption. They pick the wrong side. Some characters don't deserve to be hurt, but they get hurt anyway, while some characters don't deserve to find love, but they find love anyway. The innocent are wronged by the guilty, and the guilty remain innocent. The good die young and the bad live on, while I'm left wondering where everything went wrong.

Since Dad passed a month ago, I've become an empty vessel, a feather in the wind. Tish took me in, and though it hasn't been long, I can already tell I won't be able to repay her for everything she's done for me. She took time off work so I wouldn't be alone, and it's given us a chance to be there for each other.

Within a week of Dad's death, the lawyers were calling. I answered, nodding at Tish's living room wall. Shortly after, a man with a monotone voice and a rehearsed sympathy speech visited to tell me what Dad left behind. He didn't stay long, considering everything Dad left for me was lost in the fire. He did, however, give me a check for an amount the insurance companies thought would compensate for losing the only family I had left.

"What the hell am I supposed to do with this?" I asked Tish the moment the man left. "The last thing on my mind is money."

"When the time comes, you'll know," she told me.

I don't want money. I want my dad back.

The investigator overseeing the cause of the fire documented it as "accidental." I guess an old building full of books catching fire isn't uncommon, no matter my suspicions of Abel. I made sure to voice those suspicions, and the investigator still ruled it as an unfortunate event. To me, it's another case where the innocent were wronged by the guilty, and the guilty got away with it.

Luca hasn't been the same since the night of the fire. The band hasn't performed. He hasn't surfed. He *is* drinking again, though. It doesn't matter to me at this point. Everyone copes in different ways and he found his. I'm still finding mine. My gut says that the night he left to speak to Abel, he got the answer he was looking for. He never told me what that answer was, which was an answer in and of itself.

The silence

was

deafening.

I hardly recognize the girl in my bathroom mirror as I make final arrangements before Dad's funeral. Tish's black dress is tight around my frame, the fit and color foreign to me after wearing white my whole life. I've always been comfortable in white. To me, the color white is hopeful and pure. It lightens and complements all other colors, but all Tish owns is black. I feel like I'm dressed in the shadow of everything I've lost, and I must say that it suits the bags under my eyes after the sleepless nights.

A light knock on the bathroom door pulls me from my trance. I turn to see Tish peeking around the door frame, her gaze soft. "You look beautiful," she says, though we both know I don't feel it.

I nod, having no strength to thank her with words.

She steps to the middle of the doorway and holds up a white dress that catches the light seeping in through the window. It's simple yet elegant, carrying a shimmer that offers quiet comfort. The neckline is modest, the hem grazing below the knee. "I thought you would want to maybe wear this instead."

I raise a palm to cover my lips. My fingers tremble as I reach out to touch the fabric. The cool silkiness beneath my fingertips stirs something fragile within. All I can do is look at Tish, hoping she can comprehend my gratitude while I can't form the words to express how grateful I am for her.

"You shouldn't have," I finally whisper. She hands the dress to me, and it becomes an invitation, a reminder of who I am below all the sorrow. She lays it over my outstretched arms, the smooth fabric cool at the touch. My eyes meet hers, my vision blurred by tears. "Thank you."

Tish offers a subtle nod as if she's giving me permission to be myself again. Without saying a word, she smiles and steps back into the living room. After changing dresses, I meet Tish with newfound hope.

"There she is," she says, standing to her feet. "Ready?"

I force a smile.

I've passed this cemetery a million times, and not once did I think I would step foot in it so soon after Mom died. I've seen groups of all sizes standing over graves as their loved ones are lowered into the ground, and not once did I think another one of mine would join them.

Our small procession makes its way up the hill in silence. Tish keeps her arm locked in mine, my eyes locked on the hearse ahead as it rolls up the winding cemetery road. I can't look away, nor can I fully comprehend that Dad's urn is just behind the tinted glass. I have read countless books in my lifetime full of unfathomable imaginary characters and worlds, and yet, losing my dad is the one thing I can't fully wrap my head around.

The air is warm, the sun shining brightly in defiance of the gloom I feel within. As we reach the top of the hill, I push my shoulders back and lift my chin. I want to be strong for Dad and be the courageous and brave daughter he raised me to be. But, the closer we get to the top of the hill, the more my heart turns to stone. The marble structure at the top of the hill glistens under the piercing blue sky. Its edges are sharp, the white columns gleaming over the freshly cut grass.

The hearse slows to a stop, and a man picks up the golden urn that holds one of the last pieces of my heart. The sunlight reflects off the urn, the shimmer stopping me in my tracks before I walk up the marble stairs. I release a shaky breath, trying to be strong. Tish's hand gently grazes my arm, a simple gesture communicating that it's okay to not be okay.

I steady my breaths, regaining my composure, then walk up the steps as if I'm learning to walk all over again. We reach the top stair, and I catch sight of the rows of glass shelves lining the wide hall. Each holds an urn, each urn intricately designed in a unique way that reflects a unique life lived, a unique story told from beginning to end.

Names are etched below the urns, characters that have reached their final chapters. Dad's urn will sit among them, his own story tying into the story of this town and the world beyond.

We make our way down the hall, beams of light shining through narrow slits carved into the marble ceiling. The serene sound of a violin plays at the end of the hall where silhouettes have gathered, and when we near the back wall, I'm caught by surprise. People from all over town have gathered, forming a half-circle that faces the back wall of glass shelves beneath a colorful mosaic art piece. Locals of all ages stand side by side, some families and others individuals, all taking time out of their day to celebrate Dad's life.

Dad's urn is placed on a marble altar in the middle of the corridor, and one by one, people walk up to place items around the urn. Hand-written cards, bookmarks, small bouquets, and novels they bought from the store. It dawns on me that although Dad spent most of his time reading behind the countertop at the store, the books he stocked the shelves with each played a role in the lives of so many readers. Thanks to Dad, people could embark on adventures they never could have imagined embarking on themselves. Thanks to Dad, they rode dragons, found treasure, and fell in love time and time again.

Tish releases my arm and joins Luca in the front row of the small crowd as I step behind the altar. Pride mingles with sadness as I recognize faces from old times and new. I force a smile, unfolding my eulogy.

Be strong, I remind myself. *Be strong.*

After a quivering breath, I read aloud. "Being the daughter of a bookstore owner, my life has always been nothing short of surreal." I inhale, I exhale. "Dad would tell me that our lives are our stories. Some stories are sweet, and some are tragic. Some are pure, and some are tainted by sorrow and pain. But, all are nonetheless stories that help shape us. If you stepped into the bookstore, you could feel the magic he found in every story he would read.

"After my mom passed, Dad would talk about how their story wasn't over. They were just two characters who parted ways for a few chapters, and every once in a while, he would remind me that one day, they would find their way back to each other. He believed that God, 'The Author,' held the pen, and His story was already written. Dad would just have to enjoy every line, every paragraph, every chapter, the best he could because that's all we can do as characters in God's story. We don't get to write our own stories, but we can choose to find the good in them.

"It wouldn't be fair for me to be upset about losing my dad so suddenly because my dad wasn't upset when he lost my mom. Now, even as I struggle to come to terms with him being gone, I recognize that this is just a chapter that came to a close, and I find peace in knowing that the end of my chapter with Dad marks the beginning of a new chapter where Dad reunites with Mom." I pan around the saddened group, tears welling in my eyes as I say, "To everyone here, my dad didn't just sell books. He shared magic and adventure. If we leave here with anything, let it be this: Life is a precious, fleeting story, and it's up to us to fill each page with love, peace, and our wildest adventures. So, we get out there and we find it. We find true love, we make our peace, and we embark on our wildest adventures."

I place my hand on the cool urn, tears rolling down my cheeks. "Dad, thank you for sharing your story with me. I'll take your story everywhere I go, and when mine is said and done, I pray it be filled with the adventure you inspired."

I step back, and after a few silent beats, an attendant gently lifts the urn and places it behind a glass door next to my mother's urn. The two rest side by side, illuminated by the sunlight seeping through the ceiling. The sight stirs bittersweet peace within the depths of my being when I read not only Mom's name but Dad's, too. The attendant carefully locks the glass door and then makes their way back behind the group.

I step forward, placing my palm on the glass. "Enjoy your next adventure," I whisper over Mom and Dad. "And someday soon, I'll be right there to enjoy it with you."

The afternoon takes a toll on me in more ways than one. I'm physically exhausted from standing out in the sun and emotionally drained from receiving endless condolences for my loss. I'm grateful, truly. It just pains me to hear how much pleasure people found in my dad's company at the bookstore *after* he's gone. My dad was the happiest man, but it would've made him even happier to know that he touched so many lives by just being himself.

"Bella dear?" Ms. Rivera's voice makes itself known over the few nearby conversations.

I turn to see her wearing a lush, lavender dress. Her presence both calming and radiant, she politely greets me with a nod. The neckline of her dress curves softly, framing her collarbone in understated elegance. Tiny flowers have been sewn across the hem, her silver hair falling in soft curls along the sides of her face.

"Thanks for coming, Ms. Rivera." I hold the hand she offers me, then meet her halfway for a hug I didn't realize I needed until now.

Tears introduce themselves under Ms. Rivera's thick, purple glasses. "I've been coming to your bookstore since you were a little girl." She pats her tears with a handkerchief. "Your parents were such a light, and I have no doubt you will continue to be a light for them."

A shaky breath leaves my lips.

"Donald told me you were writing a book?"

I blink at Ms. Rivera's question, taken by surprise. "I… I am. Well, I want to."

"I would never rush you, darling." She nods, her palm grazing my forearm. "But, when you're ready to make it happen, give my daughter a call." She carefully places a small business card in the palm of my hand, then smiles. "Her name is Rachel. She's a book publisher living in Manhattan. I mention you every time I talk to her on the phone. When I lost my husband and my daughter moved away, your bookstore was the only place that brought me peace." She releases my hand and then steps around me. "Your dad was right when he said that life is a precious, fleeting story. Make the most of yours, Bella."

With that, Ms. Rivera turns and gracefully heads back down the winding road. I stand there, staring at the delicate business card in my hand. The edges are slightly frayed as if she was waiting for the perfect time to give it to me. Her daughter's name is printed across the front in bold letters, the address of the New York publishing house lining the bottom.

When I look up, Ms. Rivera has disappeared beneath the canopy of trees that loom over the winding road stretching down toward the water. I slip the card into my purse, then find Luca sitting at the top of the stairs. His hair hangs over the sides of his face. He taps a melody over his knee, deep in thought until he notices me approaching. I sit beside him, watching people head back down the hill. After hours of quick conversations, I settle in for what may be a long conversation with Luca.

"Juliet," Luca greets in a whisper. His hand meets my thigh. "How're you doing?"

"As good as I could be." I wrap his hand in mine. "You've been distant."

Luca exhales a nervous laugh, tucking a few strands of golden hair behind his ear. "I don't handle death very well."

"I can tell," I say a little too quickly.

It's easy for me to become skeptical of Luca distancing himself since the night of the fire. How could I not be? He's gone from being a stranger to wanting me, to nearly taking advantage of me, to loving me, to becoming a stranger all over again. Deep down, I've always yearned for adventure, and I thought Luca was that adventure. I'm starting to think I can't settle for whatever adventure this is.

Luca reaches into his breast pocket and pulls out a metal flask. He undoes the cap and takes a sip as if he didn't just break one of his promises right in front of me. It's one thing to have smelled it on him the past few times we've seen each other. He at least had the decency to somewhat try to hide it then, but this? This is just a whole new level of disrespect.

"You're drinking again," I say, willing to risk disturbing our peaceful moment.

"I'm coping," he snaps. He takes another sip, one longer than the last.

"Right. I forgot you lost your dad." My words leave my lips in the form of daggers. They're sharp and violent. I can't help it. He's being selfish. He's withdrawing from me during what may be the most difficult time of my life while offering himself wholly to his vices.

Luca lowers his head, disappointed. "Bella, I'm trying."

"You're not." I spring to my feet and walk down the steps to face him when I say, "Ever since the fire, you've been distant. In the days leading up to that night when you started spending more time with me and less with Abel, I was starting to see a better side of you. I saw it! You even said it yourself!"

He subtly looks around at the remaining guests still lingering around the reception. "Can we not do this right now?" he slurs.

I can no longer hold back tears I thought were used up on Dad. "I'm losing you, Luca!" I shout over him. I lean forward, my voice cracking the more I speak. "I've lost everything. My family, my home, my books. All of it just burned to the ground for no reason at all. All of it... just... burned to ash."

"Bella." Luca mumbles words under his breath, a drunken slur. I can't hold back the wave of frustration and anger that threatens a fleeting peace I once held. I love Luca, and if there's one thing I've learned, it's that loving Luca comes at the price of losing everything.

"Can't you see that all I wanted was for you to love me? Since I met you, you became all I thought about, all I could see." I clench a fist with one hand and point at him with the other. "I fell so hard for you, I didn't realize my best friend was suffering. I didn't realize that I put the rest of my life on hold. I didn't realize my world was on fire until it was too late." Luca mumbles something again louder this time, but I keep going, hoping that at some point, this will make me feel better. "Bad things aren't supposed to happen to good people, not for no reason. And now I can't help but think it's my fault."

"It's not your fault, Bella. Please, just..." Luca cries into his palms before dragging them down his face. "It's—"

STILL

10 DAYS STRANDED

"Why'd you stop?" I ask Bella when she shuts the journal. She stares down at the weathered leather, her face flushed. Her hands are trembling, sweat coating her forehead. "Bella?"

She keeps looking down, detached from the present moment. It's as if she's been trapped in her own story, bound by the very words she wrote herself. I can see the memory replaying in her eyes. Memories swirl between specks of blue and brown. I see the white dress, the cemetery, the conversation with Luca. Every scene is riddled with pain and regret, every word embedded in her mind, cemented into every fiber of her being the way ink has seeped into the pages of her journal. The words are forever there, the page poisoned by her pen and her past. In an instant, she rips out the last few pages of her journal.

"BELLA!" I shout, but it's too late. "What're you doing?!"

Bella springs to her feet and makes a beeline for the water. I sprint after her as she crumples up the pages. There's a determination in her step, a commitment she made to herself the moment she reached what may be the climax of her love story.

Just as she winds up to throw the crumpled pages into the

ocean, I grab her arm. "You can't!" I exclaim. "You can't just throw your story away!"

"You don't get it." Bella fights back. "I have to!" She yanks her arm, trying to free herself from my grip. It kills me to think I may leave a bruise the way Luca once did, but this is her life, her book, her legacy. I can't let her bury her past because we weren't brought here to bury it. We were brought here to make peace with it.

"Just listen to me," I plead.

"I thought I could do it," she whispers between sobs. "But, what I'm about to read is the reason I don't think I can move on, no matter how hard I try. It's the reason I'm stuck somewhere between my past and whatever lies ahead."

"You're not stuck," I state, keeping a firm hold on Bella's arm. "You're healing. You said it yourself. It's why we were brought here." Her tears form streams down her cheeks while she stands with one foot pointing toward me, the other toward the lapping waves. "If it weren't for you reminding me to use the hourglass, to keep digging through my past, I wouldn't be where I am right now."

"Stuck on an island?" she snaps.

"*Alive*," I correct her, our eyes locked. "And ready to love you with everything I am."

I can see my words seeping into Bella's conscience. I can feel her restraint dissolve in my own hand. As much as I want her to forget Luca, as much as I want her to throw not just the remaining pages but the entire love story they share into the deepest depths of the ocean, I can't let her. She would be cementing what may be the darkest part of her past into the depths of her heart. Loving her would be like trying to keep her afloat with a weight tied to her ankle. She cut my weight loose, and now it's my turn to cut hers.

Bella's eyes linger on mine for a few moments longer, the stream of tears drying out. When I no longer feel a trace of resistance, I cautiously release her arm. My heart calms when I see that I didn't leave a bruise on her arm the way Luca once did. Her hand quivers as she opens her palm for me to take the crumpled pages.

I carefully take the pages, fold them, then slip them into my pocket. An emotional pain sends an ache through my chest when I see the defeat in her gaze. I know Bella is stronger than this. I know her past is more difficult than I once imagined, but the angelic spirit she embodies has not once lost its light. It's because her beauty is made up of her brokenness. Her peace is made up of her pain. She's seen the darkness of night, which allows her to embrace a new light.

I take her hand in mine. "Someday soon, you're going to be stronger than you ever thought." She looks up at me with a softened gaze. I hold back my smirk, waiting for her to realize we just started playing our game. "Go on. It's your turn."

Bella's brows lift with warmth. She whispers, "Someday soon, you'll be happier than you ever thought."

"Someday soon, we'll love each other more than we thought we could."

I guide Bella under the porch of our home. I sit with my back against one of the large rocks, pulling her in so that her cheek rests against my shoulder. My fingers gently trace her hip, my nails trailing up her side and in circles over her shoulder. With every circle I trace, she relaxes just a little bit more.

"Someday soon, you'll be the best swimmer on this island," she breathes against my chest.

I struggle to hold back a smile. "You almost got me there." I look around the island to see a place that once brought pain now holding hope for a future together. Be it a day, a week, months, or years, a future together is all I can hope for. "Someday soon, I'll marry you," I promise her.

I feel her cheek rise into a smile.

"Aha," I utter softly. "You lose, ma'am."

Bella keeps smiling. "Fine by me." She presses her hand against my chest, rubbing over the fabric of my shirt as she sits up, then raises an open palm.

I sit up, legs crisscrossed. "Are you sure?"

She nods, an underlying defiance manifesting itself between us as she lifts her chin. I take out the folded pages and place them in her hand. Taking cautious, calculated breaths to calm herself, she straightens the pages and smooths them over her thigh. The atmosphere falls silent, and I wait patiently as she braces herself for impact.

Bella glances up at me, sadness flickering in her expression before she blinks it away. "Alright," she whispers. "Time to make peace, once and for all."

I place a supportive hand on her leg, using my thumb to gently graze admiration and respect over her. Regardless of what's written on these final pages, I know what awaits us on the other side–a heart set free and weightless, guilt-free love shared for eternity.

She reads…

"It's not your fault, Bella. Please, just…" Luca cries into his palms before dragging them down his face. "It's–"

"How can losing my dad not be my fault?" I press my fingers to my temples, pacing beneath the staircase where he sits watching me. "He could hardly look after himself. He needed me. He needed me to check on him and make sure he was okay. I should have been there and I wasn't and I would've seen the fire starting if I was there."

"HE DID IT!" In a sharp move, Luca stands from the stairs and grabs me. His hands are tight around my bare arms, his bloodshot eyes wild and desperate. His breath is laced with liquor as he hisses through gritted teeth, "ABEL STARTED THE FUCKING FIRE."

The words echo around the cemetery, settling all around us like scattered ash.

Abel

started

the

fucking

fire.

I remember the thought popping into my mind while in the ambulance that night. The thought became an assumption while with Luca in the hospital lobby. The assumption became an accusation while Tish was consoling me in Dad's hospital room. And now, the accusation becomes a confession, a guilty admission from the man I love.

I grew up thinking the truth sets you free. How wrong I was because the truth doesn't set you free. It binds you. The truth is twine wrapped around your neck. It's suffocating, unyielding. It cuts off the circulation between your mind and your heart, forcing you to confront what you wish you could forget. It locks you in a room where your only companion is the unforgiving reality of what actually happened. There's nothing "free" about it.

Breathing becomes a burden. Standing becomes nearly impossible. Air feels limited, and even under the clear blue sky, Abel's looming shadow overpowers us. Luca would never hurt me the way Abel has, but it's more complicated than that. Luca knew how reckless and broken Abel was, and he let me get between them, which cost my dad his life.

I press my hand against my chest to calm my pounding heart as memories of the fire pollute my existence like thick, suffocating smoke. Luca dissolves the distance between us, wrapping me in his embrace as if to fend off my impending feelings of hurt and betrayal. For a month, Luca let me believe that it was my fault. He kept his distance, knowing the truth behind his brother's actions. I feel his heartbeat against mine, sharing the pain he's carried for weeks.

I push away. "Why didn't you tell me?!"

Luca clenches his jaw, looking up to keep his tears from falling. He runs a shaky hand back through his hair. "He didn't mean to hurt your dad."

"ABEL SET OUR HOME ON FIRE!" Rage courses through me, boiling my blood. I've never known true anger before, never known true hurt. "HE'S A MURDERER. AND *YOU* LET HIM INTO MY LIFE."

Luca flinches at the blame I bestow upon him. Lowering his head, he murmurs, "He's lost."

"You're defending him."

His brows furrow. "Bella, I would never defend him for doing what he did," he says, his voice strained.

"Then go to the police," I say, a flicker of hope manifesting within. I grab his hand between mine. "Tell them what Abel did," I whisper, my words crushed under the weight of my plea. "Please. You can't let him get away with this. My dad didn't deserve to die."

Luca looks down at our hands, shadows shifting across his face under golden strands of hair. He wrestles with his loyalty to Abel and justice for the wrong Abel committed, all while I cling to him, realizing that what he decides to do will ultimately decide our fate. There's an underlying tension in his expression as if he's still holding on to something he has yet to confess.

"Abel isn't here anymore," Luca finally says, his tone low, careful.

My heart sinks. "What do you mean 'he isn't here anymore?'"

"The night I ran out of the hospital after you said you saw Abel outside your house, I confronted him." I release his hand, taking a small step back as he continues. "He wasn't in his right mind, Bella. He was under so many different drugs that night... he was drunk... he... he was angry with me for threatening to leave the band and jealous."

"Jealous of me," I cut in with a trembling breath. "Because I took you away."

"Abel was mortified. Not of the trouble he would get into, but of what he had done." Luca takes a step toward me. I raise my hand for him to stay back. "He didn't know your dad was inside."

Frustration and helplessness fill my chest. I knew I saw Abel sitting in the van outside the fire that night. His expression was sharp.

His body was too still for him to be out of his right mind. I can't help but think that Abel was lying to Luca, trying to earn his sympathy in a last-ditch effort.

"Where is he?"

"He left with Dane," Luca confesses. "They took the van, but I don't know where."

"You just let him leave?!" I fall back on the stairs, dragging my nails through my hair. My heart aches, tears, and breaks all at once. Luca knew, and let Abel get away. "How could you just let him leave?"

It's been a month since everything burned to the ground. There was no case, and there was hardly an investigation. Nobody was ruled at fault and no evidence pointed toward Abel starting the fire. I have no proof but a conversation Luca said they had. And even then, it's evident that Luca wouldn't expose his own brother.

Luca kneels before me, keeping a respectful distance. "Bella, I nearly killed Abel as soon as I made him confess. But you don't understand. When I pinned him against the wall by his neck that night, he looked me in the eyes, and I realized he wasn't in his own body. He was so far gone, so enraged and twisted. He wasn't my brother anymore."

My vision blurs behind tears. "If he's not your brother, turn him in to the police."

"He would've dragged me down with him." I tilt my head, Luca's response catching me off guard. His chin falls to his chest with sorrow. "Abel said that if he was going down for this, he would say that I took you out so he could burn the place down. You can't think for a second that this is your fault because this isn't about you. It's about Abel not having the childhood I had. It's about his jealousy. He was the reason I fought my feelings for you at first, the reason I was so reluctant to love you. With him in my life, everything I love is destroyed in one way or another." He leans forward, caressing my cheek, his thumb grazing the scar from the day we met. "But, he's gone now. He's gone for good." Tears glide down his cheeks. "I know you're hurt. I know you want justice. But he's gone. He can't hurt us anymore. I can finally give you everything, Bella. All of me."

Luca slowly reaches into his pocket and pulls out a closed fist. When he unravels his fingers, a diamond ring rests in his trembling palm. The diamond catches the sunlight in a sinister wink, a tainted promise.

I have no words. I have no thoughts. I just see a ring, another promise I'm supposed to trust he'll keep. And how can I? I don't doubt that Luca has loved me since we met, but is love enough? He has proven love to be reckless, unstable, irrational, and I'm left wondering if these are qualities love should even possess. I thought love would feel like—no—would *be* an adventure.

Luca gently lifts my hand and slips the ring on my finger before I can reply. As I stand still, the ring becomes a symbol of everything I fear and long for. The cold diamond burns against my skin, becoming the start of a storm, something beautiful and also dangerous, just as our love has been from the start. I'm now torn, the man before me embodying two spirits, one capable of loving me and one capable of destroying me.

His eyes search me, hoping for a smile or some kind of positive reaction. "We can start fresh, you know? We can go on an adventure like the ones you read about. We can go somewhere far away and build a new bookstore. It'll be a new chapter, a new story where we fall even harder for each other. We can find our happily ever after."

I look down at the ring, its gleam both alluring and daunting. I want to believe Luca and trust that this promise is different from any of the others. The wild emotional roller coaster that's made up our relationship has taken more than it's given, but I'm beginning to realize that it's what I asked for. I wanted a love worth reading about, and it couldn't be more obvious now that the best books come with the most heart-wrenching plots and twists. Loving Luca is all I know, and I don't know if I have the energy to move on and start all over again. Maybe *this is the love I deserve.*

"I need time," I manage. "To think about all of this."

Luca's lips flatten. After a silent beat, he nods. "I let you down. If it's space you need, I'll give you that. Just know that it killed me knowing what Abel did, and the only reason I kept it from you as long as I did was to protect you. I don't want that same reason to be what pushes you away. Because without you, I have nothing to live for."

As I look at Luca, I can't help but feel the pull of his reckless love. I begin to see the Romeo in him—a passionate lover driven by his emotions, drawn into the depths of devotion with no regard for consequences, purely reckless. Romeo and Juliet's love burned fast and fierce. Luca's love isn't slow. It's impulsive, intense, self-destructive. And when I look at him, I see a man who would risk even his own life just to keep us together. He would burn the world down, cut ties with the people and things he loves most to feed his obsession with me. Just as Romeo's love for Juliet turned to madness, Luca's love for me could become a storm that destroys us both.

"I need time," I say again, standing to my feet.

Luca slowly rises from his knee.

As I walk past him and down the hill, I contemplate my fate.

To love Luca is to give myself over to chaos, to let myself be consumed by the storm he's created. With every step I take, I question my destiny in the story that makes up my life. With nothing left to live for, maybe there is a part of me that's ready to surrender. Maybe I'm ready to let this storm take me, once and for all.

My entire walk home is blinded by the diamond suffocating my finger. Every few steps, the light catches the oval cut, a reminder that I've opened myself up to another one of Luca's promises. The more I look at it, the more its flashes reflect beauty and deception. There's no denying it also reflects the love Luca has offered me from the start.

Pacific Coast Highway stretches before me, winding along the rugged coastline. Tish's apartment is only a few streets away, and while she texted me asking if I wanted a ride back, I was persistent on needing a long walk alone with my thoughts. The salty air clings against my skin, mingling with the faint scent of coastal pines. I walk along the narrow shoulder of the road, panning from the hillside as it slants into the seaside cliffs below.

I watch the waves crash, one after another.

Crash.

I suddenly remember the note Dad left me, telling me to find my own adventure.

Crash.

I remember unwrapping his gift and seeing *The Wizard of Oz.*

Crash.

I remember reading Dorothy's story, feeling her yearn for adventure speak to me.

Crash.

I walk faster along the highway, a cool breeze pushing against me. For the first time in a long while, the temptation to drift sets in, to escape into the vastness of whatever lies on the other side of this life, true adventure. My walk becomes a jog, and I feel a piece of my heart come to life. I nearly trip over one of my flats as my jog becomes a sprint. I kick out the other flat, the wind now on my side as I run along the highway. Nothing holds me back, my strides swift and full. My feet pat against the warm asphalt, the sun warming my cheeks.

As I run, my eyes land on the cruise ship at the edge of the horizon. It's distant, and though it's not the first I've seen just off the coast, it's the first time it becomes an invitation to explore. The ship moves slowly and steadily as if waiting for me to catch up.

Tish's words consume my mind like the high tide. *"Promise me one day we'll leave this place. Just sail away, some place far from here,"* she told me down at Brooks Street. *"Let's just leave land for a bit and not worry about the people on it."*

I made her that promise, and now, it's our chance to make it happen, to let the ocean carry us somewhere far from everything we know. My pulse quickens. My legs move faster. The thought of leaving for a while becomes a spark of hope that ignites deep within me. I cling to this spark, protecting it with my spirit as I go up the stairs to Tish's apartment.

When I swing the door open, Tish looks up at me from the couch, surprised. I slam the door behind me, pressing my back against it as I catch my breath. Her eyes instantly drop to the ring on my hand. When they flick back up to mine, I can't stop smiling. Not because Luca proposed but because *I found my next adventure.*

STILL
10 DAYS STRANDED

Bella tucks the ripped pages back into her journal, then lays the journal on her lap. I don't know what to say. What *can* I say? In just a matter of months, Bella fell in love with a man, was assaulted by that man, and lost her dad because of that same man's twisted twin brother. And here I was, thinking that I had seen the worst of it in my own life. Here I was, judging Bella's life by her appearance like a book by its cover. I had no right.

I lower my gaze to the sand between us, guilt gnawing at me. Bella carries scars both seen and unseen, and after seeing the way she tore out those pages, it makes me wonder what other pages might be missing. If our lives are our stories, I'm sure there are parts we would all like to rewrite, skip over, or tear out. At this point, my love for Bella fuels a fire ready to burn every word that tells a story of her pain. The angel I first saw in that elevator doesn't deserve this.

I want to reach for her hand.

I want to pull her from her sorrow.

I want to shield and protect her from any more pain.

"Bella." I lean forward, threading my fingers through her hair. "I had no idea."

"I wouldn't expect you to know everything I've been through." Bella's breaths remain deep and steady. "Now you know why I've been so unsure. These last pages are the reason I didn't know how to feel about marrying Luca."

She takes my hand, and with it now resting on her palm, she studies it. She stares at my filthy fingertips, then grazes her thumb down my weathered fingers and over the veins along the back of my hand. Over the past 10 days we've been stuck on this island, my hands have grown more calloused, riddled with scars. But Bella's hands are still soft, whole, and almost restored.

"Since we've been here, you put me first," Bella whispers. Her hazel eyes meet mine while her fingertips brush over my imperfections. "You sacrificed for me. You fed me, made me laugh, helped me heal. Rome, you built me a home before you knew I lost my own. When Tish and I left Laguna Beach, we didn't know how long we would be gone. And truth be told, I didn't know if I would ever go back to Luca."

"You just wanted to find your next adventure," I say. "The day we left the cruise ship to explore the island, I remember you being so determined…"

"To do it for the plot," she chimes in with a fragile smile.

I smirk, remembering Bella skipping around town, her laughter bright and carefree. "But, now I realize there's so much more to it. You weren't just looking for some thrill. You wanted to feel alive, to find something to take your mind off of everything you lost."

Bella slowly nods, her smile replaced by vulnerability. "I needed an escape, and I knew that if no book could give me that, I was going to have to find it myself. I thought that maybe if I went far enough, if I just let go… lost control… I would find that adventure." She lifts her chin, admiring the serenity that encompasses our island. "And that's exactly what I've found, thanks to you."

I follow her gaze, admiring the palms dancing in the wind, the clear water rolling over itself as it kisses the shore. "I get it now."

Her head tilts, eyes narrowing. "You get it?"

"I understand why we're here." My hand sinks into the warm sand between us, and as I lift a handful to my chest, I see my past. "It's just like you said before. We were stranded on this island to heal."

As if all at once, the memories play out in the palm of my hands. Clem and I falling in love, having to say goodbye, Mac saving my life, and then looking for the will to keep living this life. The sand grows warmer and warmer until it's scorching hot, the memories more vivid than ever. For the first time, I don't have to force myself to relive each memory. Instead, I welcome them. I welcome each chapter that makes up the story of my life, everything that brought me to this point. The burn subsides, and the sand seeps through my fingertips–the pain, struggle, confusion–leaving me with a palm full of peace.

Bella wraps my hand in hers as if she's sealing that peace within me, anchoring it. Her touch grounds me, our heartbeats becoming one through our hands alone. My eyes meet hers, and our reality shifts, marking the beginning of a new chapter.

A genuine smile blooms across her face, her eyes shimmering with tears yet to be shed. "You really do understand," she whispers, her voice soft as a prayer. She stands to her feet, spreading her arms. The sunshine cascades around her, catching in her hair to form a halo. Her gaze shifts toward the other side of the island. "I'm ready," she says. "I don't want to wait any longer." Her words settle over me like a blessing, mending my broken heart.

I stand, then pull her close. "Close your eyes." I guide her up the slope and through the palms. Warmth flows through me when I catch sight of the sun setting just over the spot where I'll soon promise my eternity to Bella. "No peeking!" I shout playfully as I let go of her hand and run down the aisle.

The sand is cool under my feet as I make myself at home on top of the mound of sand between the standing palm leaves. I'm consumed by my excitement and yearning to promise this girl the rest of my days, no matter the amount. I adjust my distressed T-shirt and run my palms down what's left of my denim shorts. It's a valiant effort at "dressing up," although dressing up is the least of my concerns. My only concern, my only reason for living, stands at the top of the shore.

"Alright," I say, my voice carried by the ocean breeze. "You can open your eyes."

Bella lowers her hand, and I watch her heart melt before me. She nearly drops to her knees at the sight of it all, taking in every detail like the hourglass is down to its final grain and it's the last day we have on this island. Her lip quivers and the light catches the tear that glides over the tiny scar on her cheek.

You know those moments when you see the world through

someone else's eyes? Well, this is one of those moments. This is *the* moment when I see it all through Bella's eyes. I see the narrow aisle that bridges the gap between us, the thin strip of sand bordered by colorful shells and stones. I see the dark, lush green leaves reaching toward the sky on either side of me. I see myself as a man kept alive by the honor of being a part of Bella's life.

I'll love Bella in ways Luca could never.

I'll give Bella a life worth living, even if my life is all I can give.

I'll be the adventure she always wanted.

I'll be her everything, right here, right now.

There is no more *someday soon*. There is only *right now*.

And *right now* with Bella is all I want.

The setting sun casts a golden hue, causing grains of sand to sparkle between us. Bella approaches the top of the aisle, her caramel-colored hair catching the light as it forms gentle waves down to her shoulders. Her white romper clings delicately to her frame, so simple yet mesmerizing. She radiates purity as if she stepped down from the heavens to grace this world with her presence.

She looks down, excitedly tapping her feet against the sand while smoothing her hands over the white fabric. The sight of her is blurred by my tears, and I let out a laugh because never in a million years did I expect to be so lucky. People say God has a sense of humor, but you don't really think much of the saying until you start to consider yourself lucky for having ended up stranded on an island. *And God, am I lucky.*

Bella lets out a laugh, waiting for me to stop silently worshiping her God-given beauty so we can start the ceremony, but I can't. She's breathtaking in her most natural form. By merely existing, Bella has proven that God picks favorites. As much as I want to marry this girl right now, I also don't want this moment to end. I don't want time to keep ticking, don't want the sand to keep slipping through the center of the hourglass. The unfortunate part about beautiful moments like this is that the more you enjoy them, the shorter they feel.

One step at a time, Bella begins her descent down the aisle. And with every step, the memories we share unravel. So vivid, full of life.

I see the first time I laid eyes on her in the elevator. *It was the moment I met a real-life angel.*

I see her facing me on that stage. *It was the moment I first heard* her laugh.

I see the morning we met on the dock. *It was the moment our adventure began.*

The moment we washed up on this island, we began learning a new world. We caught fish, we shared stories, we fought our demons, we made peace with our pasts, and we healed. Bella taught me how to swim, she taught me how to appreciate the sunrise and sunset. She taught me how to love for the first time all over again, she taught me how to survive. And now, here she walks, our story etched into every grain beneath our feet. Her steps are slow, her eyes never leaving mine. She steps up the makeshift stage of sand, and the gentle smile on her face nearly undoes me like every time before. Tears slip down my cheeks, but I'm the happiest I'll ever be.

I let my gaze linger on hers a moment, then we both take in the world around us. We look past the palm leaves, past the fiery clouds, to a sky so alive. How is any of this even possible? How did I end up stranded with the one true love of my life? How did I go from having nothing to live for to having so much more than enough? It's not by chance. It's divine.

Bella lets me take her hands in mine.

"Bella," I say softly. She gives my hands a squeeze, beaming up at me as I speak my mind and heart. "Most of my life, I knew love. I knew how to love, how to be loved. But, you made me realize that all I knew was so wrong." Her gaze softens, her lips parting as I continue. "You taught me that I don't know love, how to love, or how to be loved, but that's the way it's supposed to be. In one of your journal entries, you wrote about your dad leaving you a note, saying, '*The adventure begins the moment the characters lose control.*' You said the same to me the day we got on that boat. And ever since we lost control, life has only gotten better. Bella, you are my adventure." I breathe her in, then exhale. "I don't know how much time we have left on this island. Whether it's minutes, hours, weeks, months, or years, I'm just happy to be spending it with you."

Silence lingers between us, heavy and fragile.

"Roman... '*Rome*,'" Bella says softly, taking a small step forward. She begins, her voice a breeze over still water. "My entire life, I wished for a love story of my own, one worth reading about. Time and time again, I would fall in love with the way characters fall in love, and yet, nothing could prepare me for loving you." She gently thumbs a tear from her own cheek. "It's different from any other kind of love, and I wish you knew how powerful it is. It transcends the love that's written about–transcends the love that's lived here on Earth."

She takes a breath, gathering the courage to peel back her soul. "You're not just someone I found. You're someone I was meant to find. I lost myself before we ended up on this island, and you brought me back to life. You helped me heal, and now, thanks to you and your love, I've found my happily ever after. So, Rome…" She inhales a deep breath. "I am yours. Not just for this lifetime, not for the days we can count. I am yours in a way that goes beyond time, the way stars are tied to the sky, the way the waves meet the shore. *I am yours.*"

Bella rises to her tiptoes as I lower myself to her, and we meet in the middle. I lift my trembling hand, cupping her cheek as my thumb swipes her single tear. Her hazel eyes search mine, daring me to believe every word she spoke.

She is mine.

I give in to the force both older and stronger than either of us, closing the gap to caress her lips with mine. In an overwhelming rush, I feel devotion and desperation, serenity and the storm, love and life, and all a human can feel when they reach the climax of their story. Souls bound by the mere touch of our lips, our kiss deepens. My hands glide down to the small of Bella's back, and I pull her closer than I could in any possible way.

When we part, my forehead rests upon hers, our breaths mingling in the warm air. I cradle her face in my palms like she's sacred. I smile through my tears like she's… just… like she's everything. Like she's the answer to every question, the reason my heart continues to beat, the reason the sun rises and sets amid the vast darkness that makes up the universe.

And in an instant, thoughts of *someday soon* or any flicker of our future fade because all that matters is now. Since I met Bella, our relationship has been built on a promise.

"*We can do this,*" we would say.

And now here we are, having done it.

11 DAYS STRANDED

The morning light spills through the palm leaves above. I'm greeted by the warmth of the rising sun and the softness of the sand beneath my back. Bella is curled beside me, her hair cascading over my bare shoulder. Her face is peaceful as she sleeps, her lashes fluttering faintly against her cheeks as she keeps dreaming. I watch her, careful to keep her from waking.

For a long moment, I just watch, doing my best to memorize every detail. The slight curve of Bella's lips, the fragile rise and fall of her chest, the way her fingers rest along my side as if to keep me from leaving her side.

My wife.

The sky just outside our home is a flawless blue, the clearest it's ever been. It's as if the island itself has been blessed this morning. Everything feels different. It's subtle, the way the world has shifted since Bella finished the last page of her journal. Everything has finally fallen into place the way God, The Author, intended.

The sun is well into its climb over the horizon. The water shimmers in a way that's both inviting and calm, as fresh as the words that begin a new chapter. For the first time since we've been stranded here, the ocean doesn't feel like a barrier separating us from civilization. It's merely our view, a divine painting.

I shift, and Bella's eyes flutter open, still full of sleep. "Good morning, angel," I whisper, brushing a strand of hair from her face.

The corner of her lips curls up. "Morning." She resettles herself, holding me tighter. "How long have you been awake for?"

"Not too long." I press a soft kiss to the top of her head. "Are you hungry? I might get a head start on fishing for the day."

"Of course," she replies, resting her chin on my shoulder. "But my heart's full after yesterday."

We kiss, and I stroke her arm. "Wife," I say because it feels so damn good now that it's what she is to me.

Bella giggles. "Husband." I gently move out from under her, rising to my knees. She cups a hand over her eye, shielding her view of the rising sun as she looks up at me. "We should swim today."

"We should," I say, patting my shorts dry. "And we will."

I pick up my spear and head down to the water. My growing relationship with Bella seems to have replaced the growing fatigue in my body. I've adapted to this new way of life. I've embraced the chaos with open arms, and even managed to make some order out of it. My mind has wrapped itself around my new life, and my heart has wrapped itself around my new love.

I playfully spin my spear in circles over my head while on my way down to the water. I pretend-strike left, then right, the sand crunching beneath my stride. A smile stretches across my face. I'm lighter than ever before, feeling higher than ever before. Knowing Bella has fully opened herself up to me, and I with her, I see no boundaries or barriers.

I would have never thought love could have this effect. It's the antidote that heals all, the reservoir of strength that never runs dry. The gentle waves sway with me, and I stab the first fish with ease and precision. I fasten it to the rope around my waist, then get right back to swaying.

The morning passes in a euphoric blur, and when I return home, Bella spreads her arms over the freshly made fire pit. "We might have been made for island life," she chirps, eyes fixated on the two fish hanging at my side.

I stab my spear into the sand, securing the fish with a practiced knot. Without missing a beat, I scoop Bella into my arms and spin her around. Her surprised laugh rings out, joy lighting up her face. "Who would've thought?"

As I lower her, she gives me a peck. "I always thought."

"What do you mean?" I begin striking stones over the small pile of sticks and leaves.

She lowers herself to her knees beside me. "Since the beginning, I knew you could do this," she whispers, almost to herself.

"You knew *we* could do this," I correct her as a few embers catch over the debris. "I swear, Bella. If you don't stop giving me all the credit," I tease. "We did this. We're *doing* this. Together."

Bella sits back, eyes fixed on the growing fire. Her lips twitch into a faint smile, the silence and stillness lingering between us. The warm breeze sweeps a few brown strands of her hair across her lips, which she quickly tucks behind her ear.

I lower the fish over the fire, cooking both at once. I give her a light nudge. "What're you thinking?"

She blinks her focus back to me, but the flicker in her eyes hasn't left. It's one of reluctance, as if she's holding something back. "I'm just... proud of you," she says like the words cost her something.

It's a simple answer, and while it's not the whole truth, I let it slide. There's no need to push Bella or to draw conclusions when we have forever to speak our minds. Instead of saying another word, I take her hand, squeezing it softly as the fire grows.

"You finish up without me," she says softly, letting go of my hand. "I'm ready to swim!" She springs to her feet, looking up through the trees. "I'll be waiting for you on the other side of the island."

"*Waiting for me*?!" I scrunch my face, surprised at her abruptness. "You don't want to eat?!"

Bella runs up the shore, stopping between the palms. "Too excited!" she shouts back to me. "Just come after you eat!" With a smile on her face, she says, "I'll be waiting for you on the other side."

I squint up at her, trying to figure her out. The sunlight cascades through the palms, the white beams illuminating a smile I may never grow tired of. I exhale a laugh and shake my head. I married a girl I may never fully understand, and that's fine by me. Not knowing what happens next with Bella is part of what makes our relationship an adventure. It's what makes her my adventure. "Alright, alright. I'll be right there."

"Rome," Bella says. "I love you."

I let out a laugh, my heart brimming with satisfaction. "Love you, angel."

Bella slowly turns, then disappears behind the bushes. I rake my eyes over the shore, fixating on the blackened fish meat at the end of my spear. A small flame licks the fish and it catches fire. I quickly reel the stick to my chest, blowing small gusts of air against the burnt meat. *Dammit, Rome.* I blow and blow. The wisp of smoke spirals before my eyes until a final blow clears the air, and that's when I see the dot on the horizon.

No.

It can't be.

My heart starts pounding at a rhythm I can't control, loud and uneven. My spear falls to the sand as I lean forward. My lean becomes a slow and steady crawl around the fire as I squint at the line separating the sky from the sea.

A ship.

IT'S A SHIP!

The realization slams into me like a tidal wave, my brain still struggling to process what this means. My breath catches, panic overwhelming my mind, heart, and gut. A million thoughts cross my conscience at once until one stands out among the rest. The thought grips me by the head and pulls me forward, the thought of being rescued.

"Bella," I manage to choke out. My voice is hoarse, my throat tightened by the rush of adrenaline. "BELLA!" I whirl in circles, scanning the beach. I see our home. I see the fire pit. And in the distance, I see the large pile of sticks I built up back when I saw the plane. "BELLA!" I call out again.

The panic creeps in when I see that the ship is moving across the horizon and not toward us. It slowly glides from right to left. I blink, aggressively rubbing my eyes. The ship is still there, but it won't be for long. Like sand slipping from the top of the hourglass to the bottom, I feel time running out.

I sprint back to the fire pit, tripping over the soft sand. As I light the fish meat on fire, I scream Bella's name over and over again. *No response.* I grind my teeth, my head on a swivel between the ship and now-flaming fish. Without wasting another second, I run to my emergency stick pile, then throw the flaming tip of my spear over it. A small part ignites, and I drop to my knees, ferociously blowing into the flame. With every gust that leaves my stomach, the flame grows stronger and higher.

"BELLA!" My voice cracks, now hardly a voice at all.

It suddenly dawns on me that she's swimming on the other side, waiting for me.

The entire pile is now consumed by flames, black smoke rising from the base up to its highest point, which isn't high enough. I rise to my feet, stumbling down the slope of the shore. I wave my hands and jump up and down like a madman. "HEY! HHEEYY! OVER HERE!" I scream, my voice swallowed by the vastness of the ocean.

The ship keeps moving, right to left.

I spin around, dropping on all fours. I'm crawling in all directions, throwing small sticks and leaves into the fire. "It needs to be bigger." It needs to be louder it needs to be a fire they can see so they know we're here and they can save Bella and me and we can get out of here I can't find anything else to feed the fire. "BIGGER."

The ship keeps moving, right to left.

As I pan around the island, I'm consumed by the realization that there's nothing left to feed the fire, but there's everything to burn. The home we built to shield us from the storms, the palms and greenery that have kept us alive.

Tears fall as I pick up my spear, the fire still dancing along the opposite end. I feel for the wooden cross hanging around my neck, lifting my chin toward the sky. "What do I do?" I pray.

My eyes fall to the palms, down their slim trunks to the bushes, our home only a few feet below the lush green. I once told Bella that this is all that matters. *"Right here, right now."* All that matters is the life we created for ourselves out here, one far more forgiving than the lives we once lived. Bella became my anchor, keeping me grounded in this new life. She restored my faith, and I used the newfound strength that came with that faith to turn this deserted island into our home. It's our everything.

I turn back to the ship as it continues crossing the open ocean, completely unaware of our existence. Everything I once believed about hope and survival is being tested, the stress consuming my thoughts as I weigh my options: *Destroy the life we made to be saved, or save the life we made and watch the ship sail away.*

The fire at the end of my spear flickers, the moment weighing on me. I grip the spear tighter. It feels like a lifetime ago that Bella and I washed up on this island. Since then, there was no way back, no way forward. But, together we found a rhythm. We befriended the tides, lived off the land, weathered storms. We made peace with solitude, found purpose in the silence. We became enough for each other, then created a life together.

But now, a ship looms on the horizon. The tides have shifted, forcing me to consider that Bella and I may have another shot at getting out of here together. I think of Bella, her laughter echoing in the breeze on the other side of the island. She's on the other side, waiting for me. She has no idea our next chapter is being written as I stand here, split in two like a torn page, fragile and fraying at the edges.

My hands quiver as I slowly lift the spear. Hope and Doubt–two foes who last met when I saw the plane–wage war in my mind again, each fueled by the sight of the ship. Hope constricts my heart, a new reality setting in, one where we're rescued. One moment, Hope tugs at my heart while I lock on to our home. *Get their attention, get off the island.* The next moment, Doubt pulls the opposite way. *Even if you burn it all, there may not be enough smoke to get their attention.*

Tears sting my eyes and I can hardly breathe.

Sweat coats my arms and I can hardly stand.

It's a choice I wish I didn't have to make.

But, I can't deny the feeling...

in my mind, heart, and gut.

WHOOSH!

The flames consume our home as I hold the tip of my spear over the palm leaves and branches. Within seconds, the roof is engulfed in flames, then spreads down the sides. Black smoke sweeps my face, nearly blinding me as I stagger up to the bushes. More flames catch the branches, vines, and roots. The green turns to black before my eyes. The heat rises in wavering tendrils, their shimmering dance distorting the air in all directions. Fire climbs up the palms, embracing the leaves that hang over the middle of the island.

With my shirt pressed over my mouth, I throw my spear into the flames and stumble down the shore toward the ship. "HHEEYY! HEY!" I wave my arms, my fleeting voice protesting my pleading for help. "OVER HERE! PLEASE!" The breath leaving my chest scrapes the back of my throat. "PLEASE! SAVE US!"

It's subtle at first, a gentle shift.

Then, like an unfolding promise,

the ship carves a new path,

toward us.

I watch in frozen disbelief as the vessel drifts closer as if the hand of God is drawing it in. I can hardly breathe, my chest tight, my hands shaking uncontrollably. My legs feel like they're about to give out beneath me, but I fight through my state of shock. I keep waving my hands. I keep trying to scream. I won't stop until they're here. I won't stop until I know for sure.

With my hands still raised, my tears fall in warm streams down my face.

I'm sobbing before I even know it.

I'm shocked.

I'm relieved.

The ship keeps coming, growing clearer with every passing second. The hull is a stark white, marked with bright red crosses. They're symbols of hope, life, and rescue. As it draws closer, I can make out figures on the deck, shifting in the late afternoon sun. They're there. They're real. And they're coming for me–*us*. I look back over my shoulder. A wall of black smoke has swallowed the island behind me, separating me from Bella. She has to have seen the smoke. The fire has grown so wild by now, it's impossible to ignore.

"ROME!" My eyes widen at the sound of the voice. "ROME!"

I spin back toward the water. A figure jumps off the side of the ship, landing with a heavy splash.

"Mac," I whisper. "Mac?"

Mac is soaked from head to toe, the water rushing up to his knees as he trudges through the lapping waves. His eyes are wide, his face a mix of disbelief and desperation. His boots are heavy in the sand until he finally reaches me. He pulls me into him with such a force, the air is knocked from my lungs.

"Mac," I manage in another whisper. I stumble against him, my knees buckling slightly under the weight of the moment.

"I KNEW IT." His voice is thick with emotion. "I KNEW YOU WERE STILL ALIVE." His grip is so tight I feel the tremor in his arms. "I'm so sorry, Rome. This is all my fault." His voice falters, choked with tears he can hardly hold back.

I'm still so shocked, I can hardly speak. 11 days. For 11 days, I saw the same view. I ate the same food. I slept on the same sand. I... *WE... BELLA.*

"Bella," I breathe.

A crease shows between Mac's brows. "What is it, Rome?"

"Bella," I whisper, grabbing his shoulders. "BELLA," I force through the rasp. "BELLA!" I shout, shaking him. "SHE'S HERE. SHE'S ON THE OTHER SIDE. WE HAVE TO GO GET HER."

I try to turn back, but Mac's grip keeps me from moving. "Rome, Rome," he says softly. My body submits to his hold, reminding me of the toll it's taken.

The ship's crew disembarks, their orange vests popping against the darkening sky. Their boots squelch in the wet sand as they run up the shore. They fan around the beach, scanning the area. Some head toward remnants of the fire, while others move along the shoreline.

"What're you doing?! Let go!" I try to jerk myself away from Mac, but he refuses to let me. My voice cracks as I force myself to speak, "She's waiting on the other side." One of the crew members approaches us. I point a shaky finger in her face, then toward the fire. "Bella's on the other side. She's waiting for me."

She reluctantly steps back, her eyes flicking between Mac and me.

"Rome," I hear Mac say softly.

A bearded man steps up behind the woman. After she whispers something to him, he looks out to the crew who are still spreading out, continuing their search. They need to get to the other side. They need to bring Bella back to the ship so we can sail home and we can be saved and we can find the happily ever after she always wanted and…

"Rome, Bella's gone." Mac's hands remain firm on me, but his gaze softens.

I squint at him. "She's here. She's waiting for me on the other side."

Mac clenches his jaw, then lowers his head. His eyes twitch, his unspoken words cementing themselves to the back of his throat. Pain is etched in his expression as he lifts his chin, fixating on me. "Another rescue team found what was left of the boat you were on. They found Bella and the captain tied to the wreckage." His welling eyes lock on mine. "The people who saw you board… they said you three were the only ones who boarded that boat. When the first rescue team returned, they said only two bodies were recovered. We organized this team to do one last search for *you*." He shakes me, but I no longer feel his touch. "And then we found you. It's a fucking miracle, man. You're a fucking miracle."

I tilt my head, Mac's words bouncing right off of me.

He's wrong, it's all wrong.
I spoke to her.
I held her.
I kissed her.
I married her.
Bella was here with me.

Mac's lips keep moving, but I can't register a single word he's saying. I think he's trying to calm me down I think he's trying to hold me still I have no idea because I can't feel a fucking thing or think a fucking thought and I'm losing no I've lost my mind I can't think a goddamn thought clearly until it suddenly clicks.

"You've been off your meds, Rome." Mac looks at me like I'm broken glass, like I can't be fixed. "You've been off them for almost two weeks now." His glossy eyes flick toward the shore, as if he can't stomach the sight of me processing reality. "Bella never made it to the island."

The reality slithers through my ears, twisting thoughts, memories, and dreams, blurring what's real with what's a hallucination. My blood thickens, freezing me in place. I no longer try to turn away.

I was alone this whole time? No, Bella was here. She was the reason I kept fighting and surviving. I picture her sitting beside me near the fire, sound asleep in our home, teaching me how to swim, lying with me through the storm. And now Mac tells me none of it was real? That everything–the days, hours spent together, fights, love shared, the healing–was my own mind betraying me?

"No." My voice cracks in a way I've never heard before. "No, you're wrong. You're wrong. Bella was here. She's real. She was with me." Mac's grip loosens, but I now reach for him, wanting for him to tell me that I'm right. I want him to tell me that Bella is waiting for me on the other side of the island. I grab at his shirt, my hands desperate, pulling him closer. "She talked to me! She loved me!"

Mac and I are both sobbing as he shakes his head. My vision blurs as he pulls me in again, holding me tighter than ever before. "You're gonna be alright, brother." His voice is strained but steady.

"Mac, am I crazy?" I whisper into his shoulder, my tears seeping into his orange vest. "Did I lose my mind?"

I close my eyes, seeing Bella standing between the trees just this morning, before she left for the other side. I still see the sunlight cascading through the palms, the white beams illuminating a smile as real as reality itself. My chest tightens as if a dagger has been thrust through my heart when I remember the details that no longer add up. Her unwavering grace, the untouched fabric she wore, the way she moved through the sand and water without leaving a footprint or ripple. *Was she really never here?*

"You're not crazy," Mac assures me. "You're just a little unwell." I take a shuddering breath. I want to believe Mac so badly, to see his arrival and my survival as the miracle it should be. But it's not. It's not going to be okay. Not right now, not all at once. "Let's get you home," he says, his voice softer now.

I try to nod, but the weight of it all is still too much. I don't know how to move forward, what to think or feel or believe. Mac shifts, his hand rubbing my back as he guides me toward the ship. My head hangs low, and that's when the wooden cross reveals itself, dangling from my neck, the cross Bella gave me.

"Wait," I whisper. "WAIT."

Mac senses my urgency and releases his grip. I turn and make my way up the shore, the weight of exhaustion pulling every muscle. The fire has nearly burnt out, leaving a charred wasteland where life once thrived. Everything once alive on this island–the thought of Bella included–is now dead, cloaked in ash and shadow. My stomach turns as I force myself to look at the fire pit, its remains glowing faintly in the twilight. There's no sign of Bella, nothing but her brown, leather-bound journal lying beside the pit.

Miraculously, the journal remains untouched by the flames. I drop to my knees, my trembling hands reaching out to pick it up. The leather is warm against my palms as if it absorbed the heat of our world burning around it. But it survived. I run my thumb over the edges. I can still hear Bella's voice reading to me, still see her hazel eyes glowing in the light, her caramel-colored hair catching the breeze as she shared her story with me. The same story gave me hope, a will to live, to survive.

I hold the journal tighter, the weight of her happiness and sorrow etched into pages, grounding me where I kneel. I fear that if I let it go, I'll lose her for good.

So, I won't let go.

The journal is coming with me.

Not just as a reminder of what I endured,

but of what Bella gave me–hope, purpose, and love when I had nothing at all.

Real or not, she kept me alive.

And maybe, just maybe, when I read these pages again…

I'll find answers I'm too afraid to find right now.

I tuck the journal under my arm and rise to my feet.

I shake my head, swallowing the lump in my throat as I walk back toward the ship with Mac. The waves lap gently over my feet, and with the journal now pressed against my chest, I take one last look at the barren island. "Someday soon…" I whisper. "I'll see you again."

Here and now, I accept that Someday Soon was never just a game we would play.

It was a lifeline.

I force a smile and while I accept that I lost this round, I also accept the second chance I've been given to keep healing the way Bella taught me. *And to find my next adventure.*

2 MONTHS LATER

"You look like you're gonna throw up," Mac says as I step out of the taxi.

I ignore his comment, craning my neck to look at the towering buildings. People swarm the sidewalk in front of me as I stand at the curb, each one of them consumed by their own lives, their own stories. Even as they walk along the bustling city road by the hundreds, they keep to themselves. I stumble back against the taxi, my palm pressed against the cool yellow door.

Only a few months ago, I was alone on an island in the middle of the Caribbean. Now, I'm in the heart of New York City, surrounded by individuals who take their lives for granted. My breaths are shallow, my legs shaking beneath a fresh pair of jeans. Even after a few months, I haven't gotten used to wearing clean clothes. My shirt's collar digs into my neck, and I anxiously tug at it while trying to swallow my nerves.

"This should be the place," Mac says, stepping out of the taxi.

He turns and helps Tish out of the back seat. Her demeanor is timid, her somber eyes landing on Bella's journal in my hand. The three of us are dressed to impress, which is all we can hope to do when Bella's legacy is on the line. I carefully open the journal, flipping through the pages until I find the business card with the name "*RACHEL RIVERA*" written above the address of the publishing house lining the bottom. The card is nearly destroyed at this point, the ink faded after having been through as much as we have.

I glance at Tish, meeting her gaze. Her hands are clasped in front of her, her knuckles white as if she's still holding herself together. The weight of the moment hangs heavy between us, a shared silence filled with unspoken fears and also hope. "Ready?" I ask, trying to mask my own uncertainty with a steady tone.

"Bella wouldn't want us to fail," Tish says, her voice trembling but determined.

Since I made it off the island, reality has felt like a dream. Within a few days of returning to Blue Ridge, news outlets pressed my family, friends, and me for interviews. For the short time I was readjusting to regular life and getting back on my medication, I found it hard to accept that I was alone on that island for 11 straight days. The scariest part is that the more sanity I salvage, the more my memories of Bella fade.

When I look back at that time, I see myself crawling up that shore for the first time.

I see myself fishing,

I see myself building a new home,

I see myself reading Bella's journal,

and I was alone.

But when I dream about that time, I see Bella washing up on that shore the day after me.

I see us fishing,

I see her face when I surprised her with our new home,

I see her reading her journal,

and we were together.

The publishing house is comfortably tucked between two modern buildings, a stark contrast to the bustling city around it. The brick exterior is adorned with ivy that crawls up the sides, and as we approach the wooden door, I notice the golden handle shaped like a quill. A small, weathered sign on the door reads *"Rivera Press: Est. 2010,"* the gold lettering faded but still elegant.

The sounds of the city are replaced by the sudden jingle of a bell above the door as we walk through it. Bookshelves stretch from the floor to the ceiling, books of all sizes lining every wall. The faint scent of old paper and polished wood fills the air, and part of me can't help but imagine Bella's bookstore having somewhat inspired such a paradise for readers and writers alike.

The main room is lit by an antique chandelier, casting a soft golden glow over an oak desk that serves as the reception area. Behind the wooden desk sits a girl reading a book, her short brown hair framing her bubbly cheeks and purple glasses. My shoulders tense under my tailored dress shirt, my thumb brushing over the warm leather of Bella's journal.

"Hey there," I greet softly, approaching the desk. Tish and Mac remain a few steps behind, watching me interrupt whatever adventure the little girl is reading about. "I have a meeting with Rachel Rivera?"

After a few silent beats, the little girl lifts her chin, her big brown eyes meeting mine. She slides her purple glasses back up the bridge of her nose, eyeing me curiously from just above the edge of the desk. "You're here to talk to my mommy?"

A smile spreads across my face, a sense of familiarity manifesting itself in the way the girl reluctantly puts down her book. I catch a glimpse of Bella in her, judging by the way she has very little desire to stop reading, to put her adventure on hold for even a brief moment. She hops down from the chair, then walks toward the back of the room, disappearing behind a wooden door. The door stands slightly open, revealing a small office bathed in afternoon light through sheer white curtains.

We watch as the girl steps back into the room. With her eyes fixed on the book lying on the desk, she crawls back onto her chair and returns to the page she last left off. Just before I'm convinced she's returned to her fantasy world, she says, "My mommy said you can go on in."

I hesitate, turning back to Mac and Tish for some sort of direction. I've never pitched a book idea before, let alone one that doesn't belong to me. I'm in a unique place, having fallen in love with a girl through words alone. While it may not be my place to try and turn Bella's story into a book, it feels like the right thing to do.

I take a few cautious steps toward the office, then turn back to Tish. "You should be here for this," I say softly.

Mac gives Tish's hand a squeeze. She glances at me, then the office, her lips folded between her teeth. "No," she whispers. "This is your moment, Roman. She trusted you with her story. You're the one who's meant to do this."

Mac nods in agreement, his thumb running small circles over Tish's knuckles. "Do good, be good," he says with a subtle smirk.

I nod, their words settling something in me. Gripping the

journal a bit tighter, I take a deep breath, then step toward the office. Inside the office, Rachel stands by the window, her back to me. Sunlight streams through the sheer curtains, casting patterns across the spines lining the bookshelves. She turns as I enter, her kind eyes locking on mine.

"Roman," she greets, her voice welcoming but measured. "Please, sit."

I settle into the chair across her desk, the journal resting in my lap. The weight of Bella's story is almost tangible, yearning to come alive here and now.

"You know, a lot of authors are eager to write about your survival story. A young man spending 11 days stranded on an island isn't something that happens too often… in the real world, at least." Rachel sits across from me, running a hand over her cream-colored blazer. She's polished, her short hair curling over the sides of her doe-eyed face. Her eyes fall to my lap before she says, "That's it, huh?" She tilts her chin in fascination. "That's what kept you going?"

For a moment, I'm silent. I've rehearsed my pitch time and time again. I berated myself for not delivering it right in the mirror or in front of my parents, Tish, and Mac. Bella's legacy is in my hands, and all I want is for her to be remembered the way I remember her, which is full of life, love, and adventure.

I exhale, feeling for the cross under my shirt to calm my nerves. "I, uh. I wrote out my pitch… or I mean, the idea… for how I think the story should be told, I guess?"

Rachel leans forward, narrowing her gaze. She slides a sympathetic hand across her desk, just far enough to lend me some comfort. "I know you didn't do it alone."

My brows straighten, lips parting. "You know? How?"

"Well, judging by our quick phone call, you had this desire for me to know Bella's story while everyone has had a desire to know *yours*," she says. "But, more importantly, I knew Bella. I grew up in Laguna Beach, always reading in their family's bookstore. After my father passed, my mother visited the bookstore almost every day. She would always call me when she left, telling me about how much Bella reminded her of myself. The way Bella talked about books, how she loved to read, and how she dreamed of one day writing a story of her own." Rachel points to Bella's journal. "There's no need for some formal pitch. I don't publish books for the money. Just tell me why you think her story needs to be told."

I glance down, tracing the edges of the journal with my thumb. "Bella's story saved my life," I begin, my voice steadying. "My ma has this saying. She's always told me my guardian angel is watching over me. When I met Bella back on the cruise, there wasn't a doubt in my mind that she wasn't from this world. By the way she carried herself, she was above it–divine." I feel over my shirt for the wooden cross. "I know it sounds crazy because I really only spent a day with the girl. But, *this*?" I carefully lift the journal, setting it on the desk between us. The afternoon light catches it with divine allure, and we lean over it ever so slightly. "This story is the reason that even though I only spent a day with Bella, I got to know her, spend time with her, fall in love with her."

Rachel leans back, her interest magnifying. "You fell in love with Bella through her writing?"

I nod, my welling eyes meeting hers. "Before we got on that ship, I was heartbroken, just about done with life. I had no reason to get up in the morning, no strength to move on or find love." My hands tremble over the edge of the desk, my chin dropping as I voice a truth I kept buried deep within me until now. "I was planning on taking my life shortly after I got off that cruise."

Tears fall on my lap, hot and unrelenting. I can't look up, not at Rachel or the journal. The weight of my confession is too much to bear, but I press on. "It was one last trip, one last attempt to feel something, *anything*." My breath shudders, my palm now pressing over the journal. "One thing led to another, and I found myself losing control. And that's when the adventure began." When I look up at Rachel, her arms are crossed, tears gliding down her cheeks. I continue, "The doctors will say I hallucinated. They'll say the Bella I saw on that island wasn't real. But she *was* real. Be it my guardian angel or a lifeline sent from God or both, Bella was with me for 11 days and she showed me that not only can I love again, but I can also live again.

"I would be a liar if I took on these interviews, telling the world I survived by my power alone, because I didn't. God sent Bella to save me, and it was Bella's love, her support, the reminder of us finding a better future 'someday soon.' It's because of Bella's story that not only do I want to keep living, but I want her love to live on, too. I think if people got to know her the way I did, then they would understand that, 'Life is a precious, fleeting story, and we–"

"Need to make the most of ours," Rachel interrupts, leaning

forward. Her warm hands envelop mine on top of Bella's journal. "Bella's dad said that to my mother one day in the bookstore. And to this day, it's the last thing she says to me before she hangs up the phone."

I pat the journal. "It's all here."

Rachel leans back, wiping a few remaining tears. "We'll turn Bella's story into one the world will love. And if you're willing to listen, I have an idea."

I nod.

"We weave Bella's story into yours," she continues. "We show the reader that whether a character appears for the entire book or merely a page, they serve a purpose." She lifts a palm toward me. "The world will see that life can be inspired by death, that a broken heart can be fixed, that despite tragedy and the suffering we experience, we can still heal. We can still find a way out."

I sink into my chair, feeling warmth spread through me. It's as if Rachel's words have taken pieces of Bella's story and my own, making them whole, something meaningful that will live on and hopefully inspire others. I glance down at the journal, feeling as though Bella would approve if she were here.

The waves crash against the shore of my memory, each wave carrying fragments of time that seem so distant but also impossibly close. In a blink and for just a moment, I'm back on that island. I walk through the lush wildlife, my hands grazing over the bushes as the palms sway in the cool breeze overhead. When I reach the other side, I see Bella standing on the sand, wearing all white. So pure, so innocent. I stand beside her, admiring the way she reflects the afternoon sun. There is no scar on her cheek. No fear, regret, or pain. There is only love, only Bella.

"Hi, angel," I say.

Bella's hand is warm as it embraces mine, and I'm consumed by the pride in her eyes as she whispers, "We did it."

We face the horizon, feeling at home in a place that once felt foreign.

Bella taught me how to fish when I thought I would starve.

Bella showed me how to swim when the water felt like an enemy.

Bella taught me how to fight for a second chance at life.

I returned to the world, and while Bella didn't, she still found her next adventure.

"Enjoy your next adventure," I whisper, my hand tightening around hers. "And someday soon, I'll be right there to enjoy it with you."

Now, as I sit across from Rachel in her office, Bella's journal lying on the desk between us, I feel the weight of that hope, the responsibility to move Bella's story forward. Her story–*our* story–deserves to be told. Not for us, but for anyone who feels like giving up. It's for those who feel stranded, and is a reminder to have faith because help is on the way.

Rachel breaks the silence, her voice soft. "What would you like to name it?"

I trace my finger along the edge of Bella's journal, grief and gratitude swirling within.

"*Someday Soon.*"

The title comes to me in a heartbeat.

It's the product of promises made, lessons learned, and a love put on hold for now.

Bella's story will live on, and through it, so will she.

Someday soon, the world will know Bella the way I did.

And to me, that's more than enough.

ACKNOWLEDGMENTS

This novel is entirely the product of God's will during this season of my life. When the idea of writing about two characters who get stranded on an island came to me, I treated it as a joke. But over time, I couldn't get it out of my head. The joke became less funny and more of a serious concept that rooted itself to my everyday life. I became obsessed with the idea of two characters being forced into isolation in order to heal, and I quickly realized that God gave me this idea to symbolize what He was calling me to do. I thought I was writing this book alone, but somewhere along the way, God made me realize I'm never alone, and He has had His hand on me the whole time.

With the utmost confidence, I believe the purpose of this novel transcends my own journey. I believe there is a reader out there who needs to read this story in order to be reminded that even in isolation, they are never truly alone. God is always there, and it's up to us to open our hearts to His will and story.

I want to thank my family for their unwavering support. Throughout the highs and lows that come during the writing process, they continued to check on me and make sure my head and heart have remained in the right place. I love you guys.

I thank my beta-readers for taking the time to not only read this book, but to share their honest thoughts with me. It's their feedback that has taken this book to new heights. So, with the utmost sincerity, I thank Jasmine, Mia, Marianne, Samya, Ella, Sammy, Makayla, and Bitsy.

Lastly and most importantly, I thank *you* for giving this novel a purpose. By reading, you have given my characters heartbeats and brought their story to life. I mean it when I say that my books are mine until you read them. That's when they become ours.

Thank you for your time and your attention,
and as Bella's dad used to say…
Life is a precious, fleeting story. Make the most of yours.

ALSO WRITTEN BY JULIAN FONT

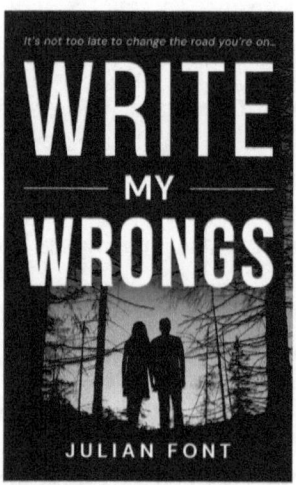

The dual POV, rockstar romance novel about two songwriters who fall in love through the songs they write together.

SCAN TO READ

The epic party novel about an up-and-coming nightclub promoter who is exposed to the dark side of the Hollywood party scene.

SCAN TO READ

The twisted psychological thriller novel about a TV show that manipulates people into taking their own lives on stage.

SCAN TO READ

www.ingramcontent.com/pod-product-compliance
Lightning Source LLC
Chambersburg PA
CBHW032028240626
47154CB00003B/823